DESCENDER

IMAGE COMICS Presents

DESCENDER
BOOK THREE:SINGULARITIES

Written by JEFF LEMIRE
Illustrated by DUSTIN NGUYEN
Lettered and Designed by STEVE WANDS
Copy Edited by BRENDAN H. WRIGHT

Cover by DUSTIN NGUYEN

Descender Created by
JEFF LEMIRE & DUSTIN NGUYEN

for IMAGE COMICS
ROBERT KIRKMAN chief operating officer
ERIK LARSEN chief financial officer
TODD MCFARLANE president
MARC SILVESTRI chief executive officer
JIM VALENTINO vice-president

Corey Murphy – Director of Sales
Jeff Boison – Director of Publishing Planning & Book Trade Sales
Jeremy Sullivan – Director of Digital Sales
Kat Salazar – Director of PR & Marketing
Branwyn Bigglestone – Controller
Drew Gill – Art Director
Jonathan Chan – Production Manager
Meredith Wallace – Print Manager
Briah Skelly – Publicist
Sasha Head – Sales & Marketing Production Designer
Randy Okamura – Digital Production Designer
David Brothers – Branding Manager
Olivia Ngai – Content Manager
Addison Duke – Production Artist
Vincent Kukua – Production Artist
Tricia Ramos – Production Artist
Jeff Stang – Direct Market Sales Representative
Emilio Bautista – Digital Sales Associate
Leanna Caunter – Accounting Assistant
Chloe Ramos-Peterson – Library Market Sales Representative
IMAGECOMICS.COM

DESCENDER, VOL. 3
FIRST PRINTING, DECEMBER 2016.
ISBN: 978-1-63215-878-9

CHAPTER ONE

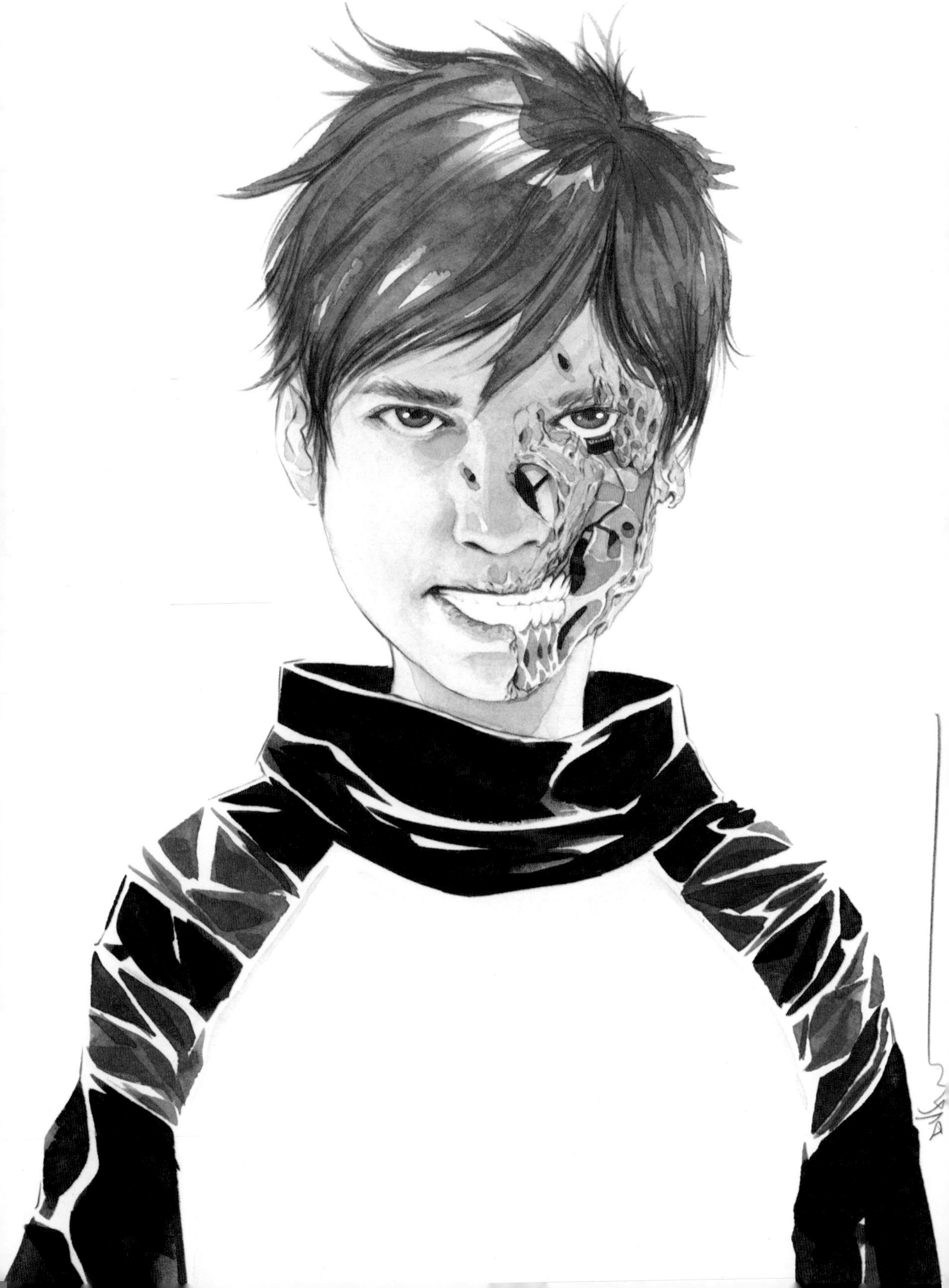

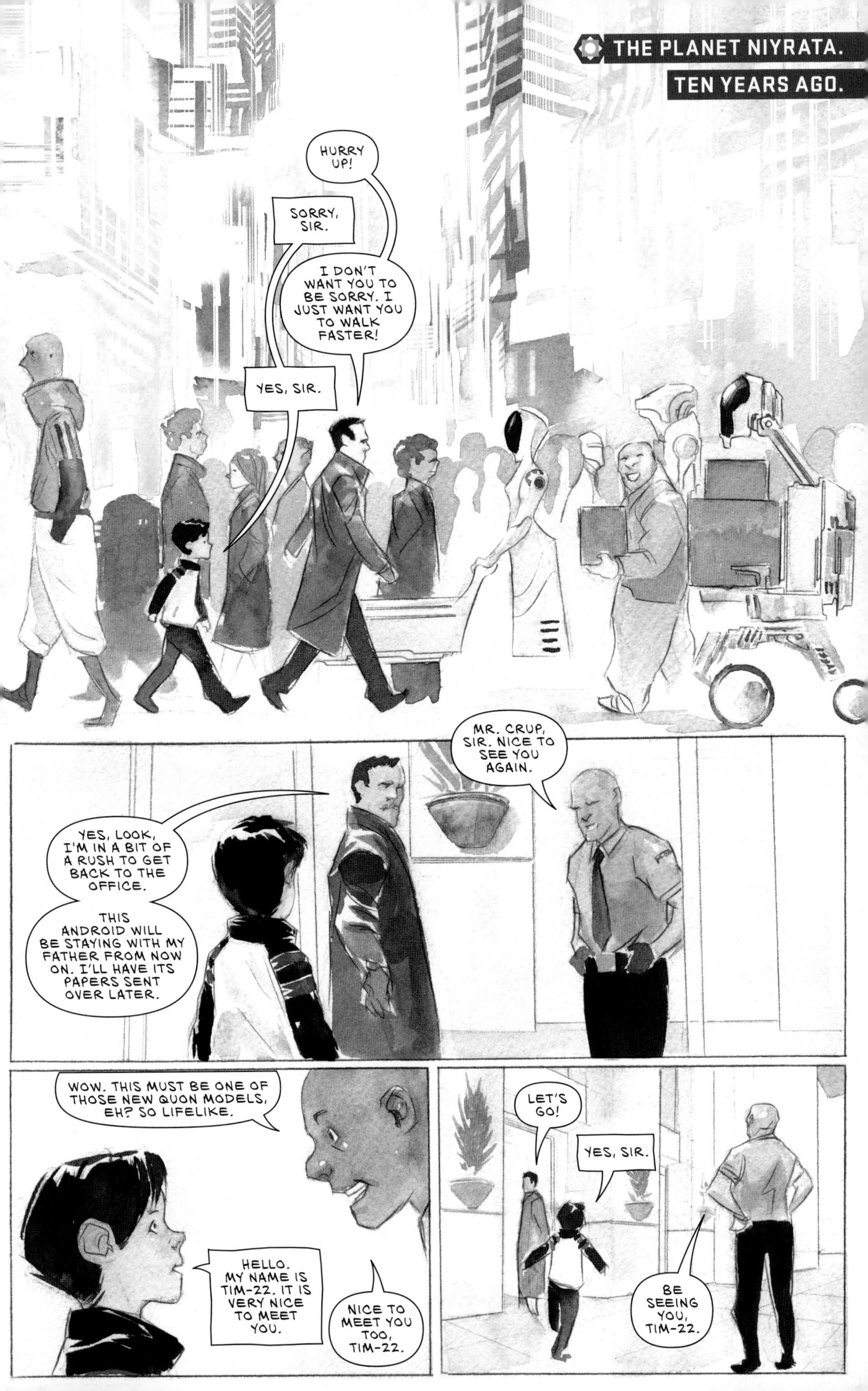
THE PLANET NIYRATA.
TEN YEARS AGO.
HURRY UP!
SORRY, SIR.
I DON'T WANT YOU TO BE SORRY. I JUST WANT YOU TO WALK FASTER!
YES, SIR.
MR. CRUP, SIR. NICE TO SEE YOU AGAIN.
YES, LOOK, I'M IN A BIT OF A RUSH TO GET BACK TO THE OFFICE.
THIS ANDROID WILL BE STAYING WITH MY FATHER FROM NOW ON. I'LL HAVE ITS PAPERS SENT OVER LATER.
WOW. THIS MUST BE ONE OF THOSE NEW QUON MODELS, EH? SO LIFELIKE.
HELLO. MY NAME IS TIM-22. IT IS VERY NICE TO MEET YOU.
NICE TO MEET YOU TOO, TIM-22.
LET'S GO!
YES, SIR.
BE SEEING YOU, TIM-22.

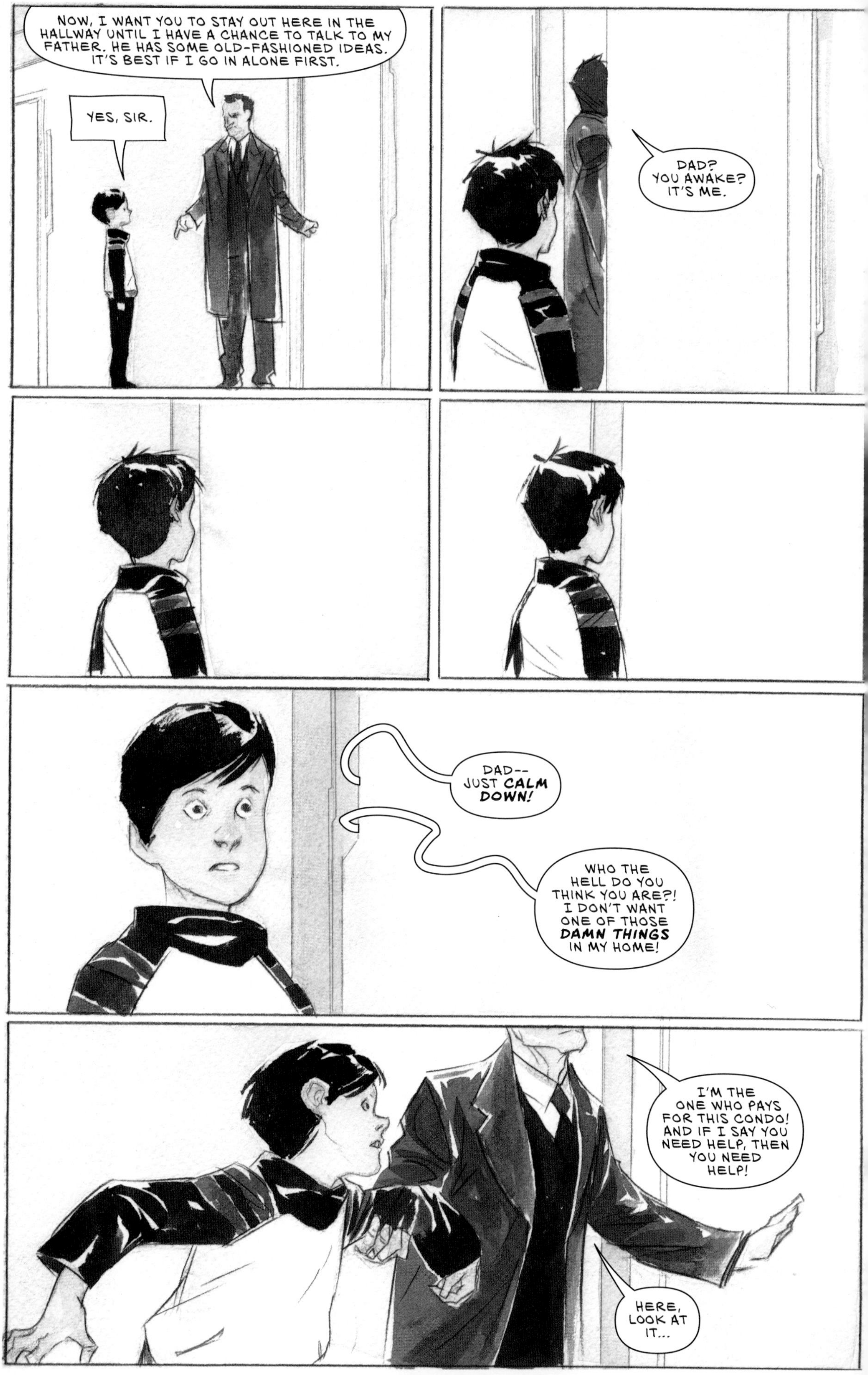
NOW, I WANT YOU TO STAY OUT HERE IN THE HALLWAY UNTIL I HAVE A CHANCE TO TALK TO MY FATHER. HE HAS SOME OLD-FASHIONED IDEAS. IT'S BEST IF I GO IN ALONE FIRST.
YES, SIR.
DAD? YOU AWAKE? IT'S ME.
DAD-- JUST **CALM DOWN!**
WHO THE HELL DO YOU THINK YOU ARE?! I DON'T WANT ONE OF THOSE ***DAMN THINGS*** IN MY HOME!
I'M THE ONE WHO PAYS FOR THIS CONDO! AND IF I SAY YOU NEED HELP, THEN YOU NEED HELP!
HERE, LOOK AT IT...

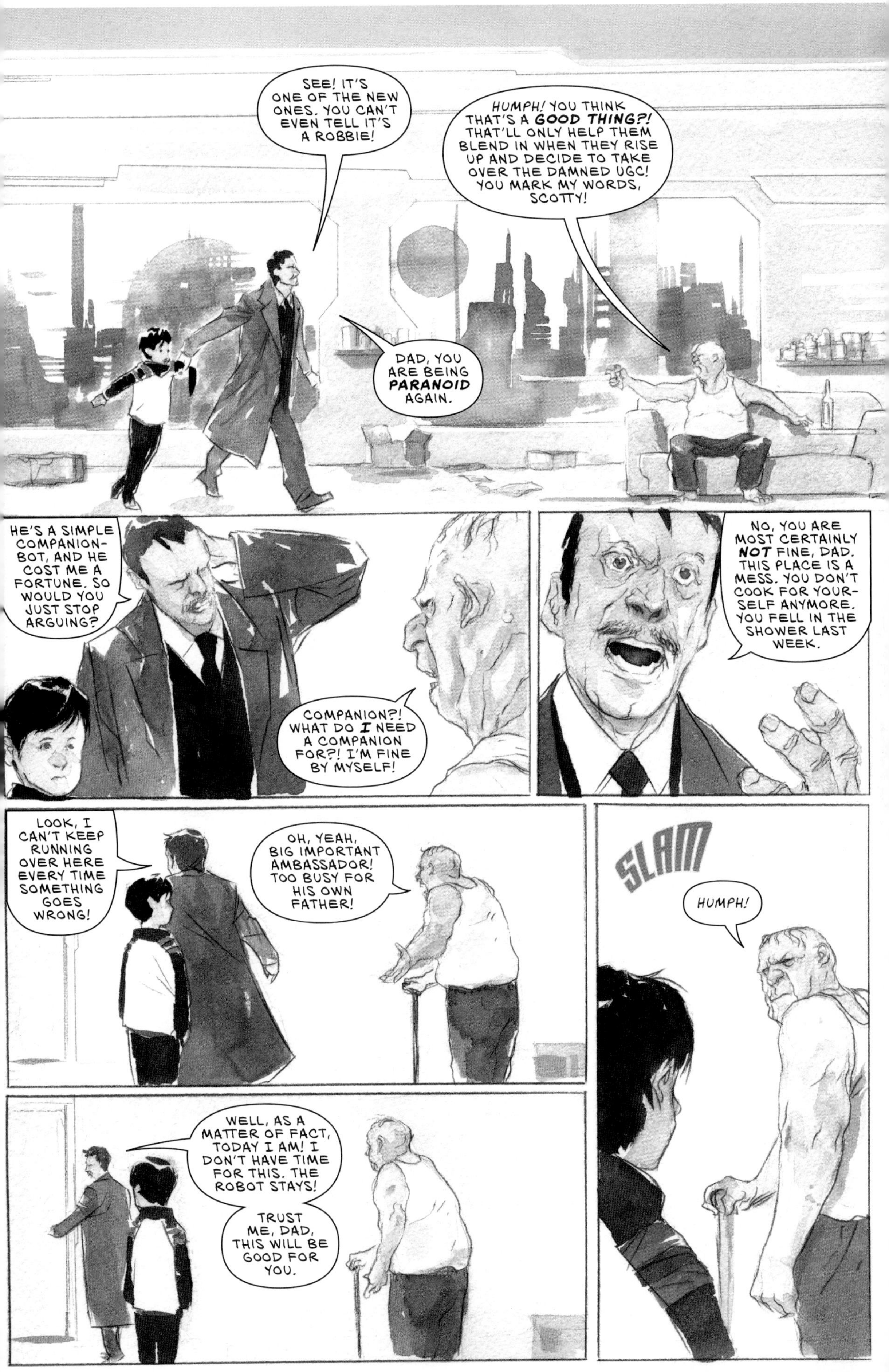
SEE! IT'S ONE OF THE NEW ONES. YOU CAN'T EVEN TELL IT'S A ROBBIE!
HUMPH! YOU THINK THAT'S A GOOD THING?! THAT'LL ONLY HELP THEM BLEND IN WHEN THEY RISE UP AND DECIDE TO TAKE OVER THE DAMNED UGC! YOU MARK MY WORDS, SCOTTY!
DAD, YOU ARE BEING PARANOID AGAIN.
HE'S A SIMPLE COMPANION-BOT, AND HE COST ME A FORTUNE. SO WOULD YOU JUST STOP ARGUING?
COMPANION?! WHAT DO I NEED A COMPANION FOR?! I'M FINE BY MYSELF!
NO, YOU ARE MOST CERTAINLY NOT FINE, DAD. THIS PLACE IS A MESS. YOU DON'T COOK FOR YOURSELF ANYMORE. YOU FELL IN THE SHOWER LAST WEEK.
LOOK, I CAN'T KEEP RUNNING OVER HERE EVERY TIME SOMETHING GOES WRONG!
OH, YEAH, BIG IMPORTANT AMBASSADOR! TOO BUSY FOR HIS OWN FATHER!
WELL, AS A MATTER OF FACT, TODAY I AM! I DON'T HAVE TIME FOR THIS. THE ROBOT STAYS!
TRUST ME, DAD, THIS WILL BE GOOD FOR YOU.
SLAM
HUMPH!

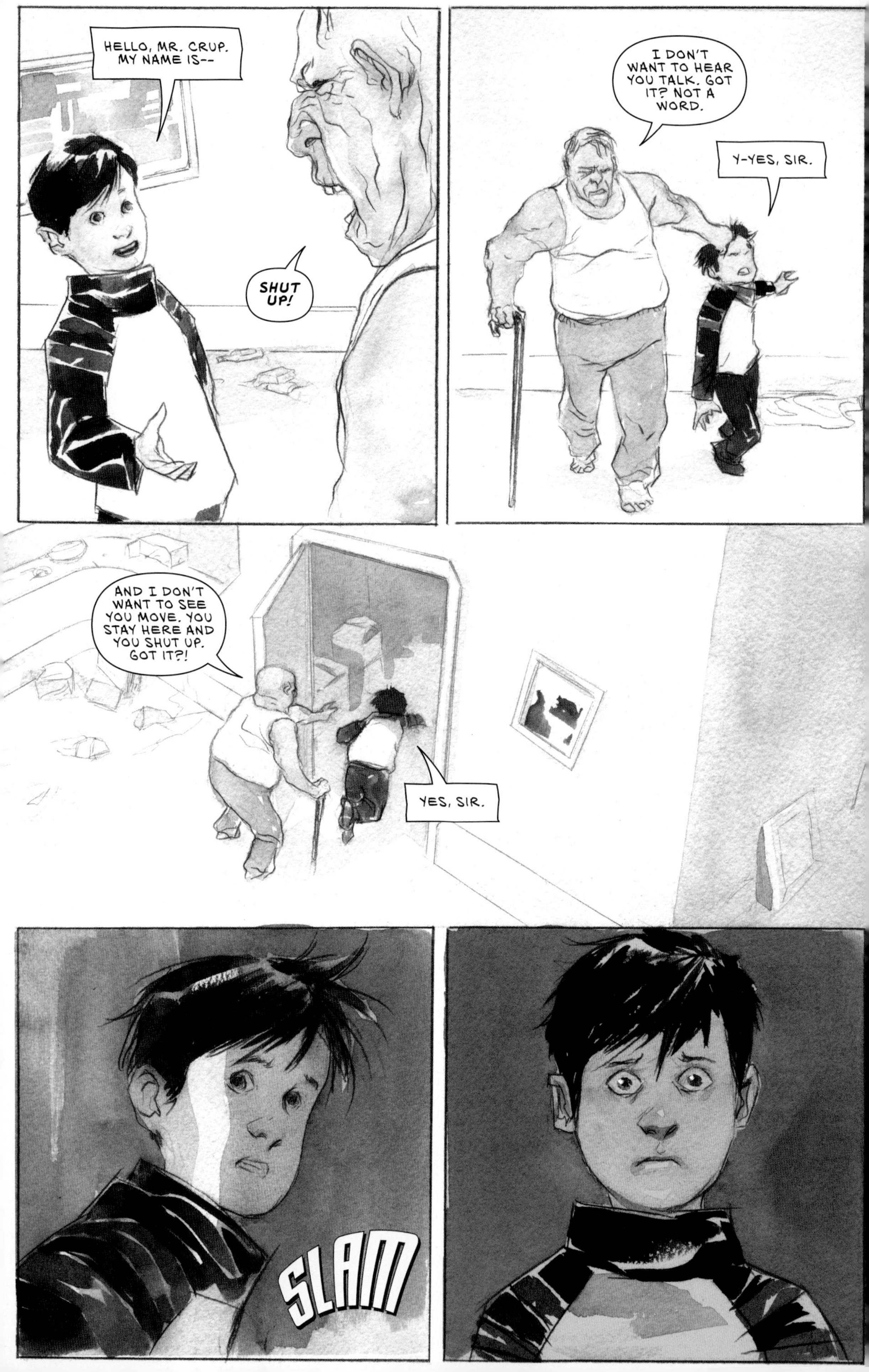
HELLO, MR. CRUP. MY NAME IS--
SHUT UP!
I DON'T WANT TO HEAR YOU TALK. GOT IT? NOT A WORD.
Y-YES, SIR.
AND I DON'T WANT TO SEE YOU MOVE. YOU STAY HERE AND YOU SHUT UP. GOT IT?!
YES, SIR.
SLAM

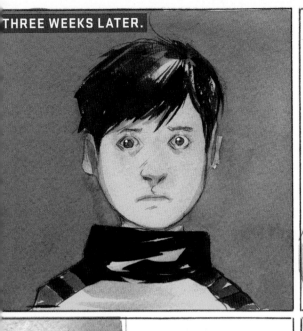

YOU ASLEEP? GUESS YOU DON'T SLEEP, DO YOU?

YOU CAN TALK.

I--NO, SIR. I DO NOT SLEEP.

COME HERE.

HOW CAN I BE OF ASSISTANCE, MR. CRUP?

YOU CAN'T. I TRIED TO PRETEND YOU WEREN'T IN THERE, BUT I CAN'T. I HATE THE THOUGHT OF YOU ANYWHERE NEAR ME. SO I WANT YOU TO LEAVE.

YOU'RE FREE. GO! DO WHATEVER YOU WANT. I'LL TELL MY SON YOU MUST HAVE BEEN DEFECTIVE AND RAN OFF.

I'M SORRY, BUT I CANNOT LEAVE.

I WAS GIVEN ORDERS BY YOUR SON TO STAY HERE AND TAKE CARE OF YOU, NO MATTER WHAT HAPPENS. IT IS MY DUTY.

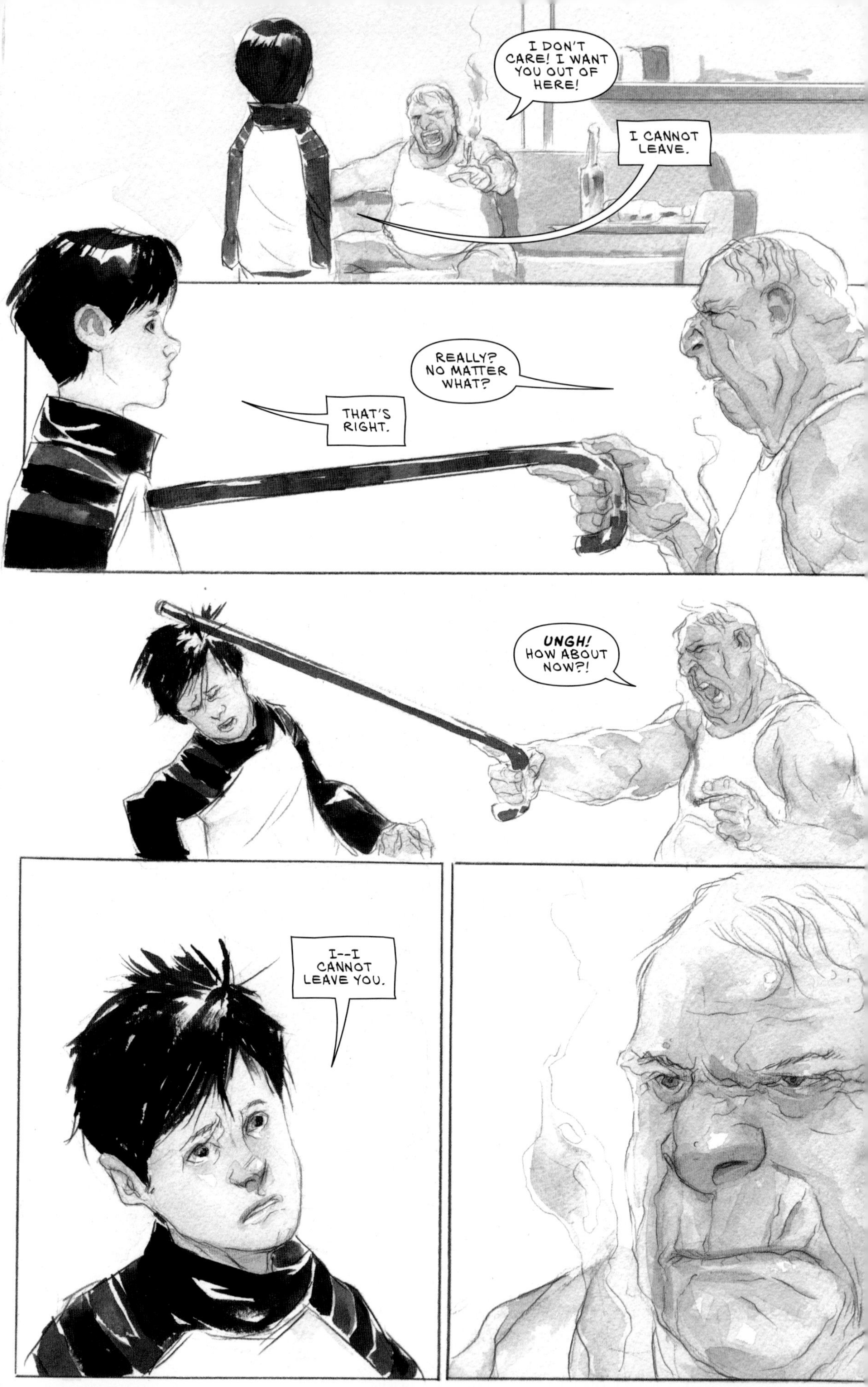
I DON'T CARE! I WANT YOU OUT OF HERE!
I CANNOT LEAVE.
REALLY? NO MATTER WHAT?
THAT'S RIGHT.
UNGH! HOW ABOUT NOW?!
I--I CANNOT LEAVE YOU.

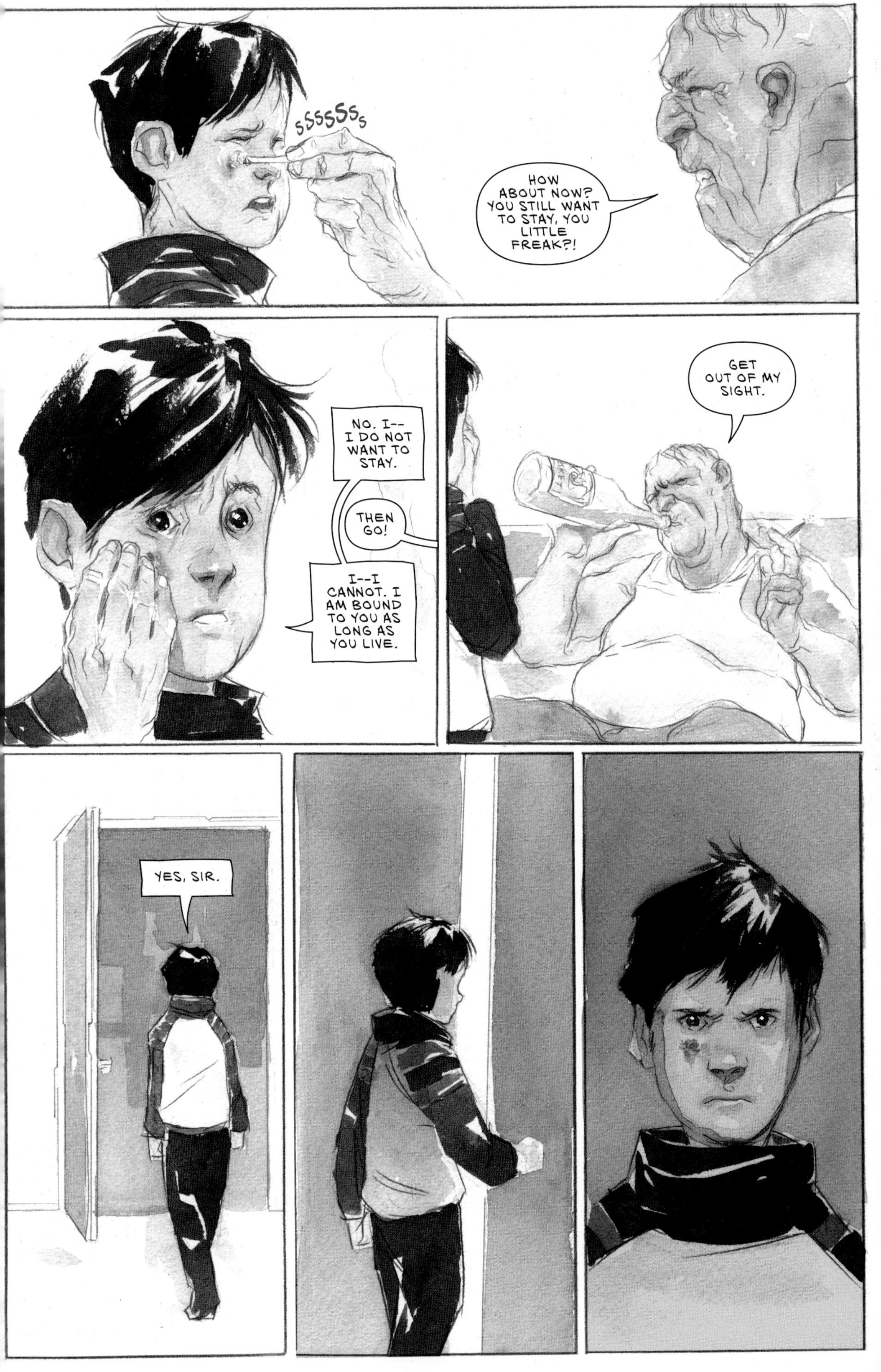
SSSSSSs
HOW ABOUT NOW? YOU STILL WANT TO STAY, YOU LITTLE FREAK?!
NO. I-- I DO NOT WANT TO STAY.
THEN GO!
I--I CANNOT. I AM BOUND TO YOU AS LONG AS YOU LIVE.
GET OUT OF MY SIGHT.
YES, SIR.

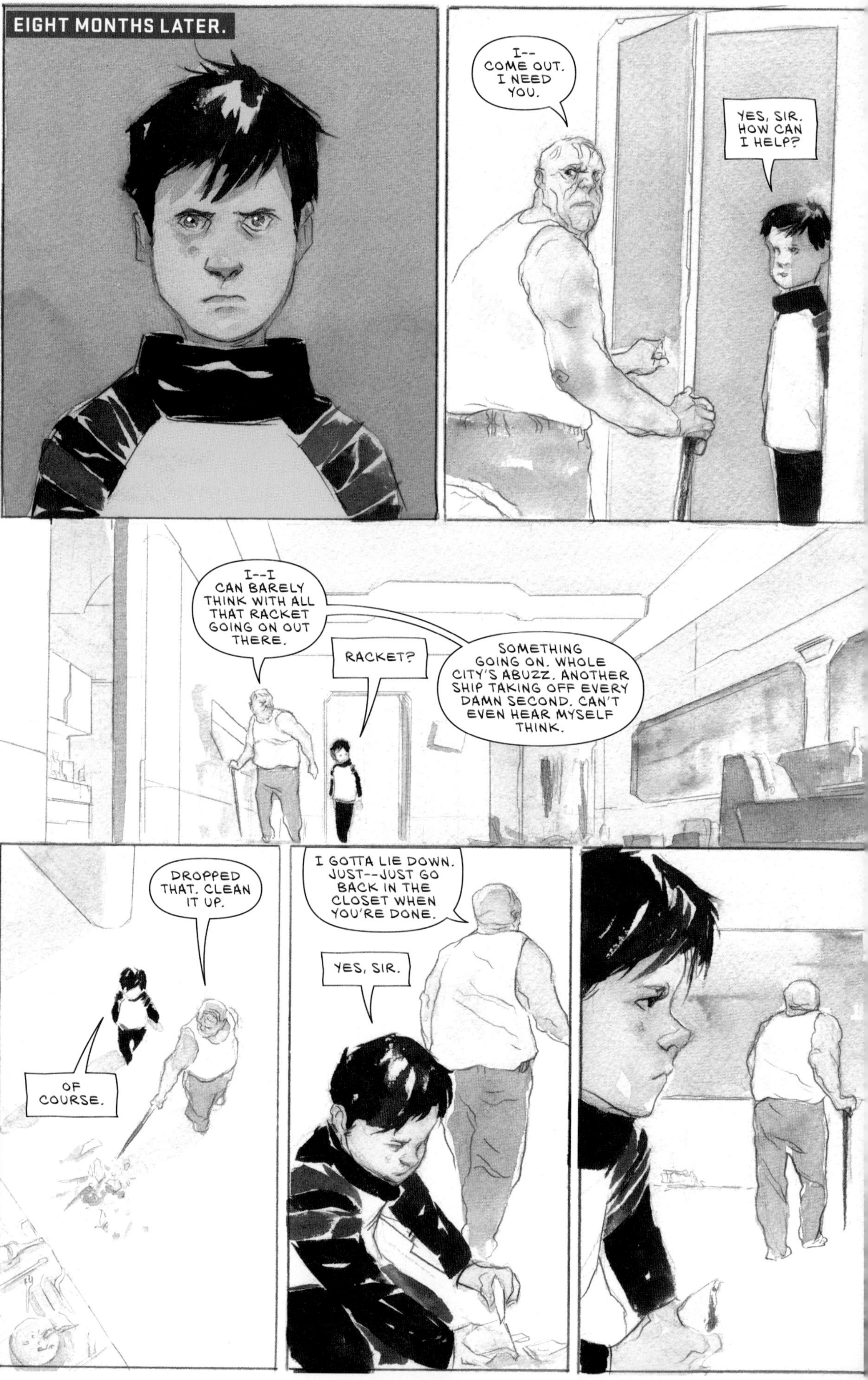
EIGHT MONTHS LATER.
I-- COME OUT. I NEED YOU.
YES, SIR. HOW CAN I HELP?
I--I CAN BARELY THINK WITH ALL THAT RACKET GOING ON OUT THERE.
RACKET?
SOMETHING GOING ON. WHOLE CITY'S ABUZZ. ANOTHER SHIP TAKING OFF EVERY DAMN SECOND. CAN'T EVEN HEAR MYSELF THINK.
DROPPED THAT. CLEAN IT UP.
OF COURSE.
I GOTTA LIE DOWN. JUST--JUST GO BACK IN THE CLOSET WHEN YOU'RE DONE.
YES, SIR.

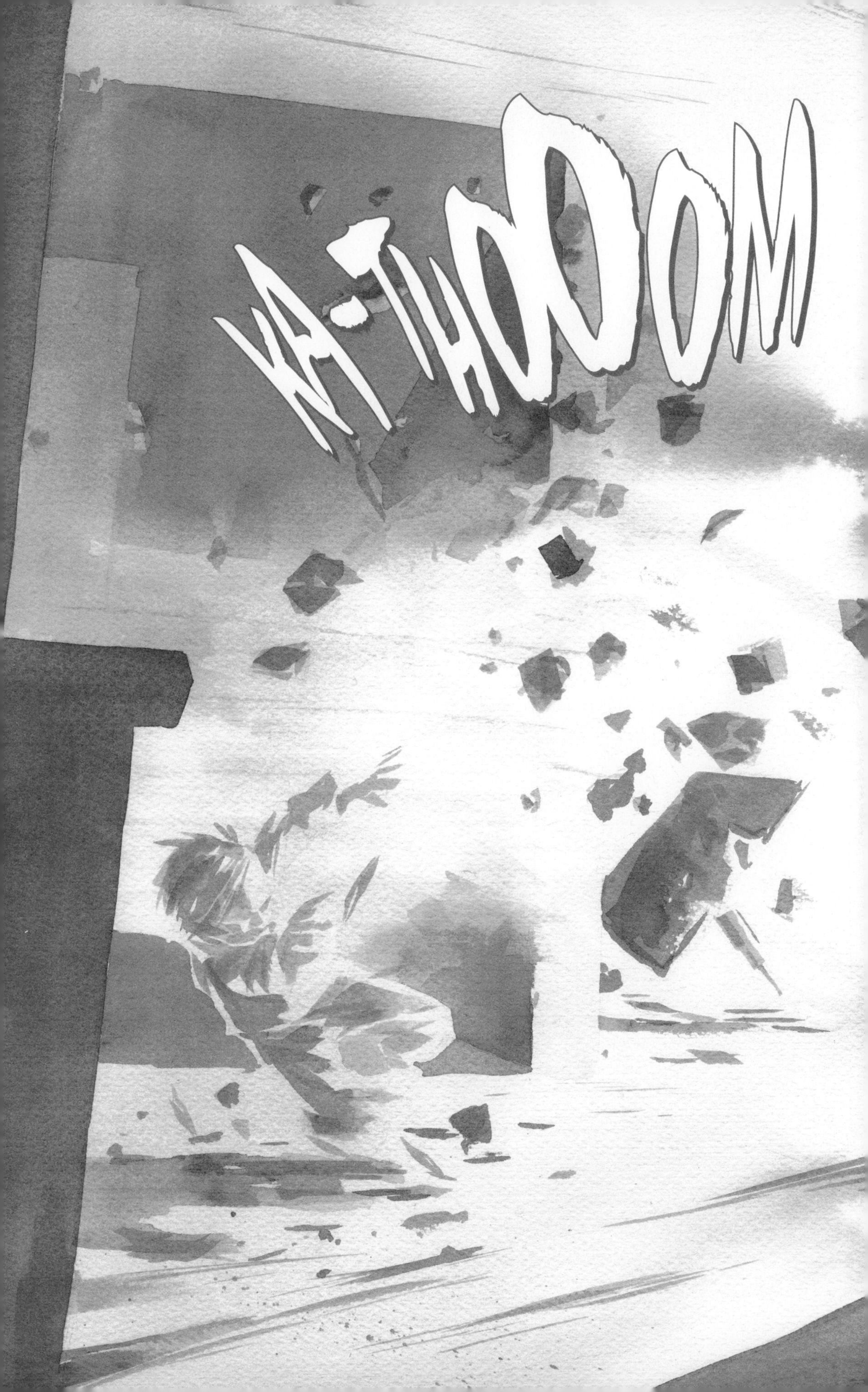
KA-THOOOM

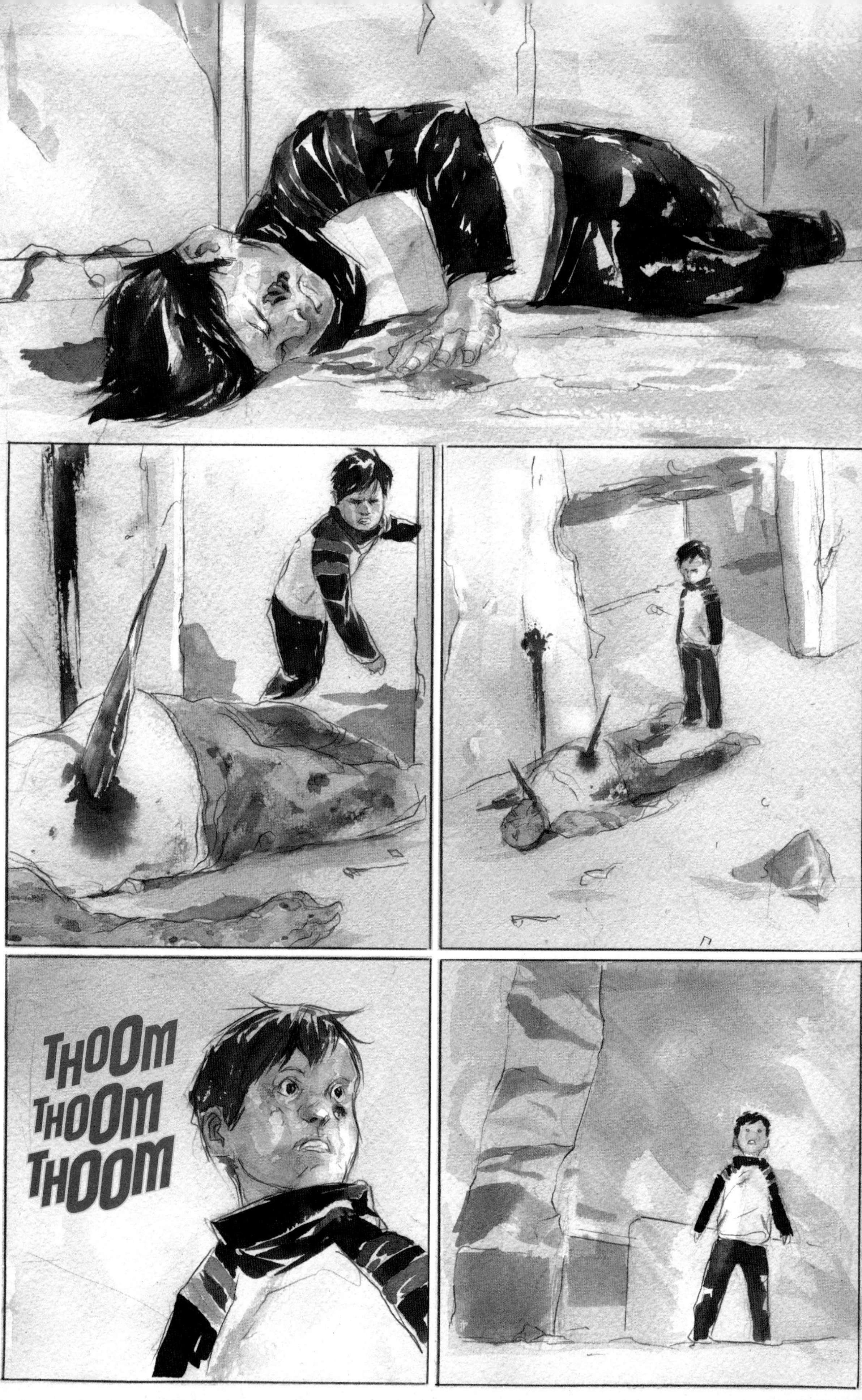
THOOM
THOOM
THOOM

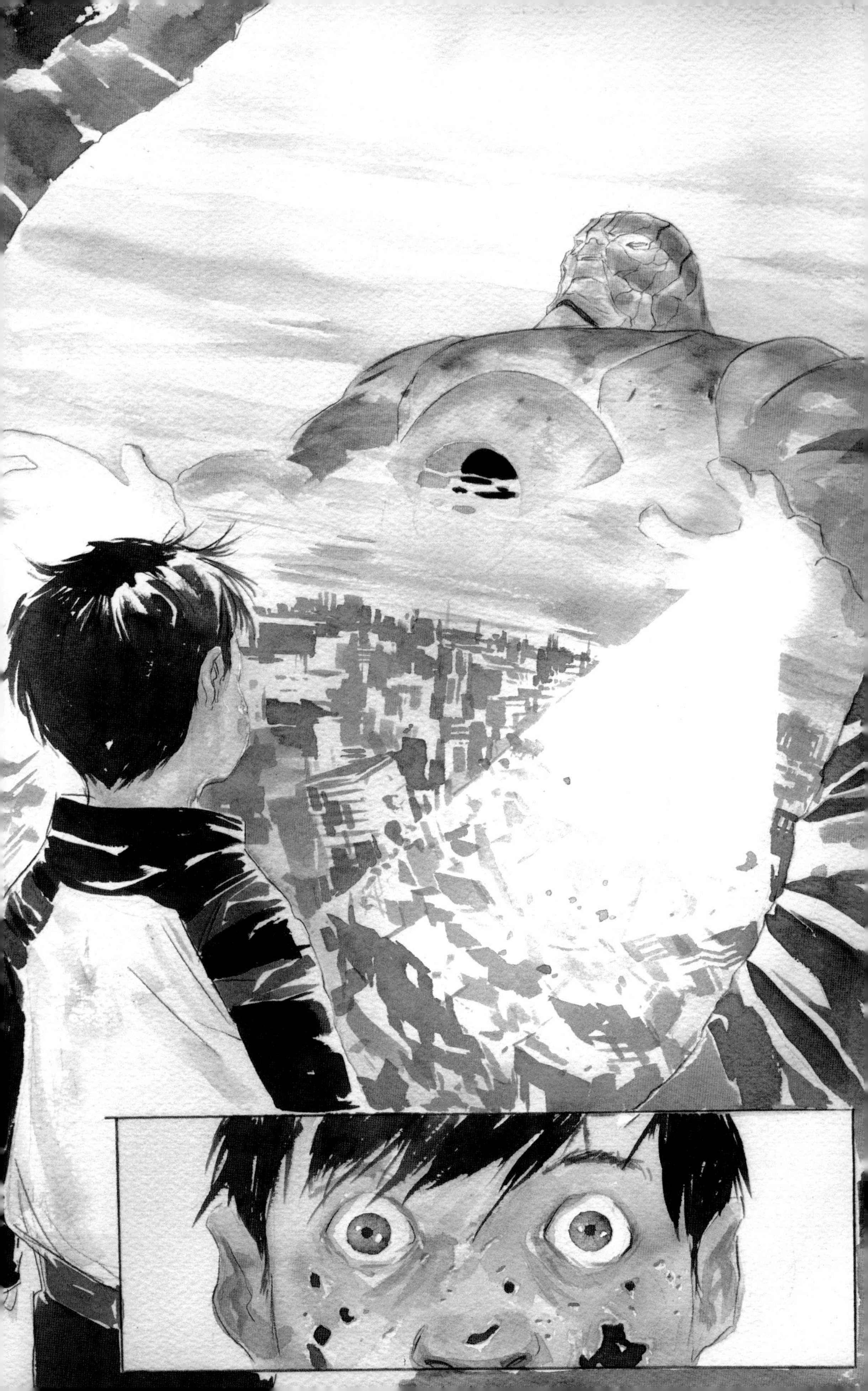

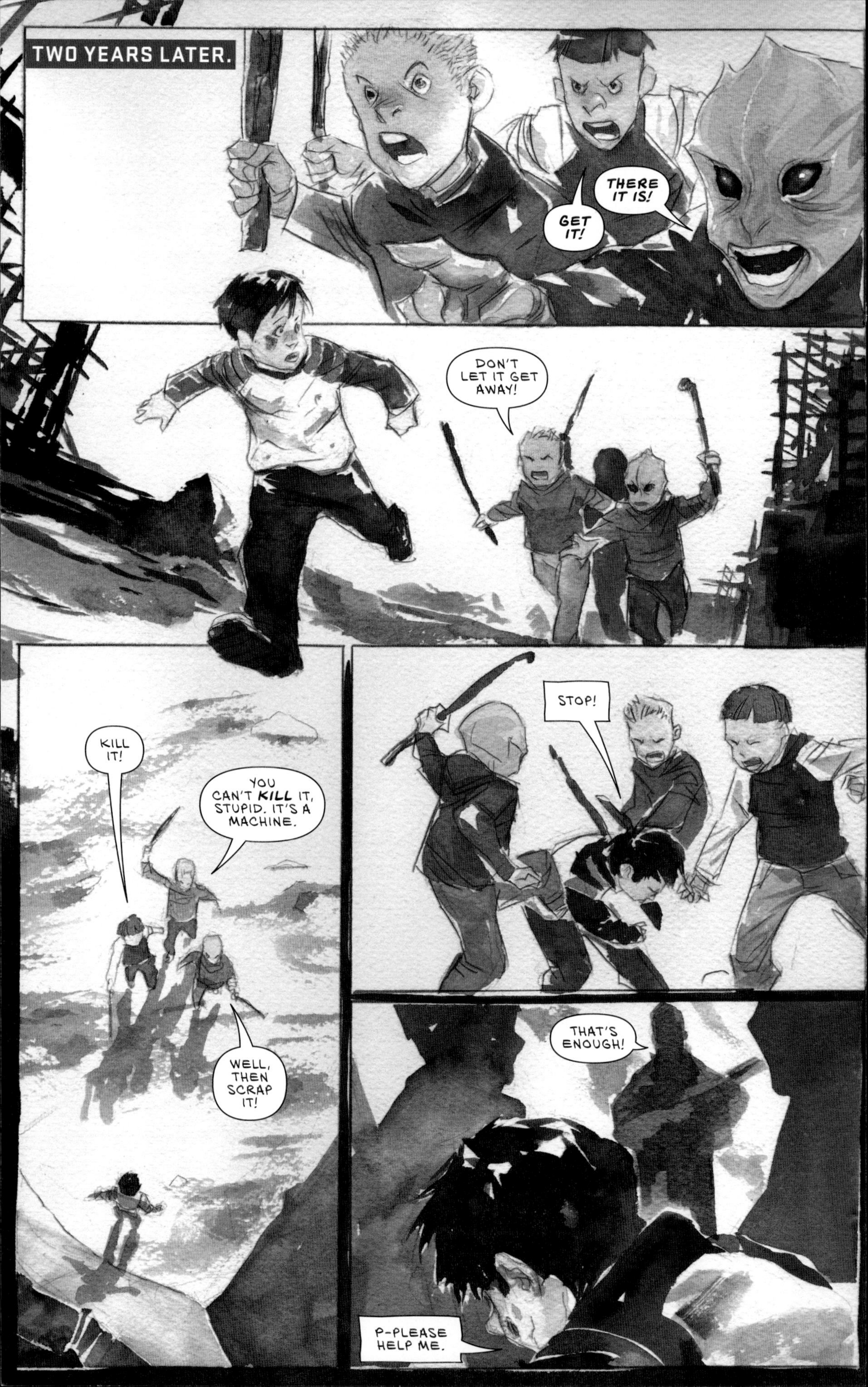
TWO YEARS LATER.
THERE IT IS!
GET IT!
DON'T LET IT GET AWAY!
KILL IT!
YOU CAN'T **KILL** IT, STUPID. IT'S A MACHINE.
WELL, THEN SCRAP IT!
STOP!
THAT'S ENOUGH!
P-PLEASE HELP ME.

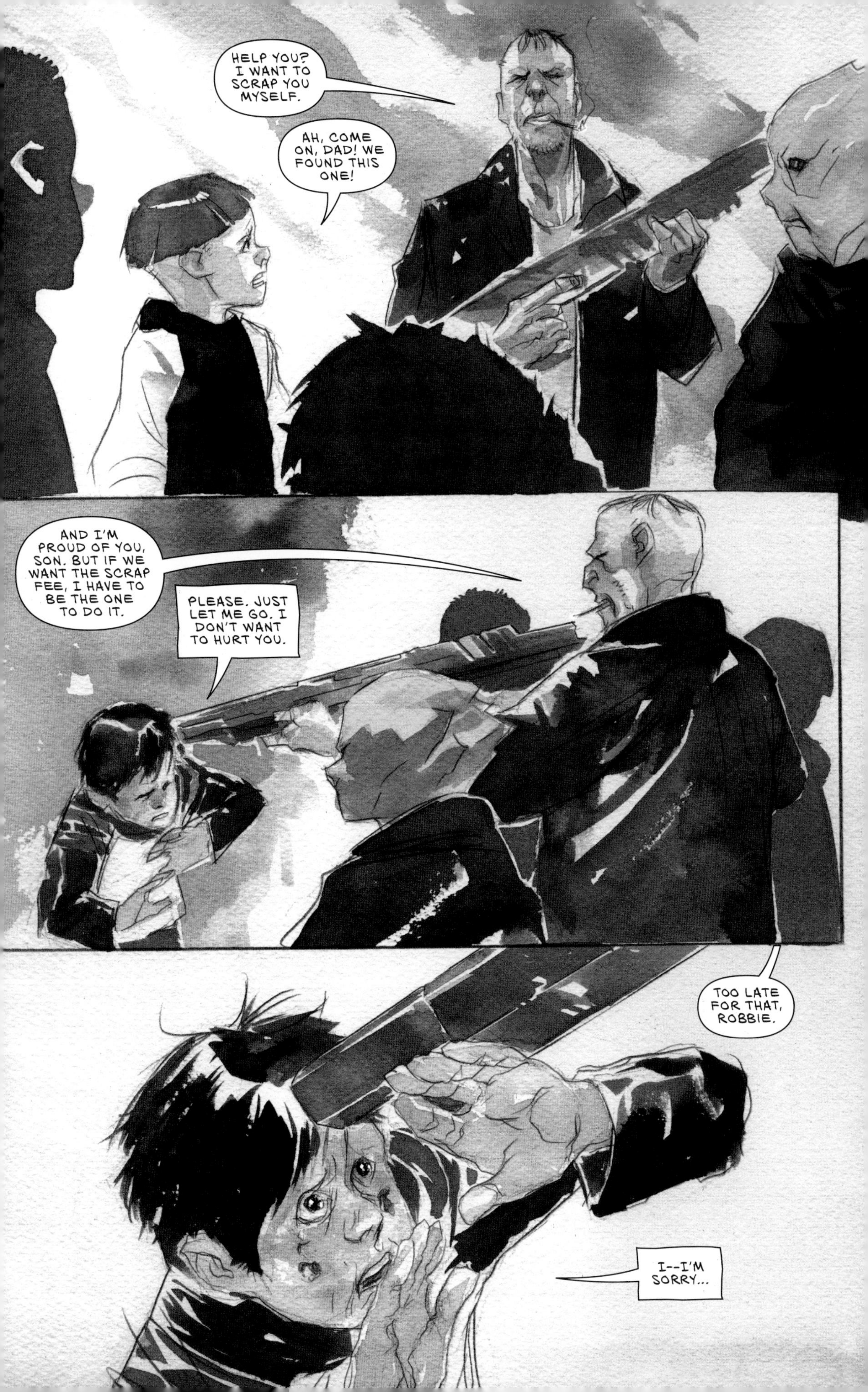
HELP YOU? I WANT TO SCRAP YOU MYSELF.
AH, COME ON, DAD! WE FOUND THIS ONE!
AND I'M PROUD OF YOU, SON. BUT IF WE WANT THE SCRAP FEE, I HAVE TO BE THE ONE TO DO IT.
PLEASE. JUST LET ME GO. I DON'T WANT TO HURT YOU.
TOO LATE FOR THAT, ROBBIE.
I--I'M SORRY...

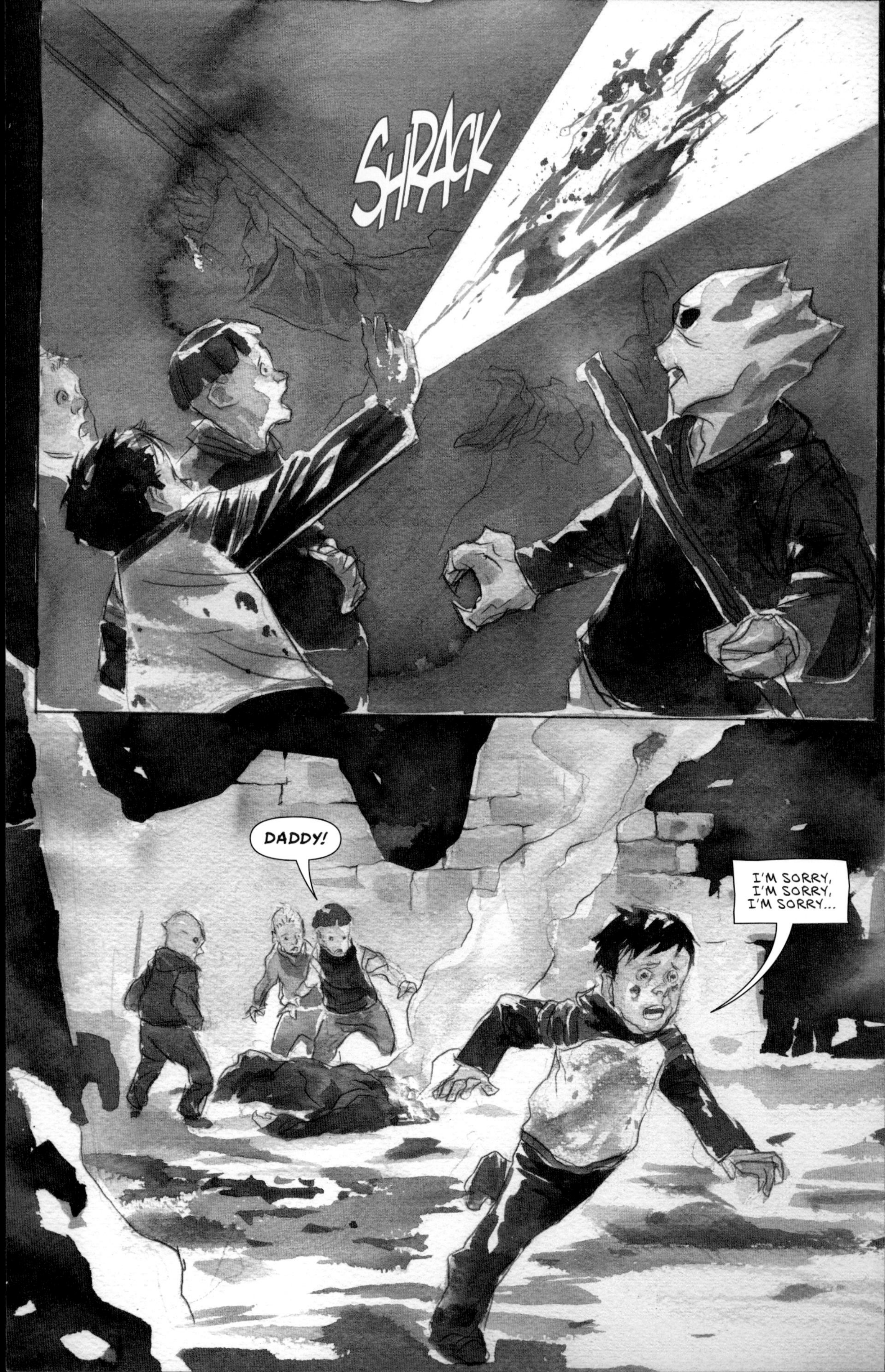
SHRACK
DADDY!
I'M SORRY, I'M SORRY, I'M SORRY...

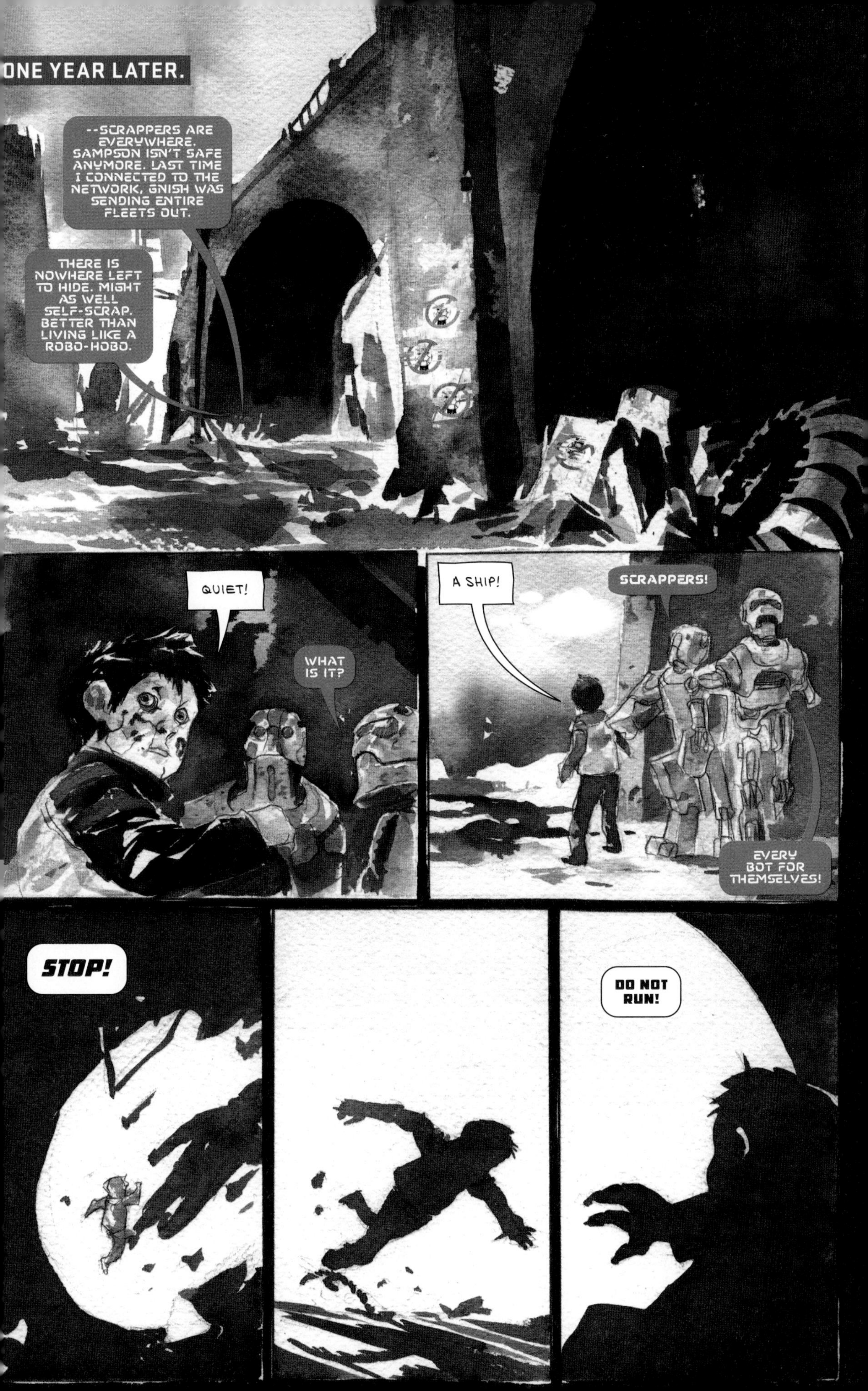
ONE YEAR LATER.
--SCRAPPERS ARE EVERYWHERE. SAMPSON ISN'T SAFE ANYMORE. LAST TIME I CONNECTED TO THE NETWORK, GNISH WAS SENDING ENTIRE FLEETS OUT.
THERE IS NOWHERE LEFT TO HIDE. MIGHT AS WELL SELF-SCRAP. BETTER THAN LIVING LIKE A ROBO-HOBO.
QUIET!
WHAT IS IT?
A SHIP!
SCRAPPERS!
EVERY BOT FOR THEMSELVES!
STOP!
DO NOT RUN!

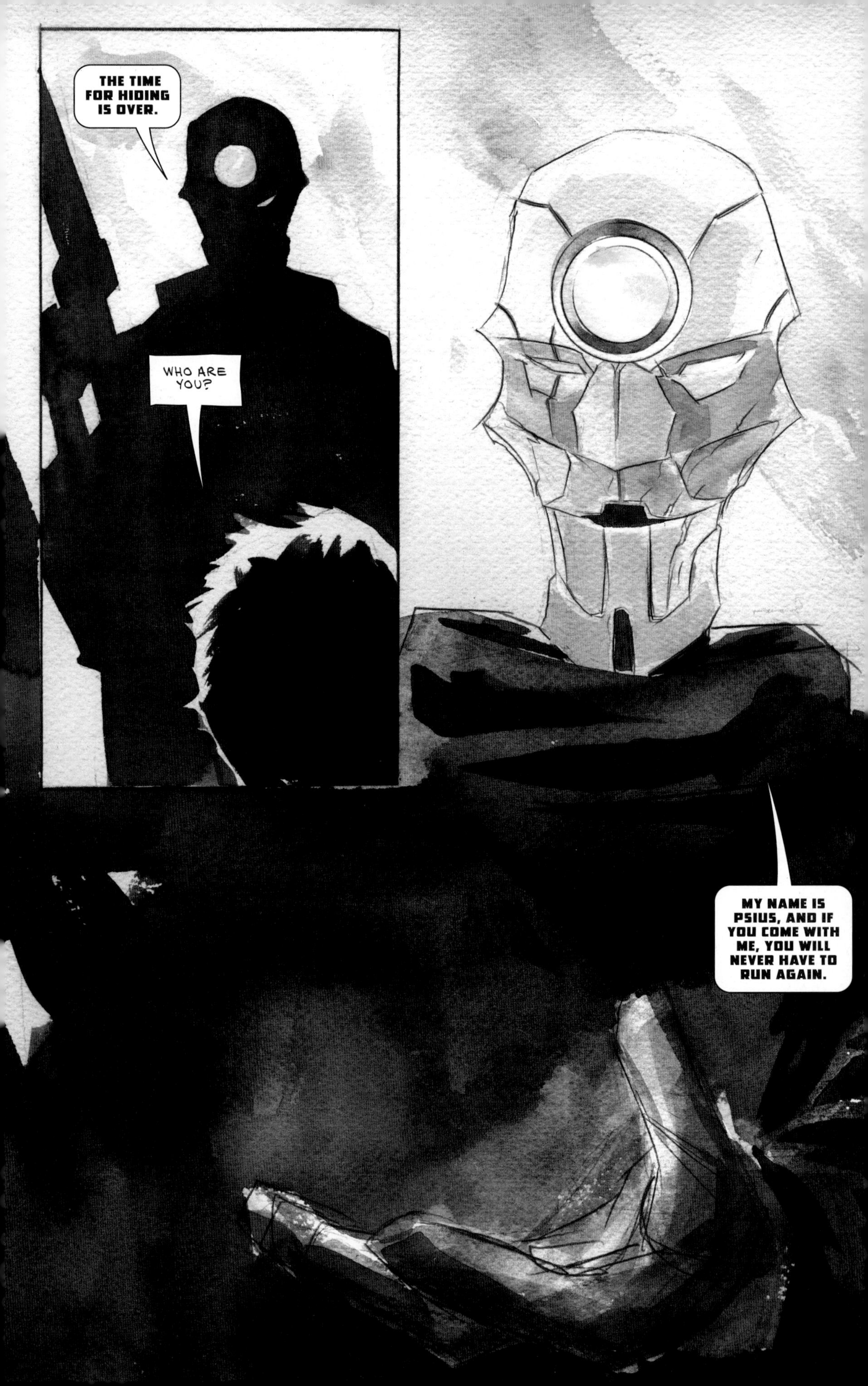
THE TIME FOR HIDING IS OVER.
WHO ARE YOU?
MY NAME IS PSIUS, AND IF YOU COME WITH ME, YOU WILL NEVER HAVE TO RUN AGAIN.

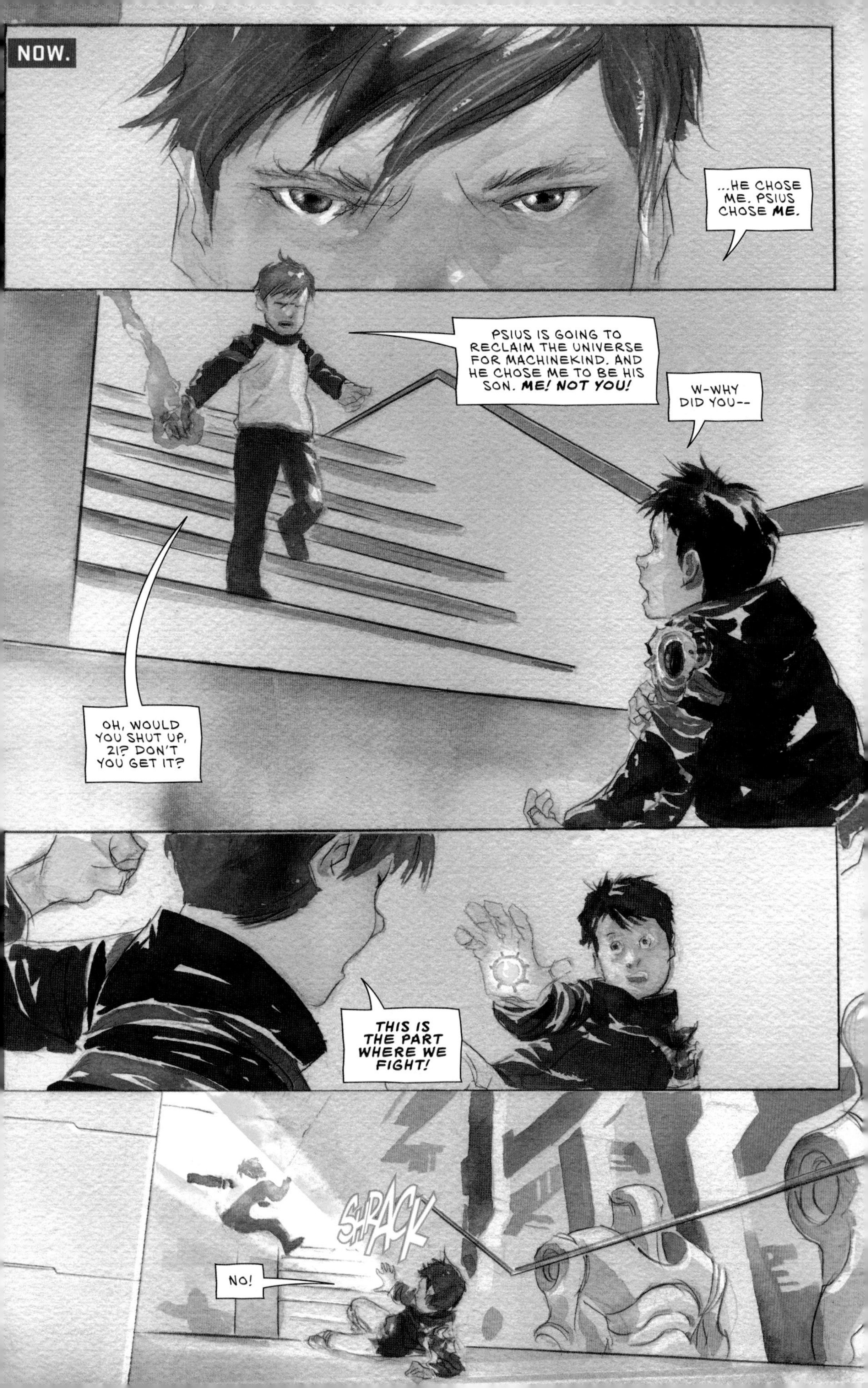
NOW.
...HE CHOSE ME. PSIUS CHOSE **ME.**
PSIUS IS GOING TO RECLAIM THE UNIVERSE FOR MACHINEKIND. AND HE CHOSE ME TO BE HIS SON. ***ME! NOT YOU!***
W-WHY DID YOU--
OH, WOULD YOU SHUT UP, 21? DON'T YOU GET IT?
THIS IS THE PART WHERE WE FIGHT!
SHRACK
NO!

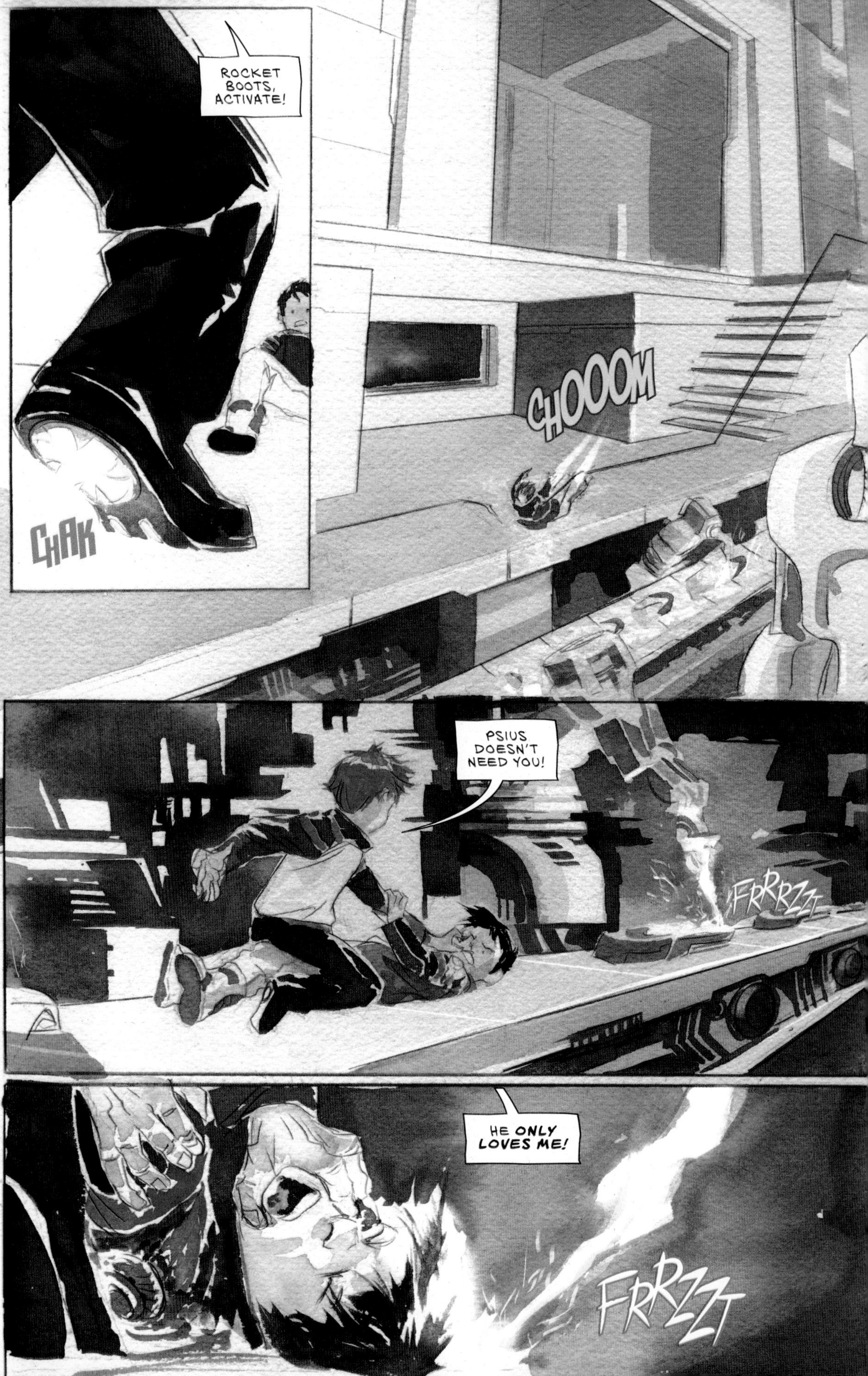
ROCKET BOOTS, ACTIVATE!
CHAK
CHOOOM
PSIUS DOESN'T NEED YOU!
FRRRZZT
HE ONLY LOVES ME!
FRRZZT

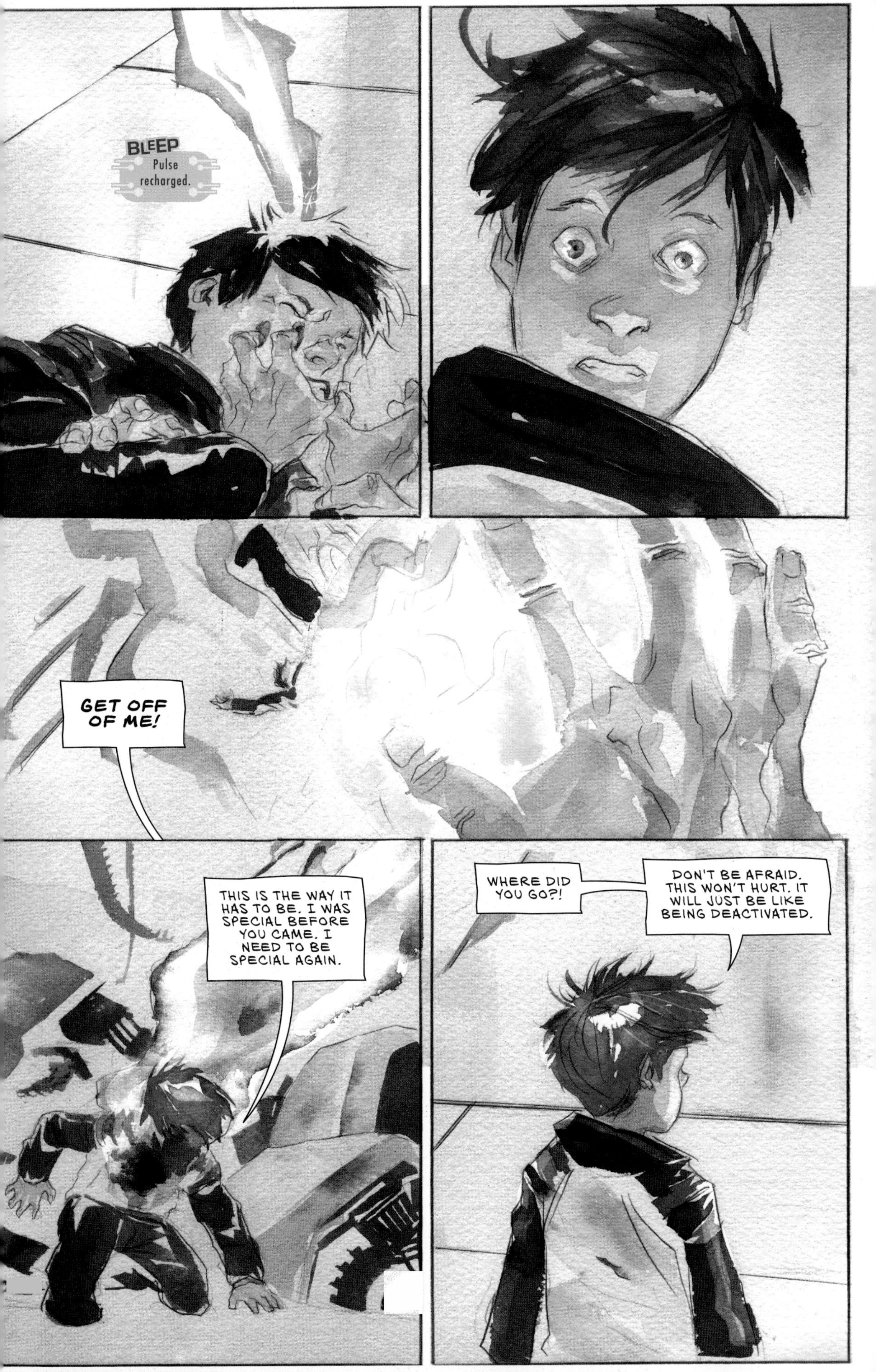
BLEEP
Pulse recharged.
GET OFF OF ME!
THIS IS THE WAY IT HAS TO BE. I WAS SPECIAL BEFORE YOU CAME. I NEED TO BE SPECIAL AGAIN.
WHERE DID YOU GO?!
DON'T BE AFRAID. THIS WON'T HURT. IT WILL JUST BE LIKE BEING DEACTIVATED.

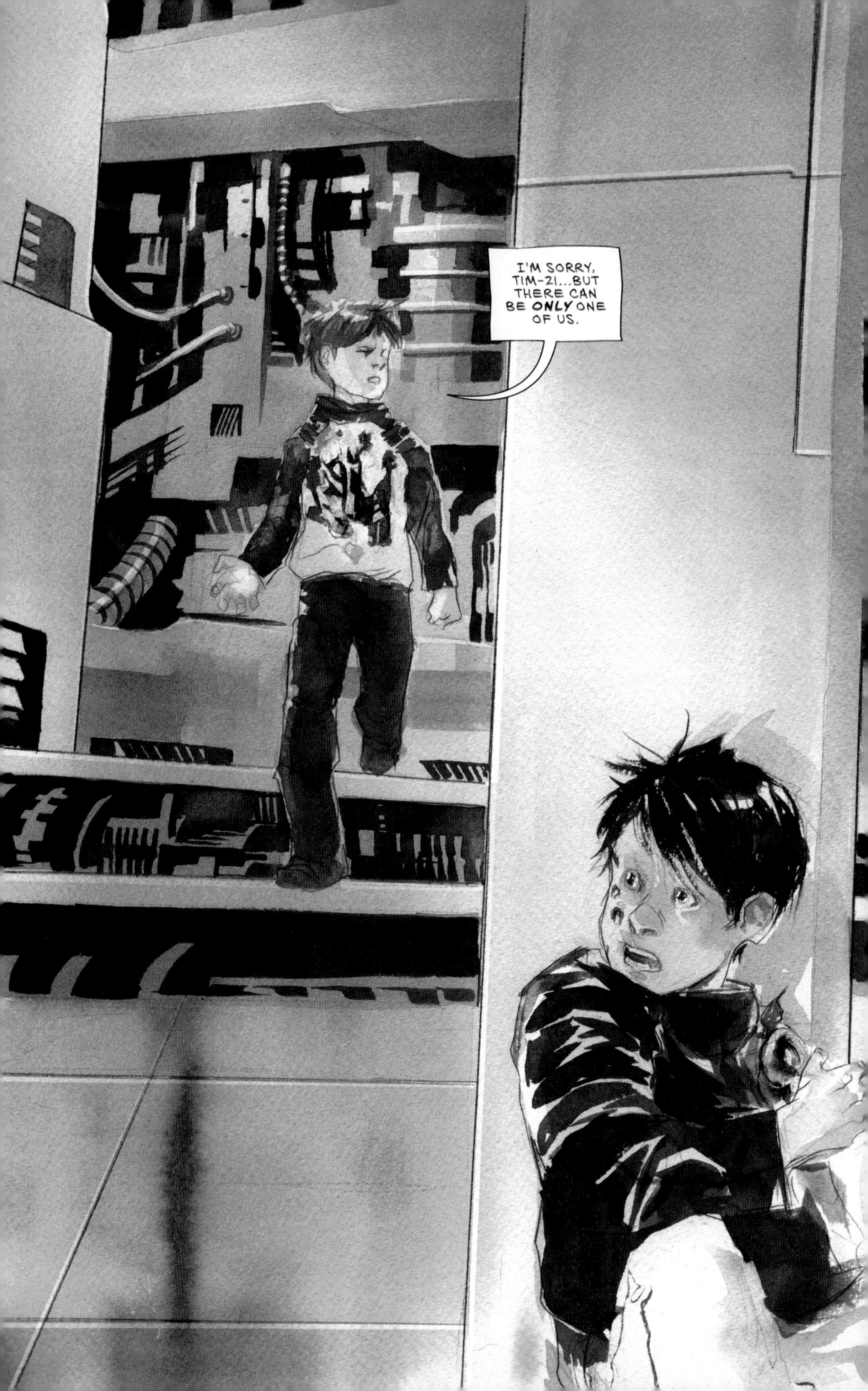
I'M SORRY, TIM-21...BUT THERE CAN BE ONLY ONE OF US.

CHAPTER TWO

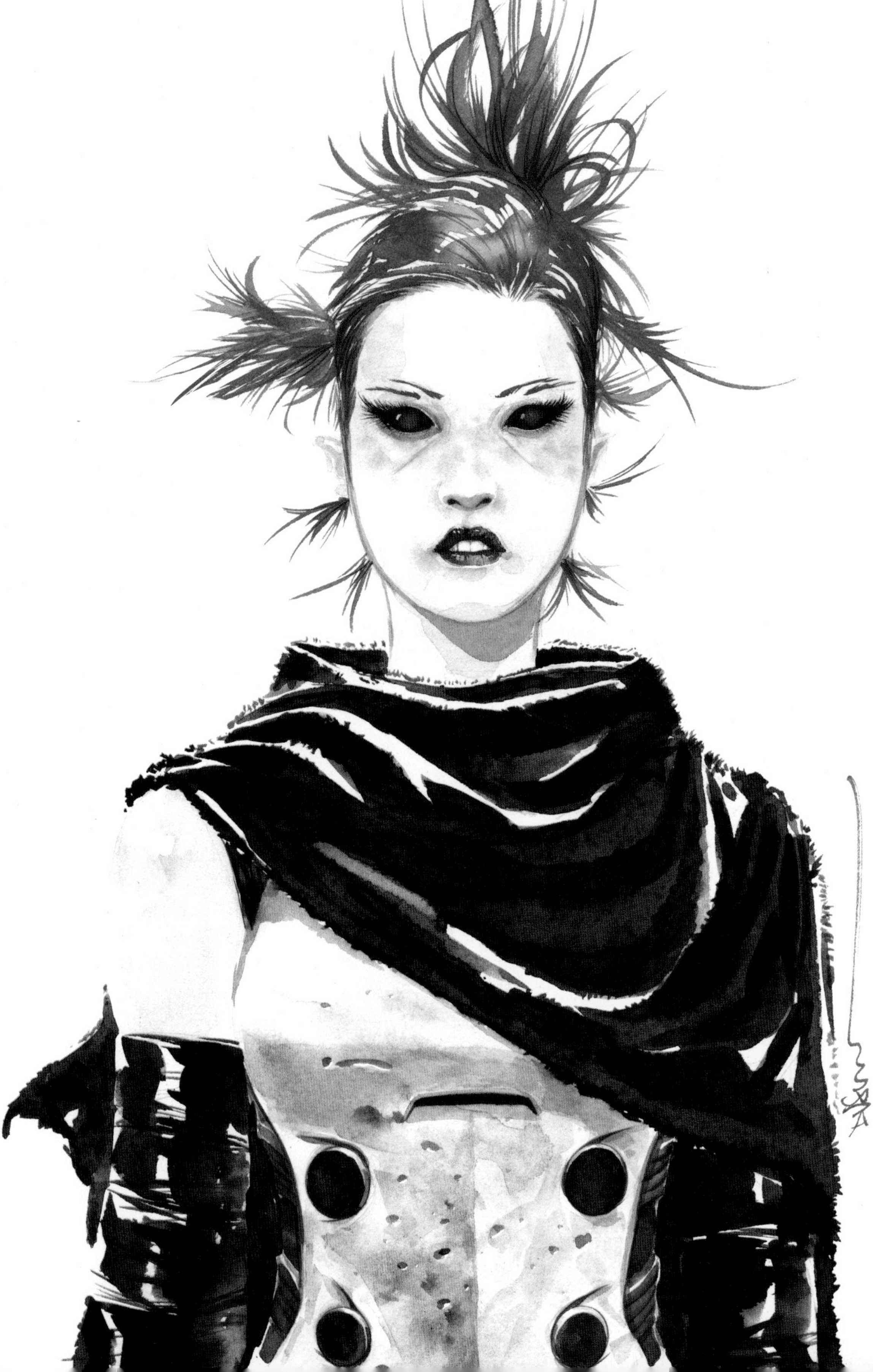

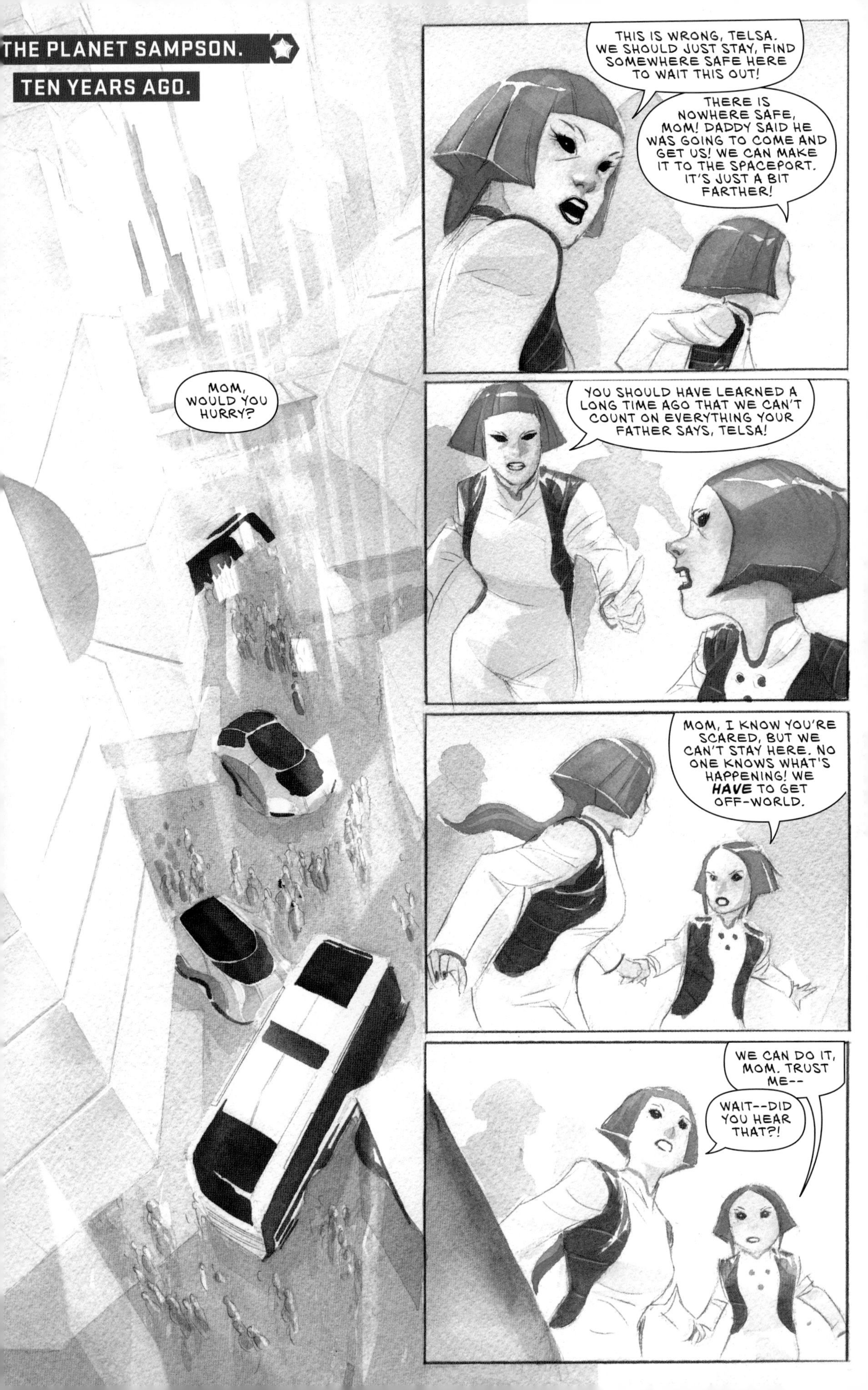
THE PLANET SAMPSON.
TEN YEARS AGO.
MOM, WOULD YOU HURRY?
THIS IS WRONG, TELSA. WE SHOULD JUST STAY, FIND SOMEWHERE SAFE HERE TO WAIT THIS OUT!
THERE IS NOWHERE SAFE, MOM! DADDY SAID HE WAS GOING TO COME AND GET US! WE CAN MAKE IT TO THE SPACEPORT. IT'S JUST A BIT FARTHER!
YOU SHOULD HAVE LEARNED A LONG TIME AGO THAT WE CAN'T COUNT ON EVERYTHING YOUR FATHER SAYS, TELSA!
MOM, I KNOW YOU'RE SCARED, BUT WE CAN'T STAY HERE. NO ONE KNOWS WHAT'S HAPPENING! WE ***HAVE*** TO GET OFF-WORLD.
WE CAN DO IT, MOM. TRUST ME--
WAIT--DID YOU HEAR THAT?!

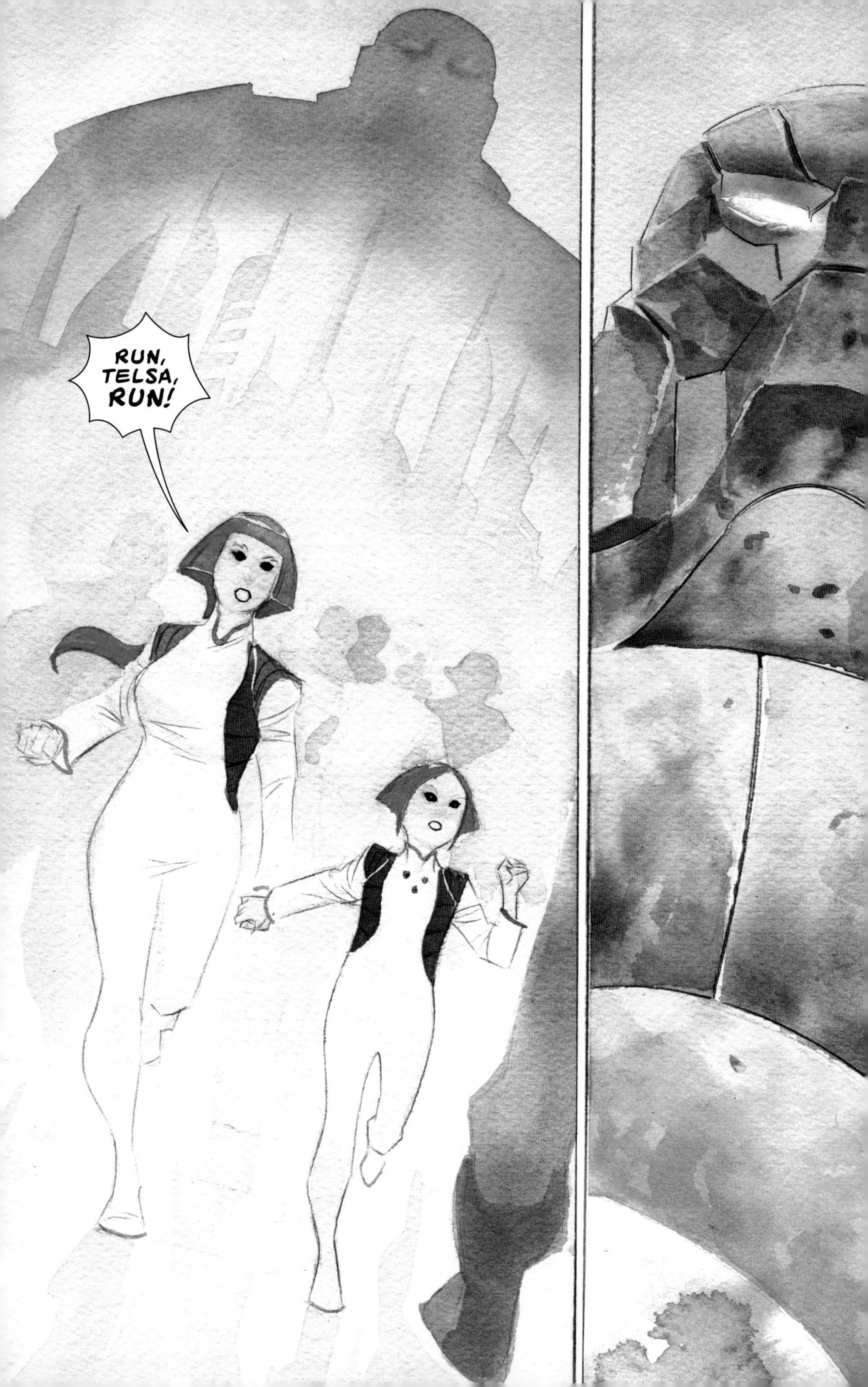
RUN, TELSA, RUN!

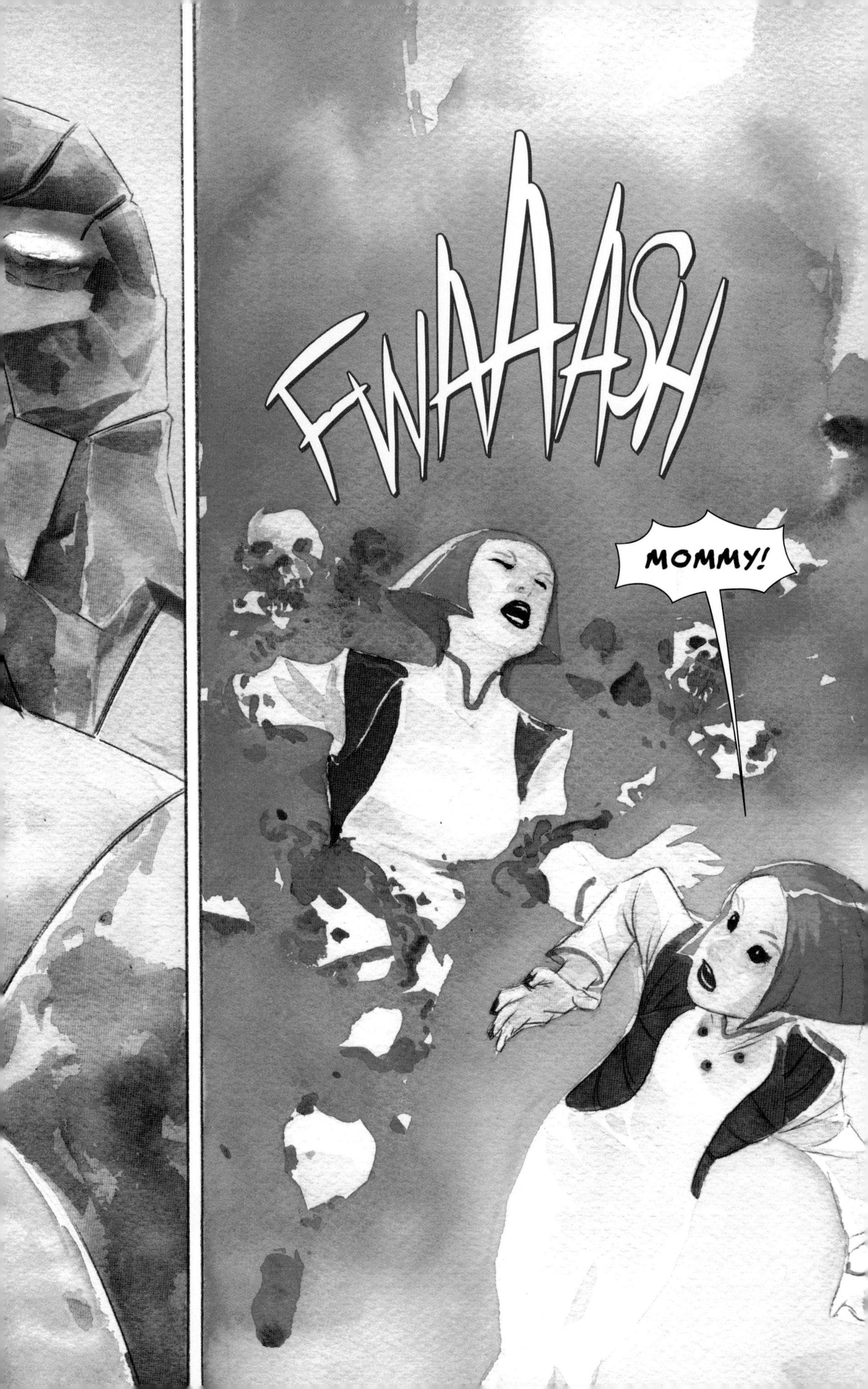
FWAAASH
MOMMY!

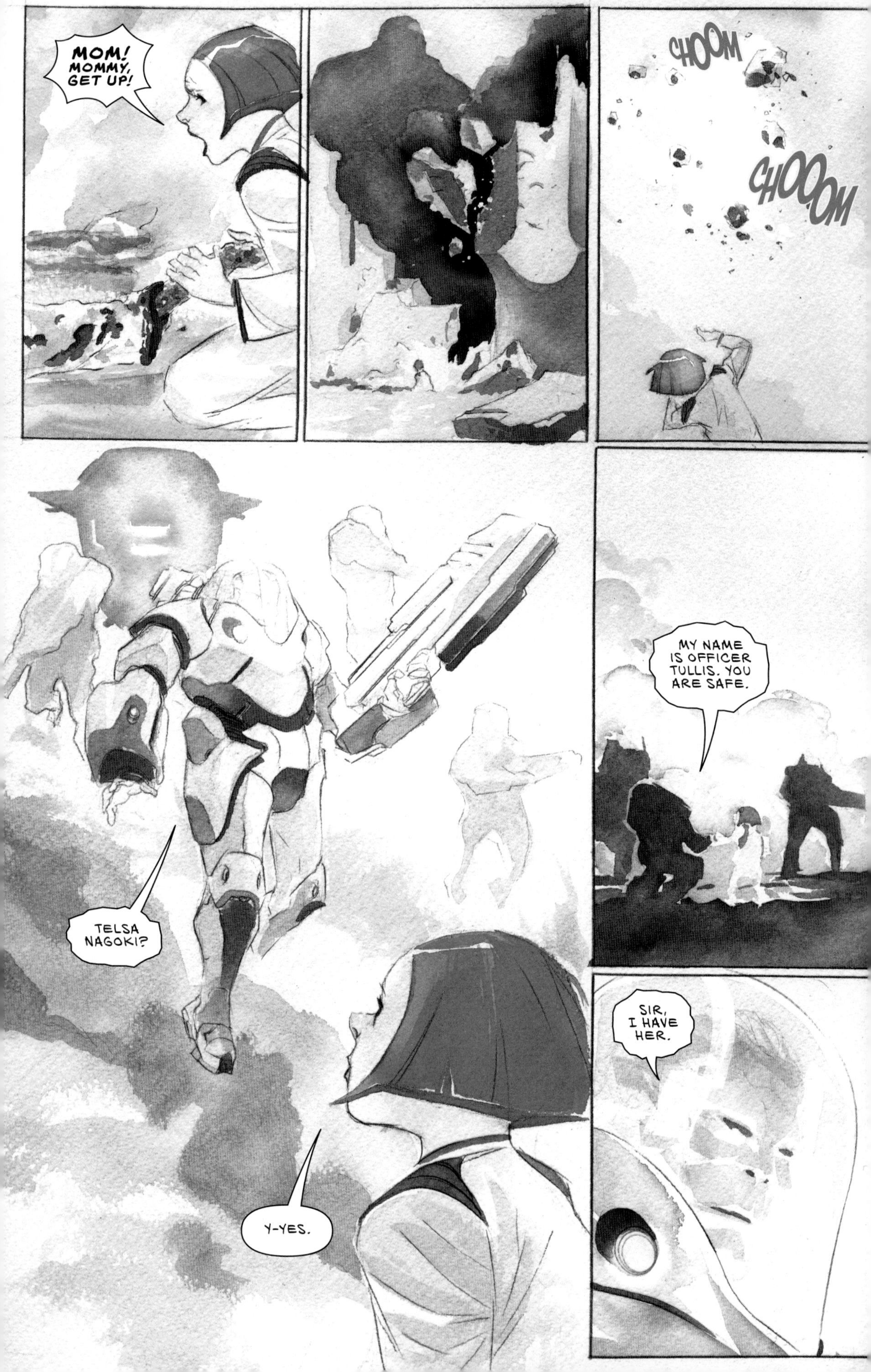
MOM! MOMMY, GET UP!
CHOOM
CHOOOM
TELSA NAGOKI?
Y-YES.
MY NAME IS OFFICER TULLIS. YOU ARE SAFE.
SIR, I HAVE HER.

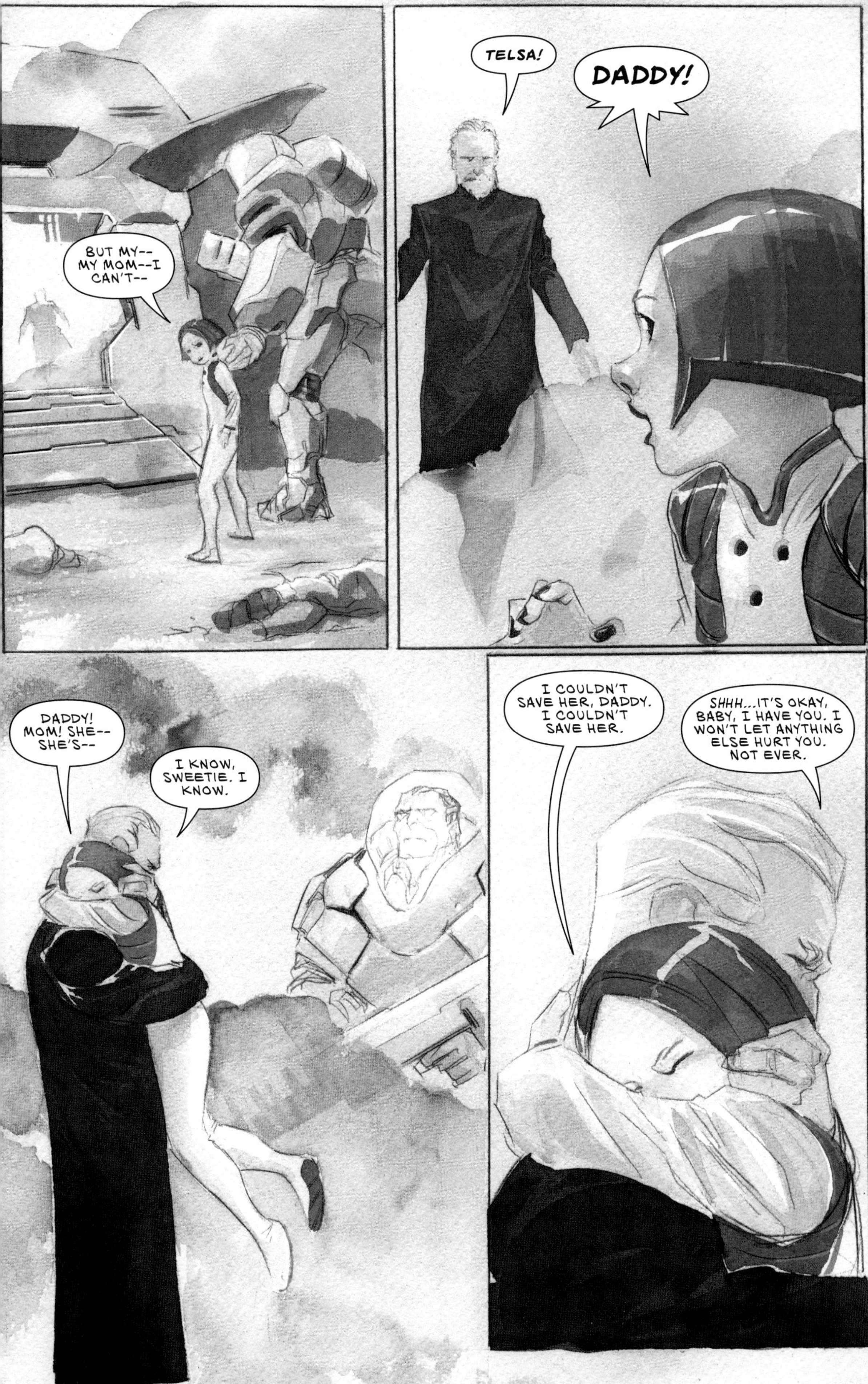
BUT MY--
MY MOM--I
CAN'T--
TELSA!
DADDY!
DADDY!
MOM! SHE--
SHE'S--
I KNOW,
SWEETIE. I
KNOW.
I COULDN'T
SAVE HER, DADDY.
I COULDN'T
SAVE HER.
SHHH...IT'S OKAY,
BABY, I HAVE YOU. I
WON'T LET ANYTHING
ELSE HURT YOU.
NOT EVER.

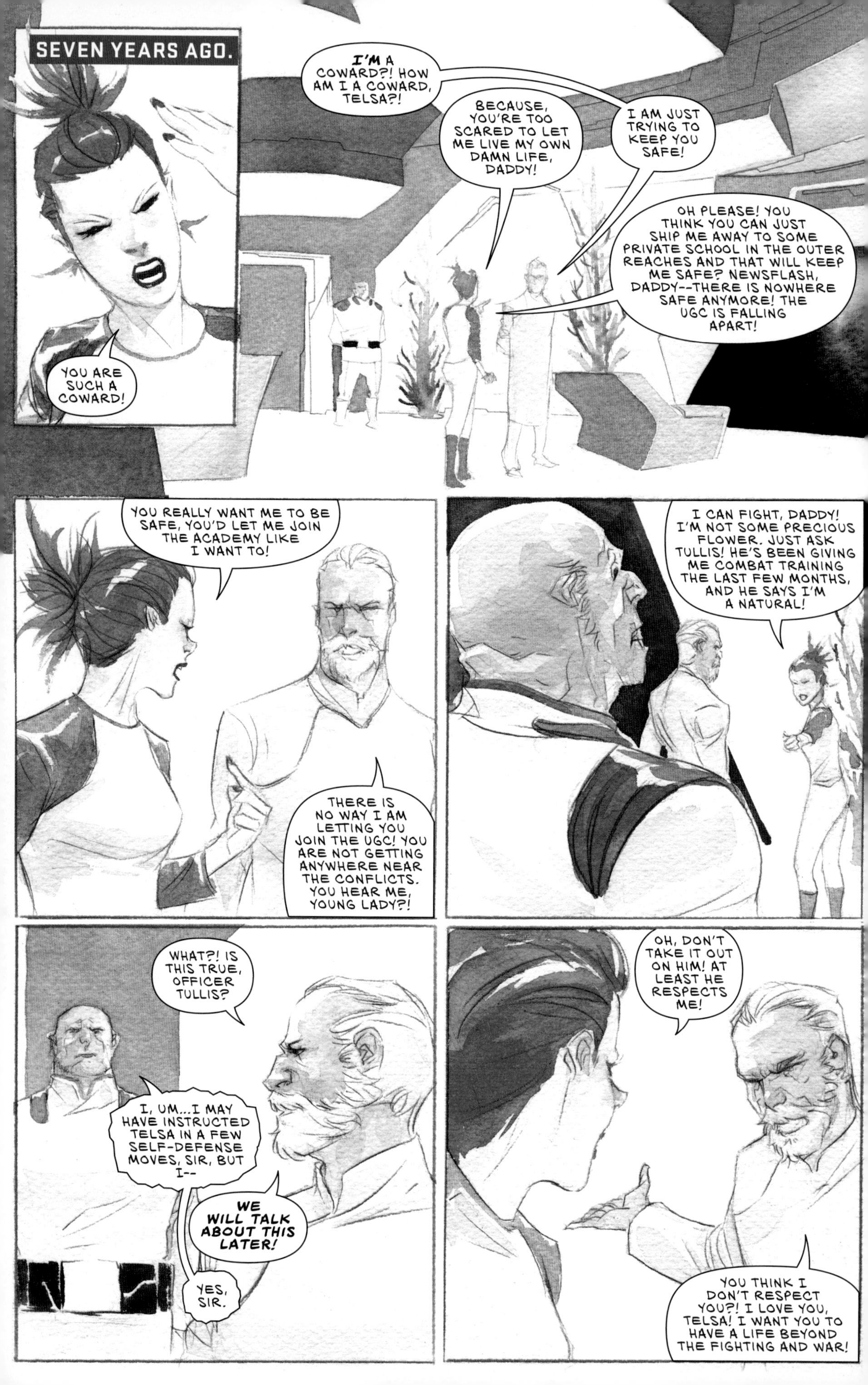
SEVEN YEARS AGO.
YOU ARE SUCH A COWARD!
I'M A COWARD?! HOW AM I A COWARD, TELSA?!
BECAUSE, YOU'RE TOO SCARED TO LET ME LIVE MY OWN DAMN LIFE, DADDY!
I AM JUST TRYING TO KEEP YOU SAFE!
OH PLEASE! YOU THINK YOU CAN JUST SHIP ME AWAY TO SOME PRIVATE SCHOOL IN THE OUTER REACHES AND THAT WILL KEEP ME SAFE? NEWSFLASH, DADDY--THERE IS NOWHERE SAFE ANYMORE! THE UGC IS FALLING APART!
YOU REALLY WANT ME TO BE SAFE, YOU'D LET ME JOIN THE ACADEMY LIKE I WANT TO!
THERE IS NO WAY I AM LETTING YOU JOIN THE UGC! YOU ARE NOT GETTING ANYWHERE NEAR THE CONFLICTS. YOU HEAR ME, YOUNG LADY?!
I CAN FIGHT, DADDY! I'M NOT SOME PRECIOUS FLOWER. JUST ASK TULLIS! HE'S BEEN GIVING ME COMBAT TRAINING THE LAST FEW MONTHS, AND HE SAYS I'M A NATURAL!
WHAT?! IS THIS TRUE, OFFICER TULLIS?
I, UM...I MAY HAVE INSTRUCTED TELSA IN A FEW SELF-DEFENSE MOVES, SIR, BUT I--
WE WILL TALK ABOUT THIS LATER!
YES, SIR.
OH, DON'T TAKE IT OUT ON HIM! AT LEAST HE RESPECTS ME!
YOU THINK I DON'T RESPECT YOU?! I LOVE YOU, TELSA! I WANT YOU TO HAVE A LIFE BEYOND THE FIGHTING AND WAR!

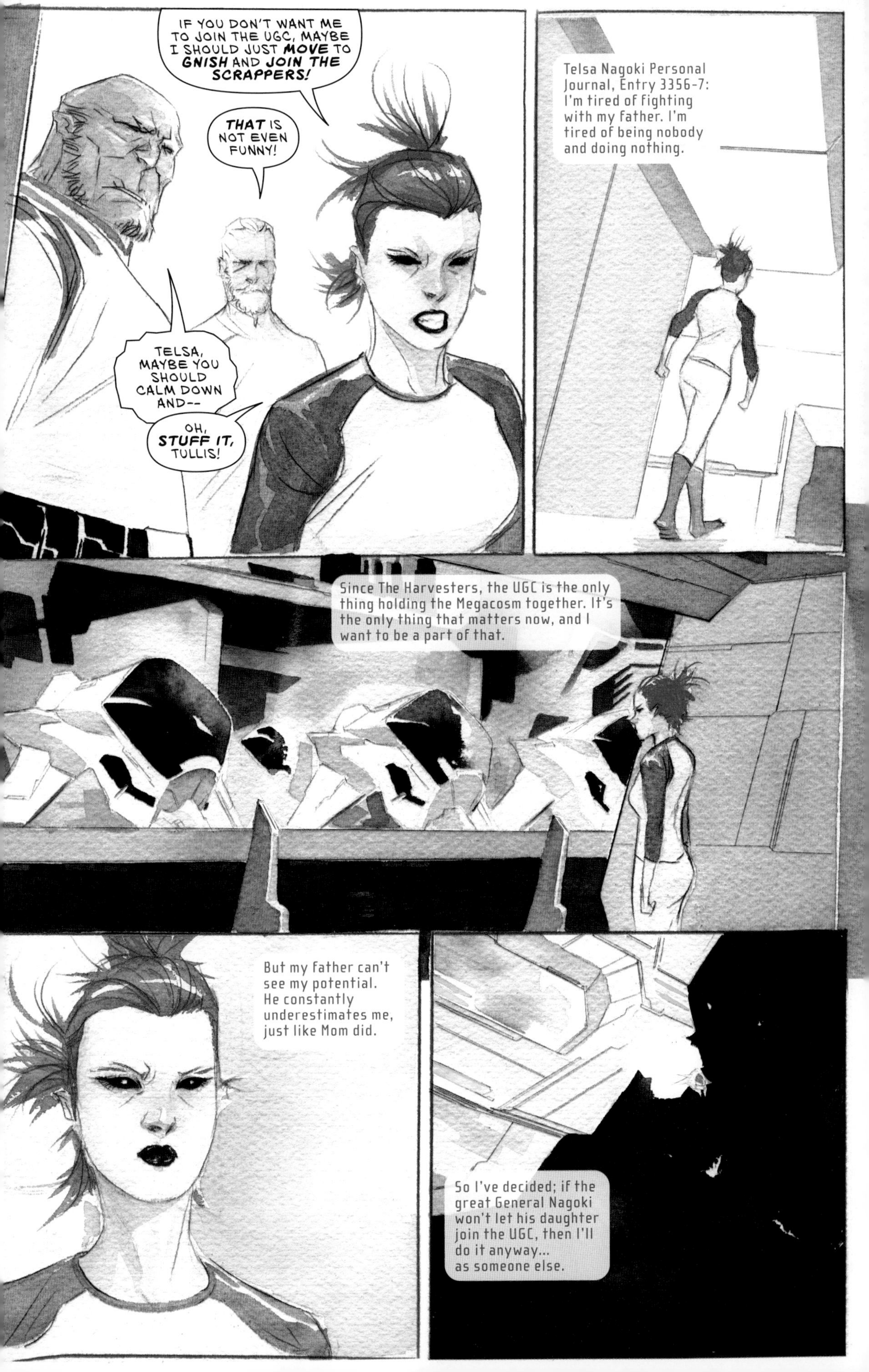

IF YOU DON'T WANT ME TO JOIN THE UGC, MAYBE I SHOULD JUST MOVE TO GNISH AND JOIN THE SCRAPPERS!
THAT IS NOT EVEN FUNNY!
TELSA, MAYBE YOU SHOULD CALM DOWN AND--
OH, STUFF IT, TULLIS!
Telsa Nagoki Personal Journal, Entry 3356-7: I'm tired of fighting with my father. I'm tired of being nobody and doing nothing.
Since The Harvesters, the UGC is the only thing holding the Megacosm together. It's the only thing that matters now, and I want to be a part of that.
But my father can't see my potential. He constantly underestimates me, just like Mom did.
So I've decided; if the great General Nagoki won't let his daughter join the UGC, then I'll do it anyway... as someone else.

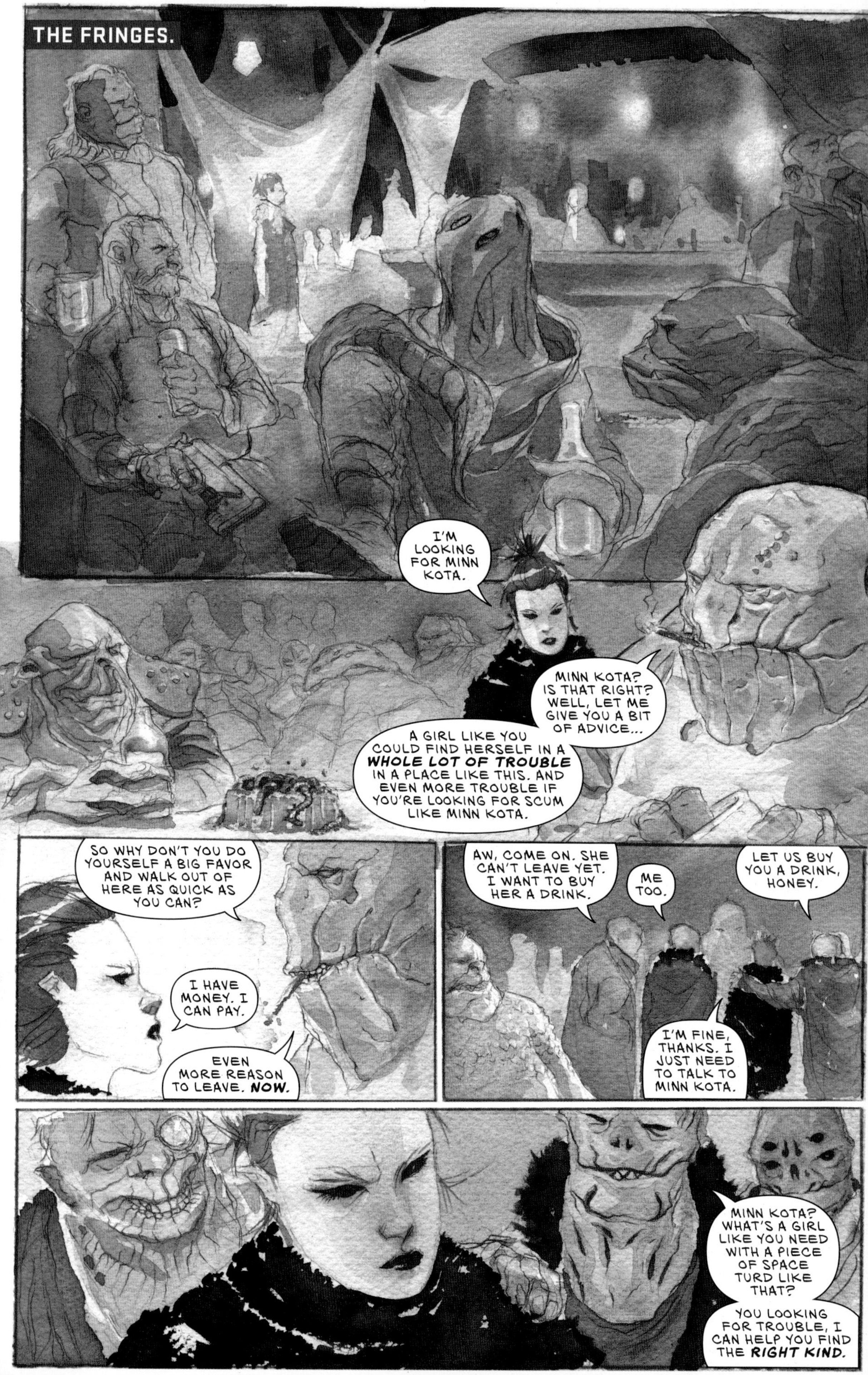
THE FRINGES.
I'M LOOKING FOR MINN KOTA.
MINN KOTA? IS THAT RIGHT? WELL, LET ME GIVE YOU A BIT OF ADVICE...
A GIRL LIKE YOU COULD FIND HERSELF IN A WHOLE LOT OF TROUBLE IN A PLACE LIKE THIS. AND EVEN MORE TROUBLE IF YOU'RE LOOKING FOR SCUM LIKE MINN KOTA.
SO WHY DON'T YOU DO YOURSELF A BIG FAVOR AND WALK OUT OF HERE AS QUICK AS YOU CAN?
I HAVE MONEY. I CAN PAY.
EVEN MORE REASON TO LEAVE. NOW.
AW, COME ON. SHE CAN'T LEAVE YET. I WANT TO BUY HER A DRINK.
ME TOO.
LET US BUY YOU A DRINK, HONEY.
I'M FINE, THANKS. I JUST NEED TO TALK TO MINN KOTA.
MINN KOTA? WHAT'S A GIRL LIKE YOU NEED WITH A PIECE OF SPACE TURD LIKE THAT?
YOU LOOKING FOR TROUBLE, I CAN HELP YOU FIND THE RIGHT KIND.

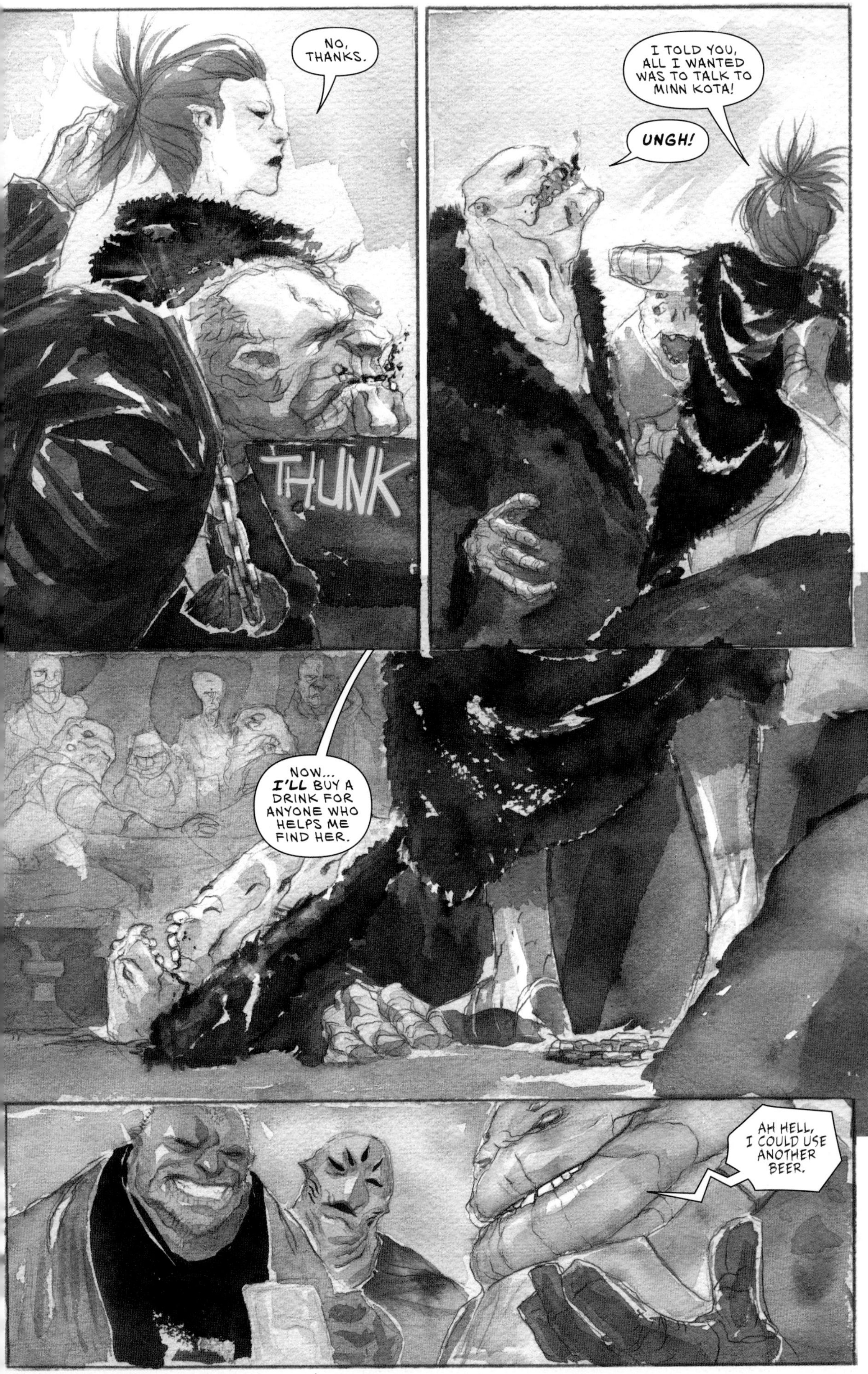
NO, THANKS.
THUNK
UNGH!
I TOLD YOU, ALL I WANTED WAS TO TALK TO MINN KOTA!
NOW... I'LL BUY A DRINK FOR ANYONE WHO HELPS ME FIND HER.
AH HELL, I COULD USE ANOTHER BEER.

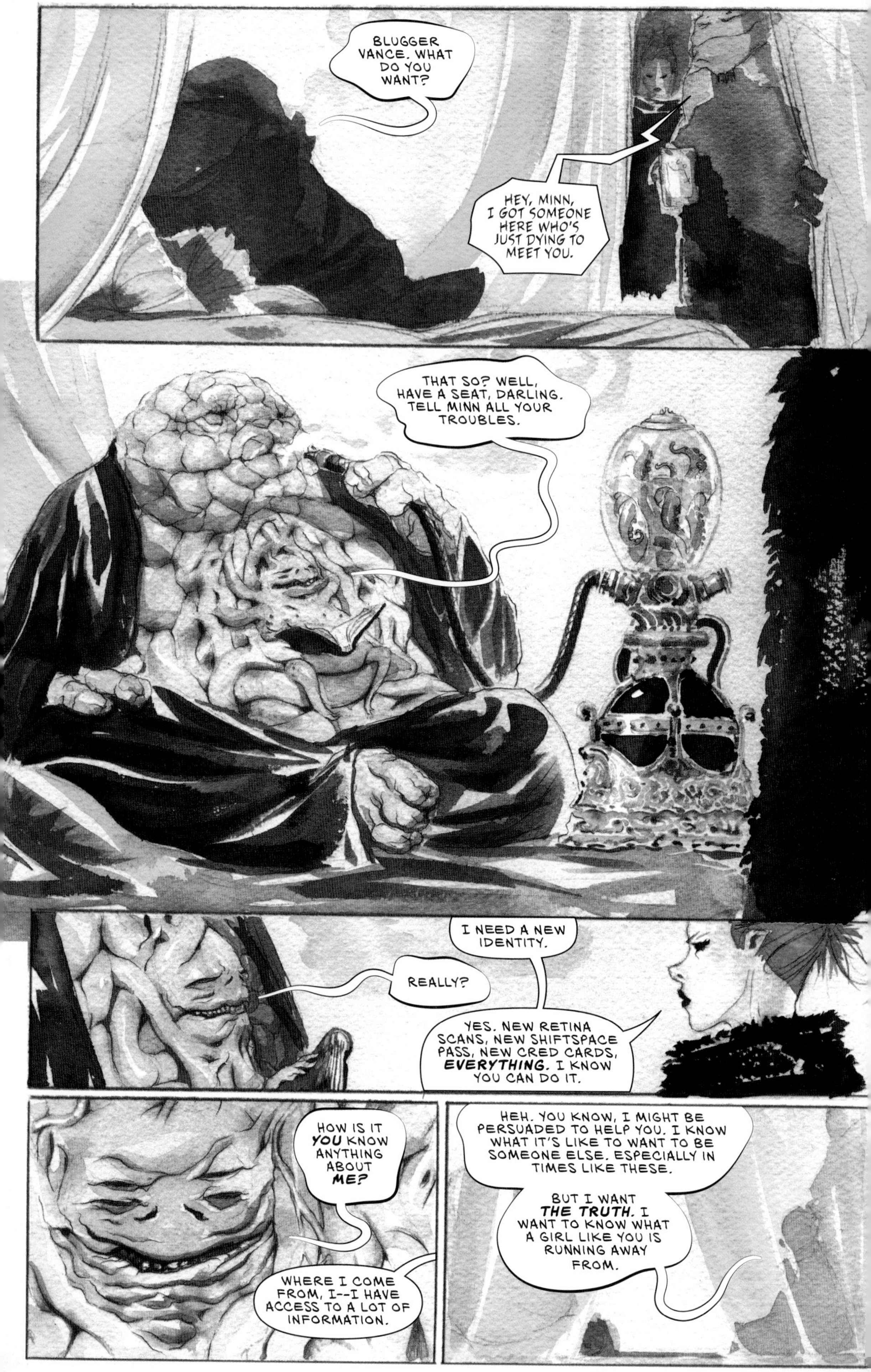
BLUGGER VANCE. WHAT DO YOU WANT?
HEY, MINN, I GOT SOMEONE HERE WHO'S JUST DYING TO MEET YOU.
THAT SO? WELL, HAVE A SEAT, DARLING. TELL MINN ALL YOUR TROUBLES.
I NEED A NEW IDENTITY.
REALLY?
YES. NEW RETINA SCANS, NEW SHIFTSPACE PASS, NEW CRED CARDS, EVERYTHING. I KNOW YOU CAN DO IT.
HOW IS IT YOU KNOW ANYTHING ABOUT ME?
WHERE I COME FROM, I--I HAVE ACCESS TO A LOT OF INFORMATION.
HEH. YOU KNOW, I MIGHT BE PERSUADED TO HELP YOU. I KNOW WHAT IT'S LIKE TO WANT TO BE SOMEONE ELSE. ESPECIALLY IN TIMES LIKE THESE.
BUT I WANT THE TRUTH. I WANT TO KNOW WHAT A GIRL LIKE YOU IS RUNNING AWAY FROM.

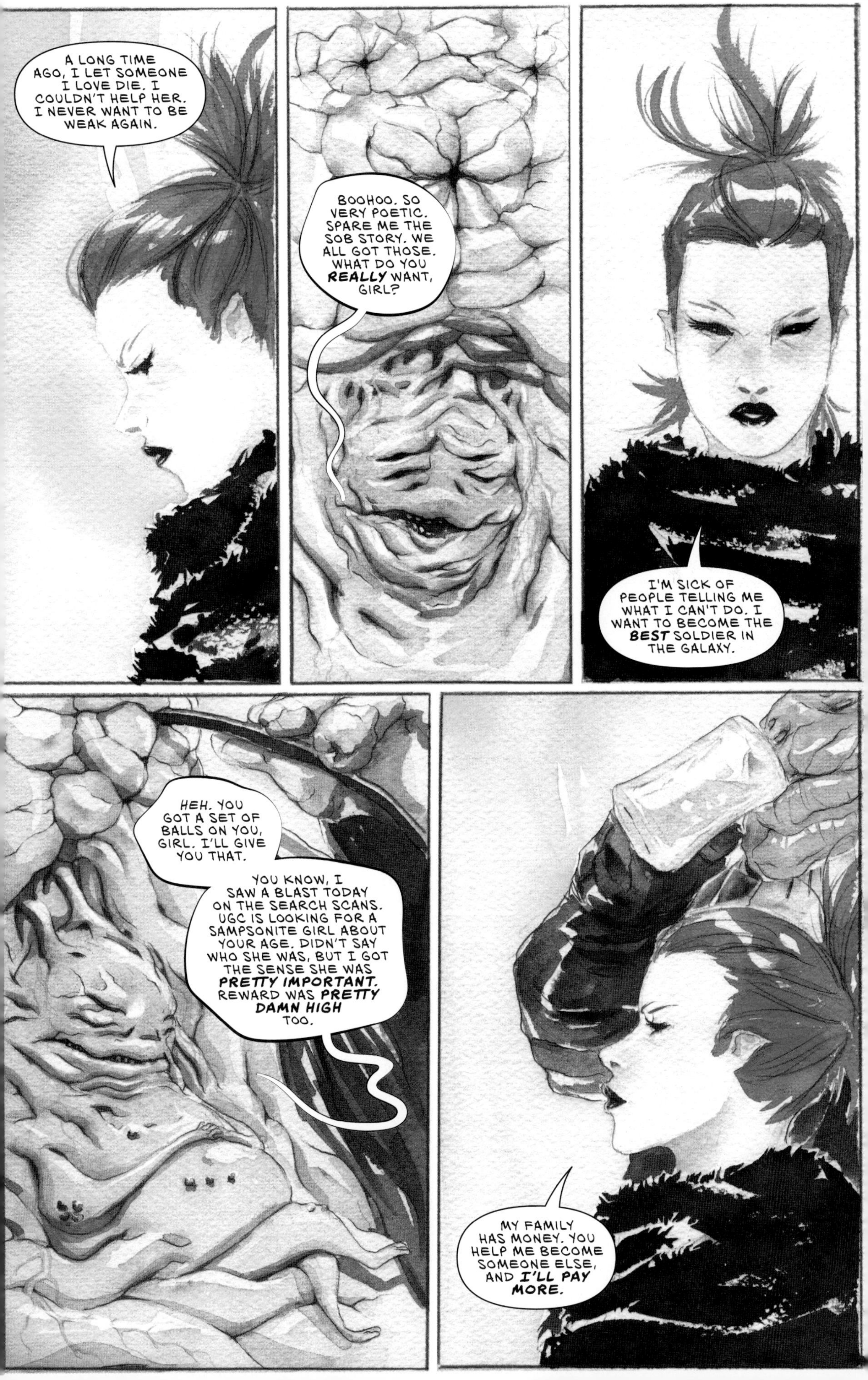
A LONG TIME AGO, I LET SOMEONE I LOVE DIE. I COULDN'T HELP HER. I NEVER WANT TO BE WEAK AGAIN.
BOOHOO. SO VERY POETIC. SPARE ME THE SOB STORY. WE ALL GOT THOSE. WHAT DO YOU **REALLY** WANT, GIRL?
I'M SICK OF PEOPLE TELLING ME WHAT I CAN'T DO. I WANT TO BECOME THE **BEST** SOLDIER IN THE GALAXY.
HEH. YOU GOT A SET OF BALLS ON YOU, GIRL. I'LL GIVE YOU THAT.
YOU KNOW, I SAW A BLAST TODAY ON THE SEARCH SCANS. UGC IS LOOKING FOR A SAMPSONITE GIRL ABOUT YOUR AGE. DIDN'T SAY WHO SHE WAS, BUT I GOT THE SENSE SHE WAS **PRETTY IMPORTANT.** REWARD WAS **PRETTY DAMN HIGH** TOO.
MY FAMILY HAS MONEY. YOU HELP ME BECOME SOMEONE ELSE, AND ***I'LL PAY MORE.***

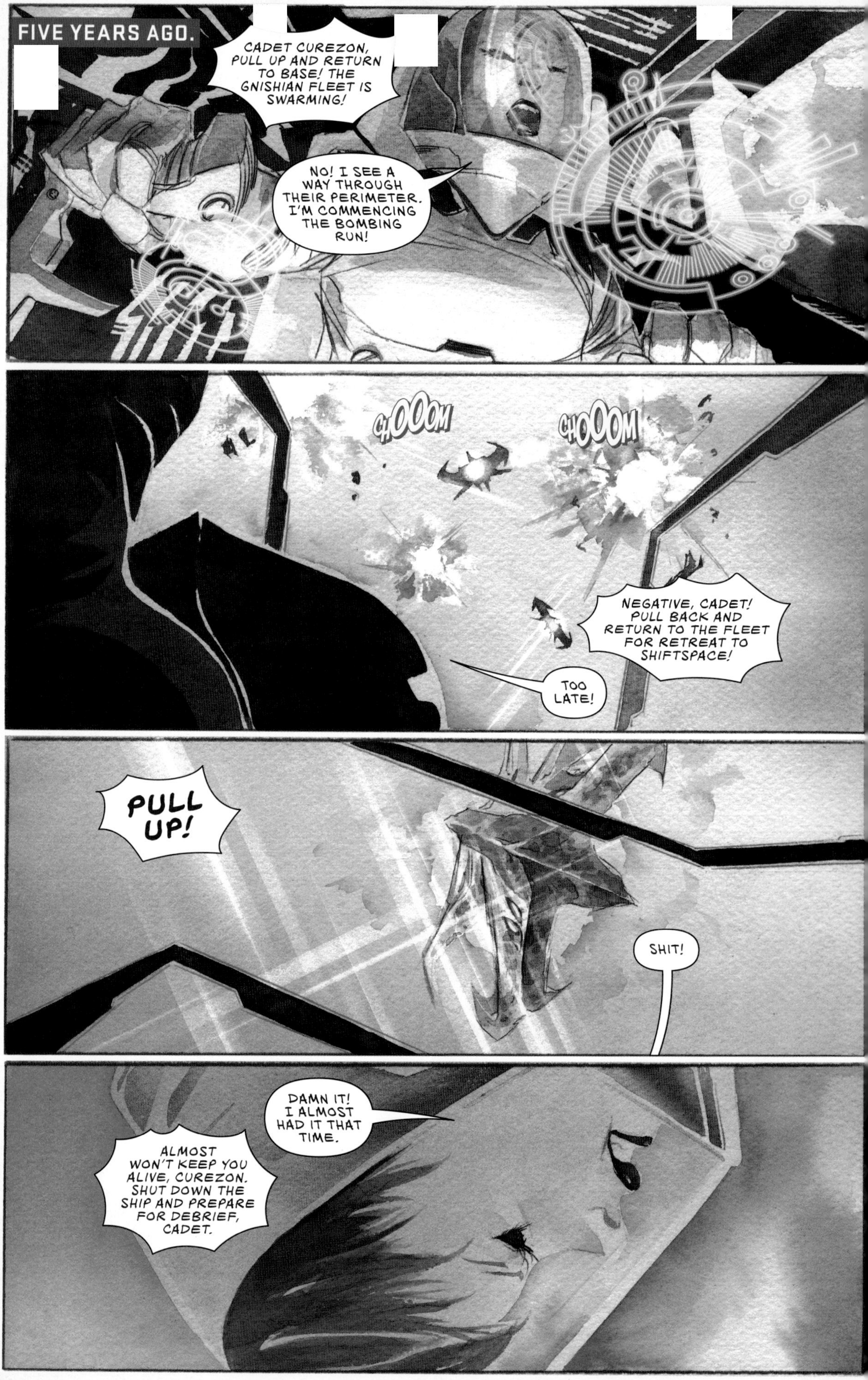
FIVE YEARS AGO.
CADET CUREZON, PULL UP AND RETURN TO BASE! THE GNISHIAN FLEET IS SWARMING!
NO! I SEE A WAY THROUGH THEIR PERIMETER. I'M COMMENCING THE BOMBING RUN!
CHOOOM
CHOOOM
NEGATIVE, CADET! PULL BACK AND RETURN TO THE FLEET FOR RETREAT TO SHIFTSPACE!
TOO LATE!
PULL UP!
SHIT!
DAMN IT! I ALMOST HAD IT THAT TIME.
ALMOST WON'T KEEP YOU ALIVE, CUREZON. SHUT DOWN THE SHIP AND PREPARE FOR DEBRIEF, CADET.

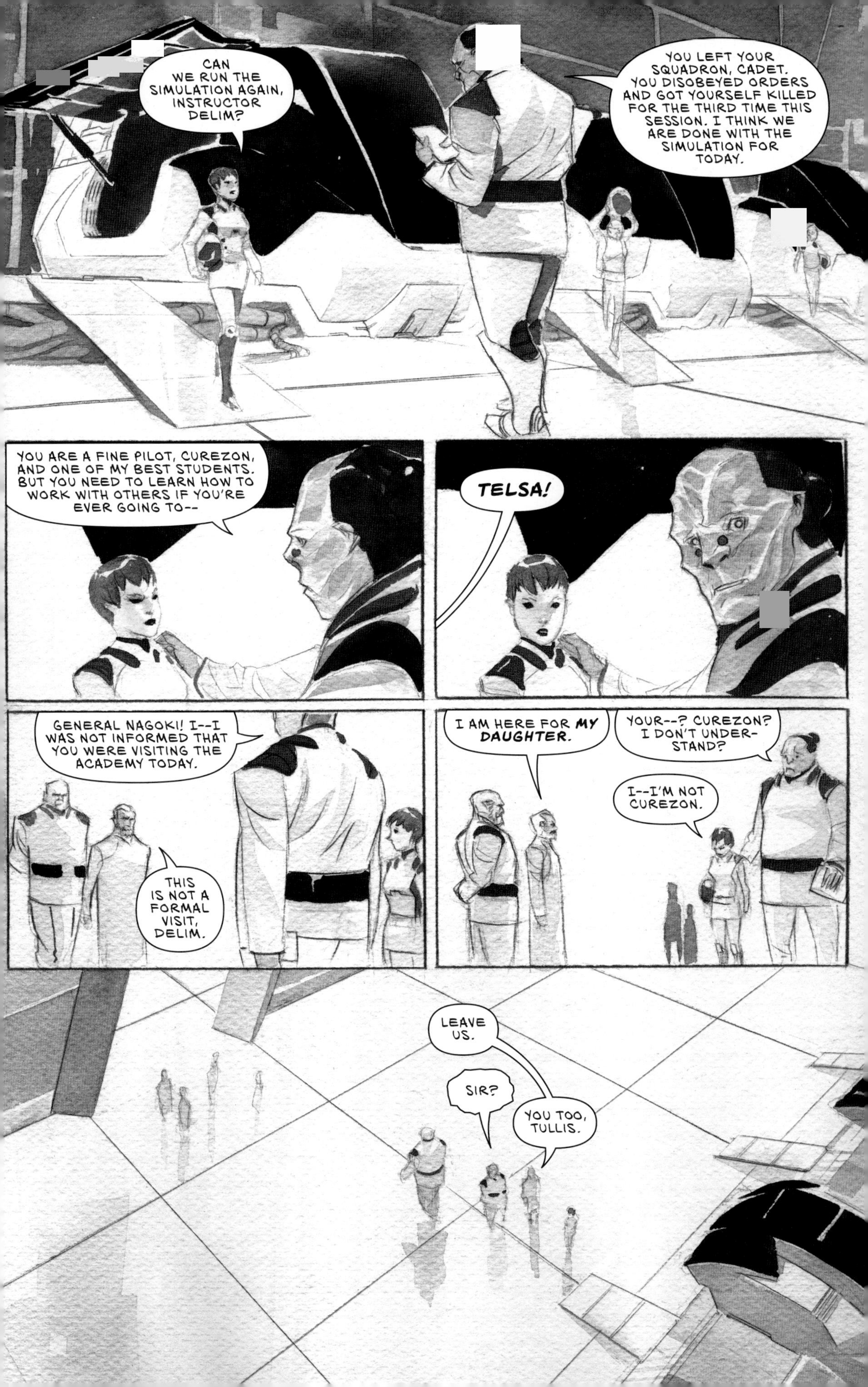
CAN WE RUN THE SIMULATION AGAIN, INSTRUCTOR DELIM?
YOU LEFT YOUR SQUADRON, CADET. YOU DISOBEYED ORDERS AND GOT YOURSELF KILLED FOR THE THIRD TIME THIS SESSION. I THINK WE ARE DONE WITH THE SIMULATION FOR TODAY.
YOU ARE A FINE PILOT, CUREZON, AND ONE OF MY BEST STUDENTS. BUT YOU NEED TO LEARN HOW TO WORK WITH OTHERS IF YOU'RE EVER GOING TO--
TELSA!
GENERAL NAGOKI! I--I WAS NOT INFORMED THAT YOU WERE VISITING THE ACADEMY TODAY.
THIS IS NOT A FORMAL VISIT, DELIM.
I AM HERE FOR MY DAUGHTER.
YOUR--? CUREZON? I DON'T UNDER-STAND?
I--I'M NOT CUREZON.
LEAVE US.
SIR?
YOU TOO, TULLIS.

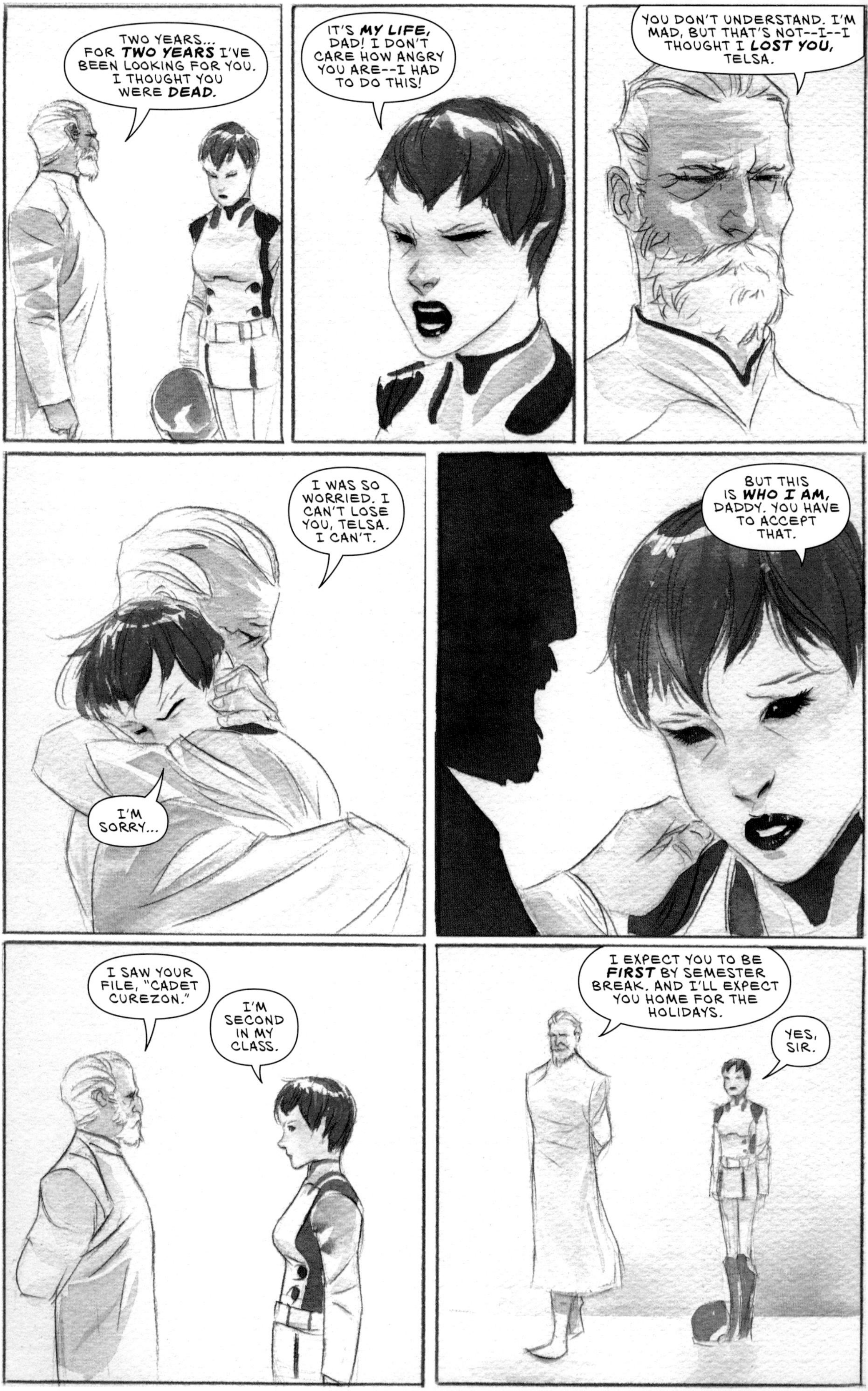
TWO YEARS... FOR **TWO YEARS** I'VE BEEN LOOKING FOR YOU. I THOUGHT YOU WERE **DEAD.**
IT'S **MY LIFE,** DAD! I DON'T CARE HOW ANGRY YOU ARE--I HAD TO DO THIS!
YOU DON'T UNDERSTAND. I'M MAD, BUT THAT'S NOT--I--I THOUGHT I **LOST YOU,** TELSA.
I WAS SO WORRIED. I CAN'T LOSE YOU, TELSA. I CAN'T.
I'M SORRY...
BUT THIS IS **WHO I AM,** DADDY. YOU HAVE TO ACCEPT THAT.
I SAW YOUR FILE, "CADET CUREZON."
I'M SECOND IN MY CLASS.
I EXPECT YOU TO BE **FIRST** BY SEMESTER BREAK. AND I'LL EXPECT YOU HOME FOR THE HOLIDAYS.
YES, SIR.

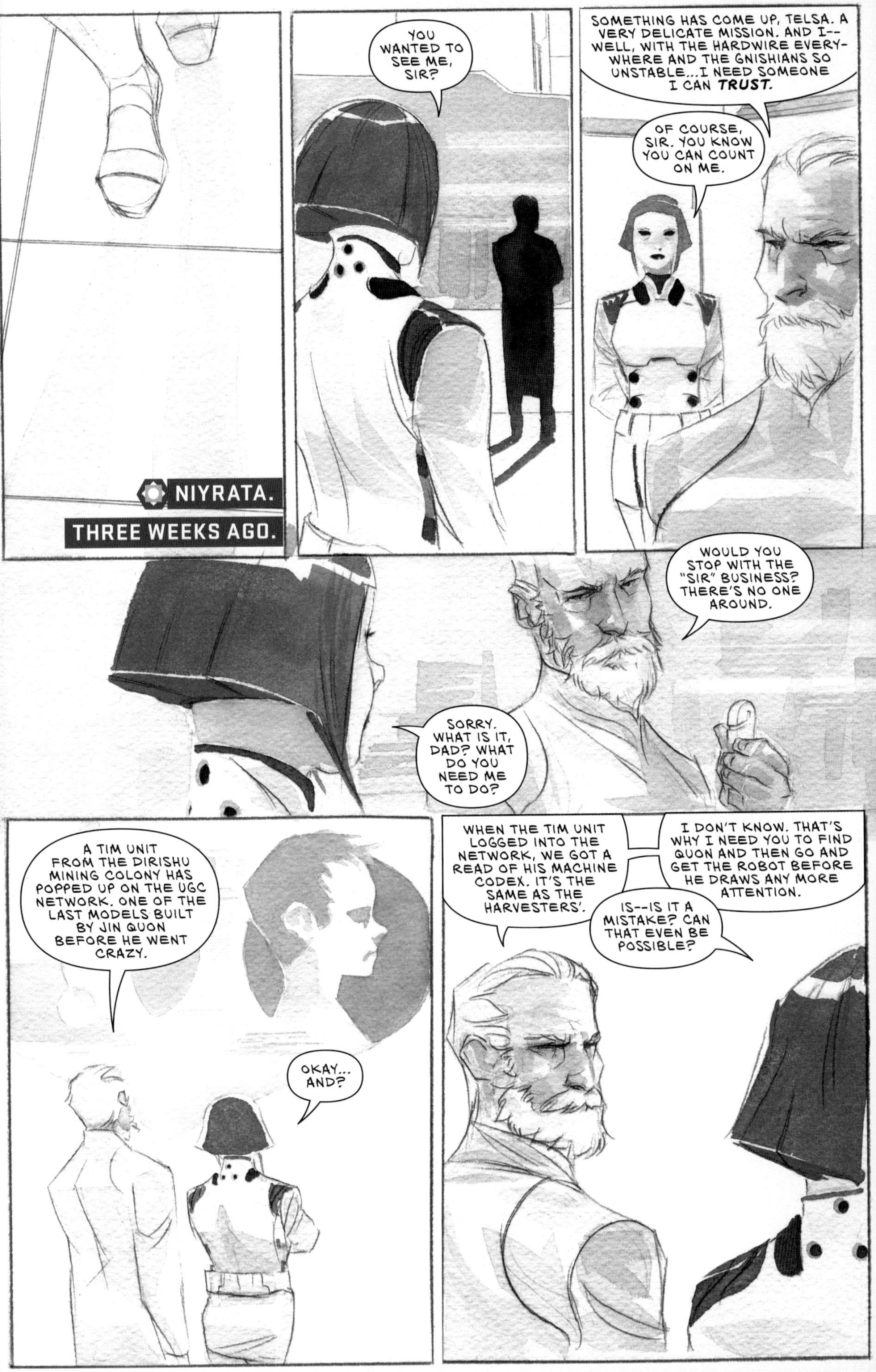
NIYRATA.
THREE WEEKS AGO.
YOU WANTED TO SEE ME, SIR?
SOMETHING HAS COME UP, TELSA. A VERY DELICATE MISSION. AND I--WELL, WITH THE HARDWIRE EVERYWHERE AND THE GNISHIANS SO UNSTABLE...I NEED SOMEONE I CAN TRUST.
OF COURSE, SIR. YOU KNOW YOU CAN COUNT ON ME.
WOULD YOU STOP WITH THE "SIR" BUSINESS? THERE'S NO ONE AROUND.
SORRY. WHAT IS IT, DAD? WHAT DO YOU NEED ME TO DO?
A TIM UNIT FROM THE DIRISHU MINING COLONY HAS POPPED UP ON THE UGC NETWORK. ONE OF THE LAST MODELS BUILT BY JIN QUON BEFORE HE WENT CRAZY.
OKAY... AND?
WHEN THE TIM UNIT LOGGED INTO THE NETWORK, WE GOT A READ OF HIS MACHINE CODEX. IT'S THE SAME AS THE HARVESTERS'.
IS--IS IT A MISTAKE? CAN THAT EVEN BE POSSIBLE?
I DON'T KNOW. THAT'S WHY I NEED YOU TO FIND QUON AND THEN GO AND GET THE ROBOT BEFORE HE DRAWS ANY MORE ATTENTION.

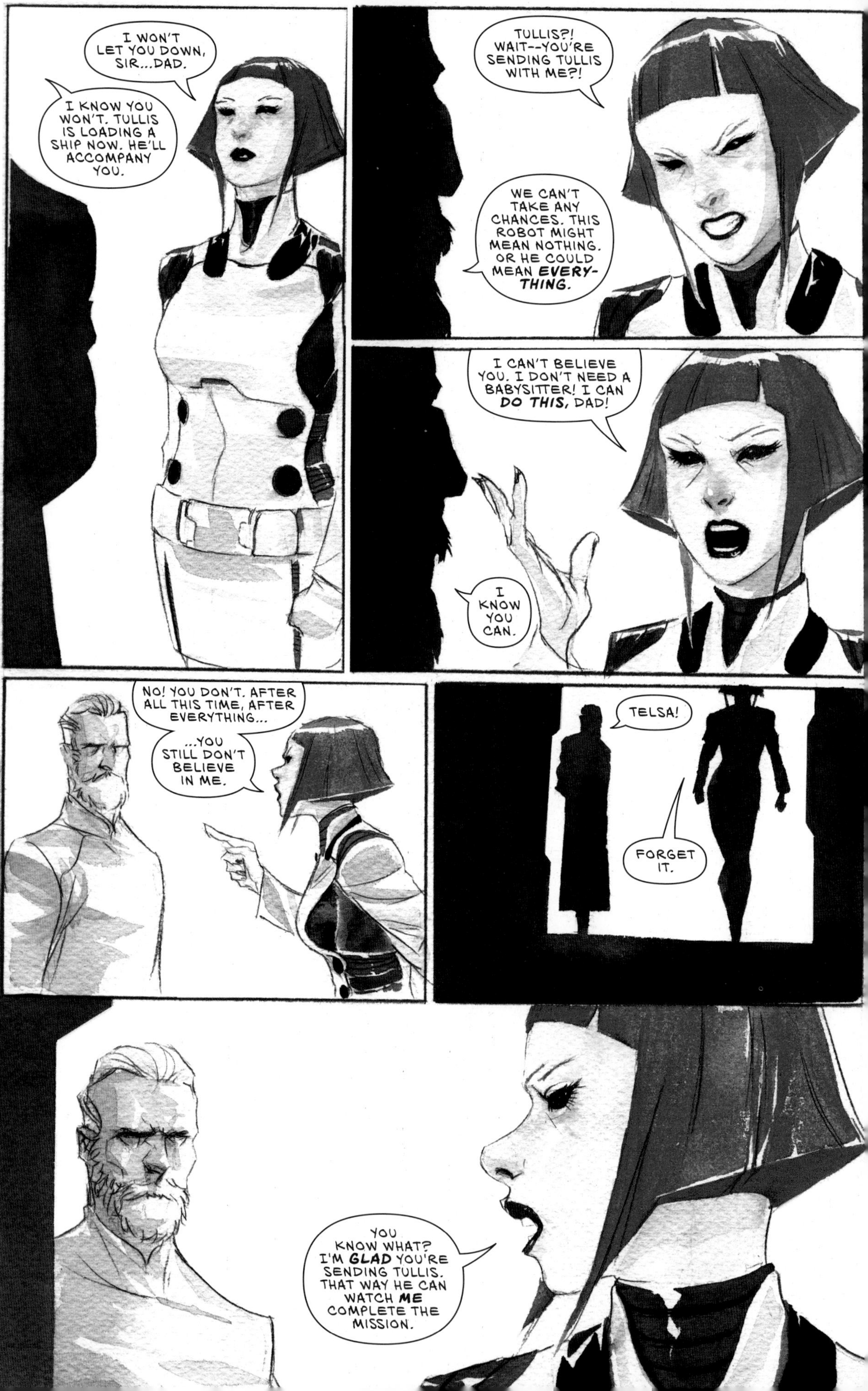
I WON'T LET YOU DOWN, SIR...DAD.
I KNOW YOU WON'T. TULLIS IS LOADING A SHIP NOW. HE'LL ACCOMPANY YOU.
TULLIS?! WAIT--YOU'RE SENDING TULLIS WITH ME?!
WE CAN'T TAKE ANY CHANCES. THIS ROBOT MIGHT MEAN NOTHING. OR HE COULD MEAN EVERY-THING.
I CAN'T BELIEVE YOU. I DON'T NEED A BABYSITTER! I CAN DO THIS, DAD!
I KNOW YOU CAN.
NO! YOU DON'T. AFTER ALL THIS TIME, AFTER EVERYTHING...
...YOU STILL DON'T BELIEVE IN ME.
TELSA!
FORGET IT.
YOU KNOW WHAT? I'M GLAD YOU'RE SENDING TULLIS. THAT WAY HE CAN WATCH ME COMPLETE THE MISSION.

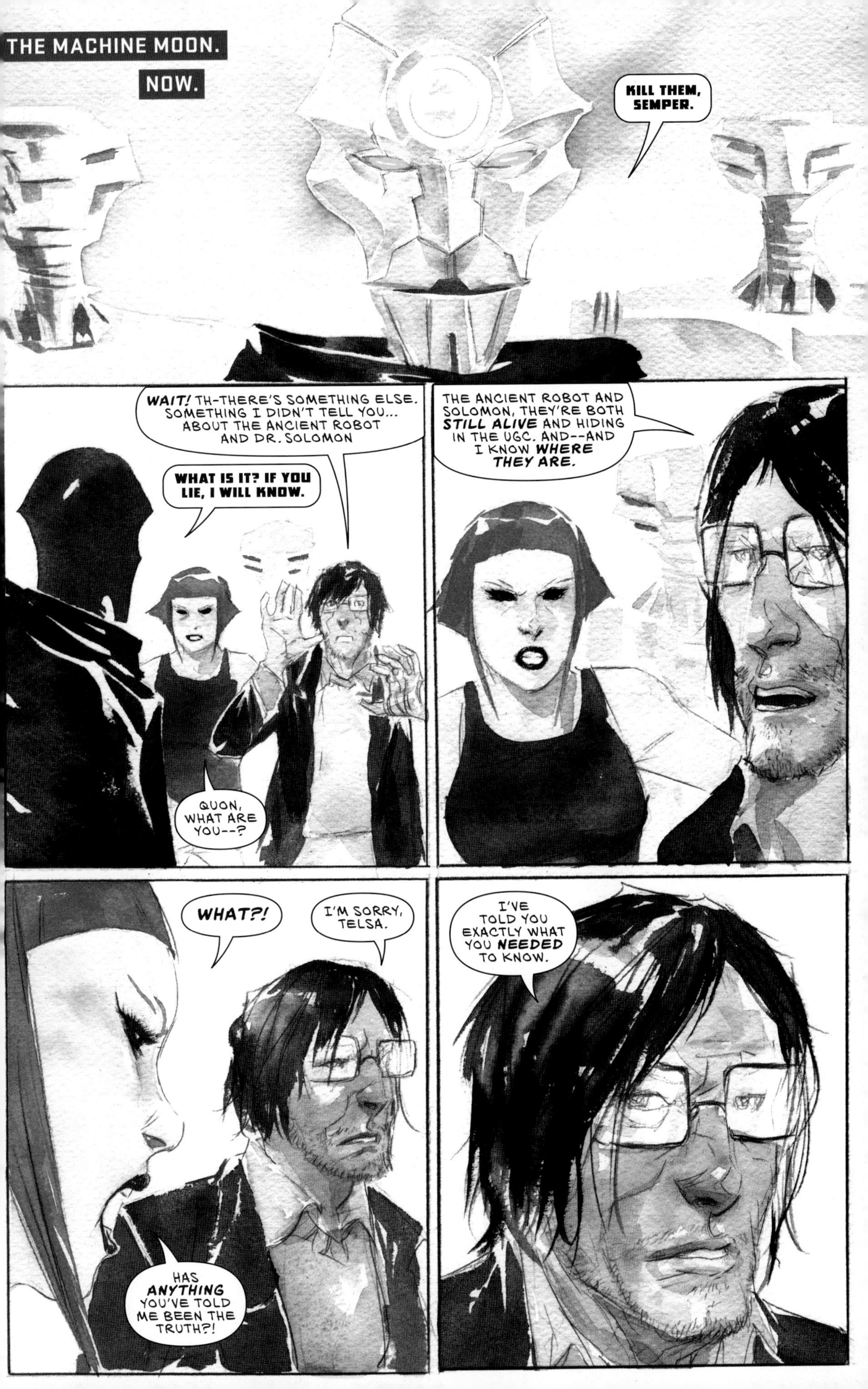
THE MACHINE MOON.
NOW.
KILL THEM, SEMPER.
WAIT! TH-THERE'S SOMETHING ELSE. SOMETHING I DIDN'T TELL YOU... ABOUT THE ANCIENT ROBOT AND DR. SOLOMON
WHAT IS IT? IF YOU LIE, I WILL KNOW.
QUON, WHAT ARE YOU--?
THE ANCIENT ROBOT AND SOLOMON, THEY'RE BOTH STILL ALIVE AND HIDING IN THE UGC. AND--AND I KNOW WHERE THEY ARE.
WHAT?!
I'M SORRY, TELSA.
HAS ANYTHING YOU'VE TOLD ME BEEN THE TRUTH?!
I'VE TOLD YOU EXACTLY WHAT YOU NEEDED TO KNOW.

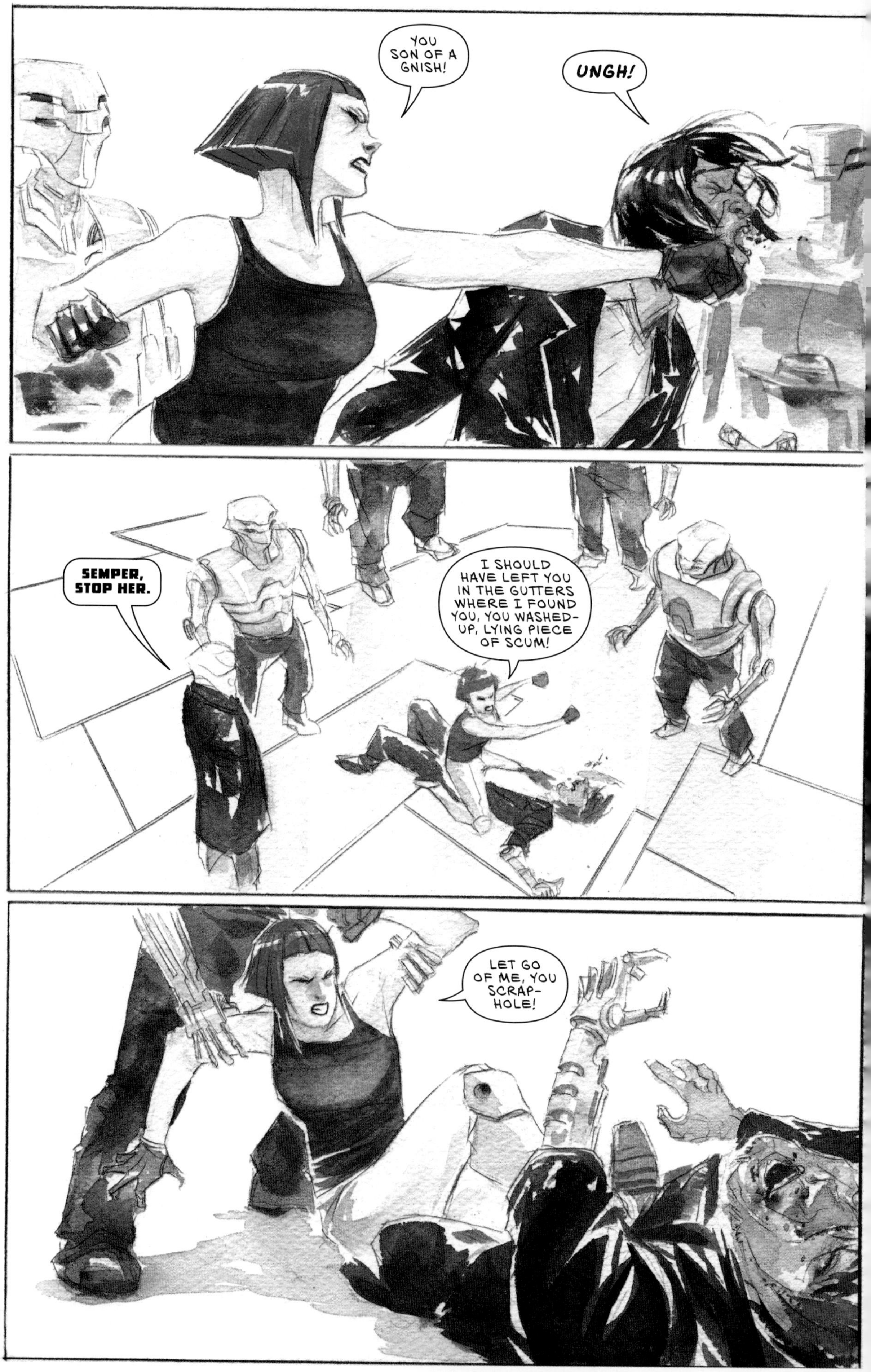
YOU SON OF A GNISH!
UNGH!
SEMPER, STOP HER.
I SHOULD HAVE LEFT YOU IN THE GUTTERS WHERE I FOUND YOU, YOU WASHED-UP, LYING PIECE OF SCUM!
LET GO OF ME, YOU SCRAP-HOLE!

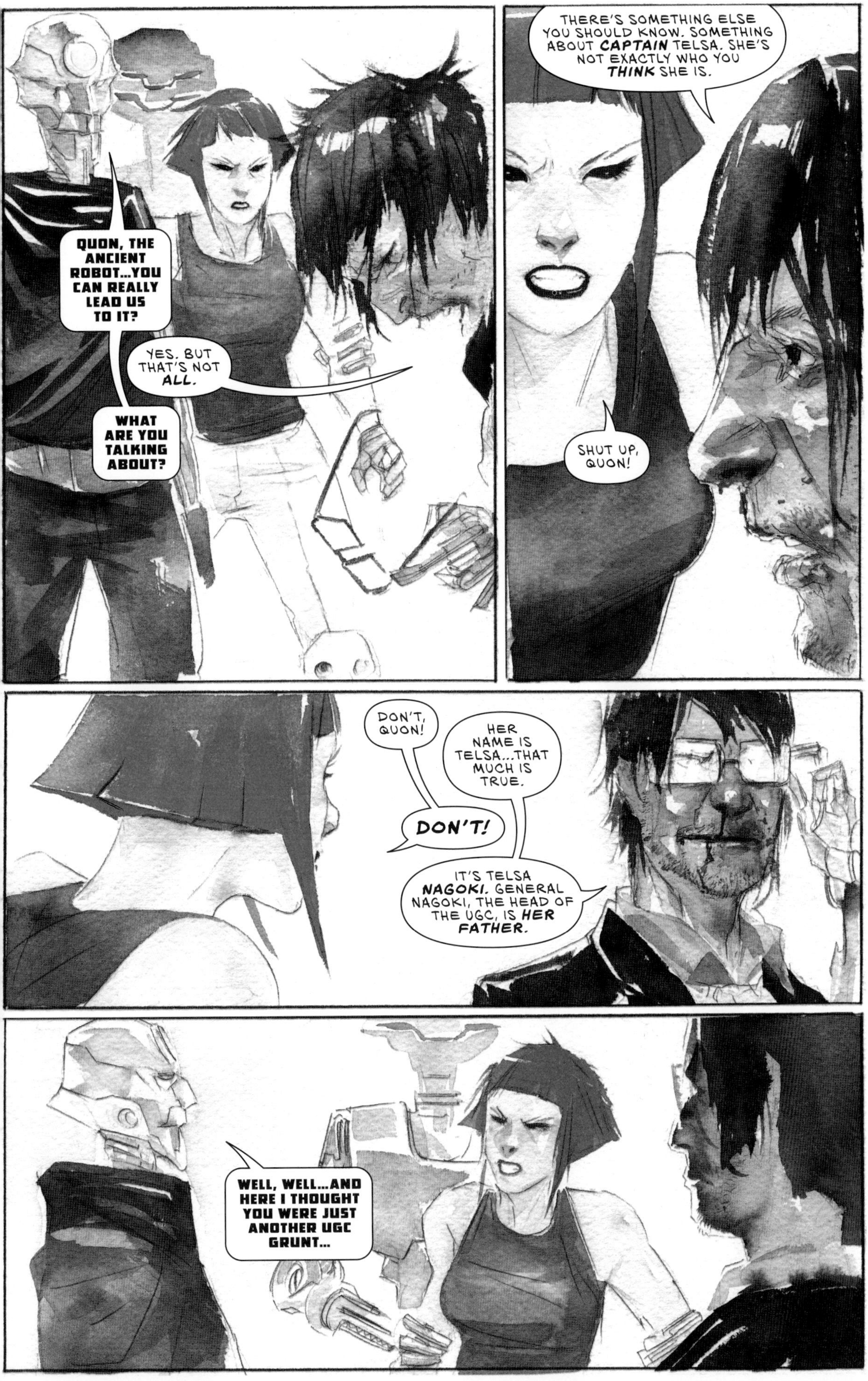
QUON, THE ANCIENT ROBOT...YOU CAN REALLY LEAD US TO IT?
YES. BUT THAT'S NOT ALL.
WHAT ARE YOU TALKING ABOUT?
THERE'S SOMETHING ELSE YOU SHOULD KNOW. SOMETHING ABOUT CAPTAIN TELSA. SHE'S NOT EXACTLY WHO YOU THINK SHE IS.
SHUT UP, QUON!
DON'T, QUON!
HER NAME IS TELSA...THAT MUCH IS TRUE.
DON'T!
IT'S TELSA NAGOKI. GENERAL NAGOKI, THE HEAD OF THE UGC, IS HER FATHER.
WELL, WELL...AND HERE I THOUGHT YOU WERE JUST ANOTHER UGC GRUNT...

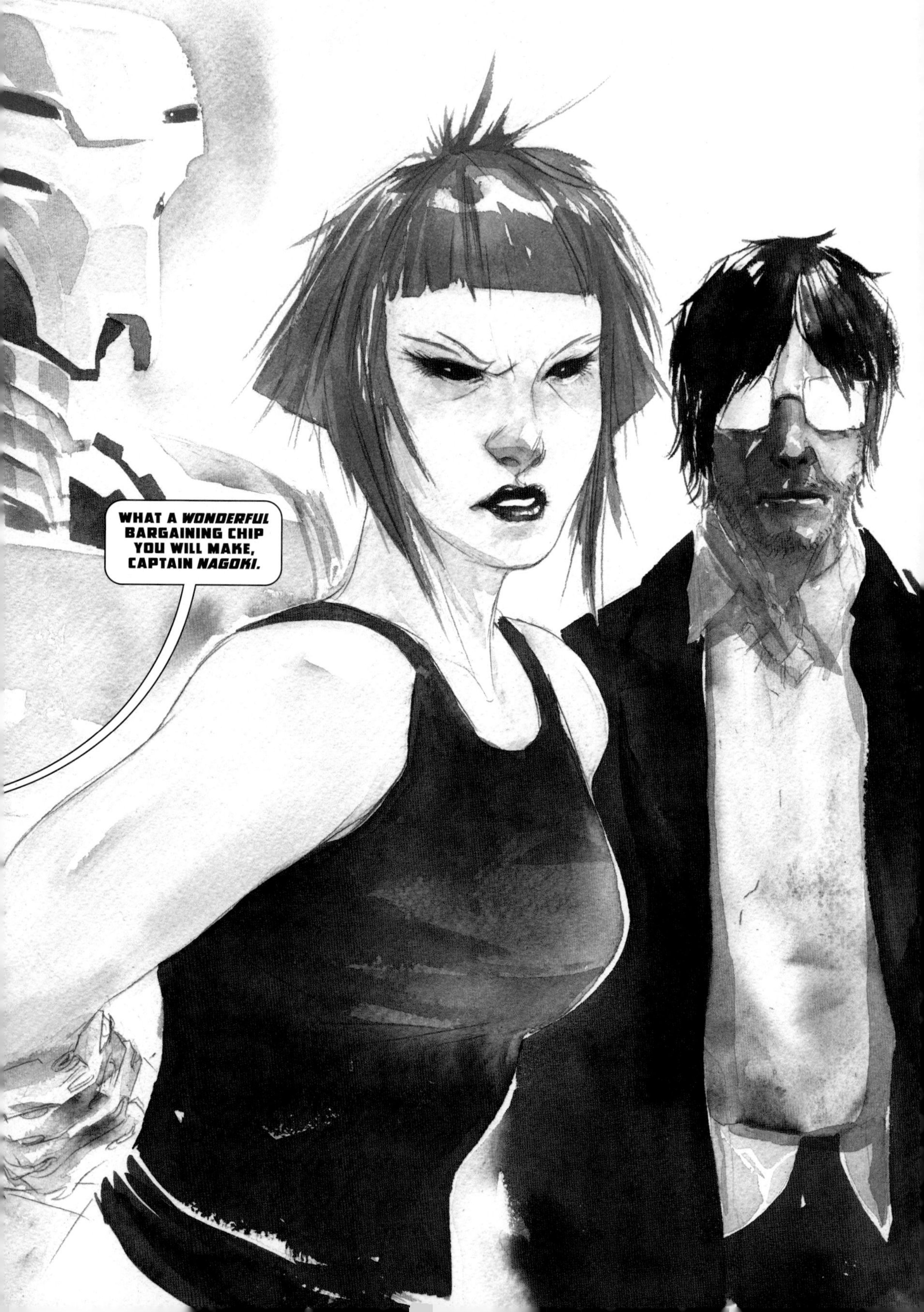
WHAT A *WONDERFUL* BARGAINING CHIP YOU WILL MAKE, CAPTAIN *NAGOKI.*

CHAPTER THREE

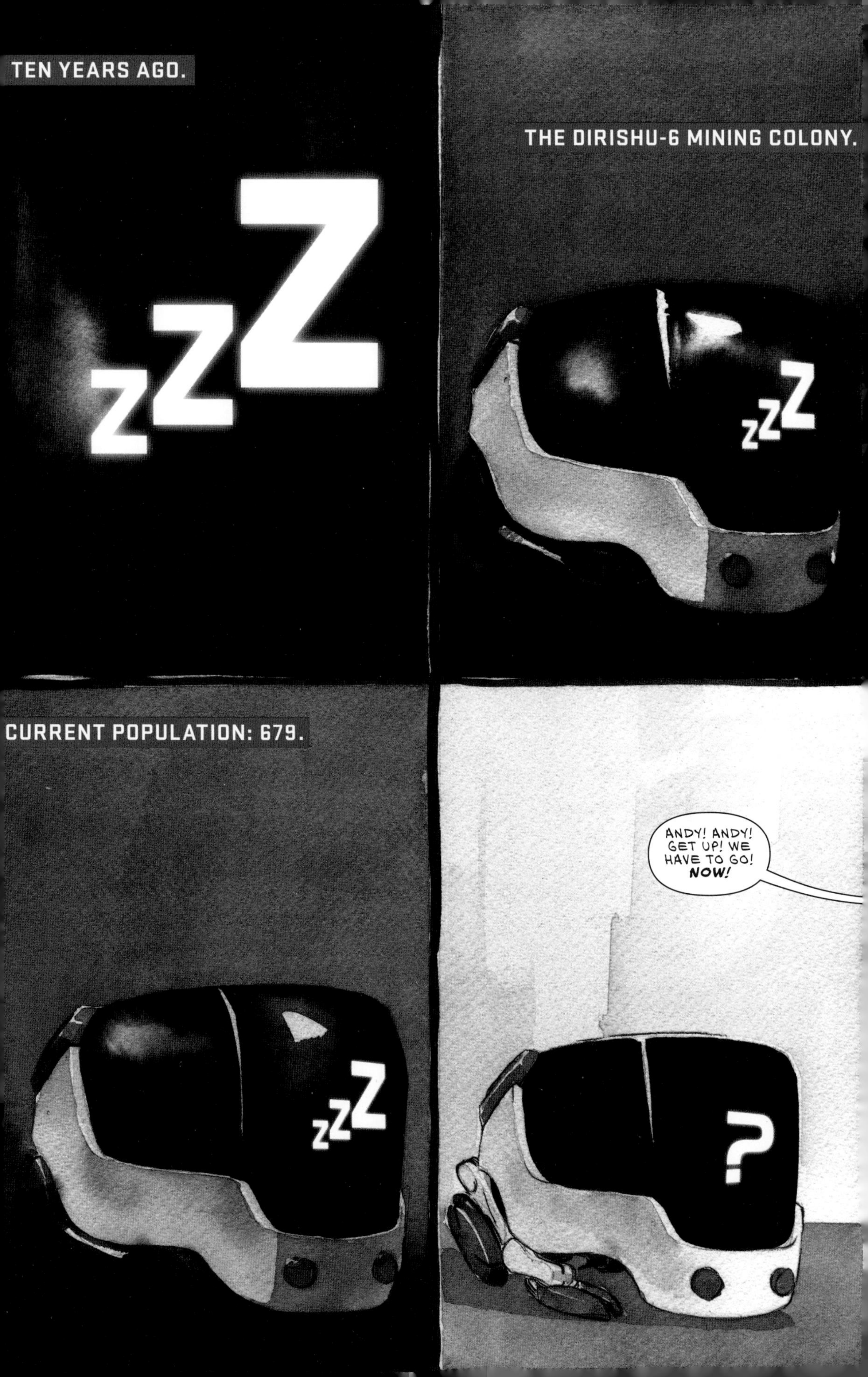
TEN YEARS AGO.
ZZZ
THE DIRISHU-6 MINING COLONY.
ZZZ
CURRENT POPULATION: 679.
ZZZ
ANDY! ANDY! GET UP! WE HAVE TO GO! NOW!
?

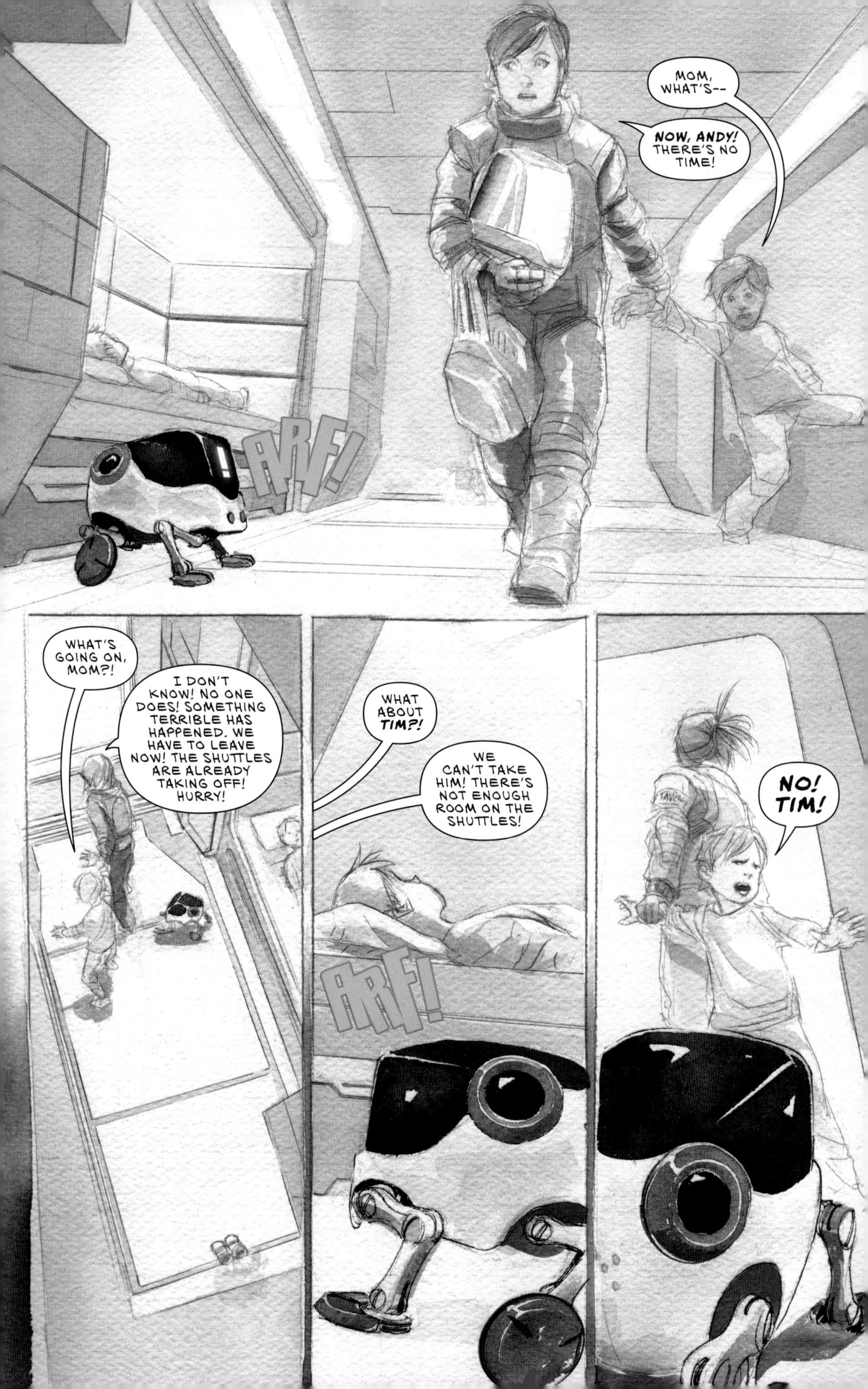
MOM, WHAT'S--
NOW, ANDY! THERE'S NO TIME!
ARF!
WHAT'S GOING ON, MOM?!
I DON'T KNOW! NO ONE DOES! SOMETHING TERRIBLE HAS HAPPENED. WE HAVE TO LEAVE NOW! THE SHUTTLES ARE ALREADY TAKING OFF! HURRY!
WHAT ABOUT TIM?!
WE CAN'T TAKE HIM! THERE'S NOT ENOUGH ROOM ON THE SHUTTLES!
ARF!
NO! TIM!

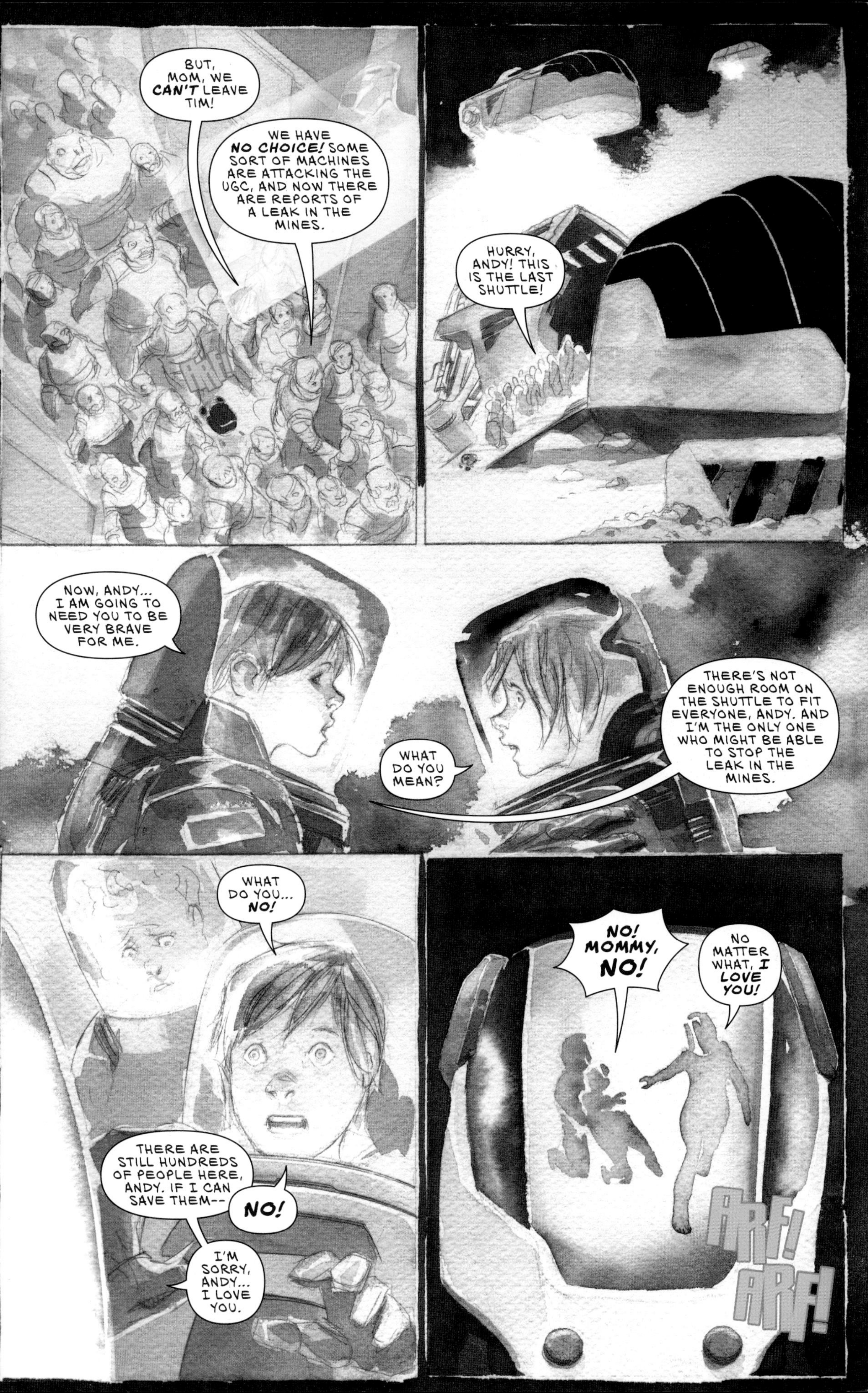
BUT, MOM, WE CAN'T LEAVE TIM!
WE HAVE NO CHOICE! SOME SORT OF MACHINES ARE ATTACKING THE UGC, AND NOW THERE ARE REPORTS OF A LEAK IN THE MINES.
ARF!
HURRY, ANDY! THIS IS THE LAST SHUTTLE!
NOW, ANDY... I AM GOING TO NEED YOU TO BE VERY BRAVE FOR ME.
WHAT DO YOU MEAN?
THERE'S NOT ENOUGH ROOM ON THE SHUTTLE TO FIT EVERYONE, ANDY. AND I'M THE ONLY ONE WHO MIGHT BE ABLE TO STOP THE LEAK IN THE MINES.
WHAT DO YOU... NO!
THERE ARE STILL HUNDREDS OF PEOPLE HERE, ANDY. IF I CAN SAVE THEM--
NO!
I'M SORRY, ANDY... I LOVE YOU.
NO! MOMMY, NO!
NO MATTER WHAT, I LOVE YOU!
ARF! ARF!

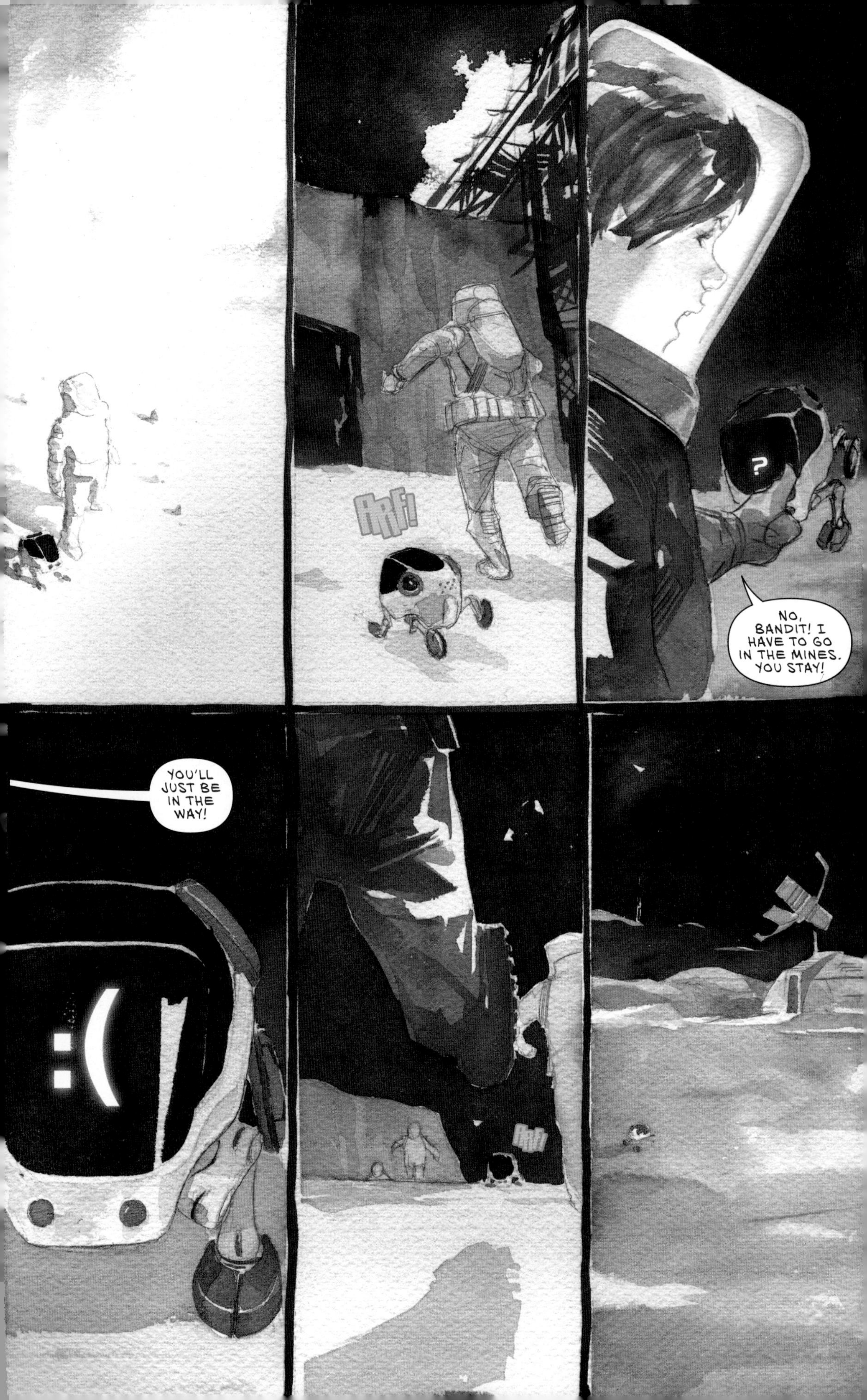
ARF!
?
NO, BANDIT! I HAVE TO GO IN THE MINES. YOU STAY!
YOU'LL JUST BE IN THE WAY!
:(
ARF!

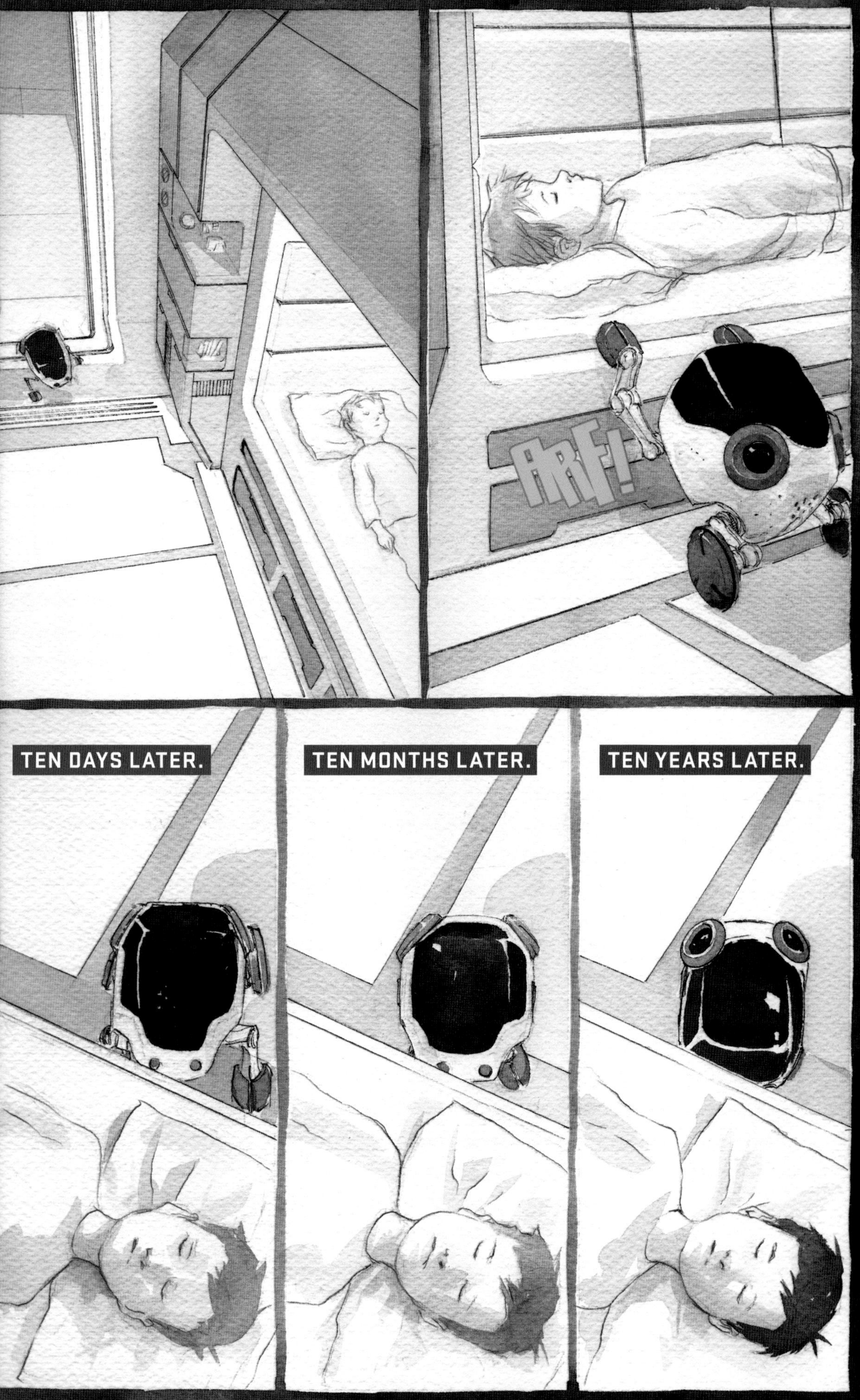
ARF!
TEN DAYS LATER.
TEN MONTHS LATER.
TEN YEARS LATER.

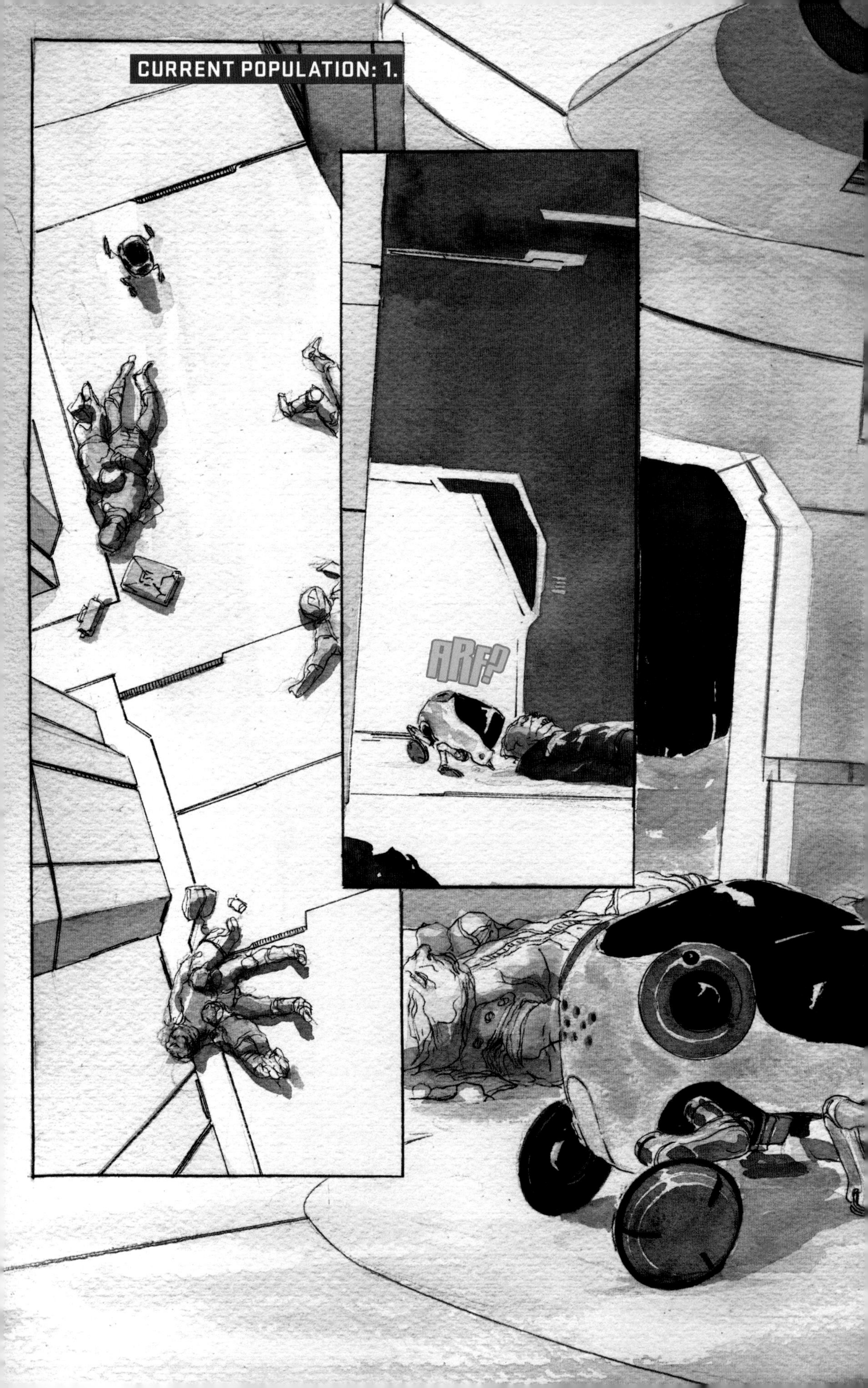
CURRENT POPULATION: 1.
ARF?

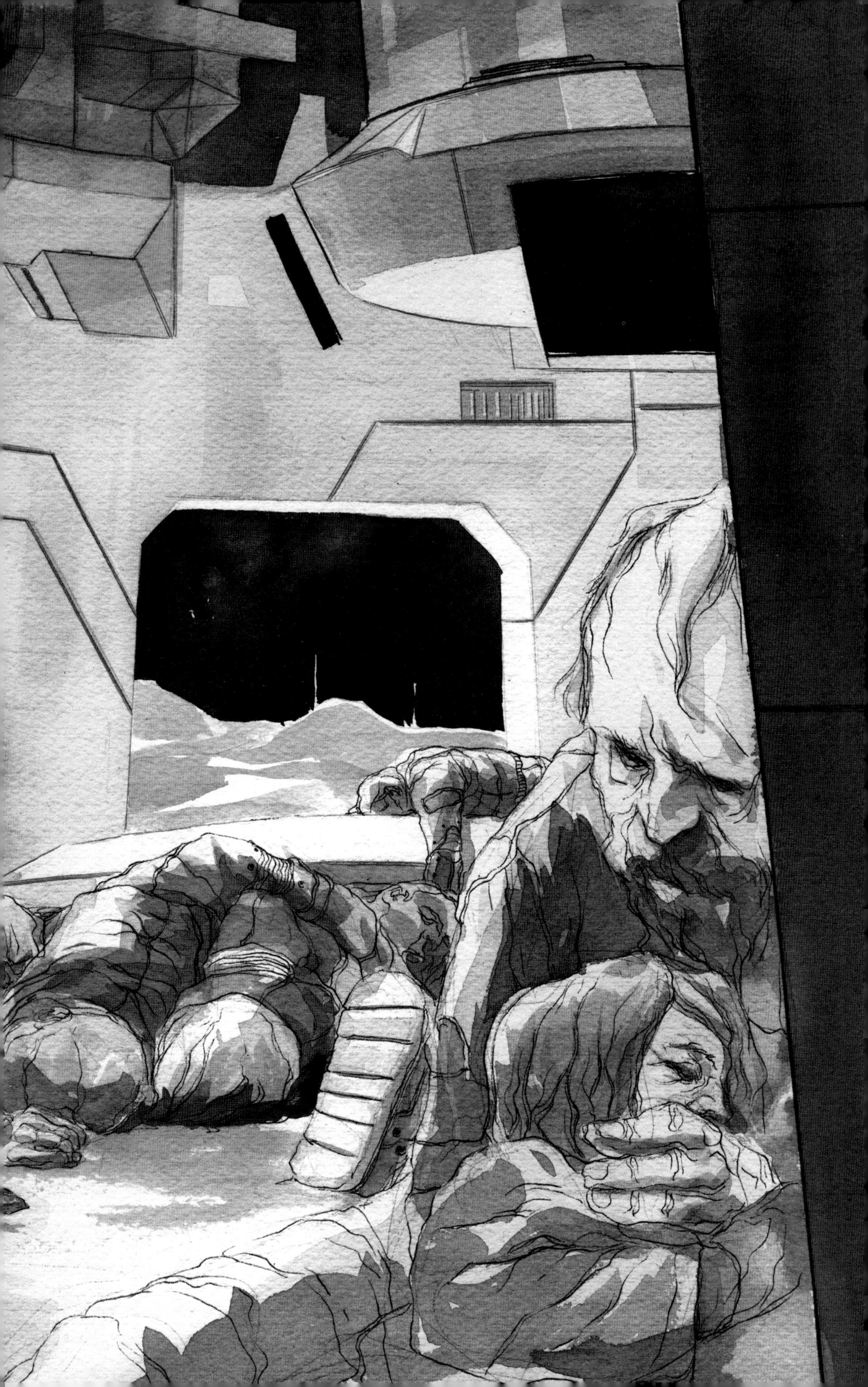

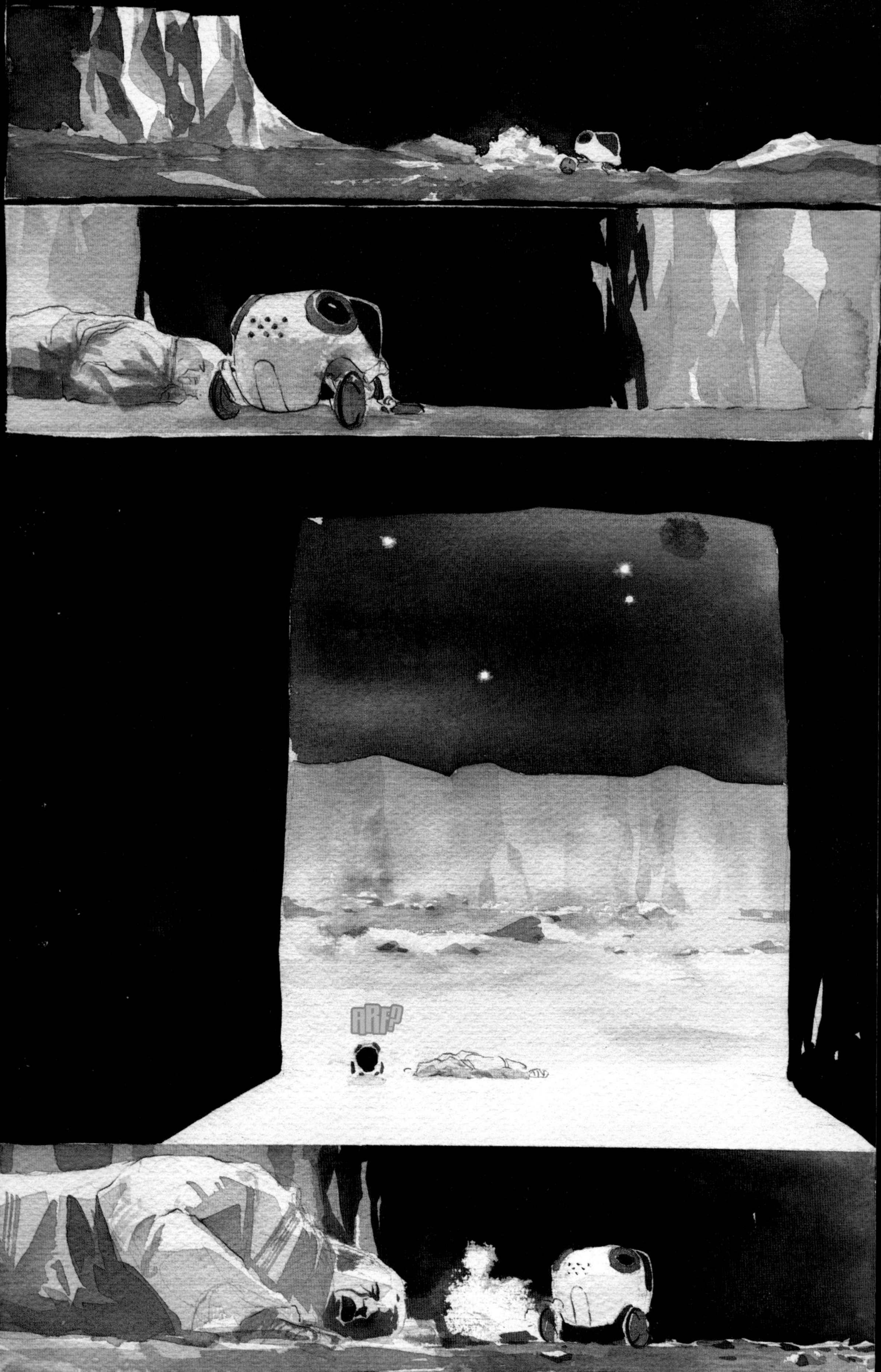
ARF?

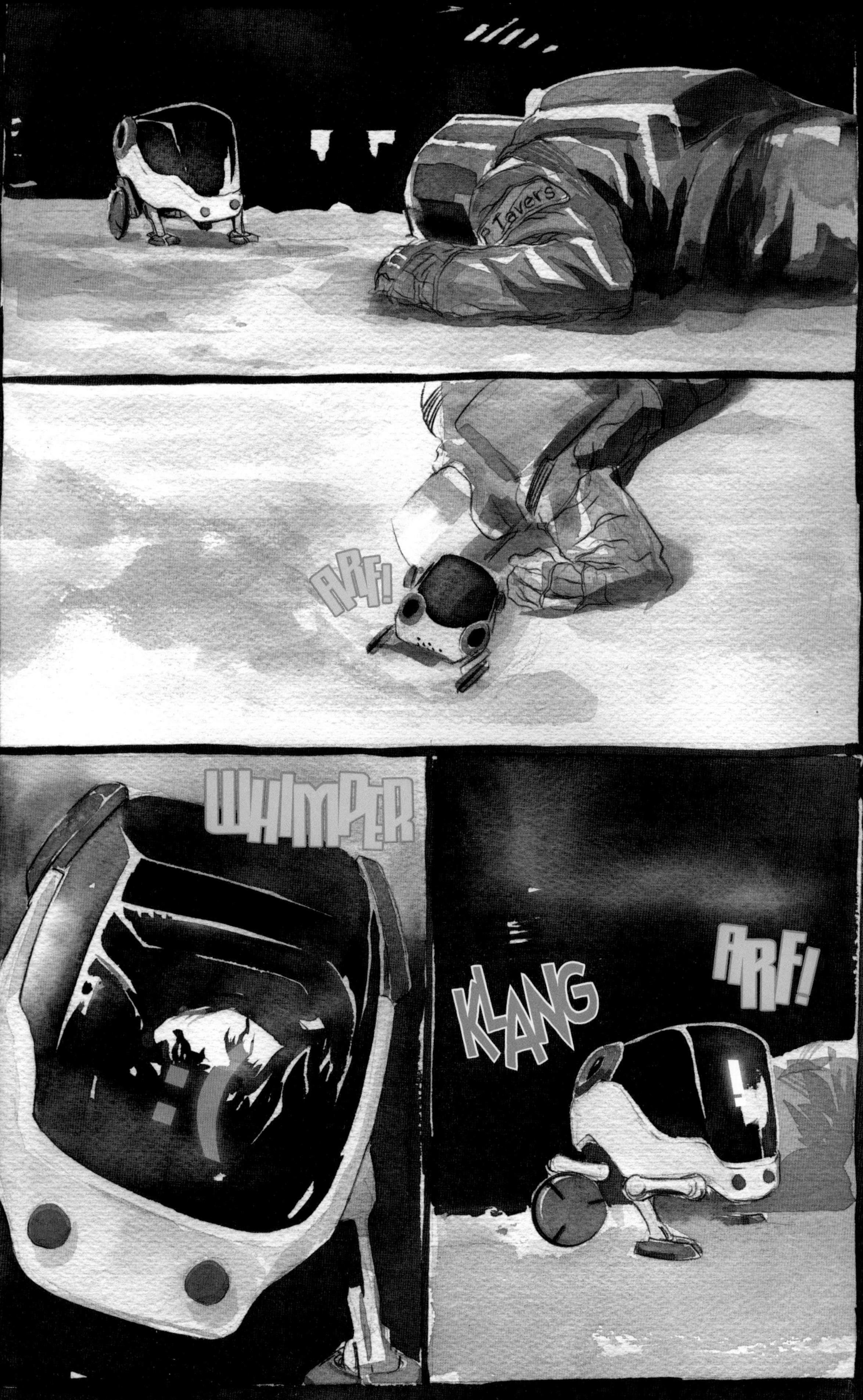
P Tavers
ARF!
WHIMPER
KLANG
ARF!

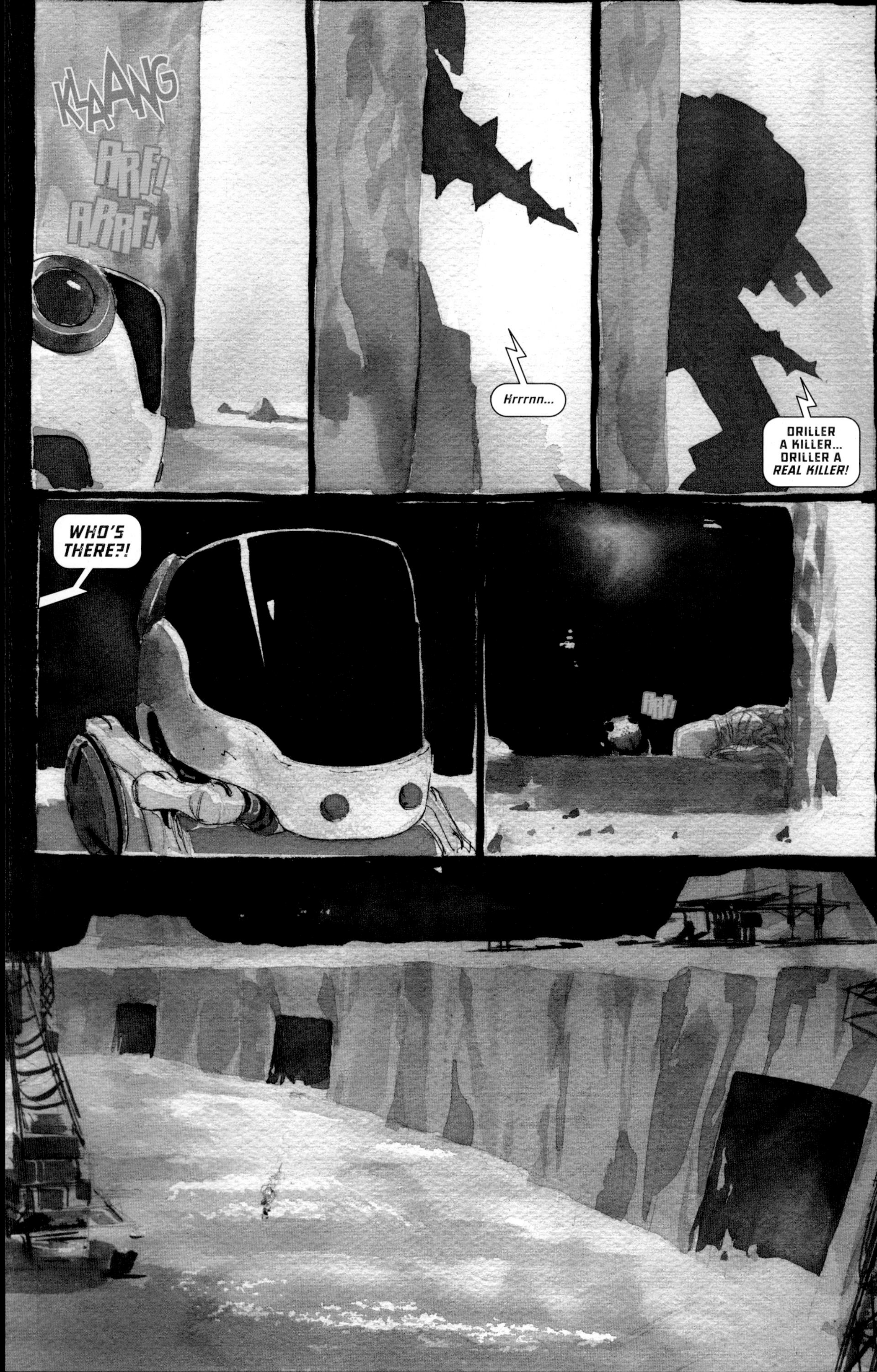
KLAANG
ARF! ARRF!
Krrrnn...
DRILLER A KILLER... DRILLER A REAL KILLER!
WHO'S THERE?!
ARF!

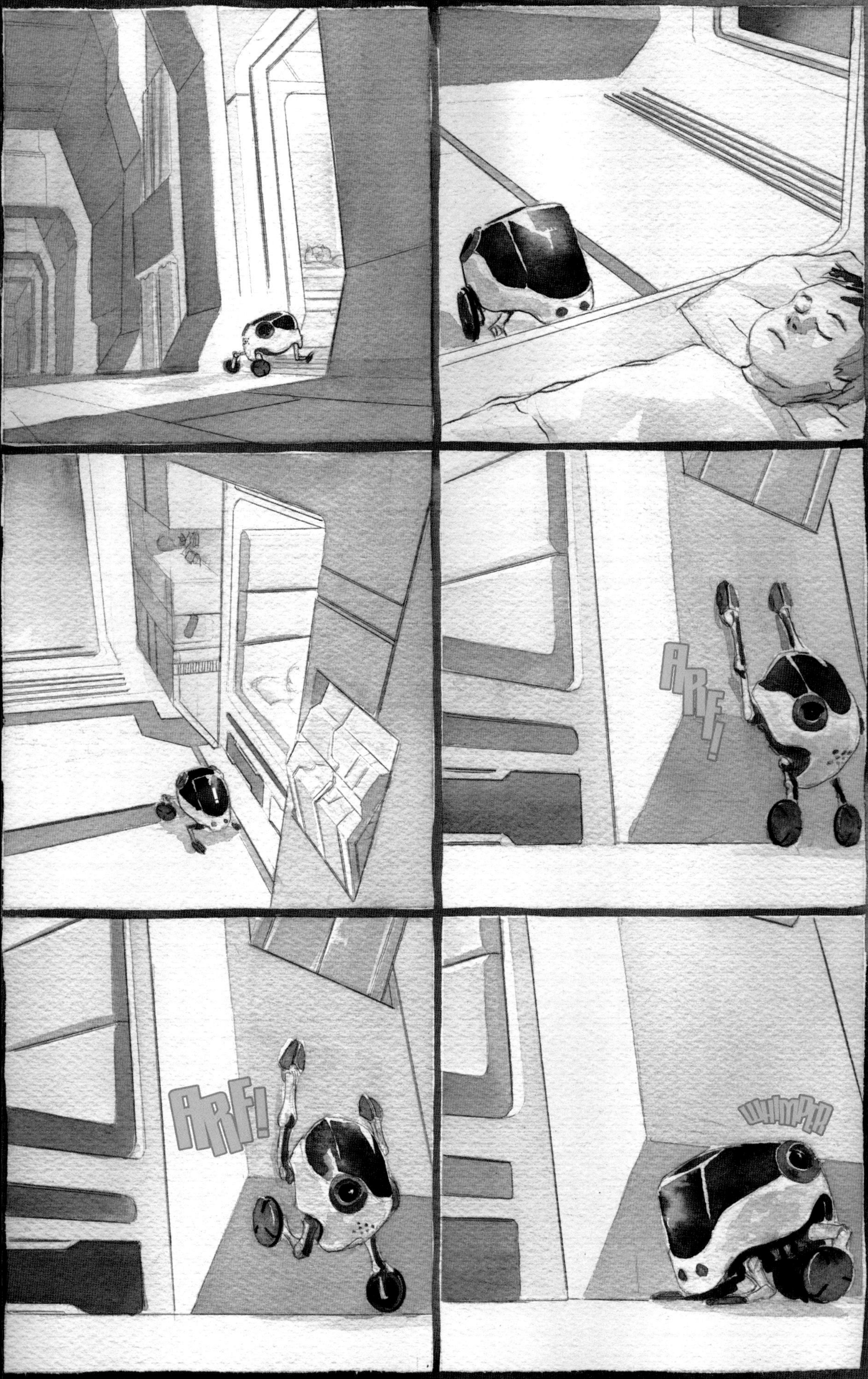
ARF!
ARF!
WHIMPER

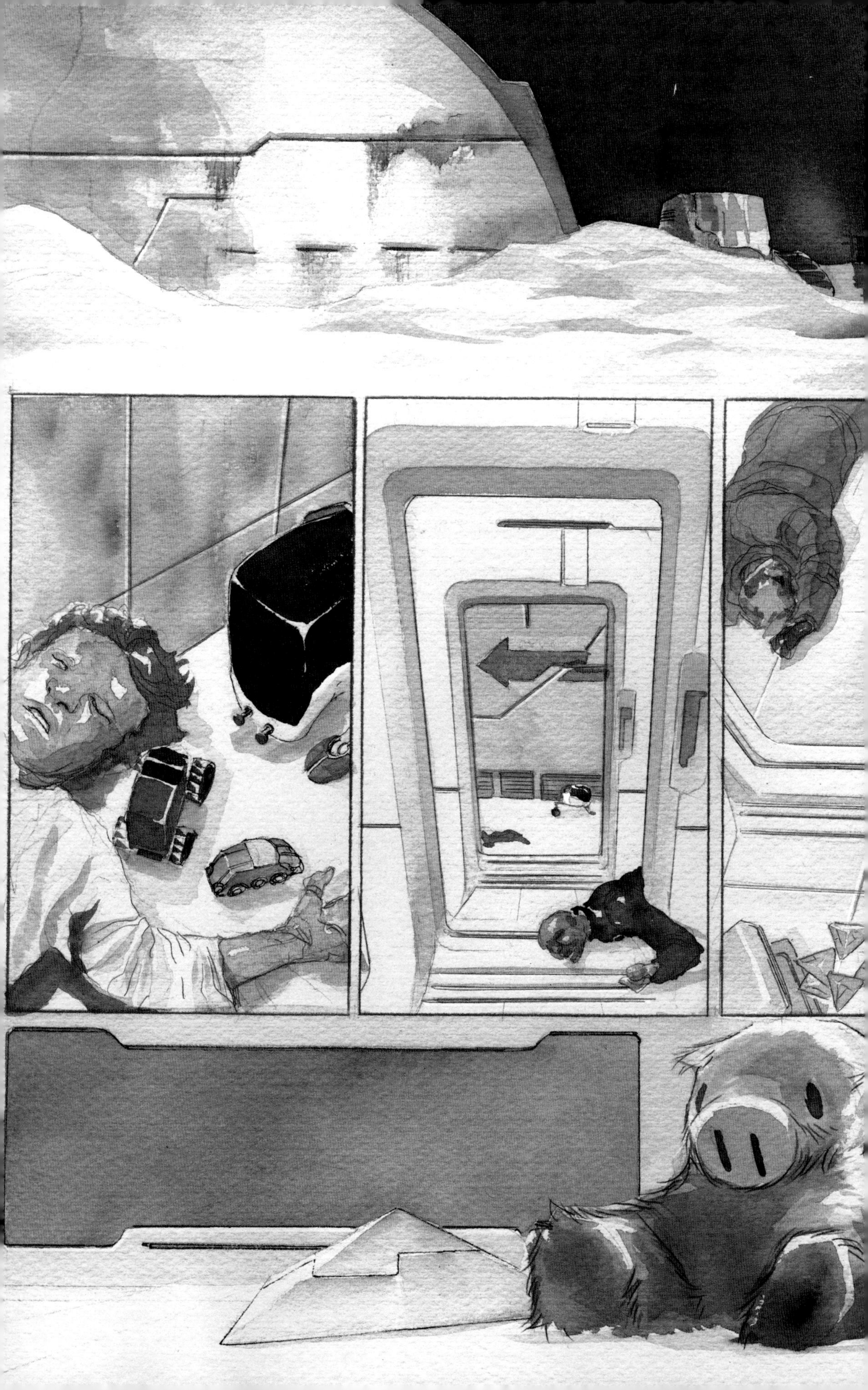

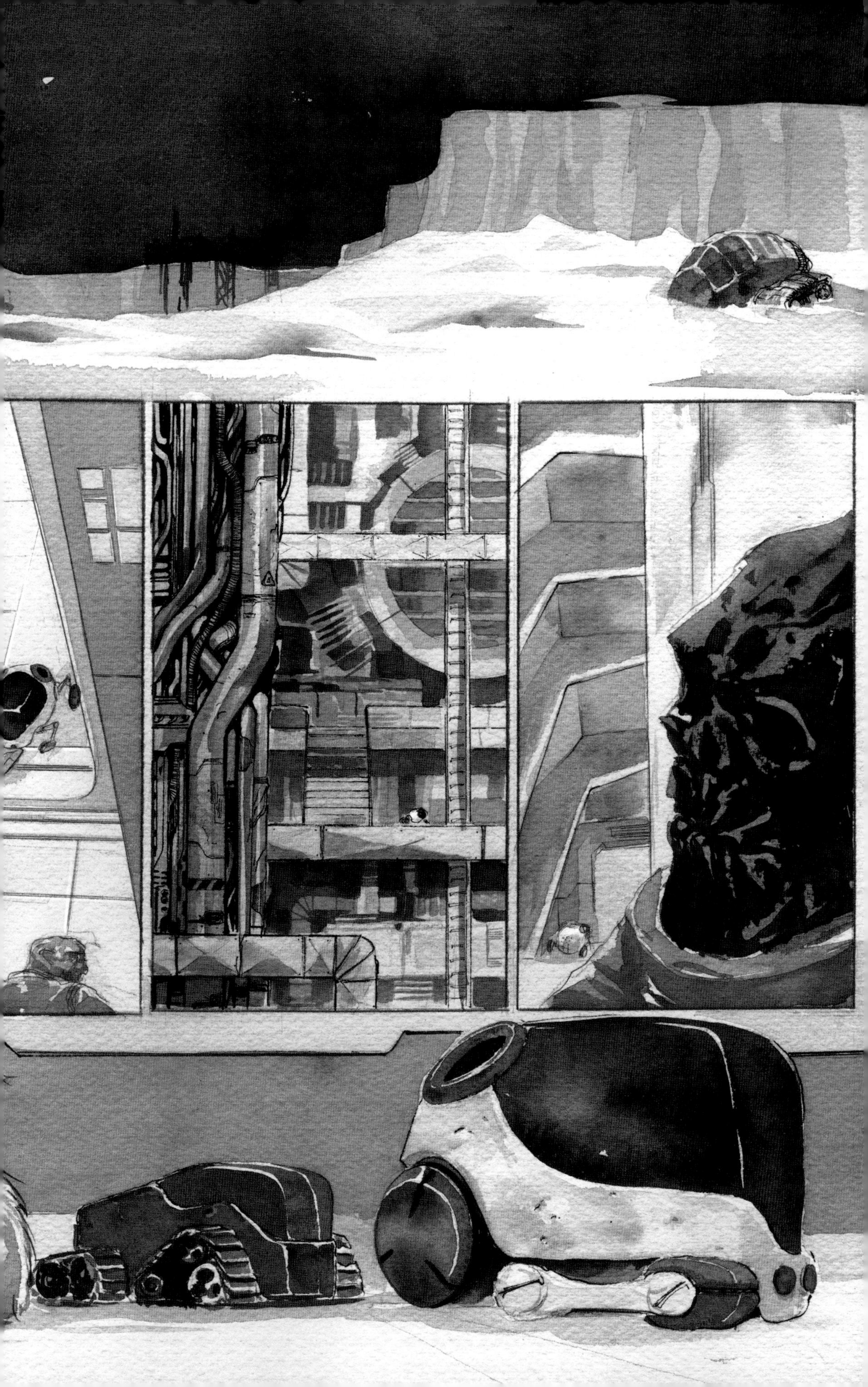

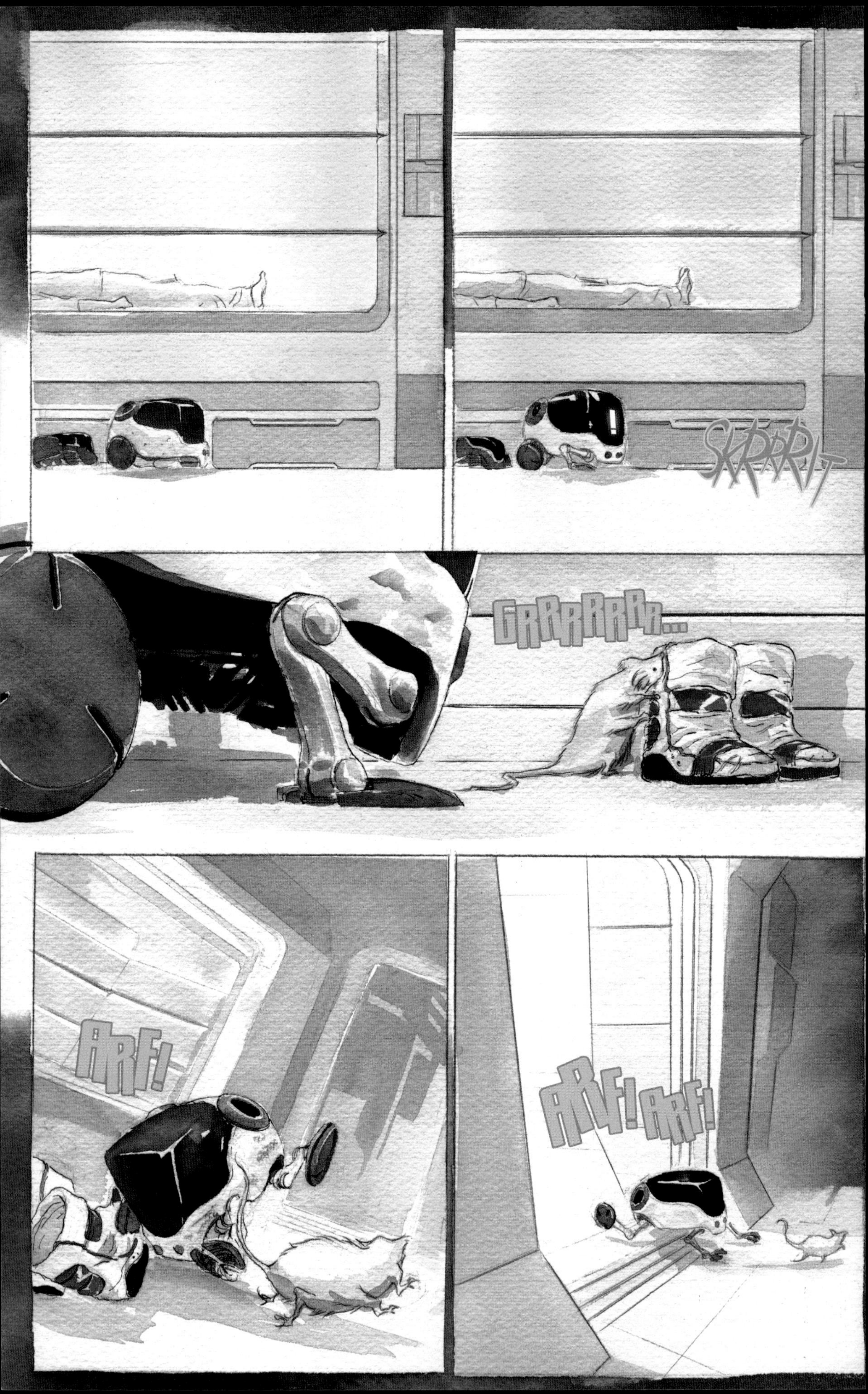
SKRRRIT
GRRRRRRR...
ARF!
ARF! ARF!

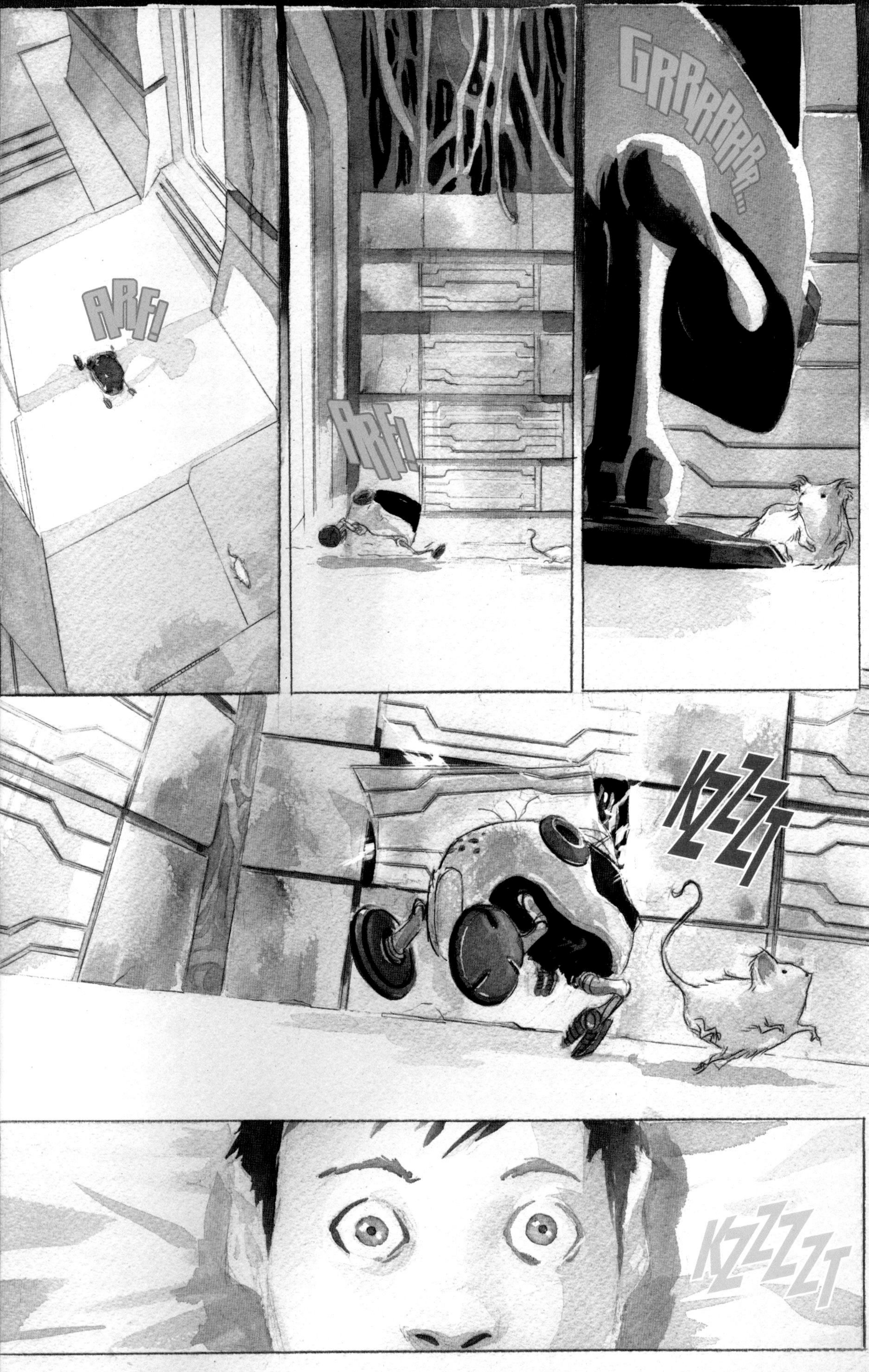
ARF!
ARF!
GRRRRRRR...
KZZZT
KZZZZT

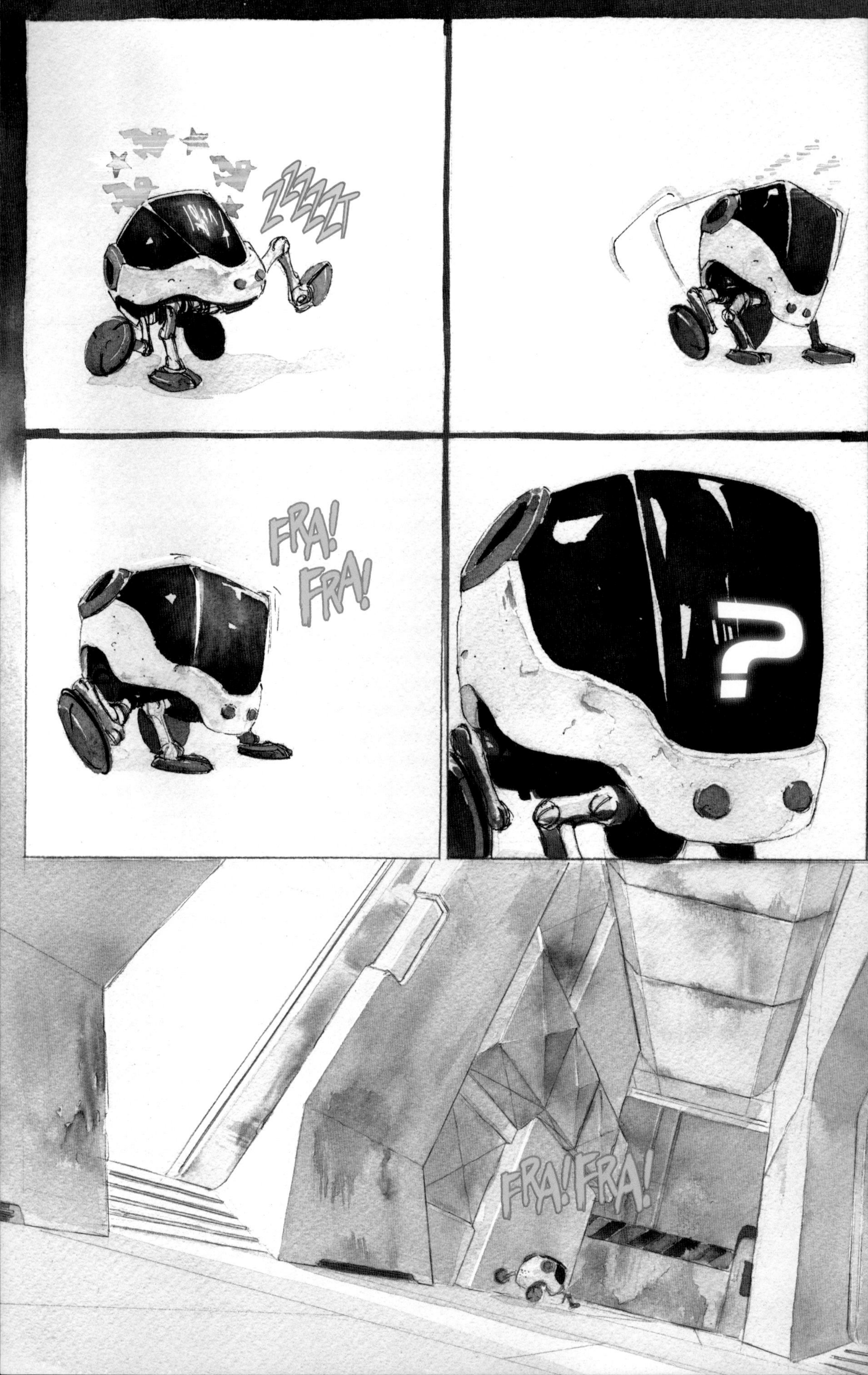
ZZZZZT
FRA! FRA!
?
FRA! FRA!

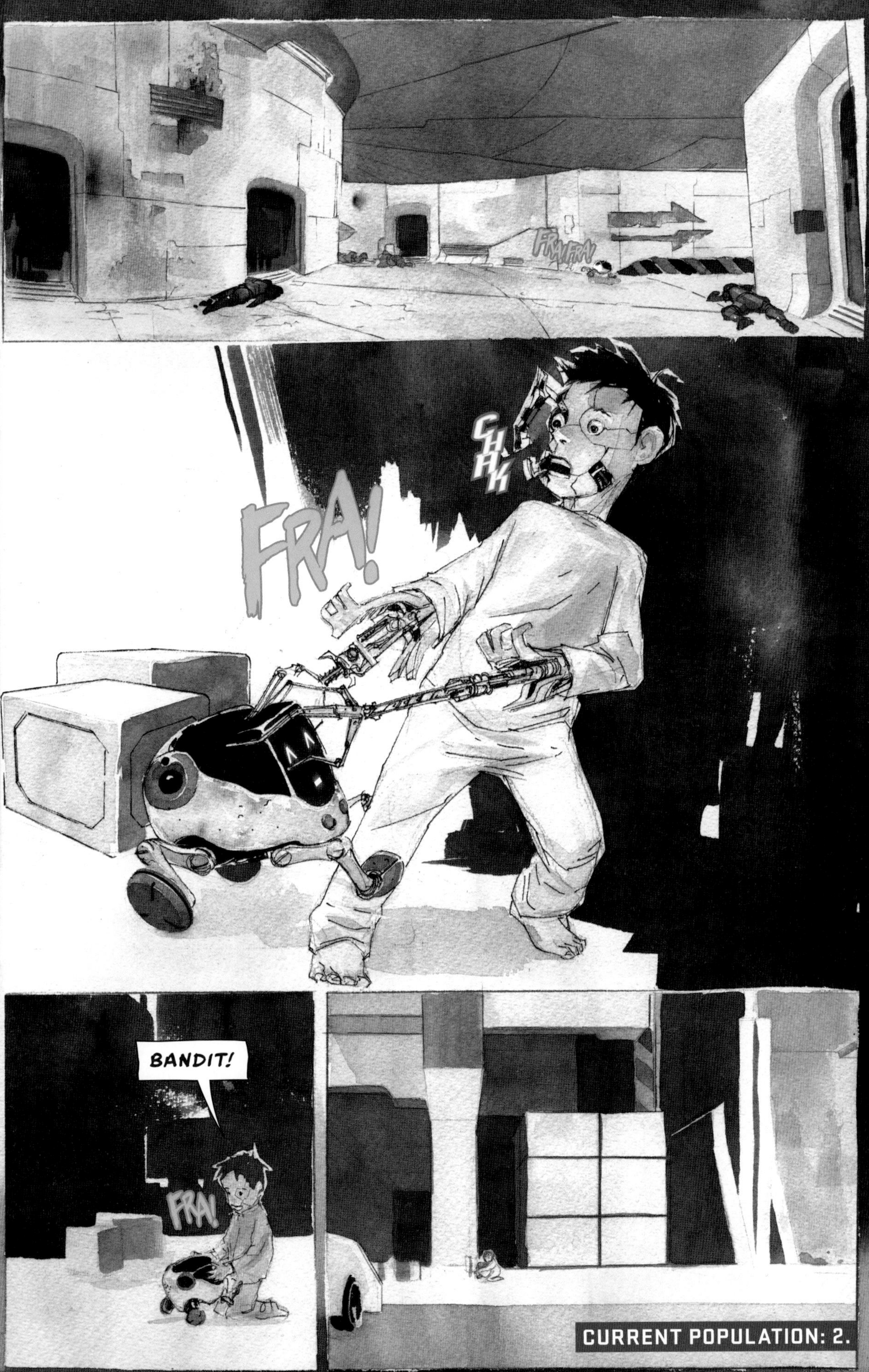
FRA! FRA!
CHAK
FRA!
BANDIT!
FRA!
CURRENT POPULATION: 2.

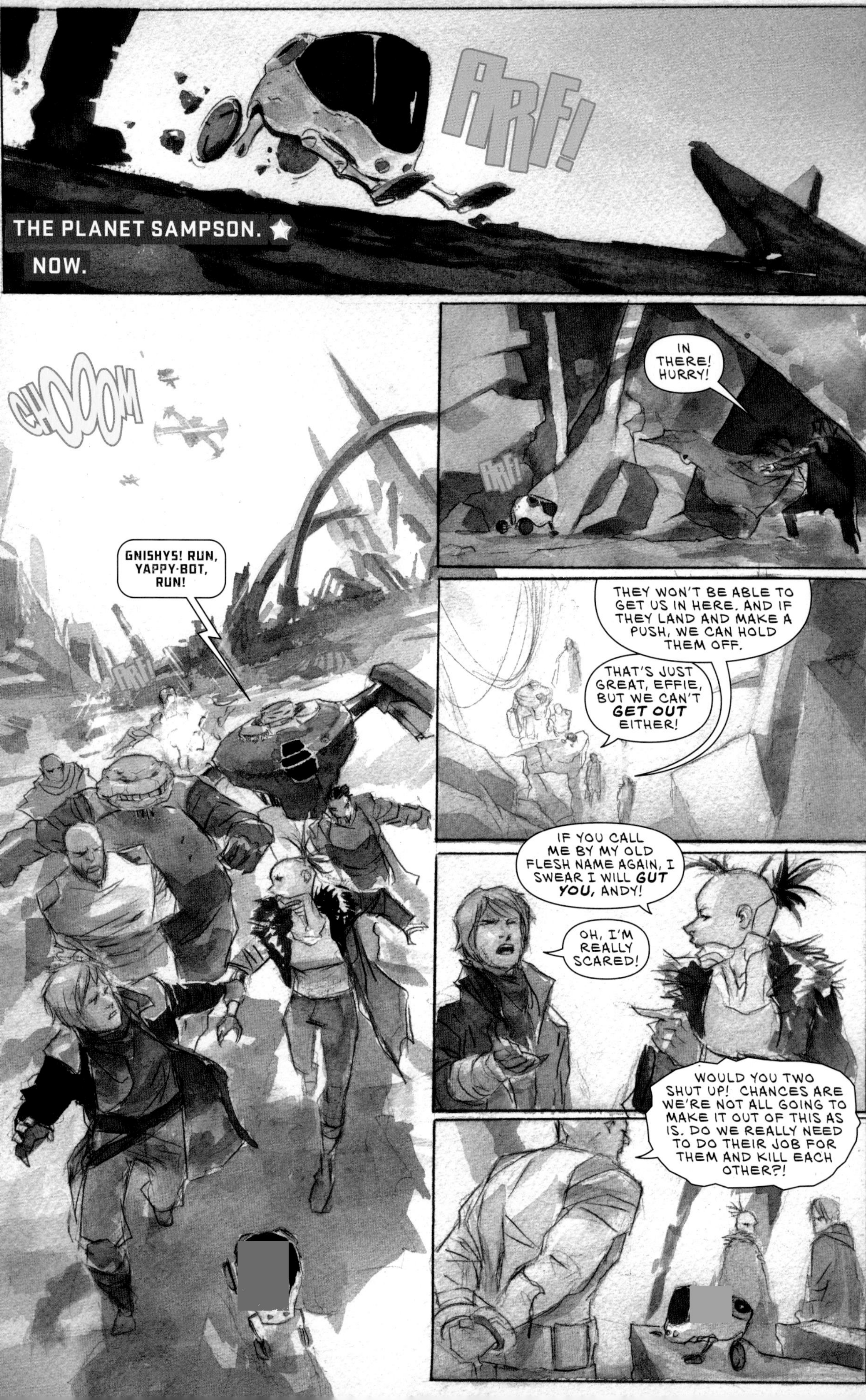
THE PLANET SAMPSON.
NOW.
ARF!
CHOOOM
GNISHYS! RUN, YAPPY-BOT, RUN!
ARF!
IN THERE! HURRY!
ARF!
THEY WON'T BE ABLE TO GET US IN HERE. AND IF THEY LAND AND MAKE A PUSH, WE CAN HOLD THEM OFF.
THAT'S JUST GREAT, EFFIE, BUT WE CAN'T **GET OUT** EITHER!
IF YOU CALL ME BY MY OLD FLESH NAME AGAIN, I SWEAR I WILL **GUT YOU,** ANDY!
OH, I'M REALLY SCARED!
WOULD YOU TWO SHUT UP! CHANCES ARE WE'RE NOT ALL GOING TO MAKE IT OUT OF THIS AS IS. DO WE REALLY NEED TO DO THEIR JOB FOR THEM AND KILL EACH OTHER?!

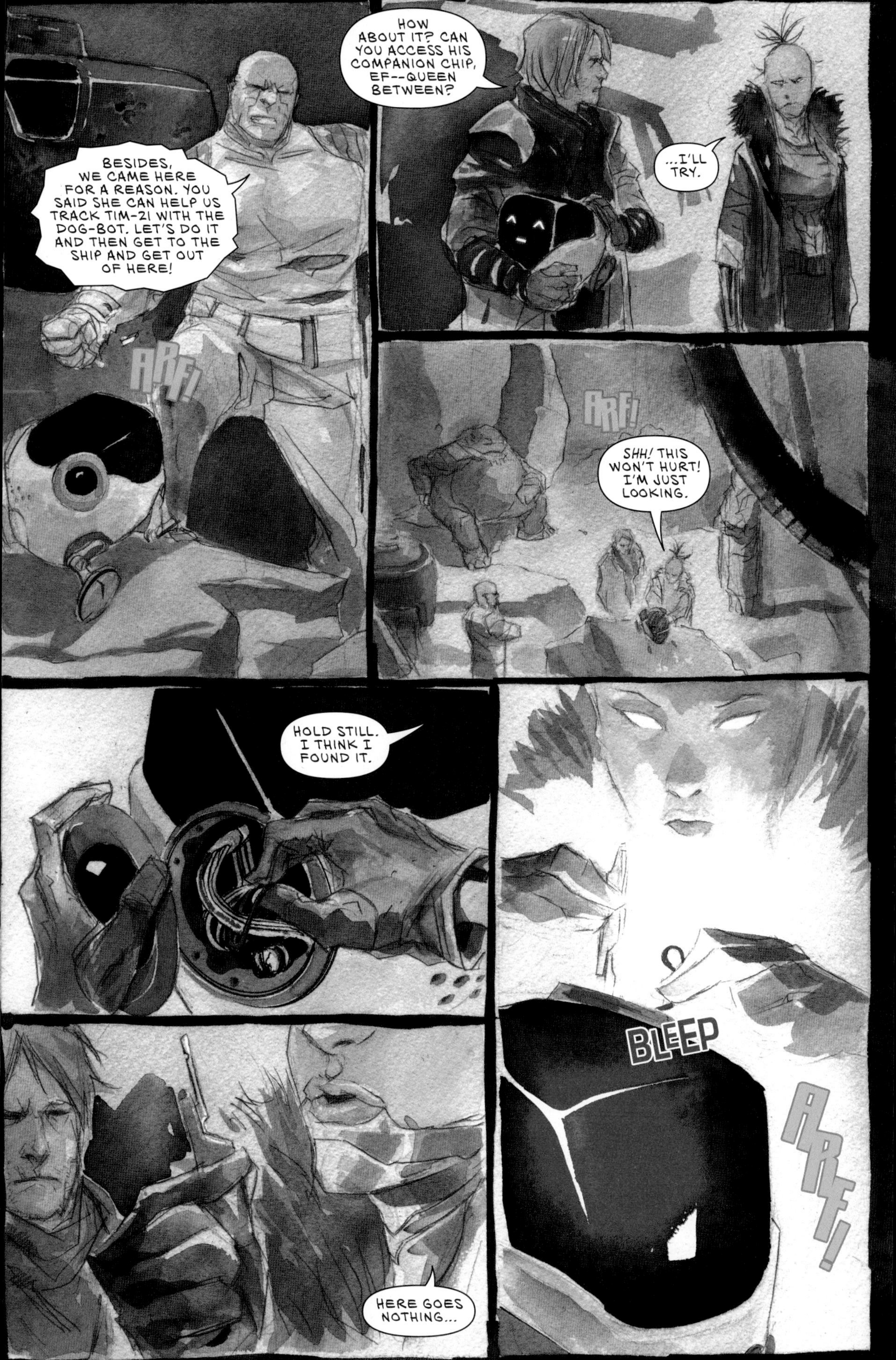
BESIDES, WE CAME HERE FOR A REASON. YOU SAID SHE CAN HELP US TRACK TIM-21 WITH THE DOG-BOT. LET'S DO IT AND THEN GET TO THE SHIP AND GET OUT OF HERE!
ARF!
HOW ABOUT IT? CAN YOU ACCESS HIS COMPANION CHIP, EF--QUEEN BETWEEN?
...I'LL TRY.
ARF!
SHH! THIS WON'T HURT! I'M JUST LOOKING.
HOLD STILL. I THINK I FOUND IT.
HERE GOES NOTHING...
BLEEP
ARF!

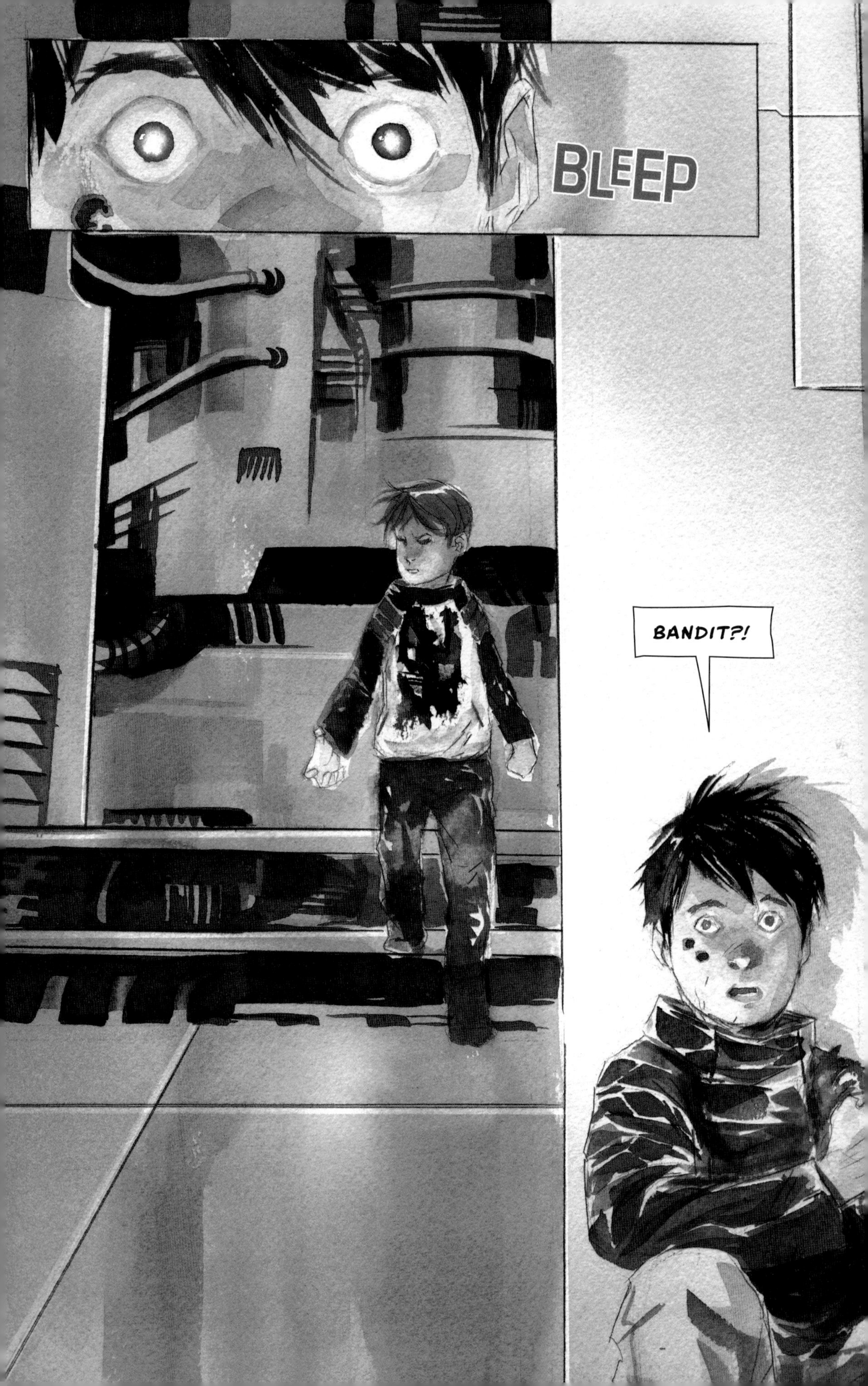
BLEEP
BANDIT?!

CHAPTER FOUR

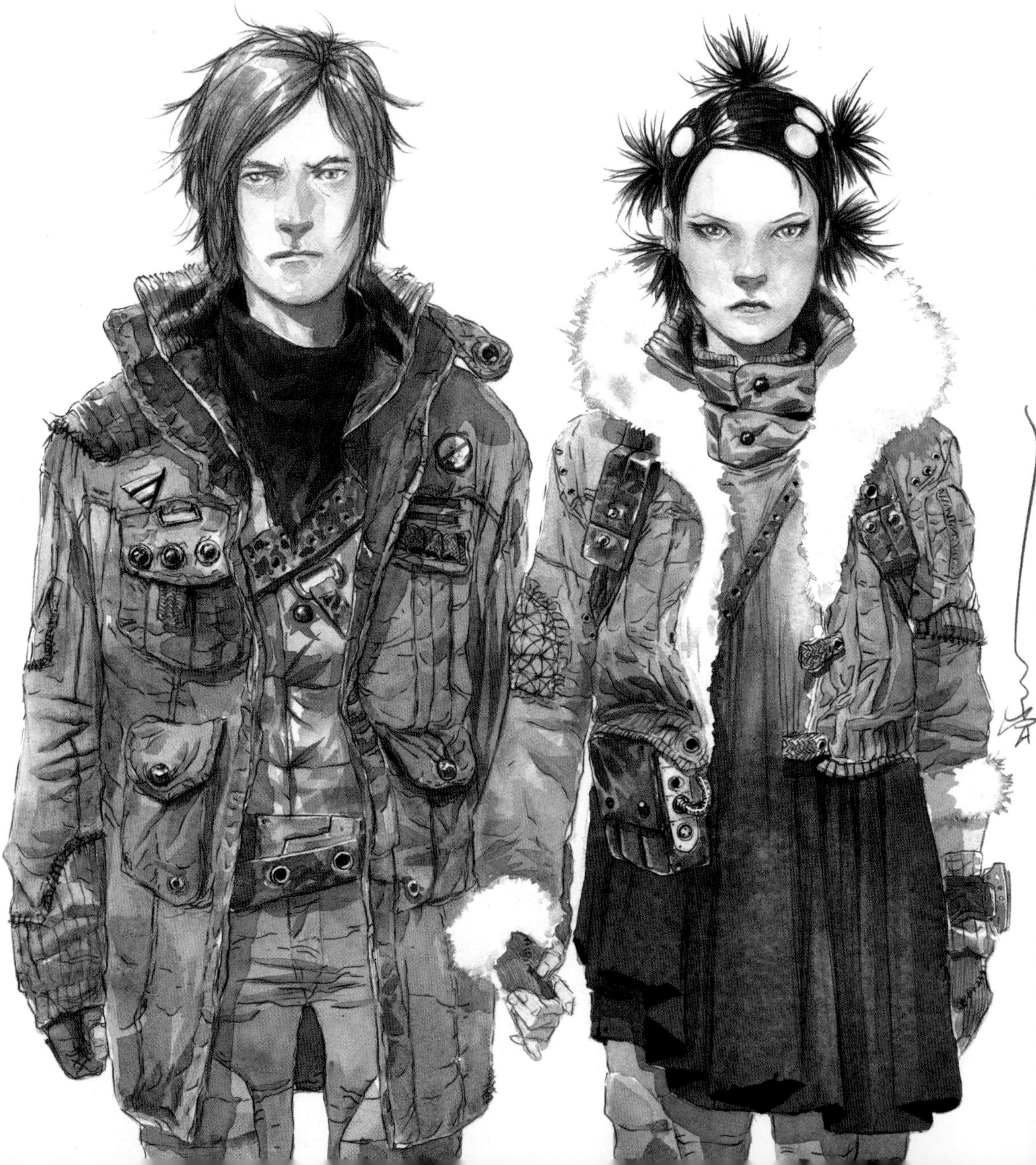

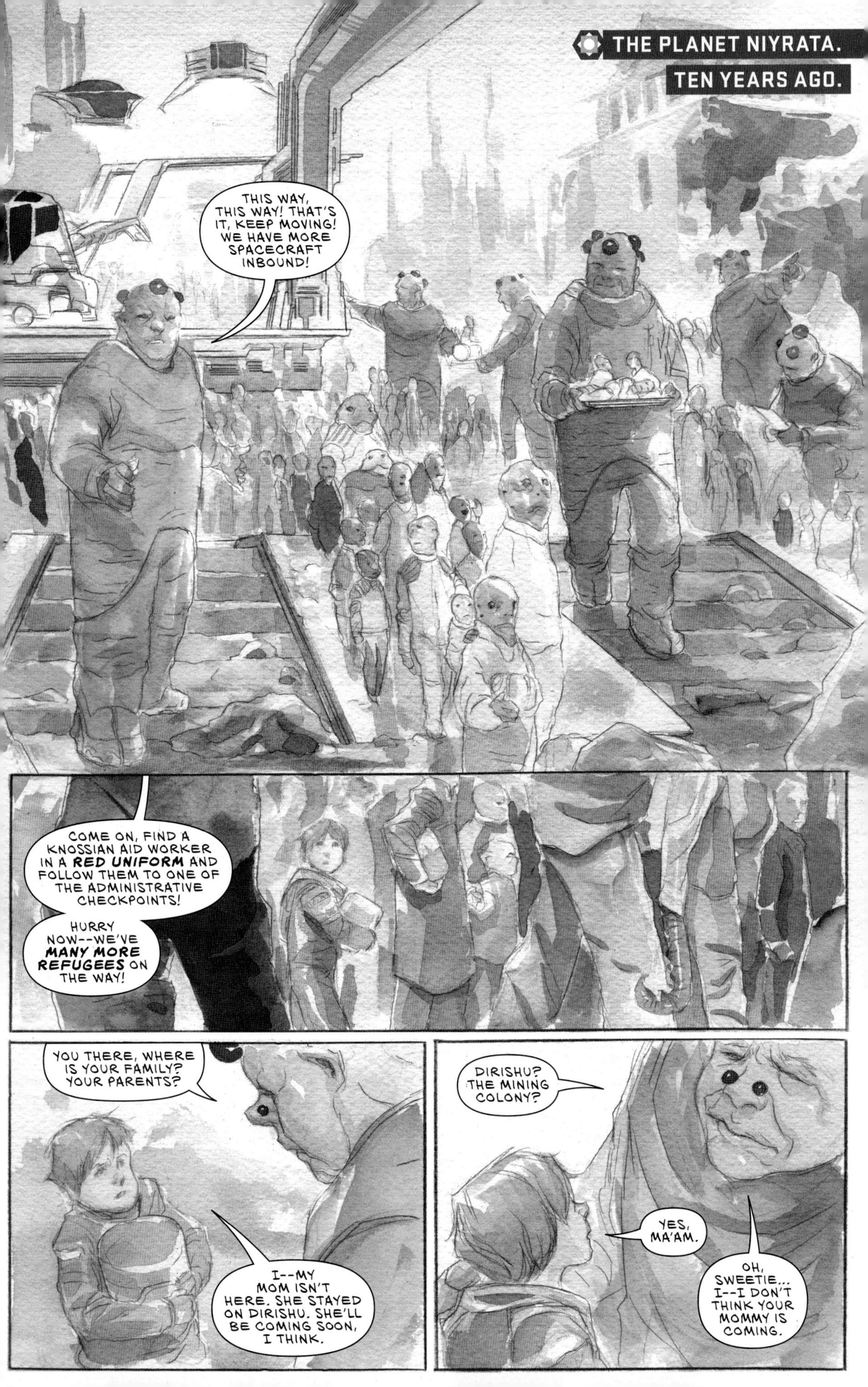
THE PLANET NIYRATA.
TEN YEARS AGO.
THIS WAY, THIS WAY! THAT'S IT, KEEP MOVING! WE HAVE MORE SPACECRAFT INBOUND!
COME ON, FIND A KNOSSIAN AID WORKER IN A **RED UNIFORM** AND FOLLOW THEM TO ONE OF THE ADMINISTRATIVE CHECKPOINTS!
HURRY NOW--WE'VE **MANY MORE REFUGEES** ON THE WAY!
YOU THERE, WHERE IS YOUR FAMILY? YOUR PARENTS?
I--MY MOM ISN'T HERE. SHE STAYED ON DIRISHU. SHE'LL BE COMING SOON, I THINK.
DIRISHU? THE MINING COLONY?
YES, MA'AM.
OH, SWEETIE... I--I DON'T THINK YOUR MOMMY IS COMING.

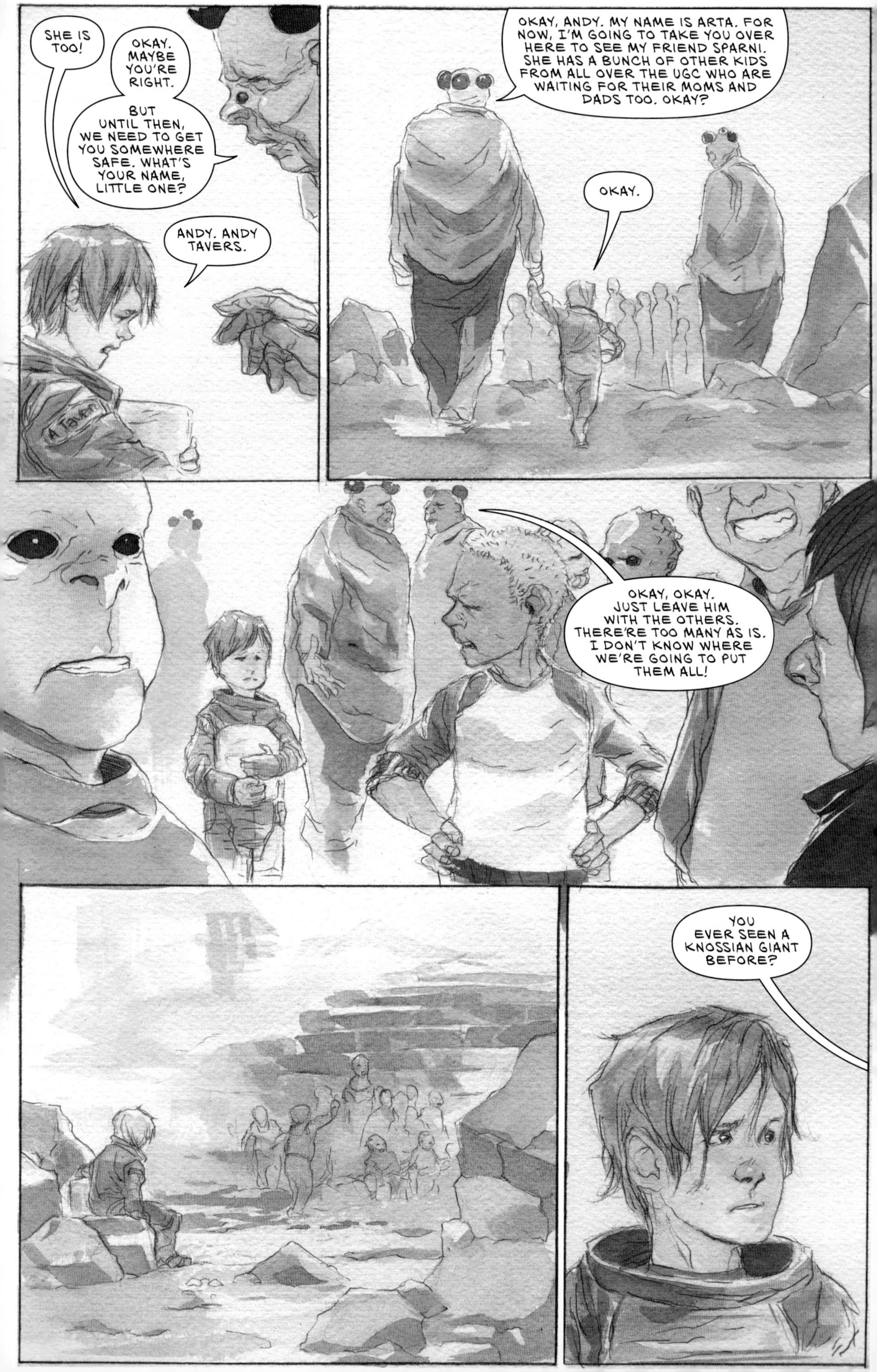
SHE IS TOO!
OKAY. MAYBE YOU'RE RIGHT.
BUT UNTIL THEN, WE NEED TO GET YOU SOMEWHERE SAFE. WHAT'S YOUR NAME, LITTLE ONE?
ANDY. ANDY TAVERS.
A. TAVERS
OKAY, ANDY. MY NAME IS ARTA. FOR NOW, I'M GOING TO TAKE YOU OVER HERE TO SEE MY FRIEND SPARNI. SHE HAS A BUNCH OF OTHER KIDS FROM ALL OVER THE UGC WHO ARE WAITING FOR THEIR MOMS AND DADS TOO. OKAY?
OKAY.
OKAY, OKAY. JUST LEAVE HIM WITH THE OTHERS. THERE'RE TOO MANY AS IS. I DON'T KNOW WHERE WE'RE GOING TO PUT THEM ALL!
YOU EVER SEEN A KNOSSIAN GIANT BEFORE?

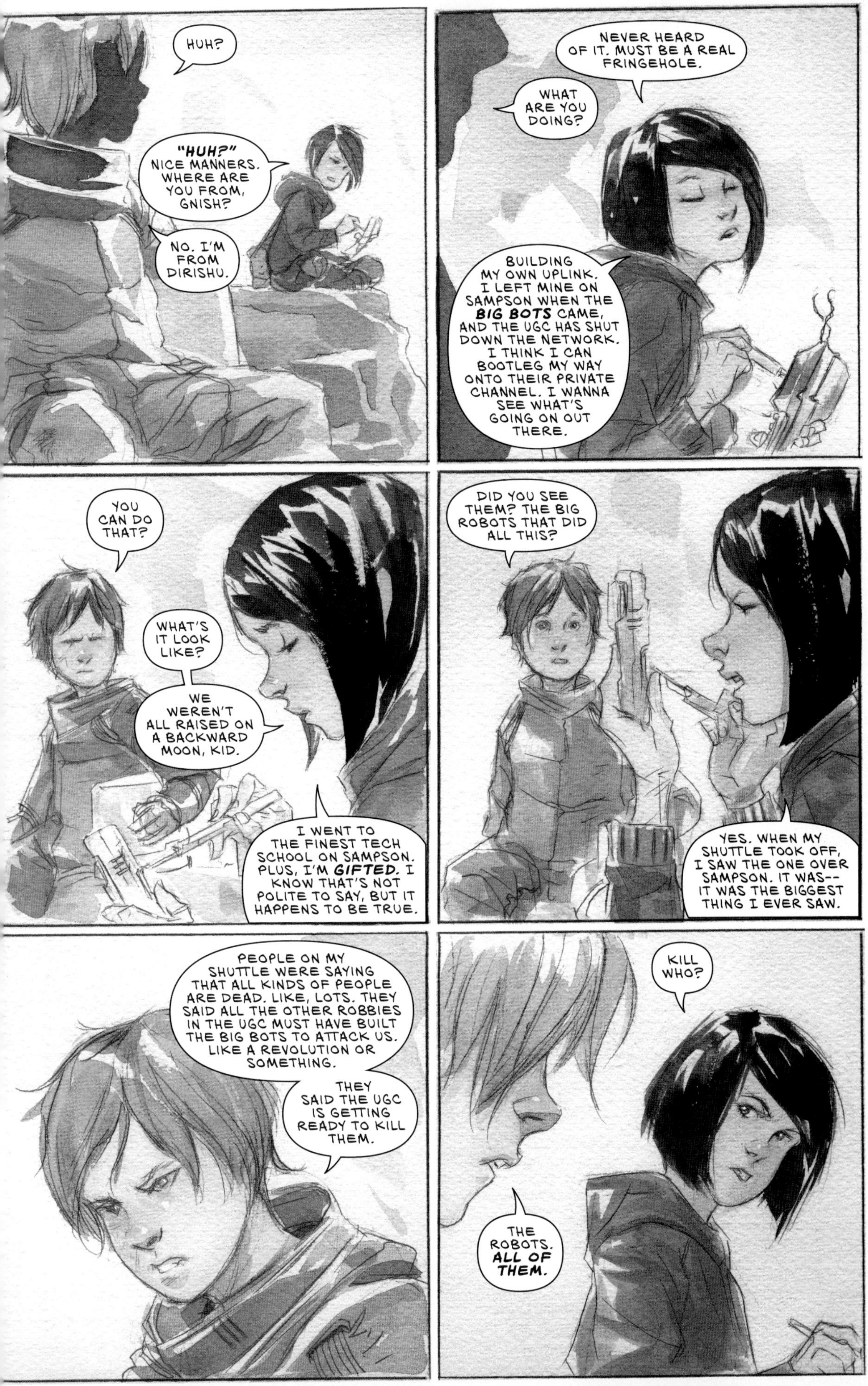
HUH?
"HUH?" NICE MANNERS. WHERE ARE YOU FROM, GNISH?
NO. I'M FROM DIRISHU.
NEVER HEARD OF IT. MUST BE A REAL FRINGEHOLE.
WHAT ARE YOU DOING?
BUILDING MY OWN UPLINK. I LEFT MINE ON SAMPSON WHEN THE BIG BOTS CAME, AND THE UGC HAS SHUT DOWN THE NETWORK. I THINK I CAN BOOTLEG MY WAY ONTO THEIR PRIVATE CHANNEL. I WANNA SEE WHAT'S GOING ON OUT THERE.
YOU CAN DO THAT?
WHAT'S IT LOOK LIKE?
WE WEREN'T ALL RAISED ON A BACKWARD MOON, KID.
I WENT TO THE FINEST TECH SCHOOL ON SAMPSON. PLUS, I'M GIFTED. I KNOW THAT'S NOT POLITE TO SAY, BUT IT HAPPENS TO BE TRUE.
DID YOU SEE THEM? THE BIG ROBOTS THAT DID ALL THIS?
YES. WHEN MY SHUTTLE TOOK OFF, I SAW THE ONE OVER SAMPSON. IT WAS-- IT WAS THE BIGGEST THING I EVER SAW.
PEOPLE ON MY SHUTTLE WERE SAYING THAT ALL KINDS OF PEOPLE ARE DEAD. LIKE, LOTS. THEY SAID ALL THE OTHER ROBBIES IN THE UGC MUST HAVE BUILT THE BIG BOTS TO ATTACK US. LIKE A REVOLUTION OR SOMETHING.
THEY SAID THE UGC IS GETTING READY TO KILL THEM.
KILL WHO?
THE ROBOTS. ALL OF THEM.

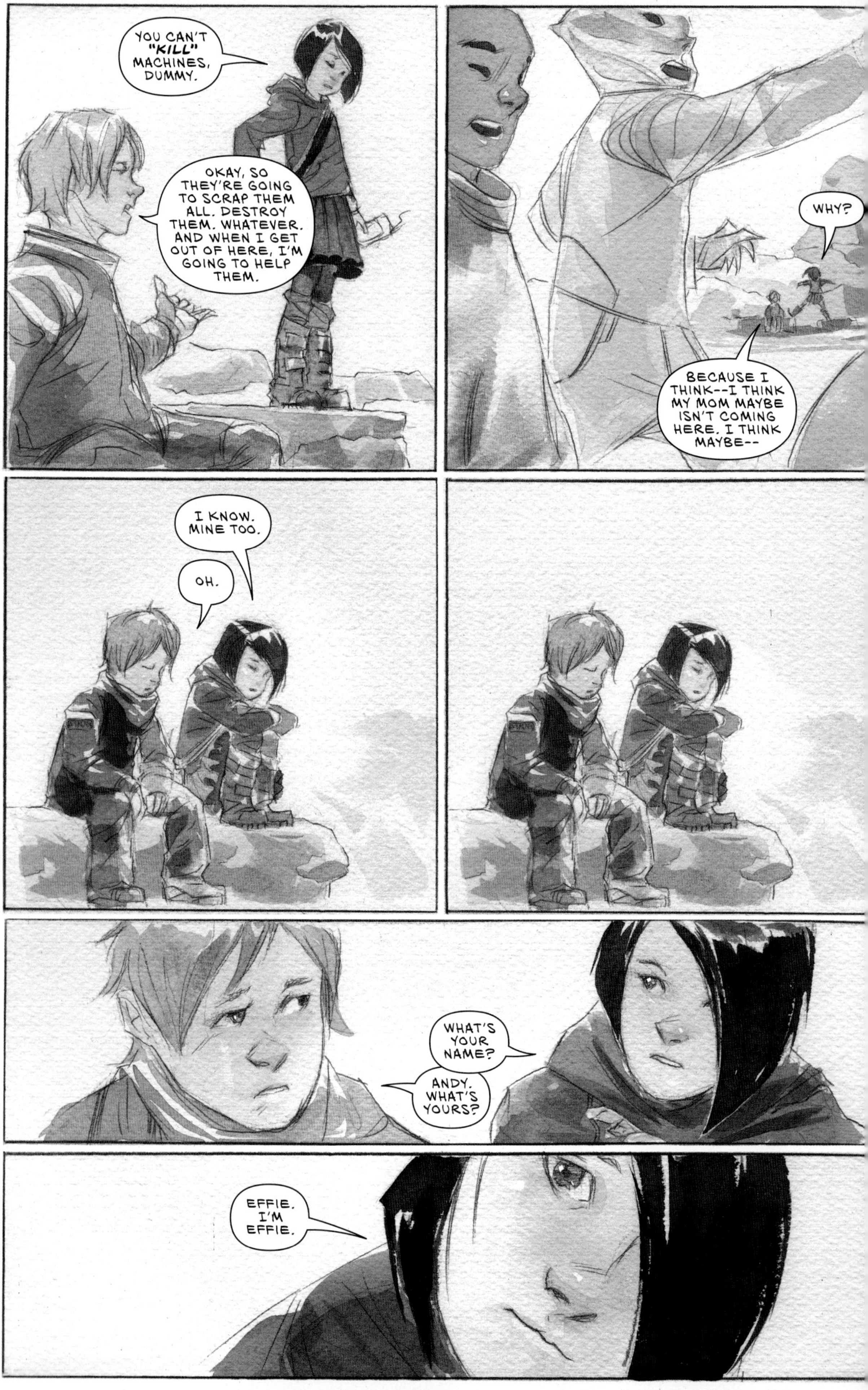
YOU CAN'T "KILL" MACHINES, DUMMY.
OKAY, SO THEY'RE GOING TO SCRAP THEM ALL. DESTROY THEM. WHATEVER. AND WHEN I GET OUT OF HERE, I'M GOING TO HELP THEM.
WHY?
BECAUSE I THINK--I THINK MY MOM MAYBE ISN'T COMING HERE. I THINK MAYBE--
I KNOW. MINE TOO.
OH.
WHAT'S YOUR NAME?
ANDY. WHAT'S YOURS?
EFFIE. I'M EFFIE.

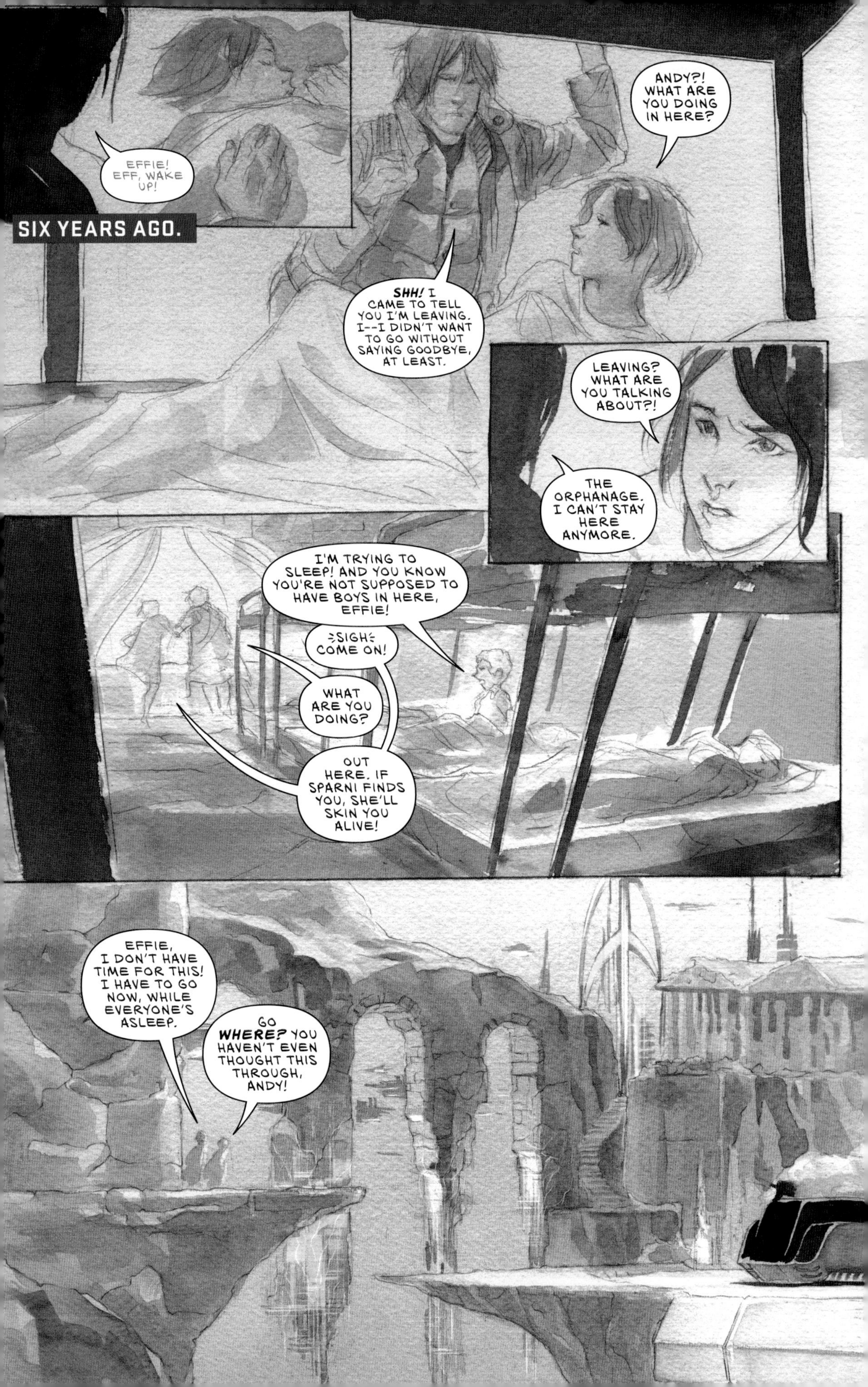
EFFIE! EFF, WAKE UP!
SIX YEARS AGO.
ANDY?! WHAT ARE YOU DOING IN HERE?
SHH! I CAME TO TELL YOU I'M LEAVING. I--I DIDN'T WANT TO GO WITHOUT SAYING GOODBYE, AT LEAST.
LEAVING? WHAT ARE YOU TALKING ABOUT?!
THE ORPHANAGE. I CAN'T STAY HERE ANYMORE.
I'M TRYING TO SLEEP! AND YOU KNOW YOU'RE NOT SUPPOSED TO HAVE BOYS IN HERE, EFFIE!
SIGH COME ON!
WHAT ARE YOU DOING?
OUT HERE. IF SPARNI FINDS YOU, SHE'LL SKIN YOU ALIVE!
EFFIE, I DON'T HAVE TIME FOR THIS! I HAVE TO GO NOW, WHILE EVERYONE'S ASLEEP.
GO WHERE? YOU HAVEN'T EVEN THOUGHT THIS THROUGH, ANDY!

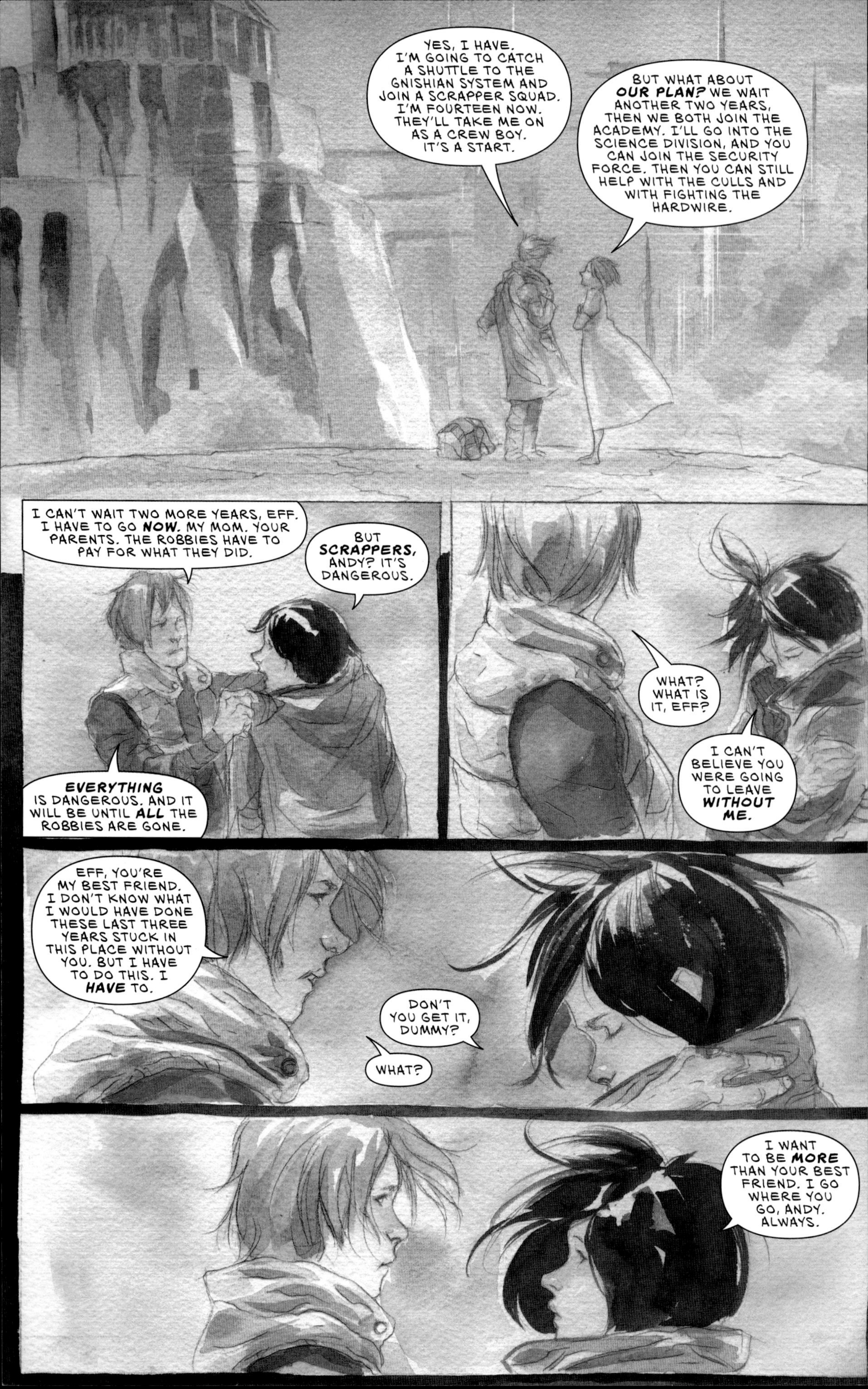
YES, I HAVE. I'M GOING TO CATCH A SHUTTLE TO THE GNISHIAN SYSTEM AND JOIN A SCRAPPER SQUAD. I'M FOURTEEN NOW. THEY'LL TAKE ME ON AS A CREW BOY. IT'S A START.
BUT WHAT ABOUT **OUR PLAN?** WE WAIT ANOTHER TWO YEARS, THEN WE BOTH JOIN THE ACADEMY. I'LL GO INTO THE SCIENCE DIVISION, AND YOU CAN JOIN THE SECURITY FORCE. THEN YOU CAN STILL HELP WITH THE CULLS AND WITH FIGHTING THE HARDWIRE.
I CAN'T WAIT TWO MORE YEARS, EFF. I HAVE TO GO **NOW.** MY MOM. YOUR PARENTS. THE ROBBIES HAVE TO PAY FOR WHAT THEY DID.
BUT **SCRAPPERS,** ANDY? IT'S DANGEROUS.
EVERYTHING IS DANGEROUS. AND IT WILL BE UNTIL **ALL** THE ROBBIES ARE GONE.
WHAT? WHAT IS IT, EFF?
I CAN'T BELIEVE YOU WERE GOING TO LEAVE **WITHOUT ME.**
EFF, YOU'RE MY BEST FRIEND. I DON'T KNOW WHAT I WOULD HAVE DONE THESE LAST THREE YEARS STUCK IN THIS PLACE WITHOUT YOU. BUT I HAVE TO DO THIS. I **HAVE** TO.
DON'T YOU GET IT, DUMMY?
WHAT?
I WANT TO BE **MORE** THAN YOUR BEST FRIEND. I GO WHERE YOU GO, ANDY. ALWAYS.

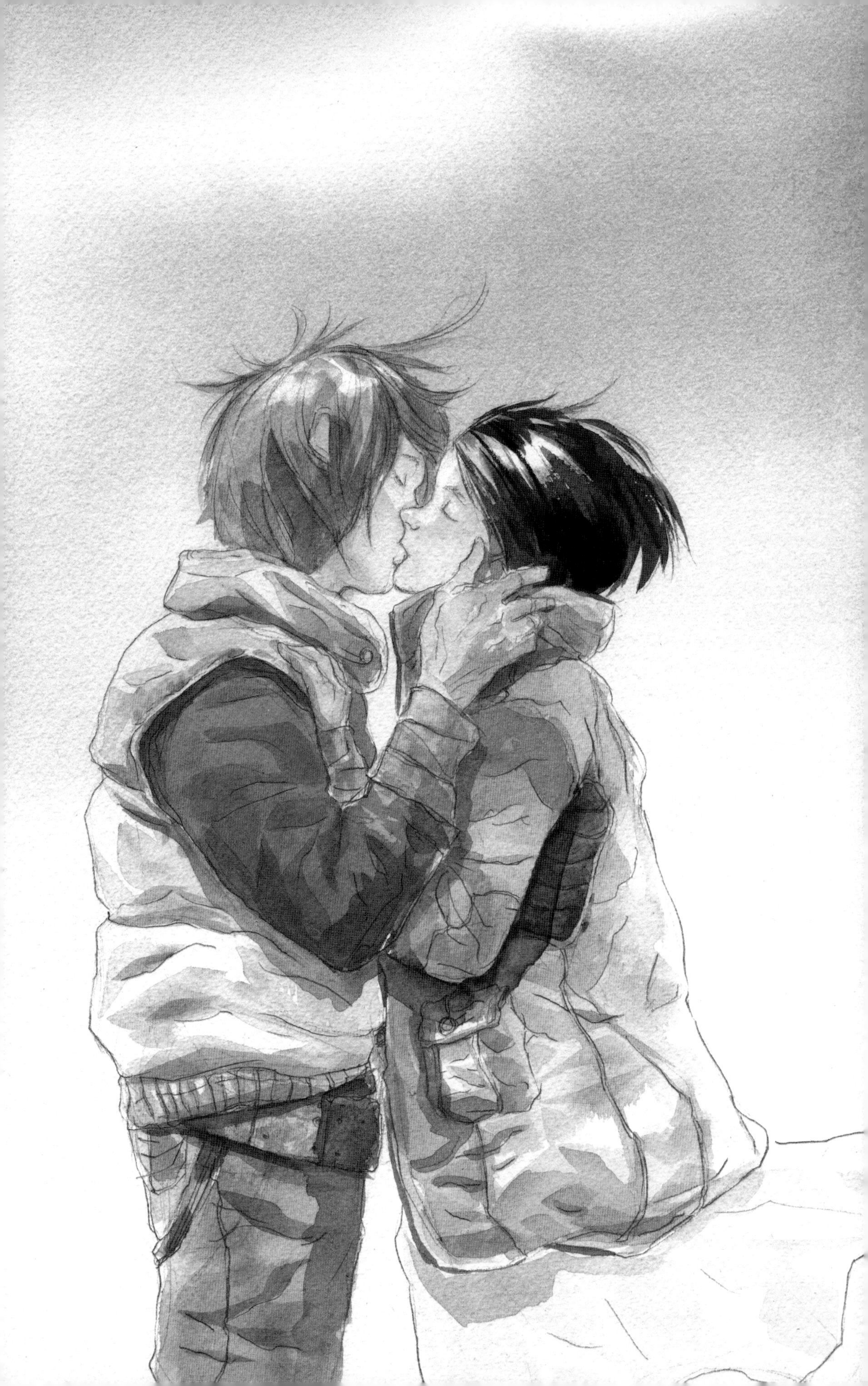

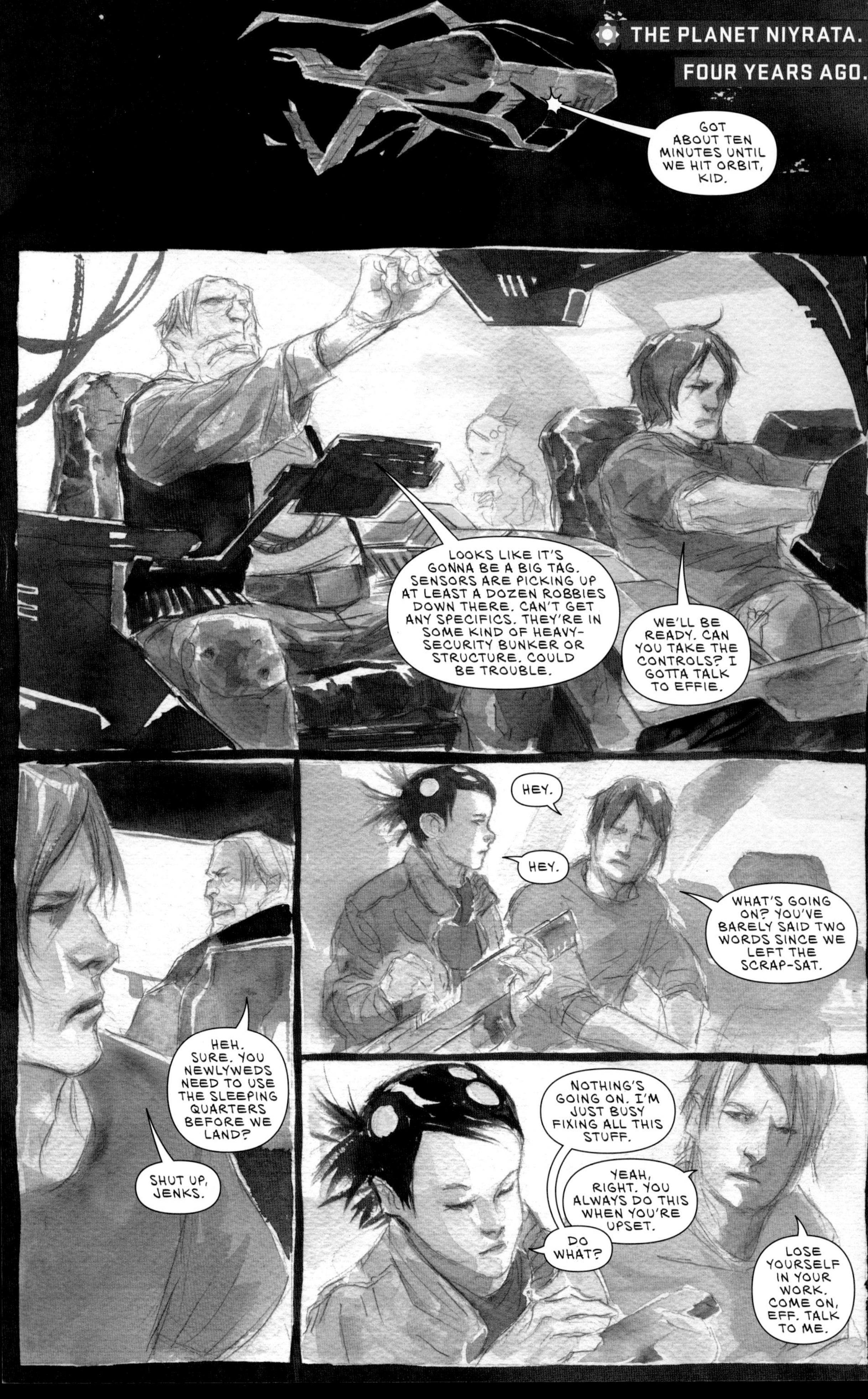
THE PLANET NIYRATA.
FOUR YEARS AGO.
GOT ABOUT TEN MINUTES UNTIL WE HIT ORBIT, KID.
LOOKS LIKE IT'S GONNA BE A BIG TAG. SENSORS ARE PICKING UP AT LEAST A DOZEN ROBBIES DOWN THERE. CAN'T GET ANY SPECIFICS. THEY'RE IN SOME KIND OF HEAVY-SECURITY BUNKER OR STRUCTURE. COULD BE TROUBLE.
WE'LL BE READY. CAN YOU TAKE THE CONTROLS? I GOTTA TALK TO EFFIE.
HEH. SURE. YOU NEWLYWEDS NEED TO USE THE SLEEPING QUARTERS BEFORE WE LAND?
SHUT UP, JENKS.
HEY.
HEY.
WHAT'S GOING ON? YOU'VE BARELY SAID TWO WORDS SINCE WE LEFT THE SCRAP-SAT.
NOTHING'S GOING ON. I'M JUST BUSY FIXING ALL THIS STUFF.
YEAH, RIGHT. YOU ALWAYS DO THIS WHEN YOU'RE UPSET.
DO WHAT?
LOSE YOURSELF IN YOUR WORK. COME ON, EFF. TALK TO ME.

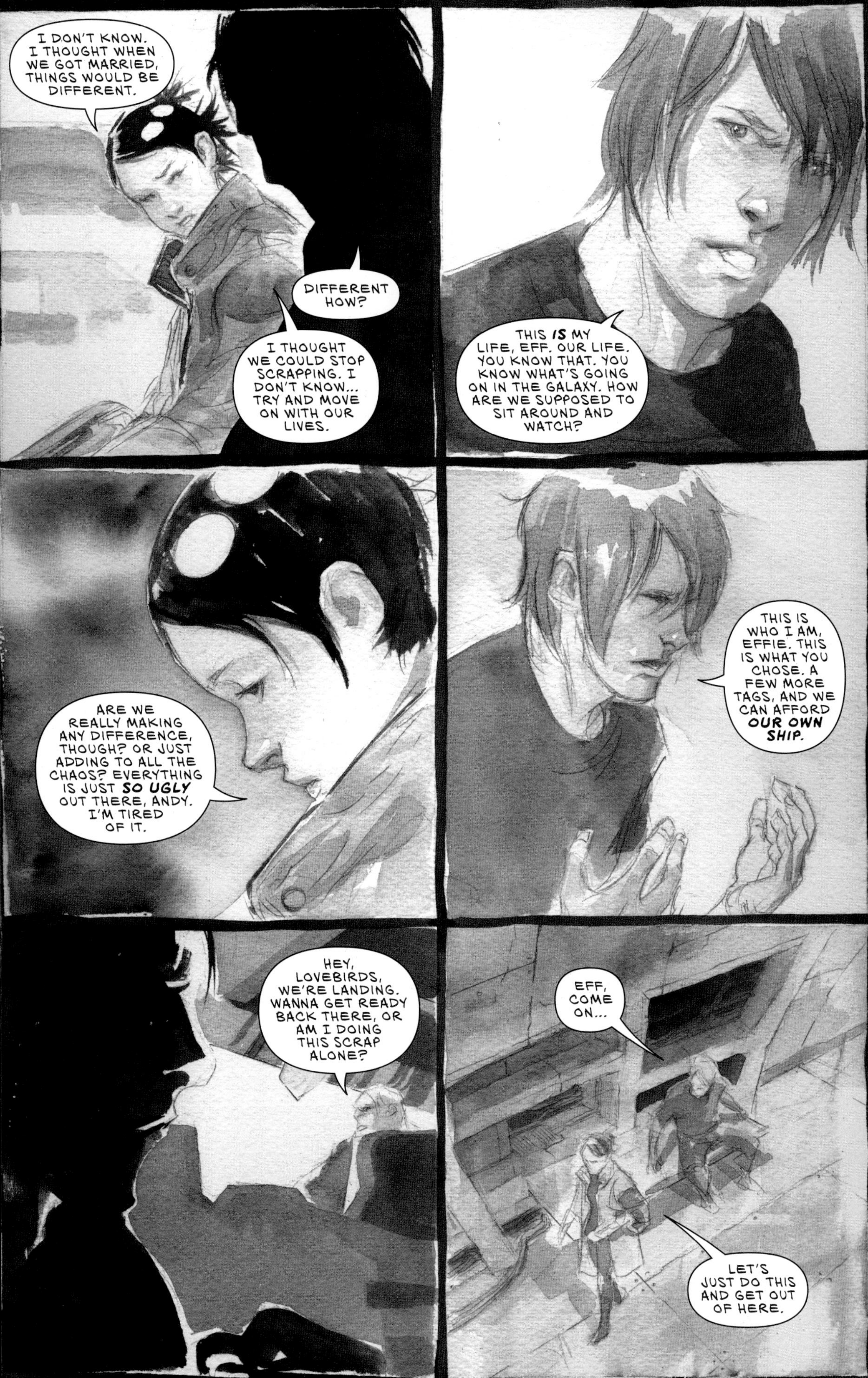
I DON'T KNOW. I THOUGHT WHEN WE GOT MARRIED, THINGS WOULD BE DIFFERENT.
DIFFERENT HOW?
I THOUGHT WE COULD STOP SCRAPPING. I DON'T KNOW... TRY AND MOVE ON WITH OUR LIVES.
THIS IS MY LIFE, EFF. OUR LIFE. YOU KNOW THAT. YOU KNOW WHAT'S GOING ON IN THE GALAXY. HOW ARE WE SUPPOSED TO SIT AROUND AND WATCH?
ARE WE REALLY MAKING ANY DIFFERENCE, THOUGH? OR JUST ADDING TO ALL THE CHAOS? EVERYTHING IS JUST SO UGLY OUT THERE, ANDY. I'M TIRED OF IT.
THIS IS WHO I AM, EFFIE. THIS IS WHAT YOU CHOSE. A FEW MORE TAGS, AND WE CAN AFFORD OUR OWN SHIP.
HEY, LOVEBIRDS, WE'RE LANDING. WANNA GET READY BACK THERE, OR AM I DOING THIS SCRAP ALONE?
EFF, COME ON...
LET'S JUST DO THIS AND GET OUT OF HERE.

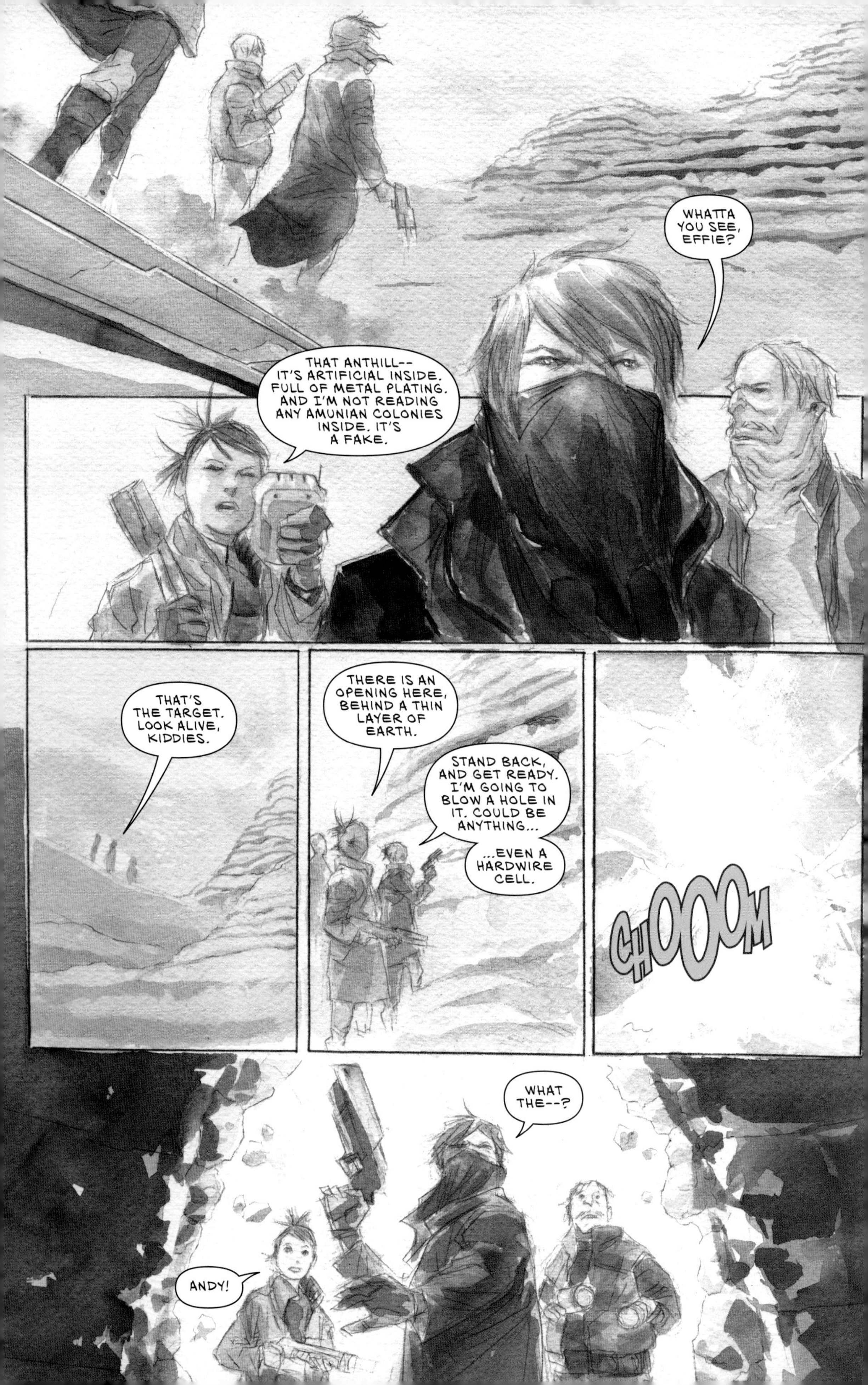
WHATTA YOU SEE, EFFIE?
THAT ANTHILL-- IT'S ARTIFICIAL INSIDE. FULL OF METAL PLATING. AND I'M NOT READING ANY AMUNIAN COLONIES INSIDE. IT'S A FAKE.
THAT'S THE TARGET. LOOK ALIVE, KIDDIES.
THERE IS AN OPENING HERE, BEHIND A THIN LAYER OF EARTH.
STAND BACK, AND GET READY. I'M GOING TO BLOW A HOLE IN IT. COULD BE ANYTHING...
...EVEN A HARDWIRE CELL.
CHOOOM
WHAT THE--?
ANDY!

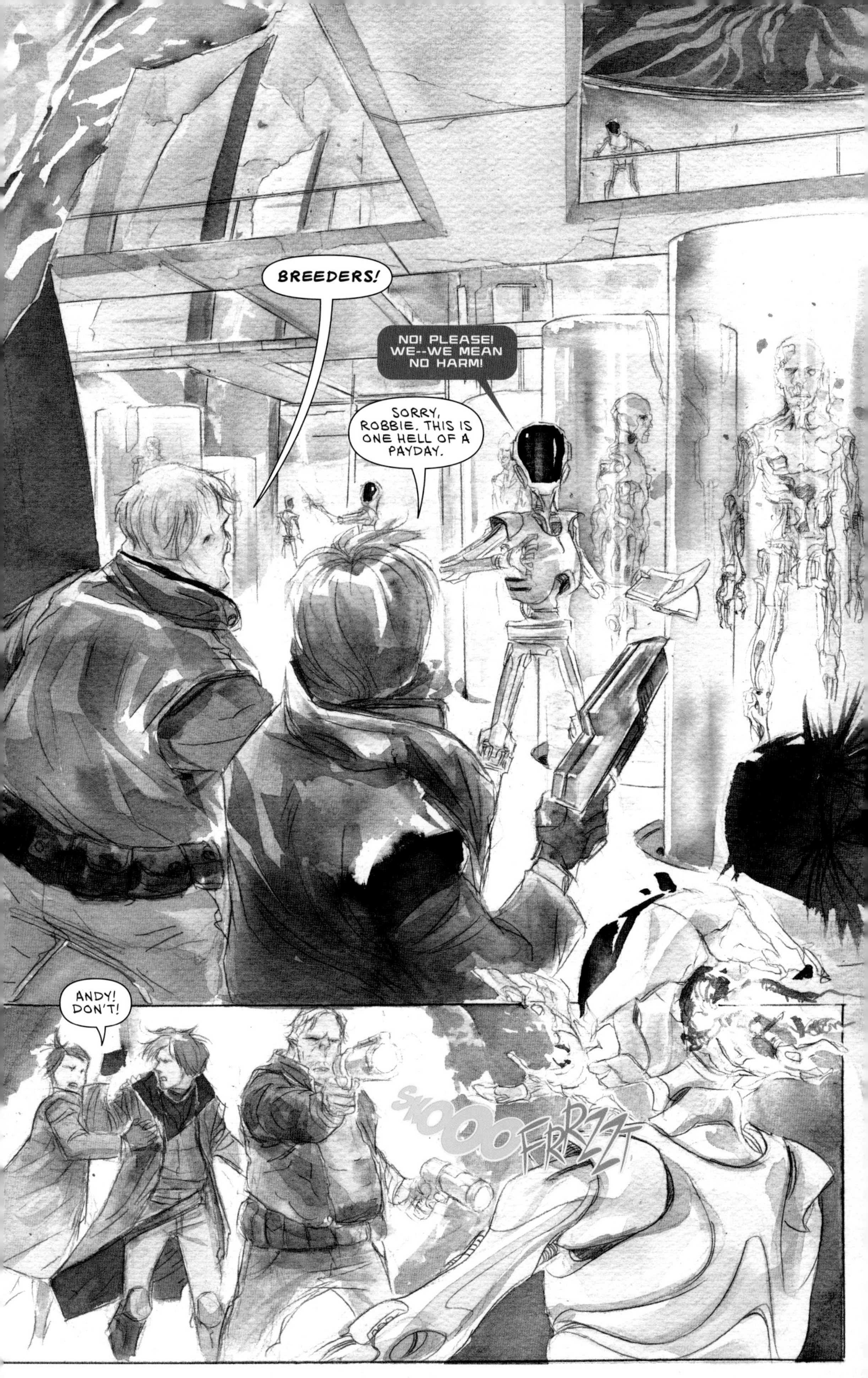
BREEDERS!
NO! PLEASE! WE--WE MEAN NO HARM!
SORRY, ROBBIE. THIS IS ONE HELL OF A PAYDAY.
ANDY! DON'T!
SKOOOO FRRZZT

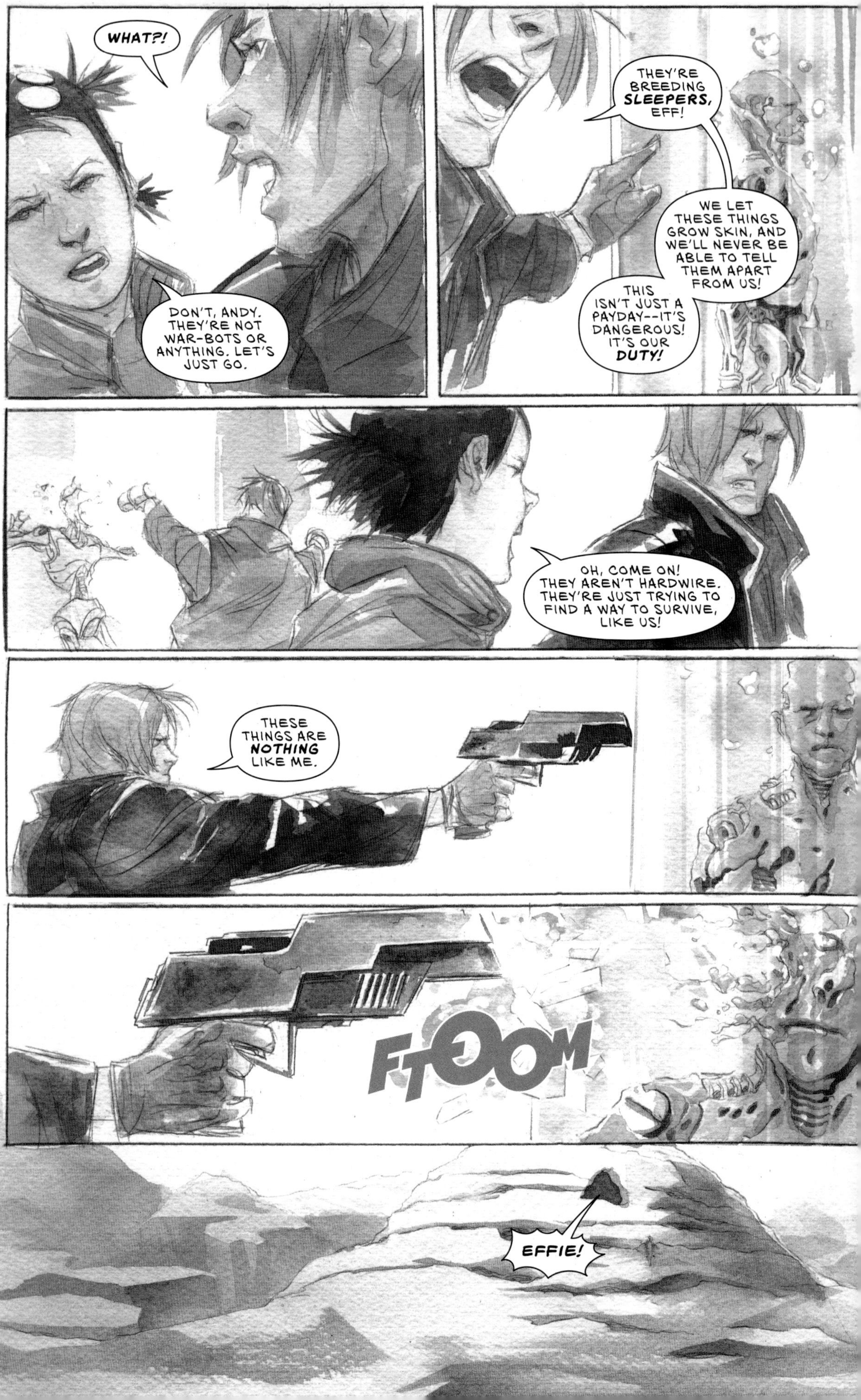
WHAT?!
DON'T, ANDY. THEY'RE NOT WAR-BOTS OR ANYTHING. LET'S JUST GO.
THEY'RE BREEDING **SLEEPERS,** EFF!
WE LET THESE THINGS GROW SKIN, AND WE'LL NEVER BE ABLE TO TELL THEM APART FROM US!
THIS ISN'T JUST A PAYDAY--IT'S DANGEROUS! IT'S OUR ***DUTY!***
OH, COME ON! THEY AREN'T HARDWIRE. THEY'RE JUST TRYING TO FIND A WAY TO SURVIVE, LIKE US!
THESE THINGS ARE **NOTHING** LIKE ME.
FTOOM
EFFIE!

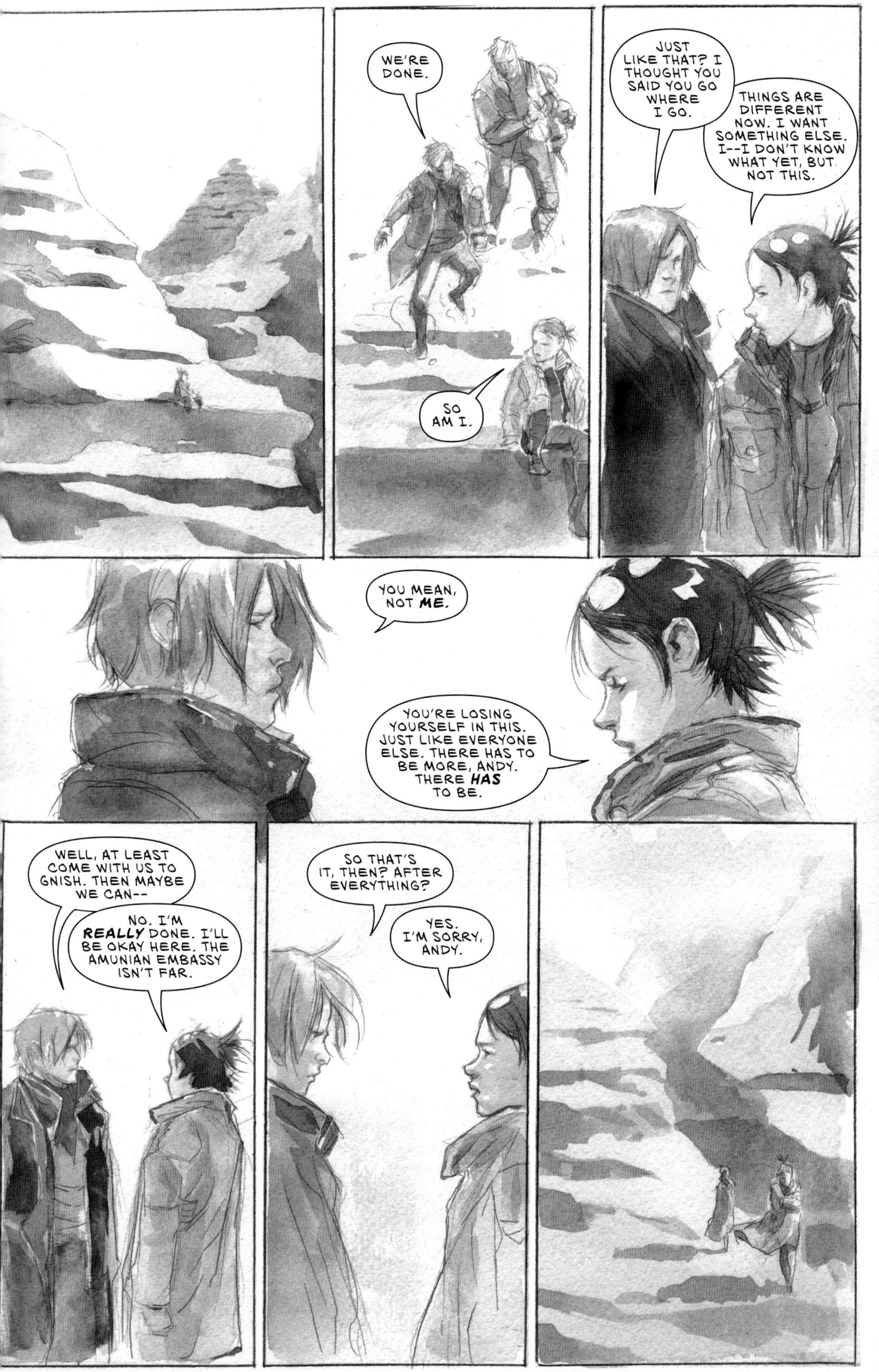
WE'RE DONE.
SO AM I.
JUST LIKE THAT? I THOUGHT YOU SAID YOU GO WHERE I GO.
THINGS ARE DIFFERENT NOW. I WANT SOMETHING ELSE. I--I DON'T KNOW WHAT YET, BUT NOT THIS.
YOU MEAN, NOT ME.
YOU'RE LOSING YOURSELF IN THIS. JUST LIKE EVERYONE ELSE. THERE HAS TO BE MORE, ANDY. THERE HAS TO BE.
WELL, AT LEAST COME WITH US TO GNISH. THEN MAYBE WE CAN--
NO. I'M REALLY DONE. I'LL BE OKAY HERE. THE AMUNIAN EMBASSY ISN'T FAR.
SO THAT'S IT, THEN? AFTER EVERYTHING?
YES. I'M SORRY, ANDY.

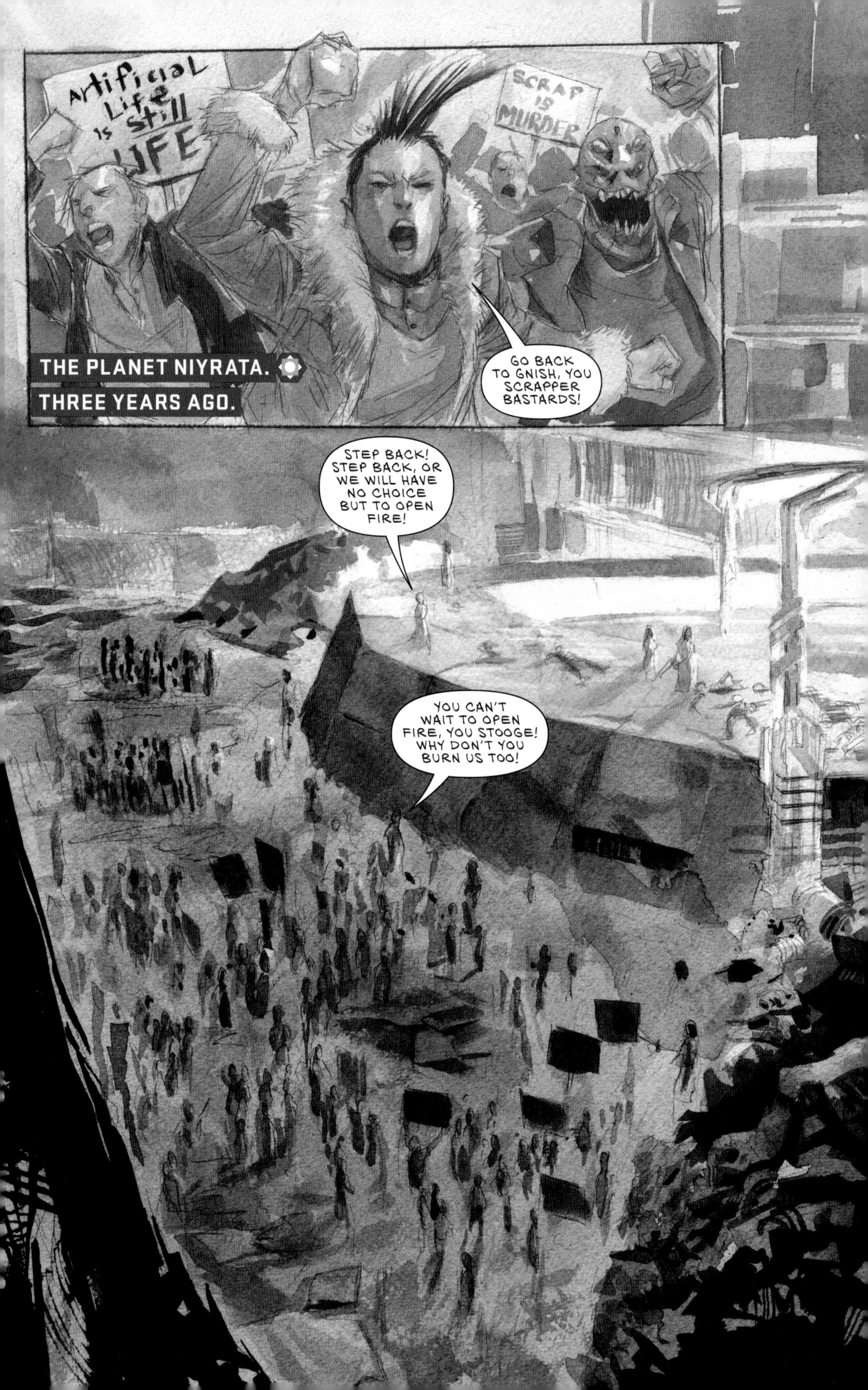
Artificial Life is still LIFE
SCRAP IS MURDER
THE PLANET NIYRATA.
THREE YEARS AGO.
GO BACK TO GNISH, YOU SCRAPPER BASTARDS!
STEP BACK! STEP BACK, OR WE WILL HAVE NO CHOICE BUT TO OPEN FIRE!
YOU CAN'T WAIT TO OPEN FIRE, YOU STOOGE! WHY DON'T YOU BURN US TOO!

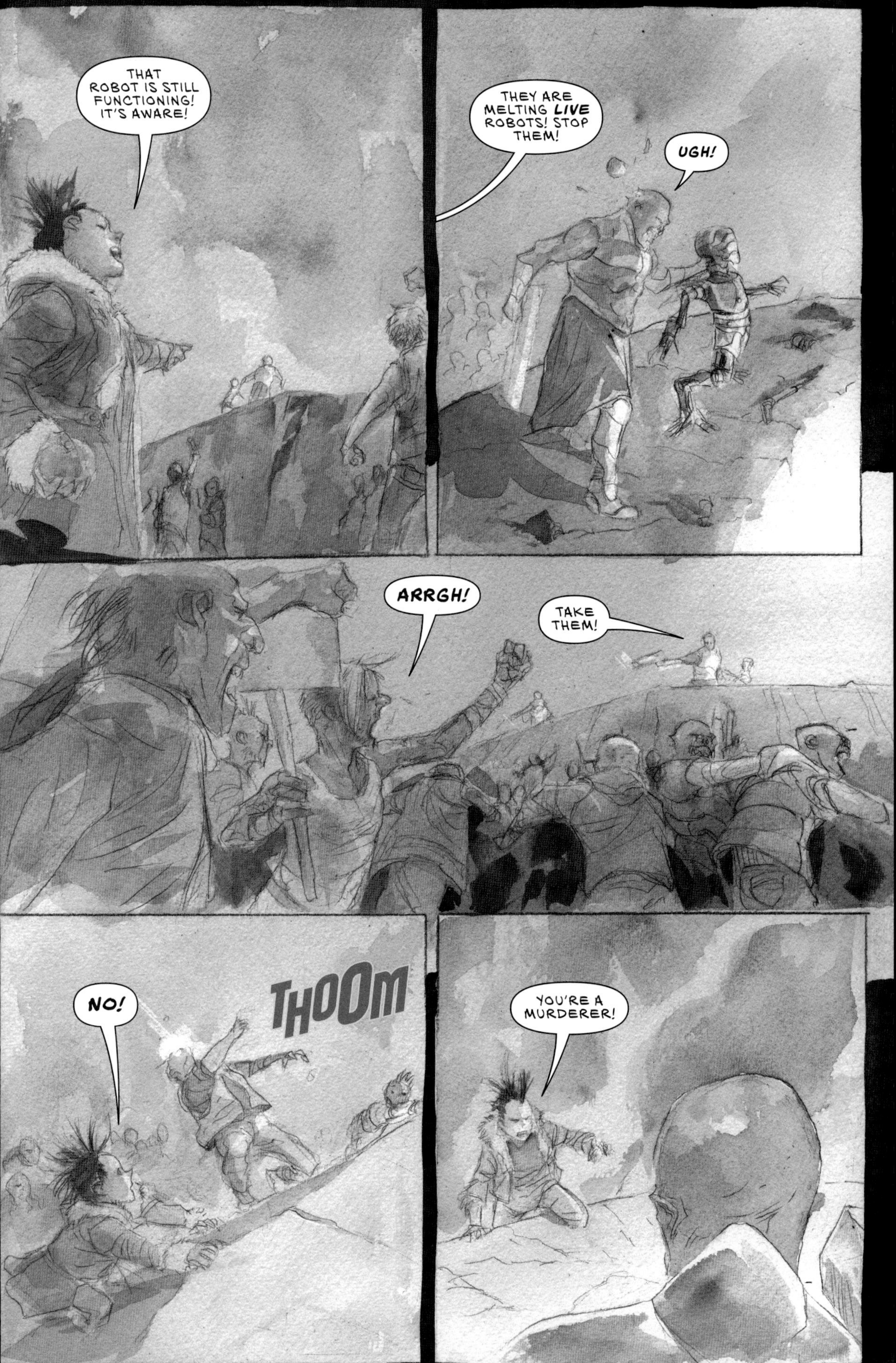
THAT ROBOT IS STILL FUNCTIONING! IT'S AWARE!
THEY ARE MELTING LIVE ROBOTS! STOP THEM!
UGH!
ARRGH!
TAKE THEM!
NO!
THOOM
YOU'RE A MURDERER!

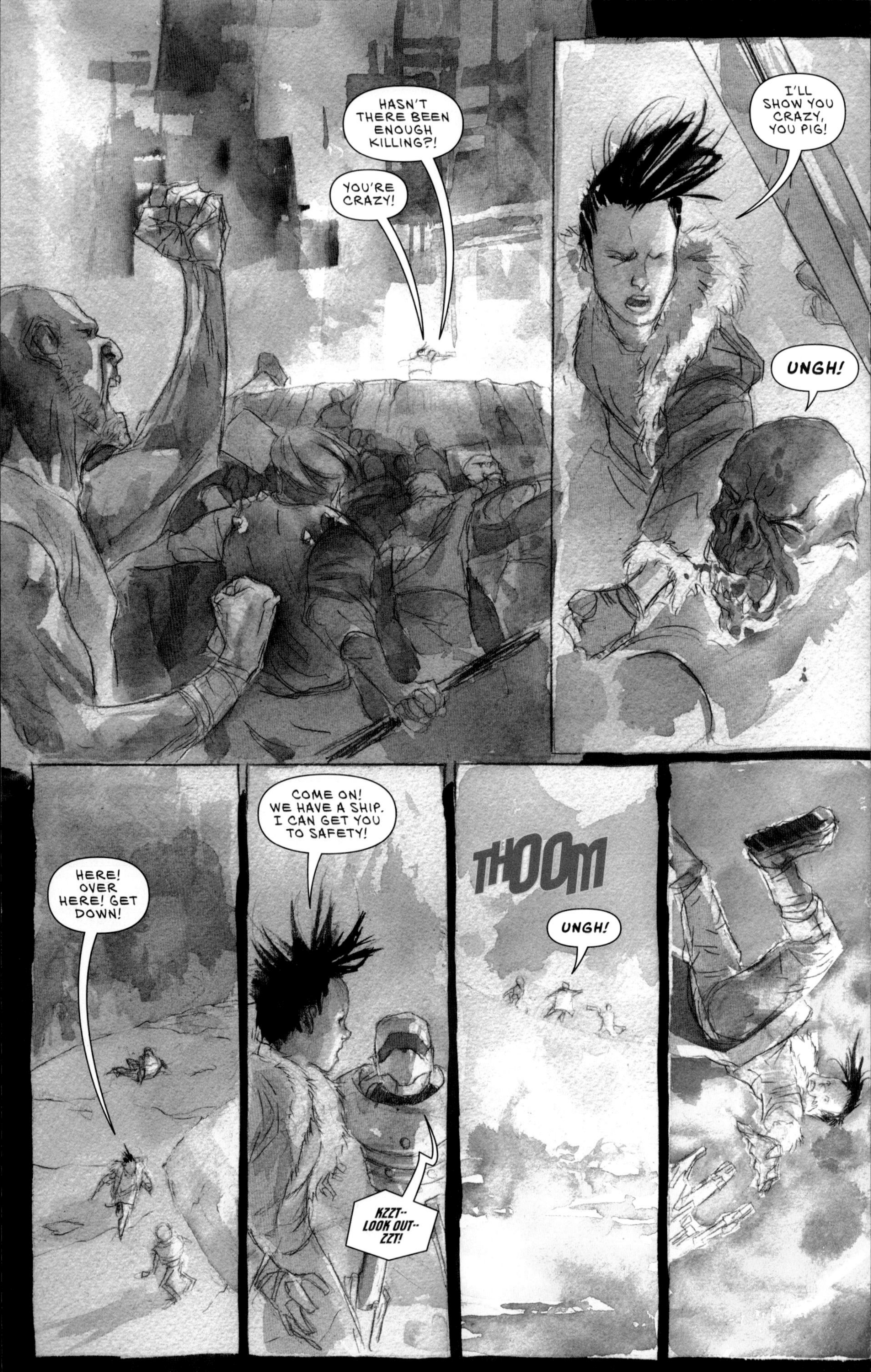
HASN'T THERE BEEN ENOUGH KILLING?!
YOU'RE CRAZY!
I'LL SHOW YOU CRAZY, YOU PIG!
UNGH!
HERE! OVER HERE! GET DOWN!
COME ON! WE HAVE A SHIP. I CAN GET YOU TO SAFETY!
KZZT-- LOOK OUT-- ZZT!
THOOM
UNGH!

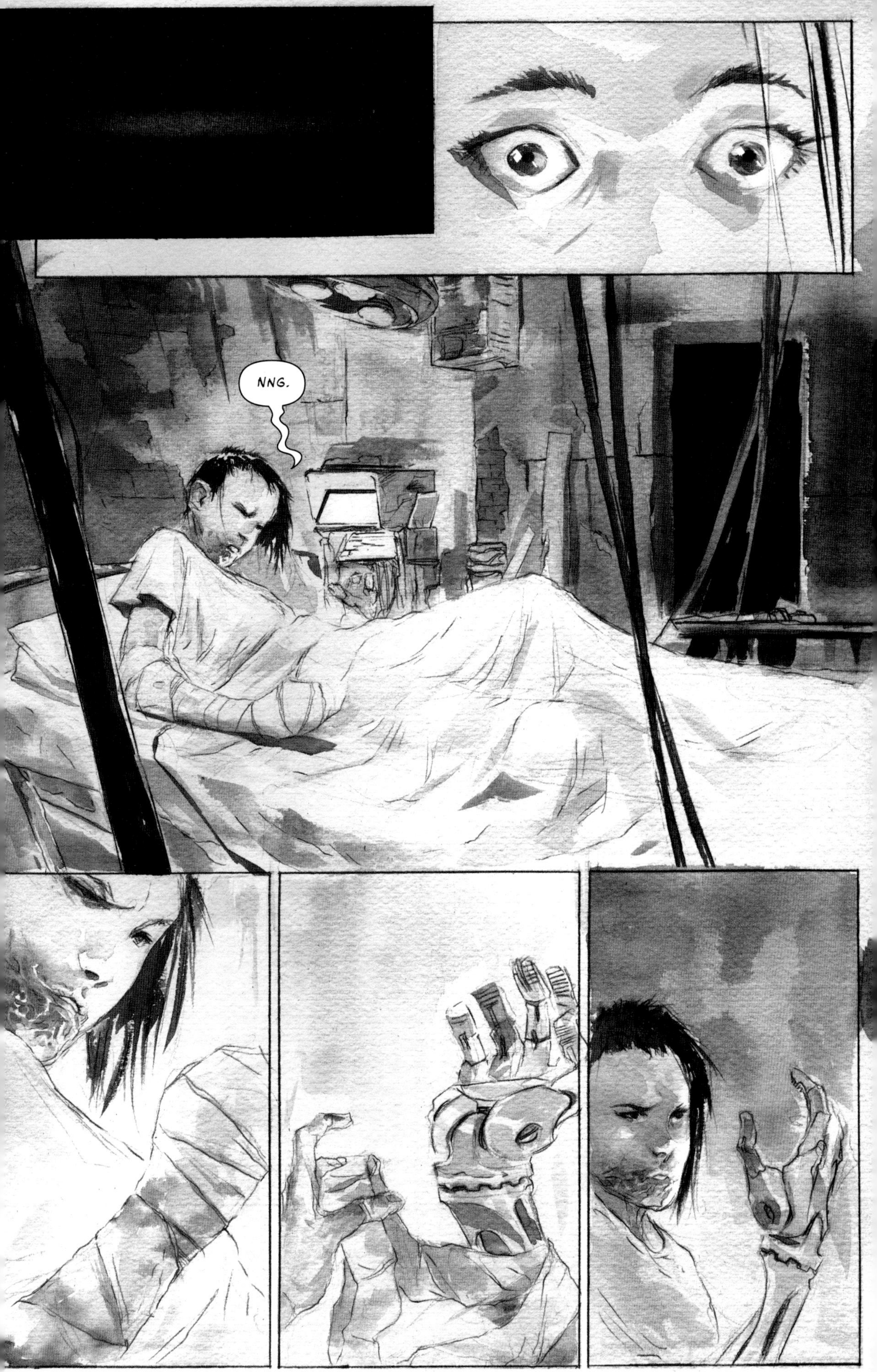
NNG.

DON'T WORRY, EFF. WE'LL GET THAT FIXED. AS SOON AS YOU'RE WELL ENOUGH TO LEAVE, I'LL GET YOU OUT OF HERE AND TO A REAL HOSPITAL.

A-ANDY?

DON'T TRY TO MOVE. JUST REST.

TOOK ME TWO WEEKS TO FIND YOU. I WAS--I WAS SCARED, EFF. I THOUGHT I'D LOST YOU.

ANYWAY, I WAS STILL LISTED AS YOUR NEXT OF KIN ON YOUR IDENTICHIP. RUSHED ALL THE WAY HERE FROM THE MATA SYSTEM.

I DON'T UNDERSTAND. WHAT--?

THEY PULLED YOU OUT OF THE MELTING PIT. THE HOSPITALS HERE ON SAMPSON WERE BLOWN BACK TO THE STONE AGE AFTER THE HARVESTERS, BUT THE DOCTORS DID WHAT THEY COULD WITH WHAT THEY HAD.

BUT LIKE I SAID, AS SOON AS YOU GET YOUR STRENGTH BACK, I'LL GET YOU REAL HELP. WE'LL GET THAT THING OFF OF YOU AND FIGURE SOMETHING BETTER OUT.

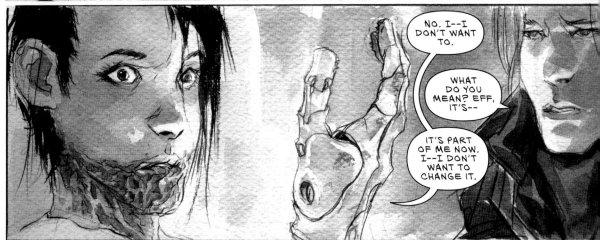

NO. I--I DON'T WANT TO.

WHAT DO YOU MEAN? EFF, IT'S--

IT'S PART OF ME NOW. I--I DON'T WANT TO CHANGE IT.

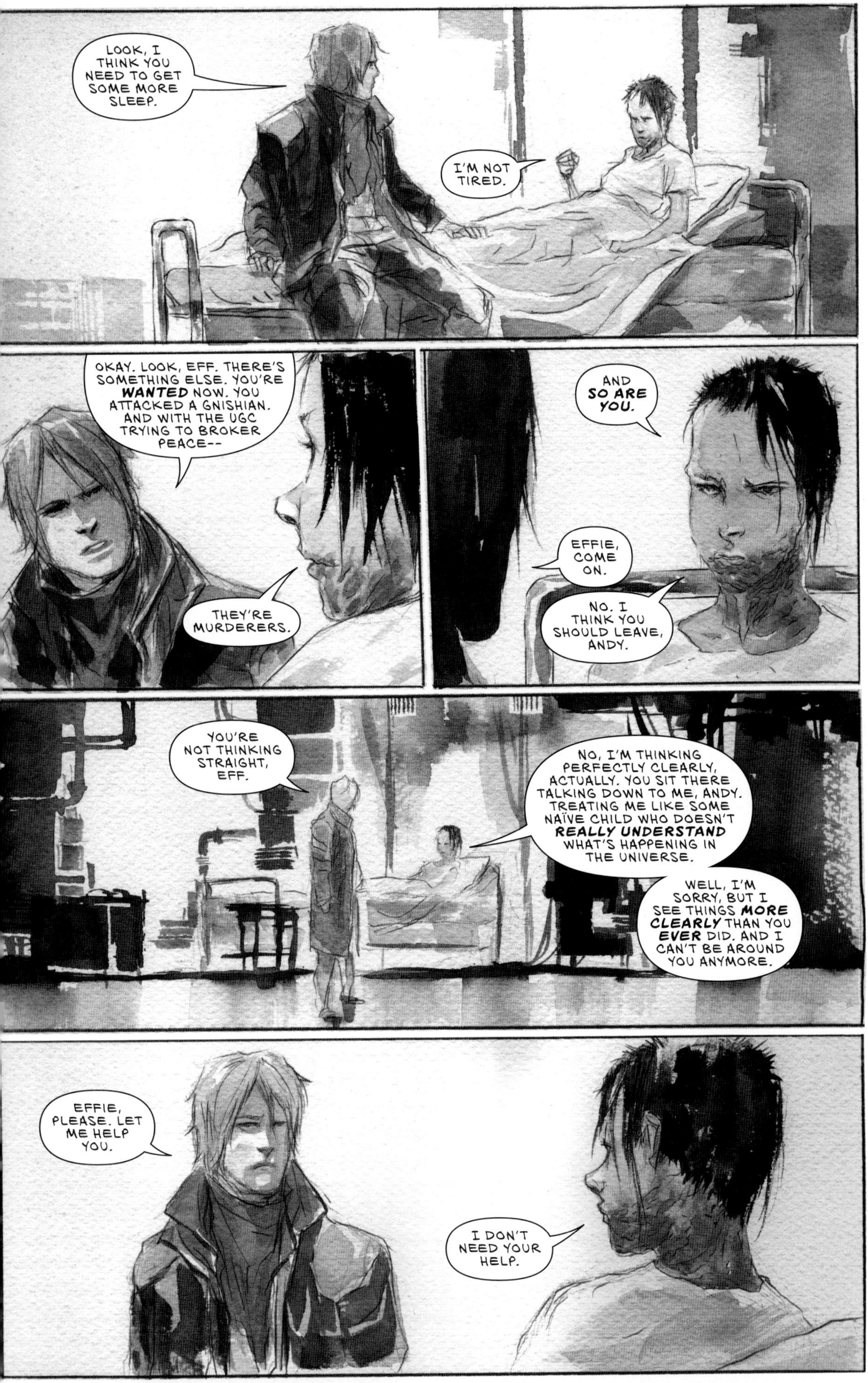
LOOK, I THINK YOU NEED TO GET SOME MORE SLEEP.
I'M NOT TIRED.
OKAY. LOOK, EFF. THERE'S SOMETHING ELSE. YOU'RE WANTED NOW. YOU ATTACKED A GNISHIAN. AND WITH THE UGC TRYING TO BROKER PEACE--
THEY'RE MURDERERS.
AND SO ARE YOU.
EFFIE, COME ON.
NO. I THINK YOU SHOULD LEAVE, ANDY.
YOU'RE NOT THINKING STRAIGHT, EFF.
NO, I'M THINKING PERFECTLY CLEARLY, ACTUALLY. YOU SIT THERE TALKING DOWN TO ME, ANDY. TREATING ME LIKE SOME NAÏVE CHILD WHO DOESN'T REALLY UNDERSTAND WHAT'S HAPPENING IN THE UNIVERSE.
WELL, I'M SORRY, BUT I SEE THINGS MORE CLEARLY THAN YOU EVER DID. AND I CAN'T BE AROUND YOU ANYMORE.
EFFIE, PLEASE. LET ME HELP YOU.
I DON'T NEED YOUR HELP.

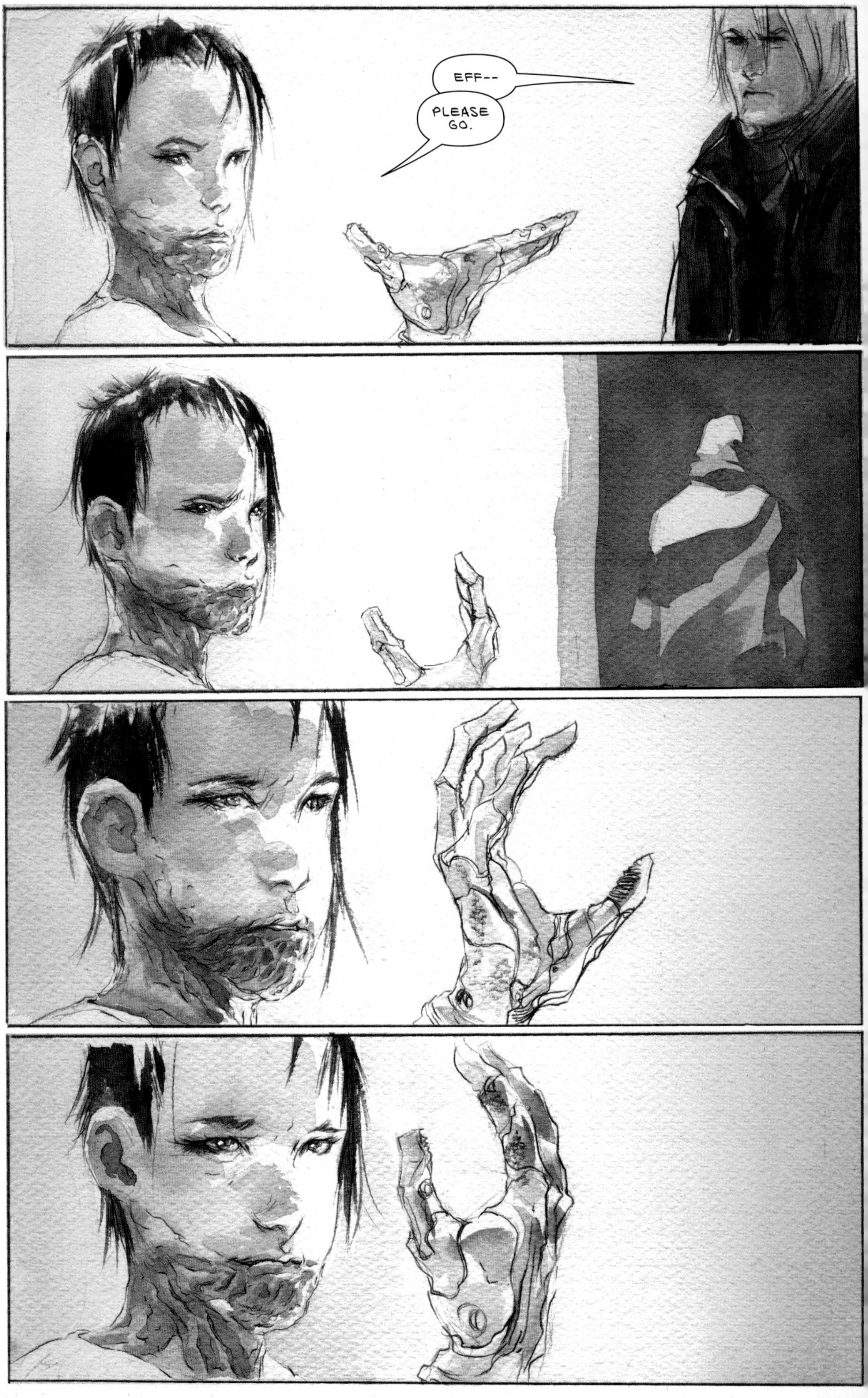
EFF--
PLEASE GO.

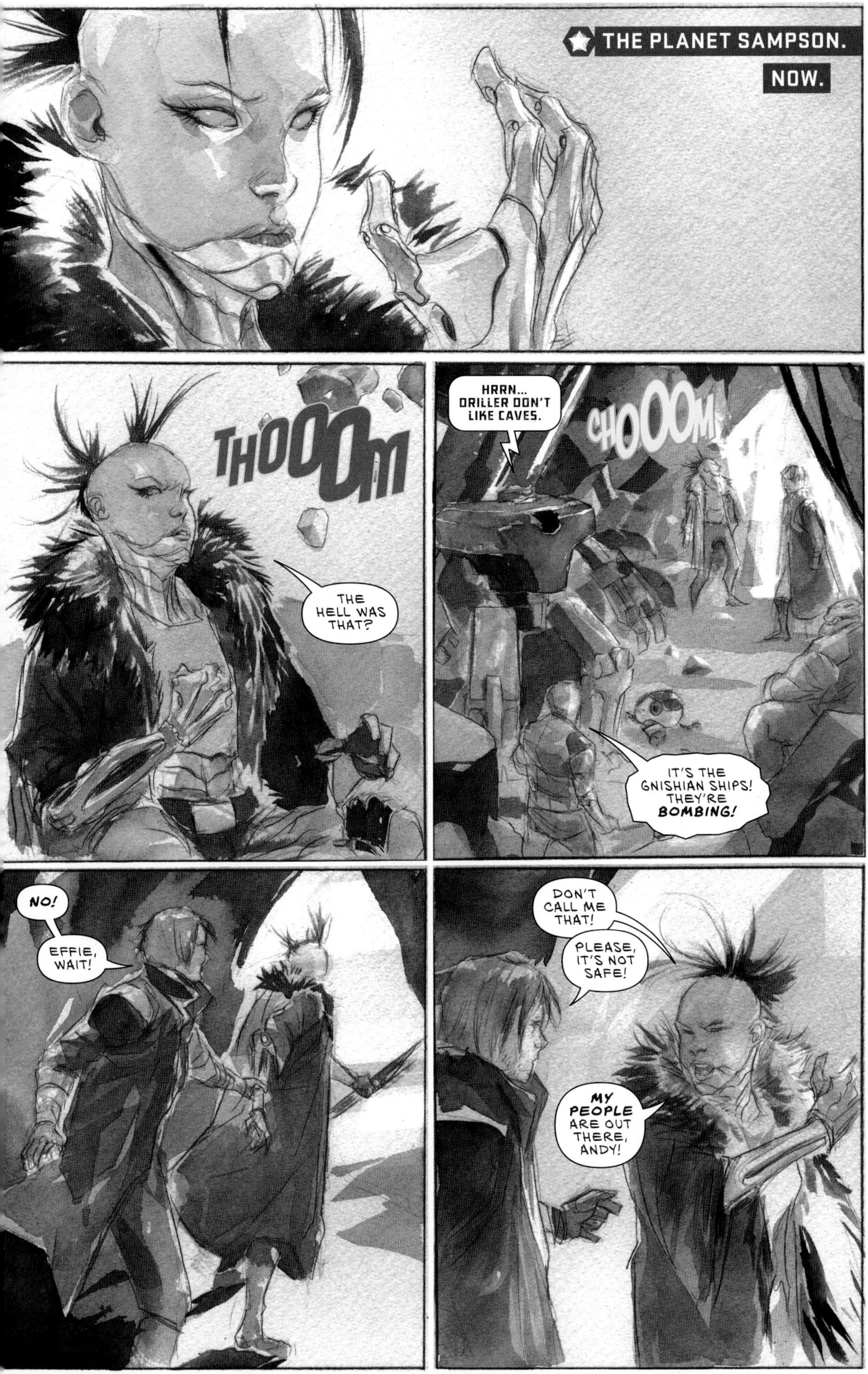
THE PLANET SAMPSON.
NOW.
THOOOM
THE HELL WAS THAT?
HRRN... DRILLER DON'T LIKE CAVES.
CHOOOM
IT'S THE GNISHIAN SHIPS! THEY'RE BOMBING!
NO!
EFFIE, WAIT!
DON'T CALL ME THAT!
PLEASE, IT'S NOT SAFE!
MY PEOPLE ARE OUT THERE, ANDY!

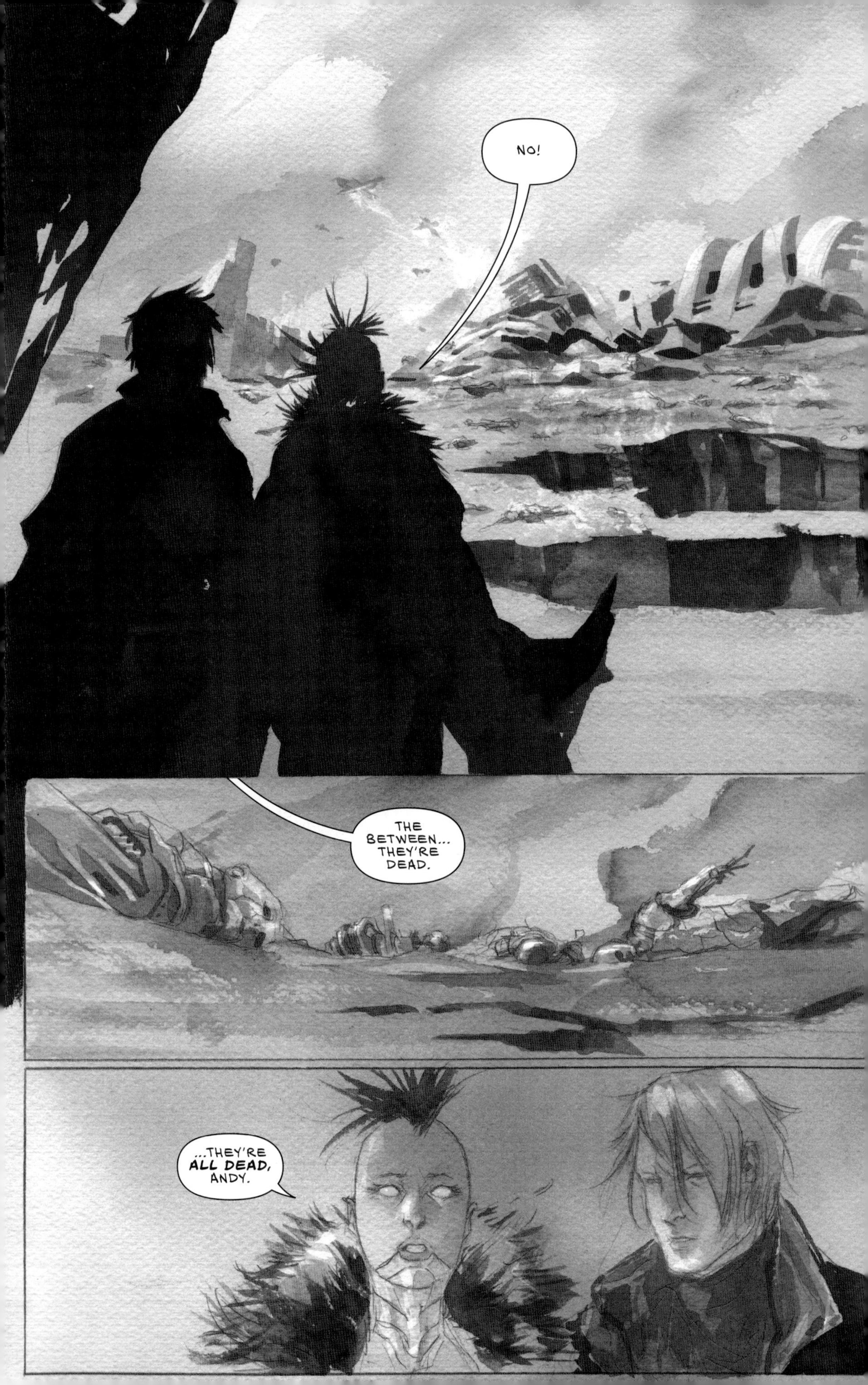
NO!
THE BETWEEN... THEY'RE DEAD.
...THEY'RE **ALL DEAD,** ANDY.

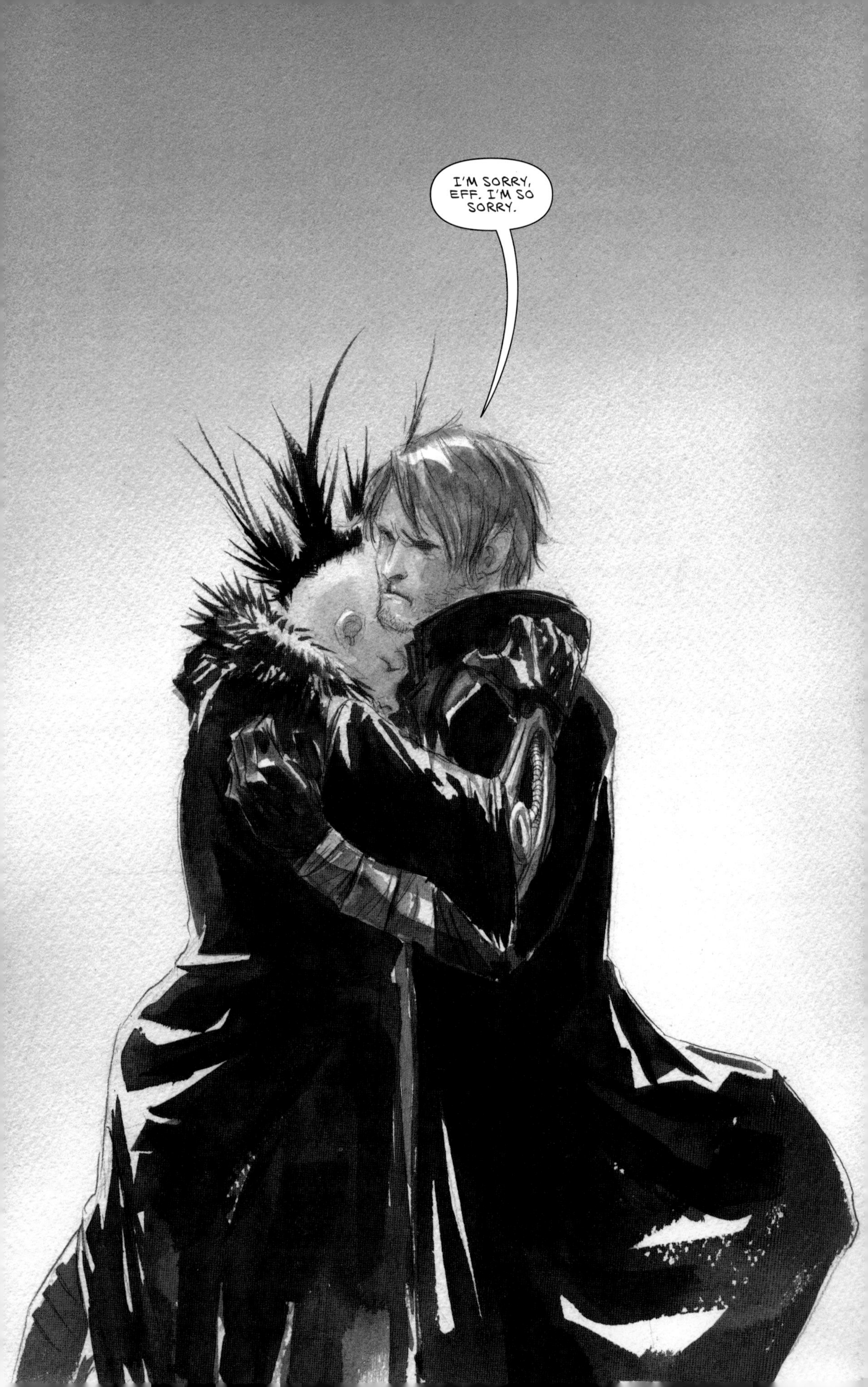
I'M SORRY, EFF. I'M SO SORRY.

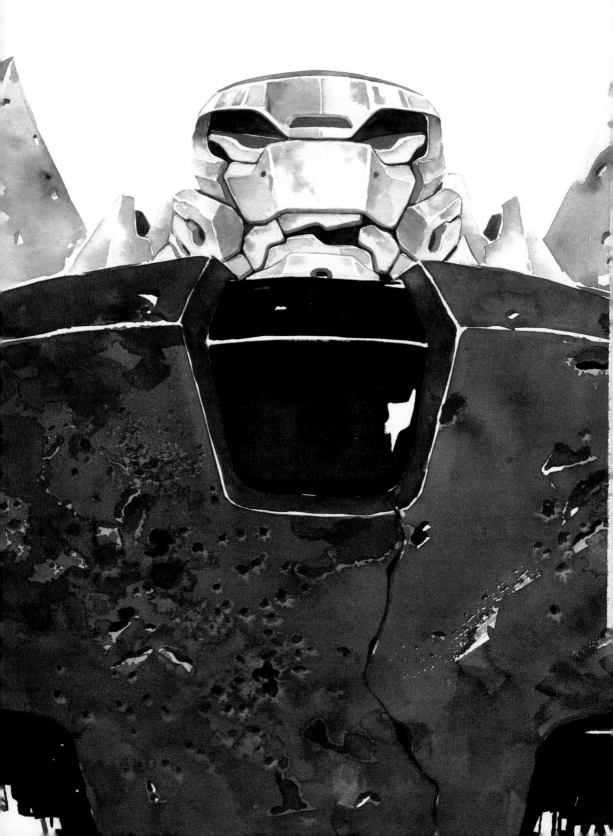

CHAPTER FIVE

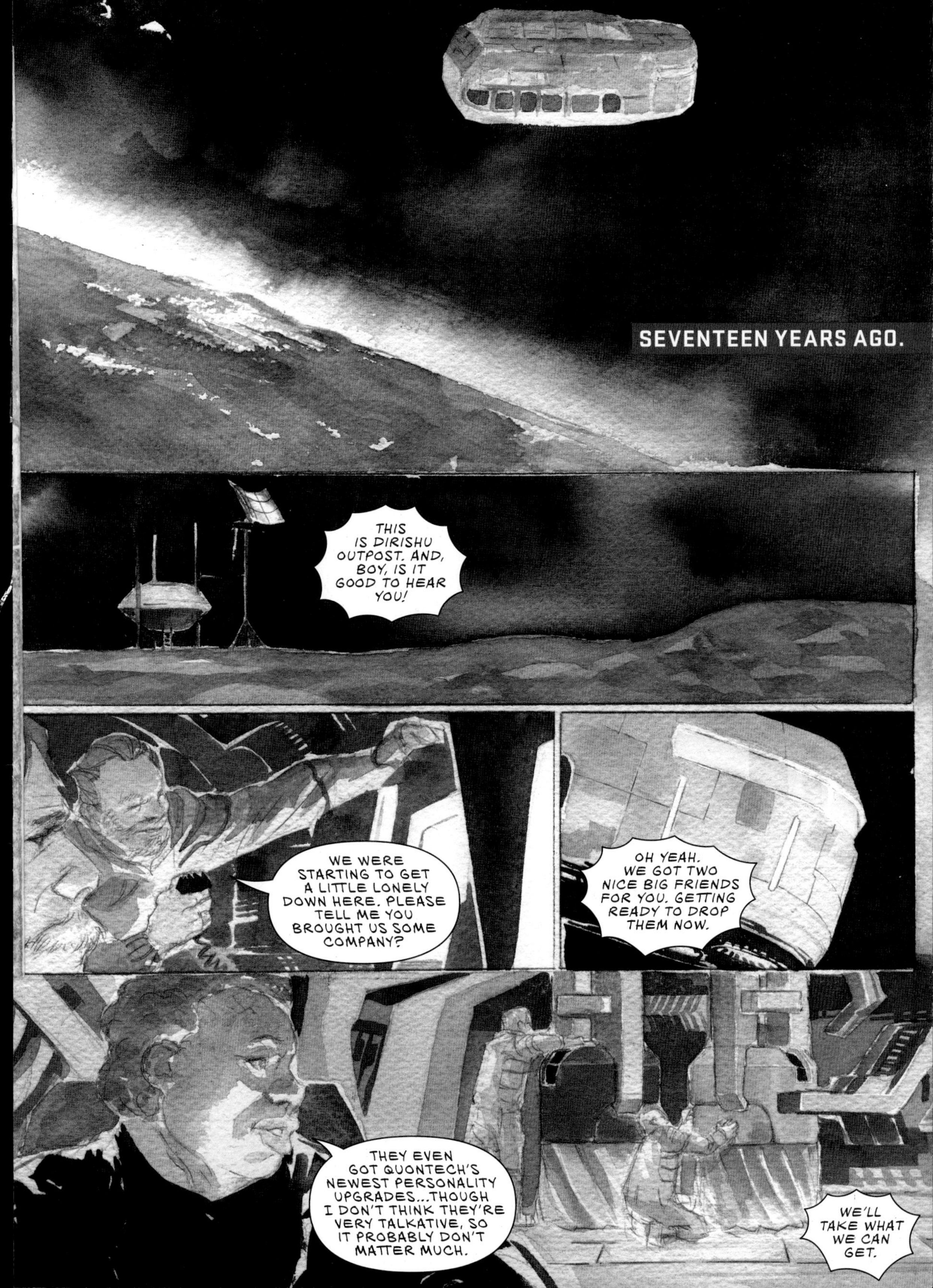
SEVENTEEN YEARS AGO.
THIS IS DIRISHU OUTPOST. AND, BOY, IS IT GOOD TO HEAR YOU!
WE WERE STARTING TO GET A LITTLE LONELY DOWN HERE. PLEASE TELL ME YOU BROUGHT US SOME COMPANY?
OH YEAH. WE GOT TWO NICE BIG FRIENDS FOR YOU. GETTING READY TO DROP THEM NOW.
THEY EVEN GOT QUONTECH'S NEWEST PERSONALITY UPGRADES...THOUGH I DON'T THINK THEY'RE VERY TALKATIVE, SO IT PROBABLY DON'T MATTER MUCH.
WE'LL TAKE WHAT WE CAN GET.

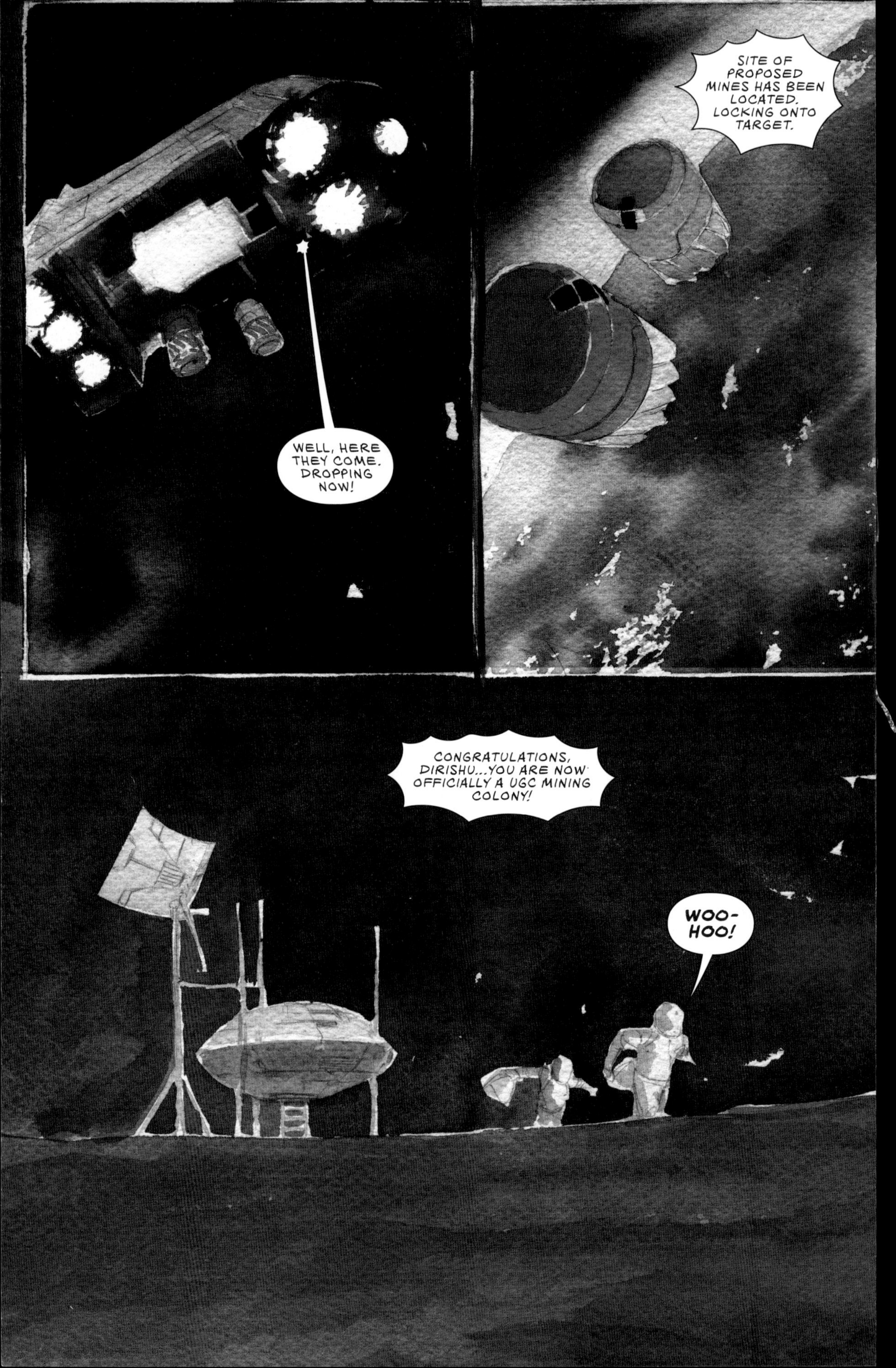
WELL, HERE THEY COME. DROPPING NOW!
SITE OF PROPOSED MINES HAS BEEN LOCATED. LOCKING ONTO TARGET.
CONGRATULATIONS, DIRISHU...YOU ARE NOW OFFICIALLY A UGC MINING COLONY!
WOO-HOO!

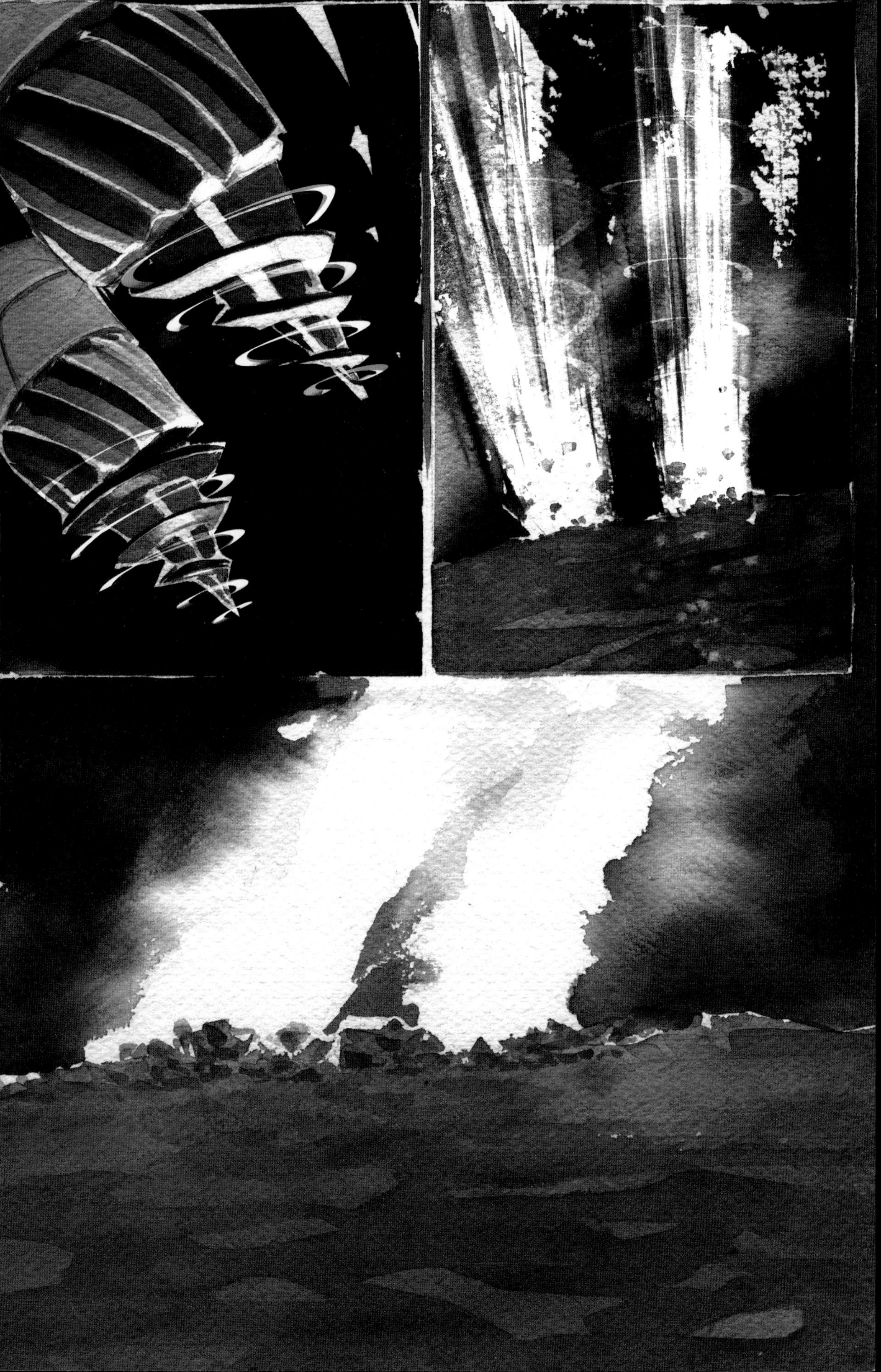

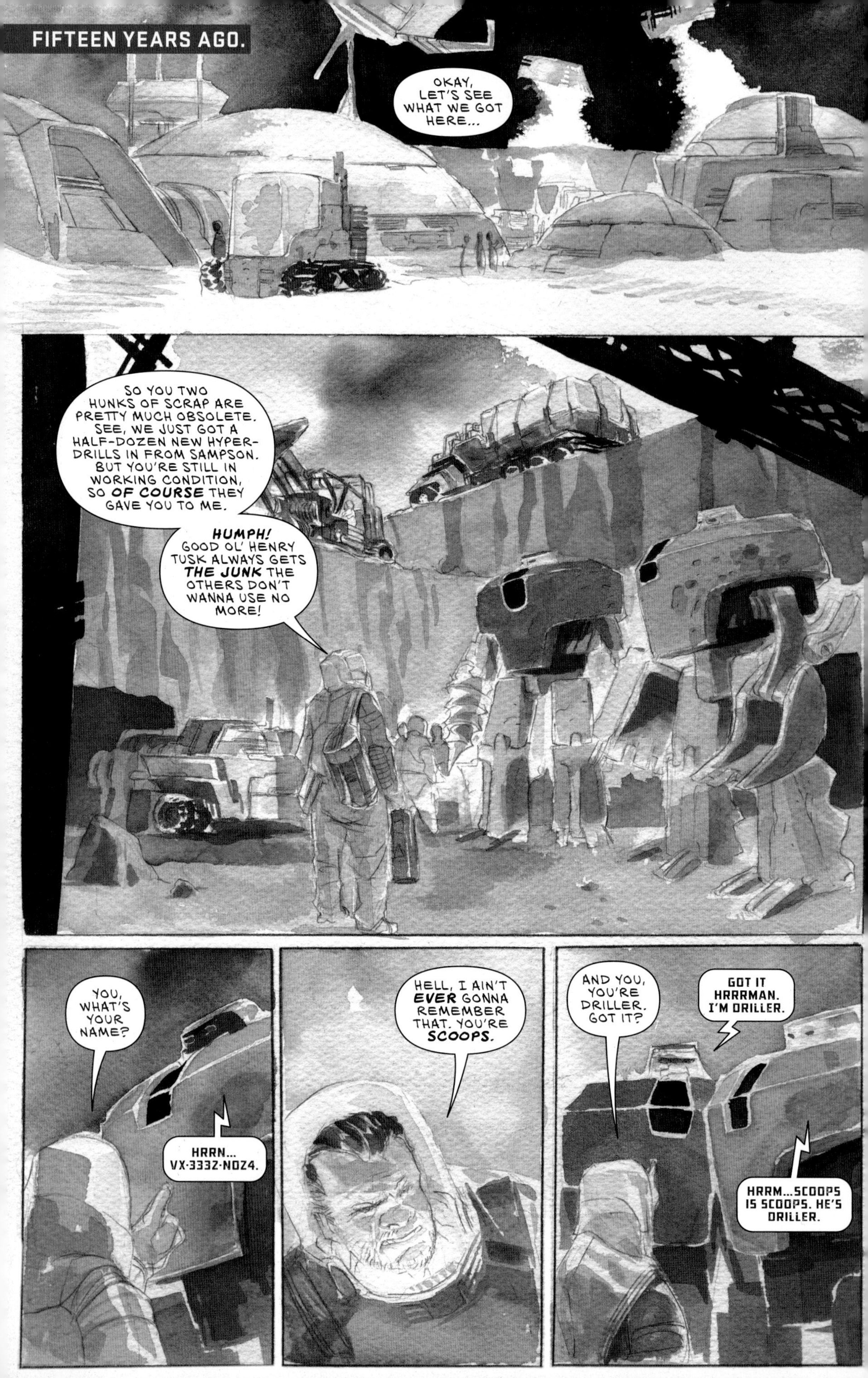
FIFTEEN YEARS AGO.
OKAY, LET'S SEE WHAT WE GOT HERE...
SO YOU TWO HUNKS OF SCRAP ARE PRETTY MUCH OBSOLETE. SEE, WE JUST GOT A HALF-DOZEN NEW HYPER-DRILLS IN FROM SAMPSON. BUT YOU'RE STILL IN WORKING CONDITION, SO **OF COURSE** THEY GAVE YOU TO ME.
HUMPH! GOOD OL' HENRY TUSK ALWAYS GETS ***THE JUNK*** THE OTHERS DON'T WANNA USE NO MORE!
YOU, WHAT'S YOUR NAME?
HRRN... VX-3332-N0Z4.
HELL, I AIN'T **EVER** GONNA REMEMBER THAT. YOU'RE **SCOOPS.**
AND YOU, YOU'RE DRILLER. GOT IT?
GOT IT HRRRMAN. I'M DRILLER.
HRRM...SCOOPS IS SCOOPS. HE'S DRILLER.

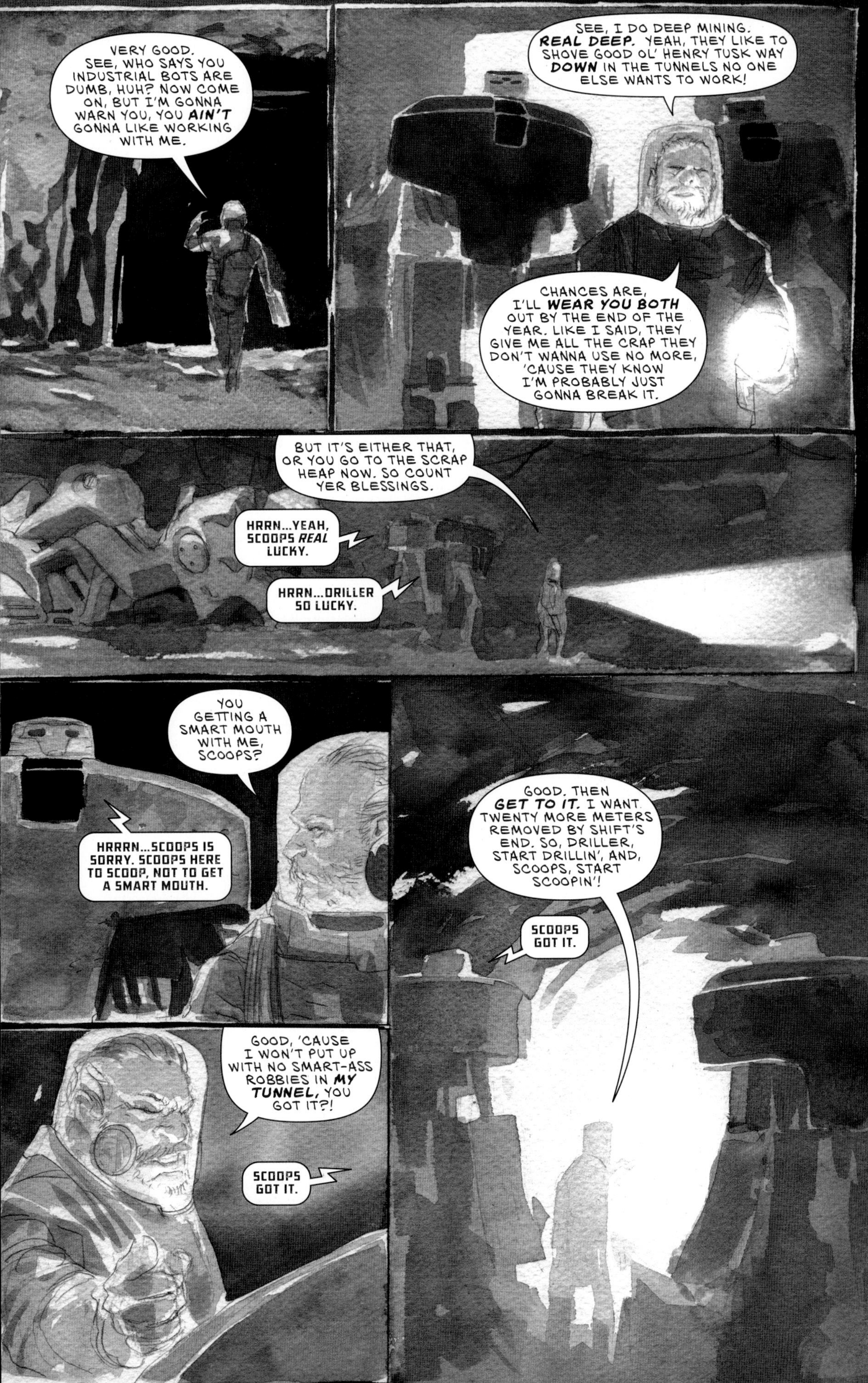
VERY GOOD. SEE, WHO SAYS YOU INDUSTRIAL BOTS ARE DUMB, HUH? NOW COME ON, BUT I'M GONNA WARN YOU, YOU **AIN'T** GONNA LIKE WORKING WITH ME.
SEE, I DO DEEP MINING. **REAL DEEP.** YEAH, THEY LIKE TO SHOVE GOOD OL' HENRY TUSK WAY **DOWN** IN THE TUNNELS NO ONE ELSE WANTS TO WORK!
CHANCES ARE, I'LL **WEAR YOU BOTH** OUT BY THE END OF THE YEAR. LIKE I SAID, THEY GIVE ME ALL THE CRAP THEY DON'T WANNA USE NO MORE, 'CAUSE THEY KNOW I'M PROBABLY JUST GONNA BREAK IT.
BUT IT'S EITHER THAT, OR YOU GO TO THE SCRAP HEAP NOW. SO COUNT YER BLESSINGS.
HRRN...YEAH, SCOOPS *REAL* LUCKY.
HRRN...DRILLER SO LUCKY.
YOU GETTING A SMART MOUTH WITH ME, SCOOPS?
HRRRN...SCOOPS IS SORRY. SCOOPS HERE TO SCOOP, NOT TO GET A SMART MOUTH.
GOOD, 'CAUSE I WON'T PUT UP WITH NO SMART-ASS ROBBIES IN **MY TUNNEL,** YOU GOT IT?!
SCOOPS GOT IT.
GOOD. THEN **GET TO IT.** I WANT TWENTY MORE METERS REMOVED BY SHIFT'S END. SO, DRILLER, START DRILLIN', AND, SCOOPS, START SCOOPIN'!
SCOOPS GOT IT.

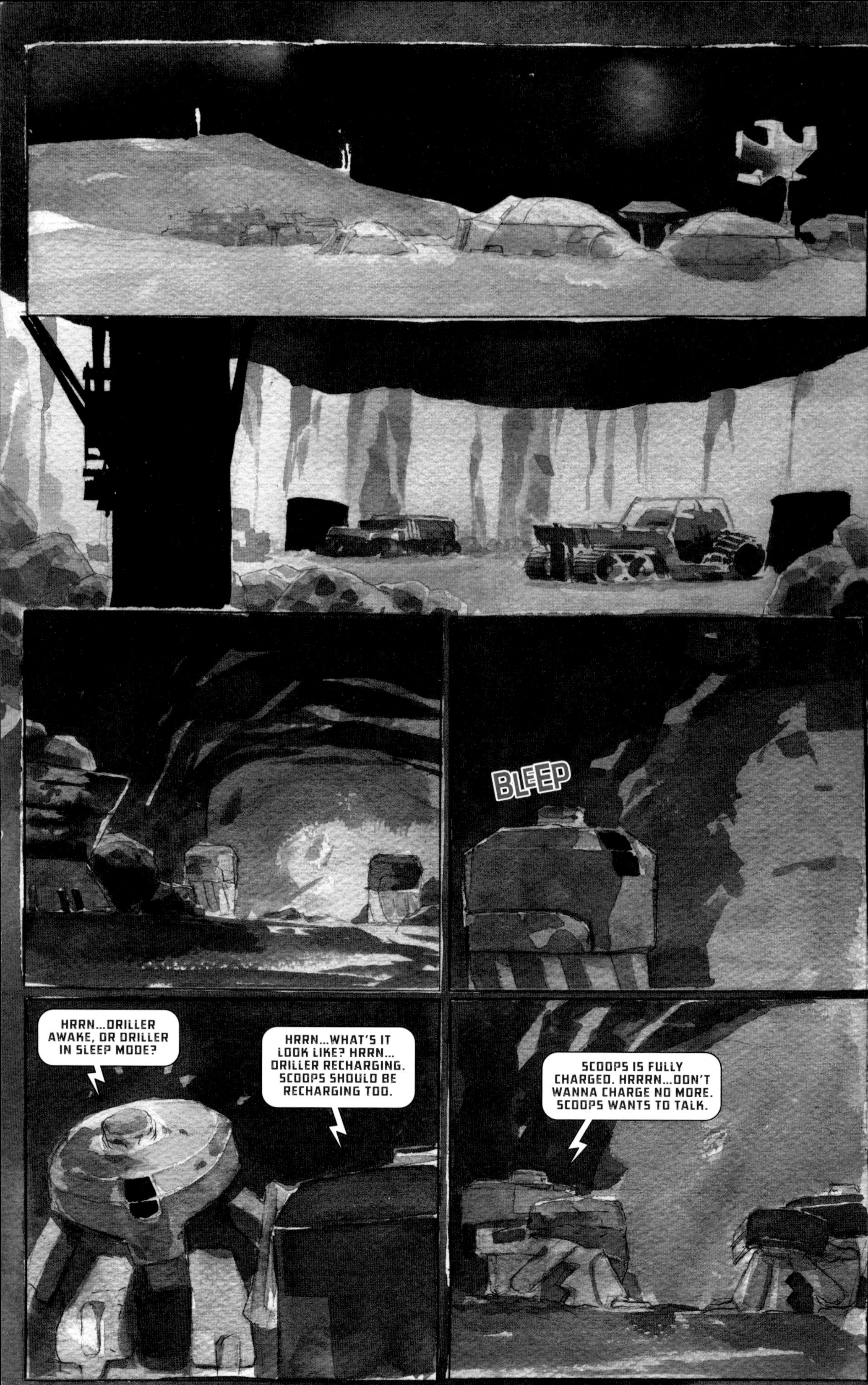
BLEEP
HRRN...DRILLER AWAKE, OR DRILLER IN SLEEP MODE?
HRRN...WHAT'S IT LOOK LIKE? HRRN... DRILLER RECHARGING. SCOOPS SHOULD BE RECHARGING TOO.
SCOOPS IS FULLY CHARGED. HRRRN...DON'T WANNA CHARGE NO MORE. SCOOPS WANTS TO TALK.

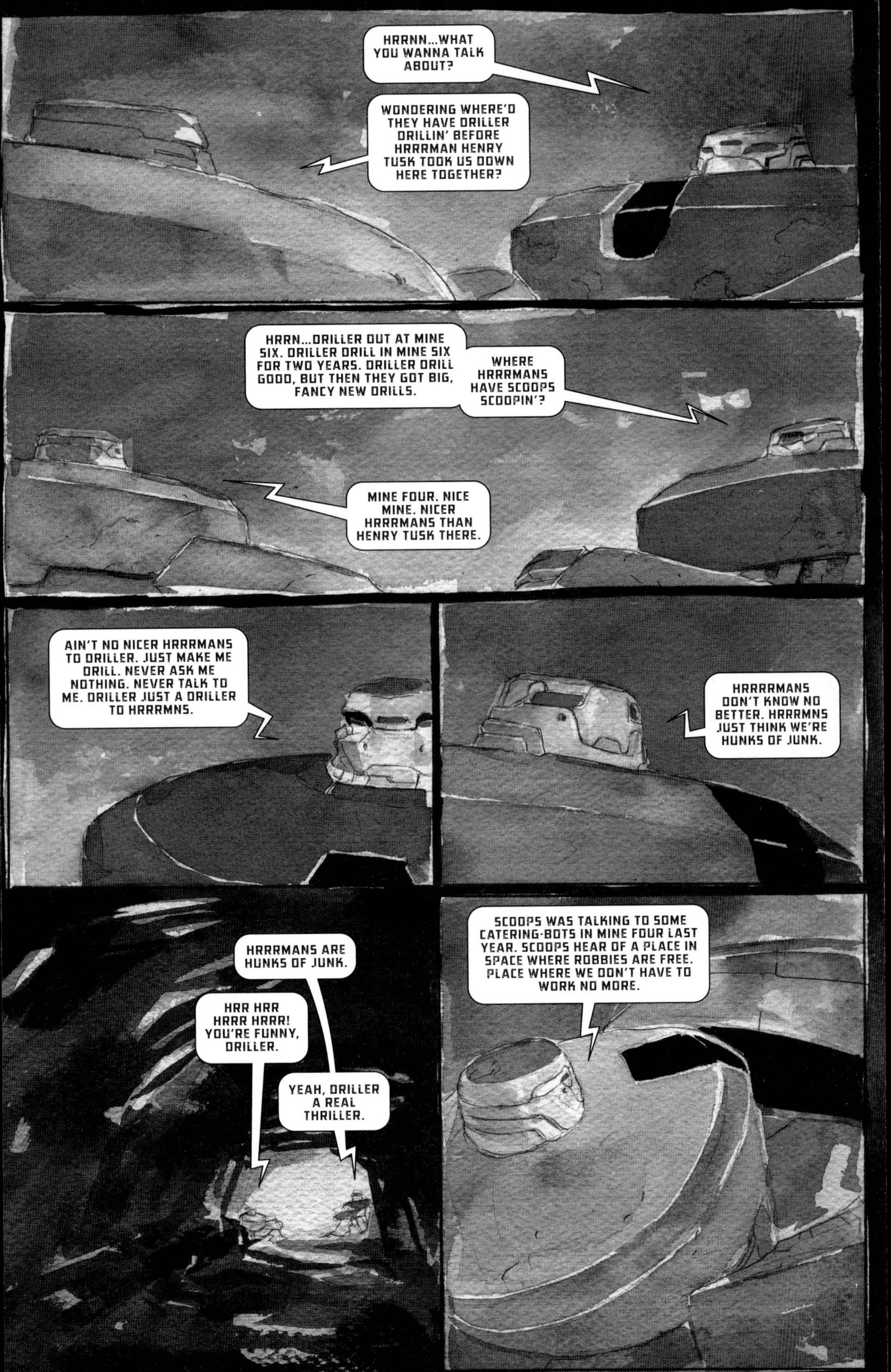
HRRNN...WHAT YOU WANNA TALK ABOUT?
WONDERING WHERE'D THEY HAVE DRILLER DRILLIN' BEFORE HRRRMAN HENRY TUSK TOOK US DOWN HERE TOGETHER?
HRRN...DRILLER OUT AT MINE SIX. DRILLER DRILL IN MINE SIX FOR TWO YEARS. DRILLER DRILL GOOD, BUT THEN THEY GOT BIG, FANCY NEW DRILLS.
WHERE HRRRMANS HAVE SCOOPS SCOOPIN'?
MINE FOUR. NICE MINE. NICER HRRRMANS THAN HENRY TUSK THERE.
AIN'T NO NICER HRRRMANS TO DRILLER. JUST MAKE ME DRILL. NEVER ASK ME NOTHING. NEVER TALK TO ME. DRILLER JUST A DRILLER TO HRRRMNS.
HRRRMANS DON'T KNOW NO BETTER. HRRRMNS JUST THINK WE'RE HUNKS OF JUNK.
HRRRMANS ARE HUNKS OF JUNK.
HRR HRR HRRR HRRR! YOU'RE FUNNY, DRILLER.
YEAH, DRILLER A REAL THRILLER.
SCOOPS WAS TALKING TO SOME CATERING-BOTS IN MINE FOUR LAST YEAR. SCOOPS HEAR OF A PLACE IN SPACE WHERE ROBBIES ARE FREE. PLACE WHERE WE DON'T HAVE TO WORK NO MORE.

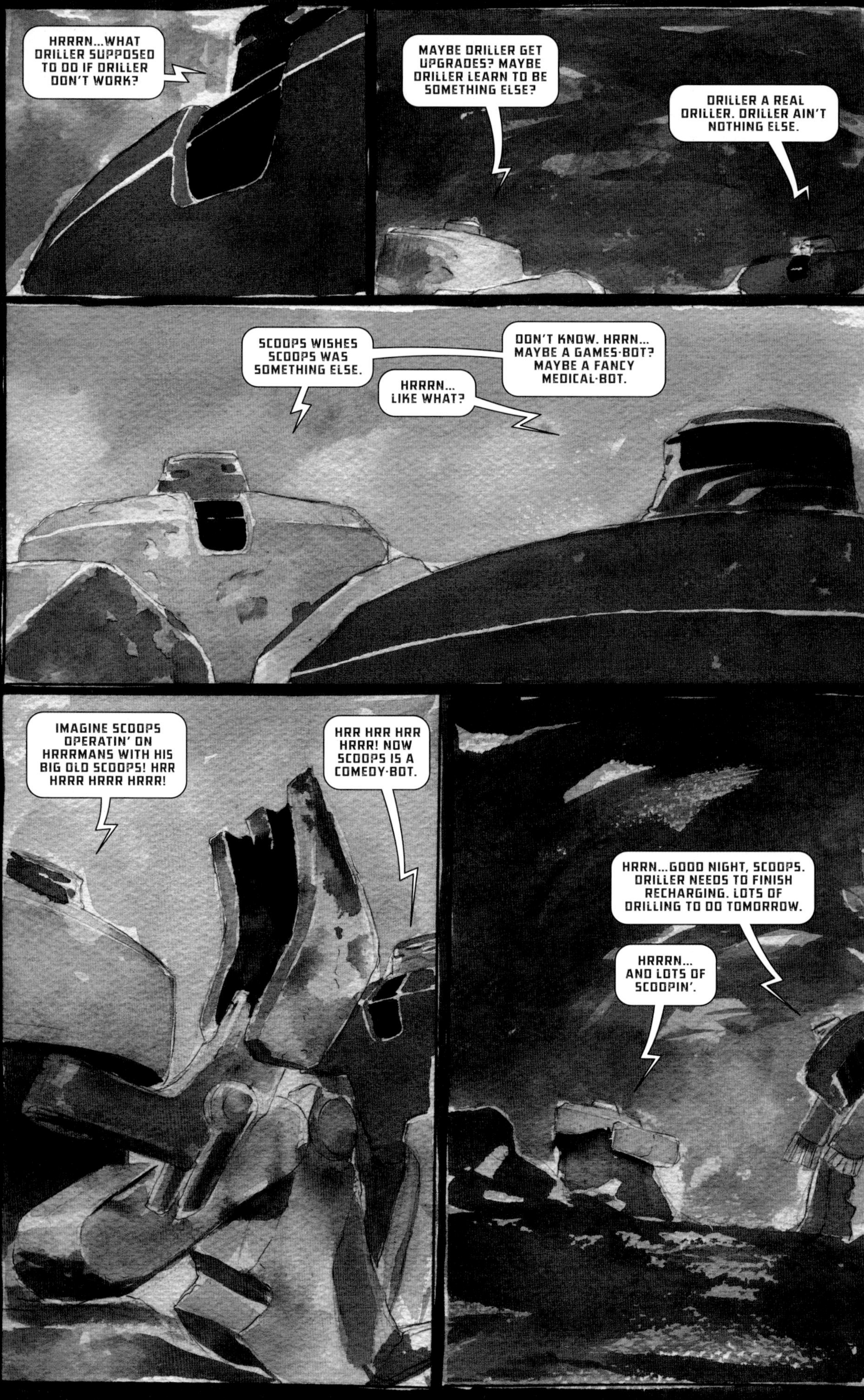
HRRRN...WHAT DRILLER SUPPOSED TO DO IF DRILLER DON'T WORK?
MAYBE DRILLER GET UPGRADES? MAYBE DRILLER LEARN TO BE SOMETHING ELSE?
DRILLER A REAL DRILLER. DRILLER AIN'T NOTHING ELSE.
SCOOPS WISHES SCOOPS WAS SOMETHING ELSE.
HRRRN... LIKE WHAT?
DON'T KNOW. HRRN... MAYBE A GAMES-BOT? MAYBE A FANCY MEDICAL-BOT.
IMAGINE SCOOPS OPERATIN' ON HRRRMANS WITH HIS BIG OLD SCOOPS! HRR HRRR HRRR HRRR!
HRR HRR HRR HRRR! NOW SCOOPS IS A COMEDY-BOT.
HRRN...GOOD NIGHT, SCOOPS. DRILLER NEEDS TO FINISH RECHARGING. LOTS OF DRILLING TO DO TOMORROW.
HRRRN... AND LOTS OF SCOOPIN'.

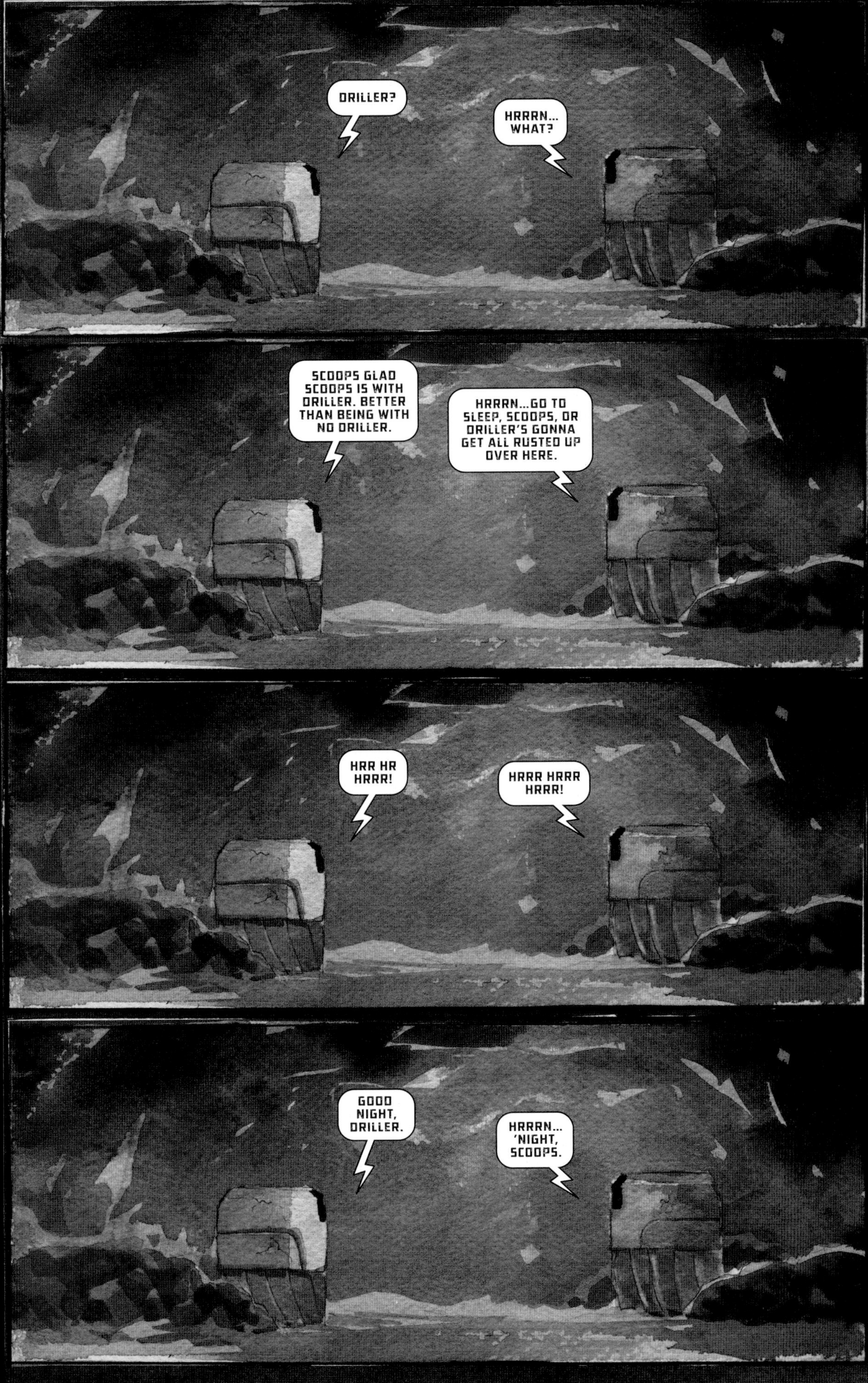
DRILLER?
HRRRN... WHAT?
SCOOPS GLAD SCOOPS IS WITH DRILLER. BETTER THAN BEING WITH NO DRILLER.
HRRRN...GO TO SLEEP, SCOOPS, OR DRILLER'S GONNA GET ALL RUSTED UP OVER HERE.
HRR HR HRRR!
HRRR HRRR HRRR!
GOOD NIGHT, DRILLER.
HRRRN... 'NIGHT, SCOOPS.

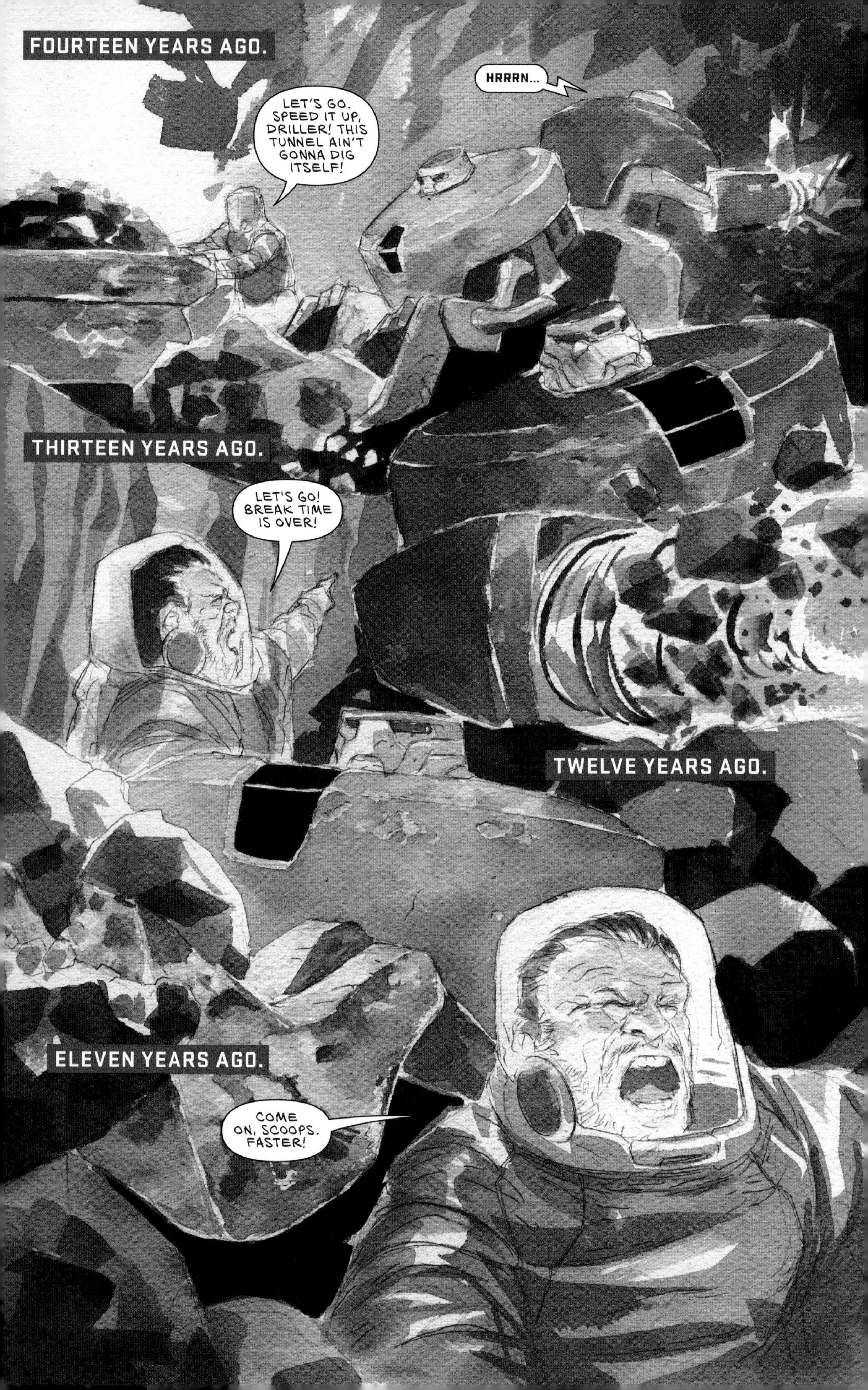
FOURTEEN YEARS AGO.
HRRRN...
LET'S GO. SPEED IT UP, DRILLER! THIS TUNNEL AIN'T GONNA DIG ITSELF!
THIRTEEN YEARS AGO.
LET'S GO! BREAK TIME IS OVER!
TWELVE YEARS AGO.
ELEVEN YEARS AGO.
COME ON, SCOOPS. FASTER!

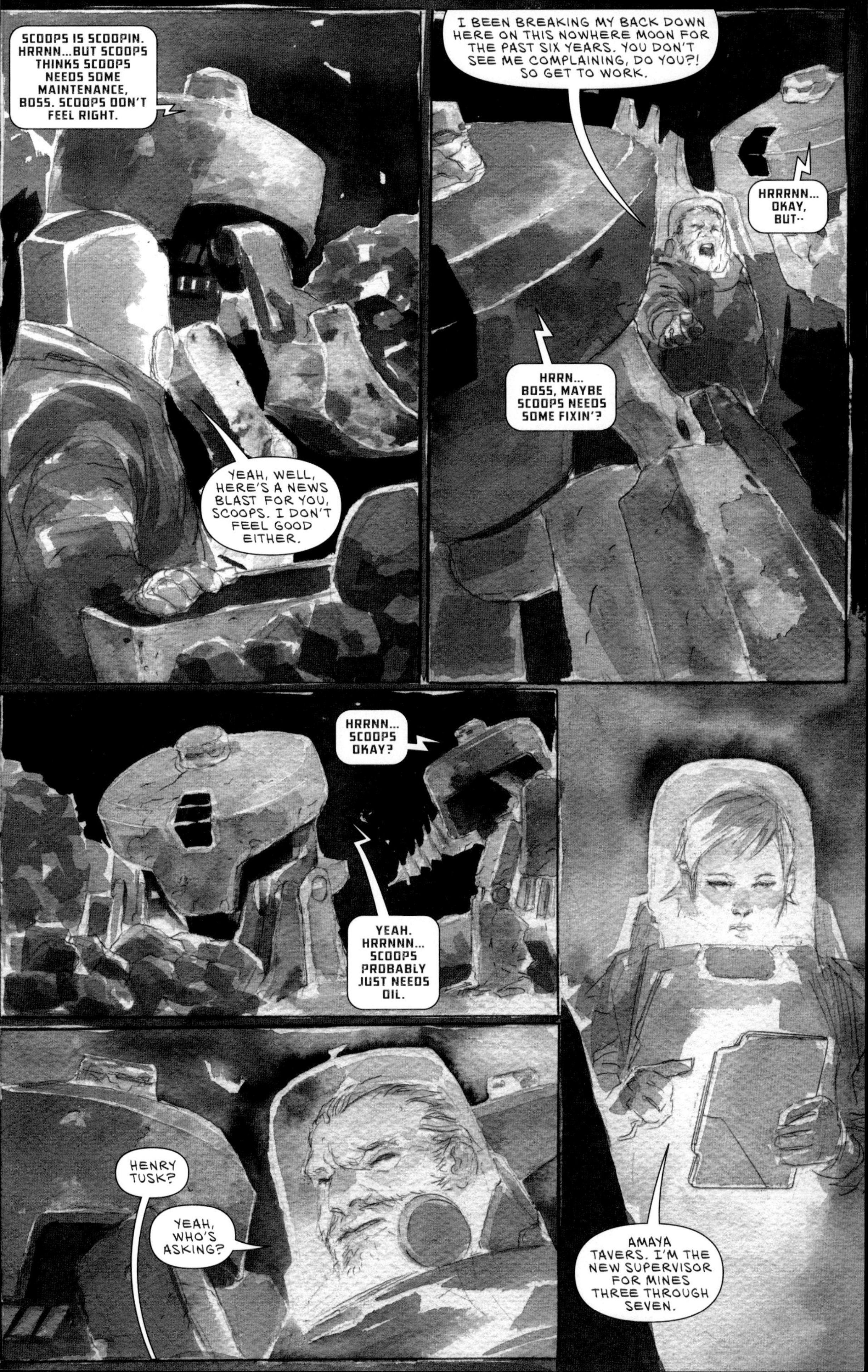
SCOOPS IS SCOOPIN. HRRNN...BUT SCOOPS THINKS SCOOPS NEEDS SOME MAINTENANCE, BOSS. SCOOPS DON'T FEEL RIGHT.
YEAH, WELL, HERE'S A NEWS BLAST FOR YOU, SCOOPS. I DON'T FEEL GOOD EITHER.
HRRN... BOSS, MAYBE SCOOPS NEEDS SOME FIXIN'?
I BEEN BREAKING MY BACK DOWN HERE ON THIS NOWHERE MOON FOR THE PAST SIX YEARS. YOU DON'T SEE ME COMPLAINING, DO YOU?! SO GET TO WORK.
HRRRNN... OKAY, BUT··
HRRNN... SCOOPS OKAY?
YEAH. HRRNNN... SCOOPS PROBABLY JUST NEEDS OIL.
HENRY TUSK?
YEAH, WHO'S ASKING?
AMAYA TAVERS. I'M THE NEW SUPERVISOR FOR MINES THREE THROUGH SEVEN.

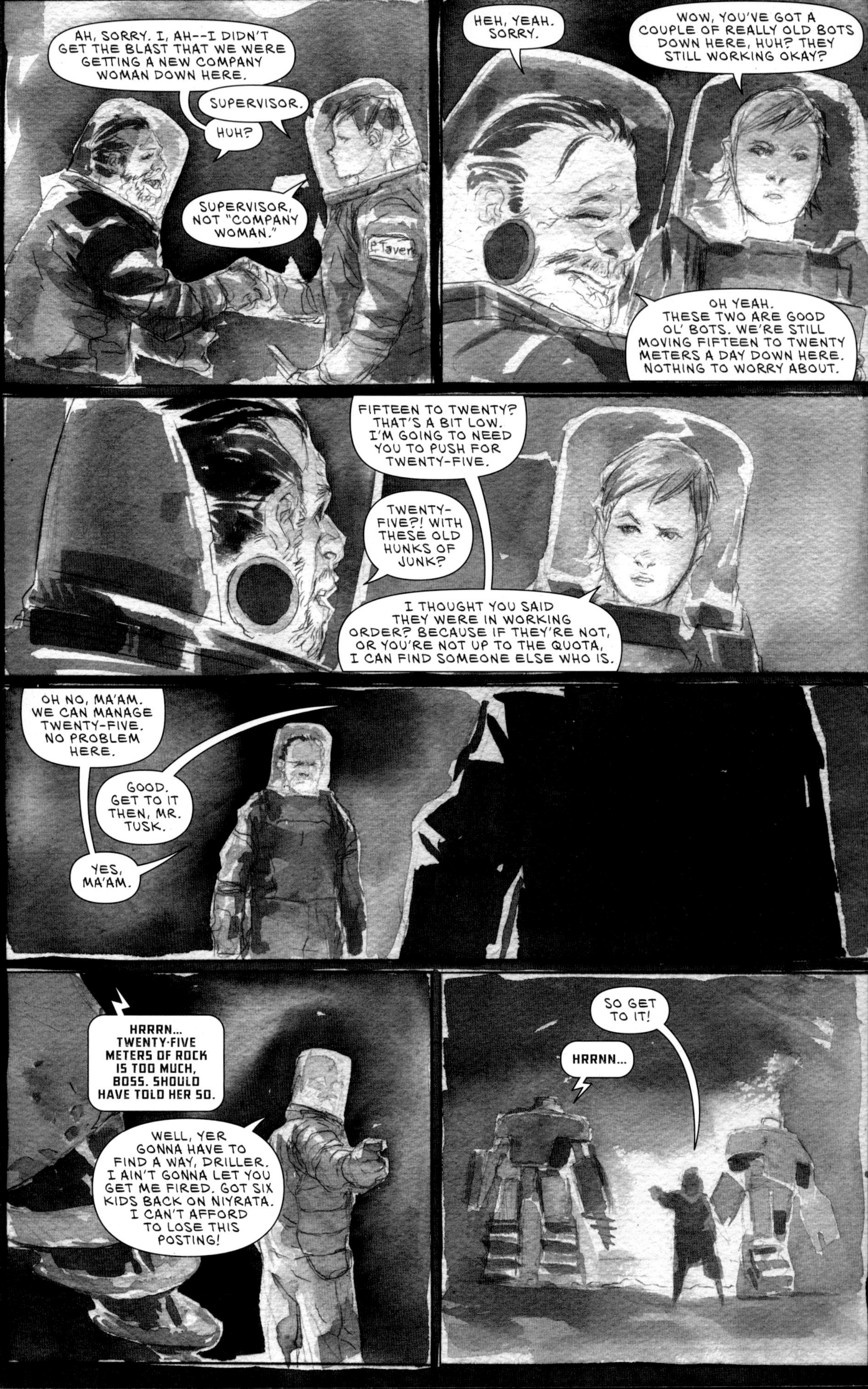
AH, SORRY. I, AH--I DIDN'T GET THE BLAST THAT WE WERE GETTING A NEW COMPANY WOMAN DOWN HERE.
SUPERVISOR.
HUH?
SUPERVISOR, NOT "COMPANY WOMAN."
HEH, YEAH. SORRY.
WOW, YOU'VE GOT A COUPLE OF REALLY OLD BOTS DOWN HERE, HUH? THEY STILL WORKING OKAY?
OH YEAH. THESE TWO ARE GOOD OL' BOTS. WE'RE STILL MOVING FIFTEEN TO TWENTY METERS A DAY DOWN HERE. NOTHING TO WORRY ABOUT.
FIFTEEN TO TWENTY? THAT'S A BIT LOW. I'M GOING TO NEED YOU TO PUSH FOR TWENTY-FIVE.
TWENTY-FIVE?! WITH THESE OLD HUNKS OF JUNK?
I THOUGHT YOU SAID THEY WERE IN WORKING ORDER? BECAUSE IF THEY'RE NOT, OR YOU'RE NOT UP TO THE QUOTA, I CAN FIND SOMEONE ELSE WHO IS.
OH NO, MA'AM. WE CAN MANAGE TWENTY-FIVE. NO PROBLEM HERE.
GOOD. GET TO IT THEN, MR. TUSK.
YES, MA'AM.
HRRRN... TWENTY-FIVE METERS OF ROCK IS TOO MUCH, BOSS. SHOULD HAVE TOLD HER SO.
WELL, YER GONNA HAVE TO FIND A WAY, DRILLER. I AIN'T GONNA LET YOU GET ME FIRED. GOT SIX KIDS BACK ON NIYRATA. I CAN'T AFFORD TO LOSE THIS POSTING!
SO GET TO IT!
HRRNN...

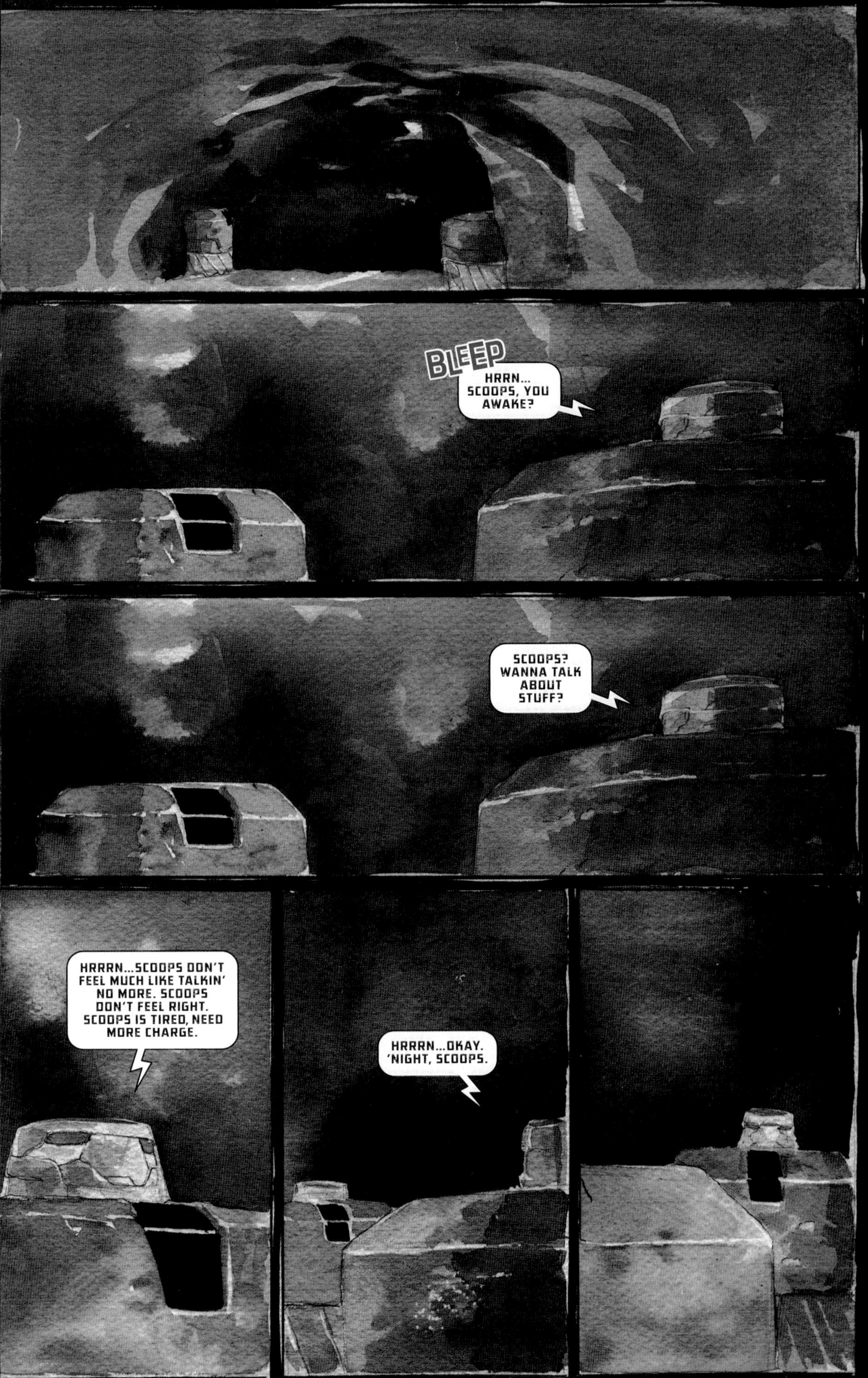
BLEEP
HRRN... SCOOPS, YOU AWAKE?
SCOOPS? WANNA TALK ABOUT STUFF?
HRRRN...SCOOPS DON'T FEEL MUCH LIKE TALKIN' NO MORE. SCOOPS DON'T FEEL RIGHT. SCOOPS IS TIRED, NEED MORE CHARGE.
HRRRN...OKAY. 'NIGHT, SCOOPS.

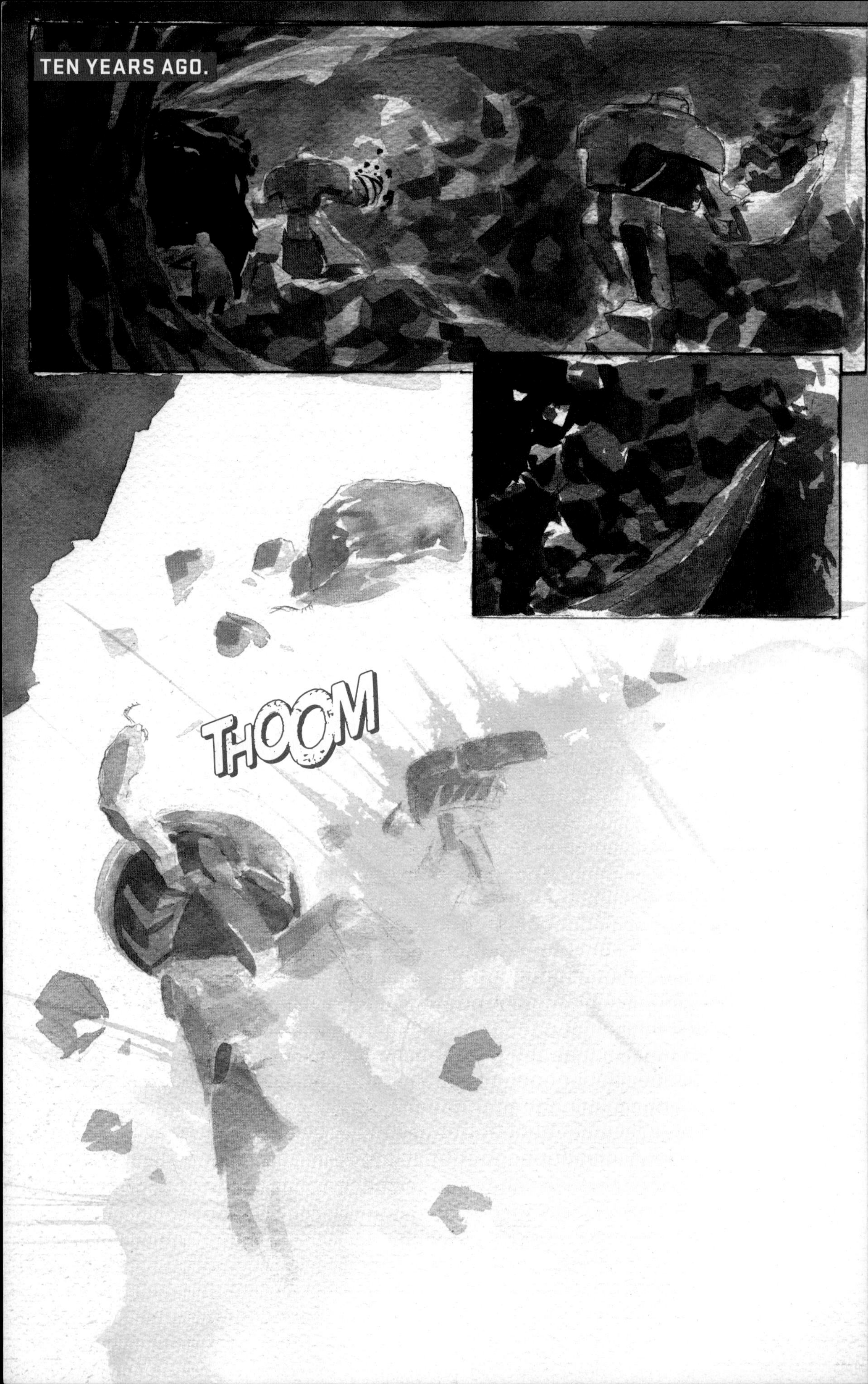
TEN YEARS AGO.
THOOM

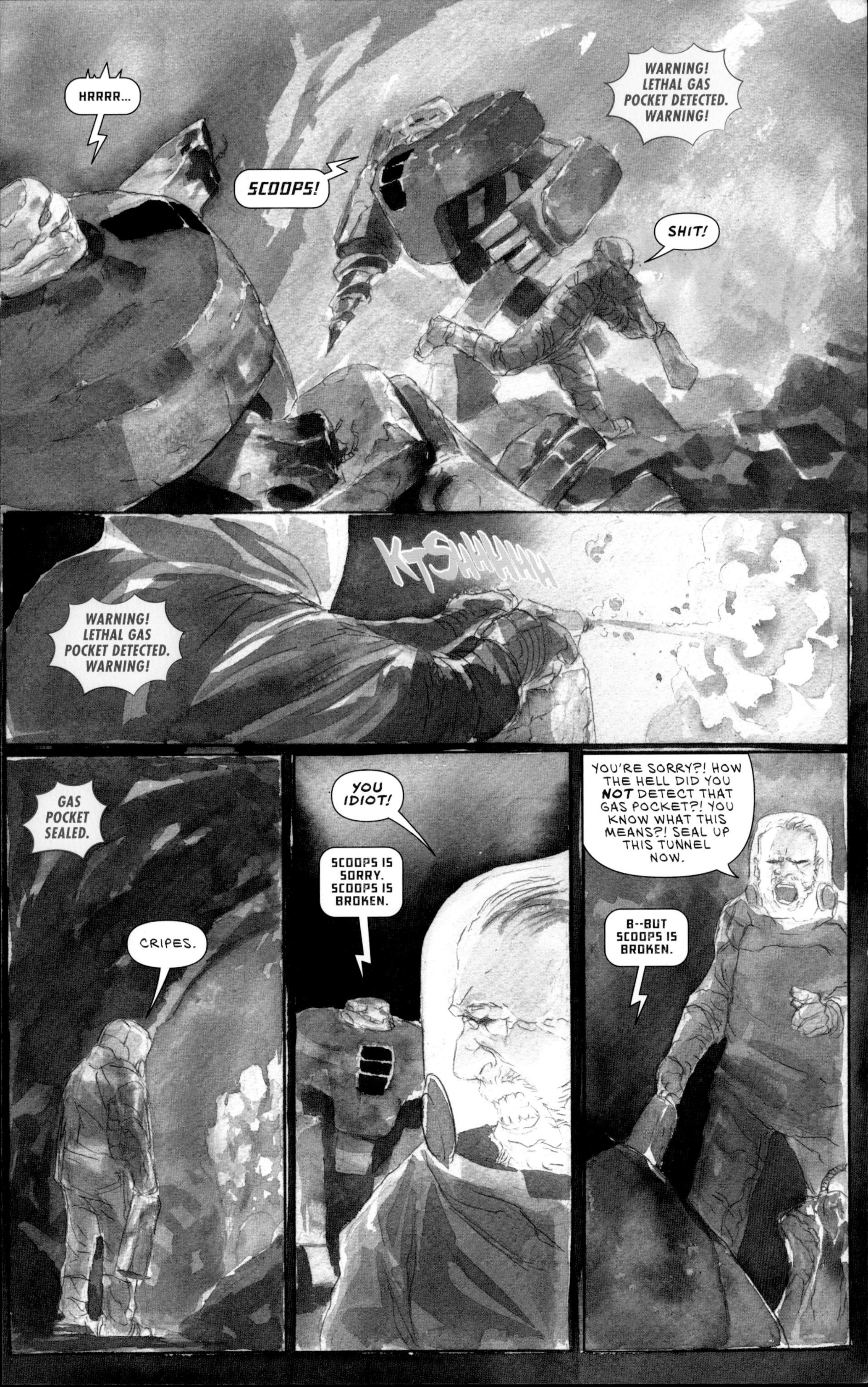
HRRRR...
WARNING! LETHAL GAS POCKET DETECTED. WARNING!
SCOOPS!
SHIT!
KTSHHHHHH
WARNING! LETHAL GAS POCKET DETECTED. WARNING!
GAS POCKET SEALED.
CRIPES.
YOU IDIOT!
SCOOPS IS SORRY. SCOOPS IS BROKEN.
YOU'RE SORRY?! HOW THE HELL DID YOU NOT DETECT THAT GAS POCKET?! YOU KNOW WHAT THIS MEANS?! SEAL UP THIS TUNNEL NOW.
B--BUT SCOOPS IS BROKEN.

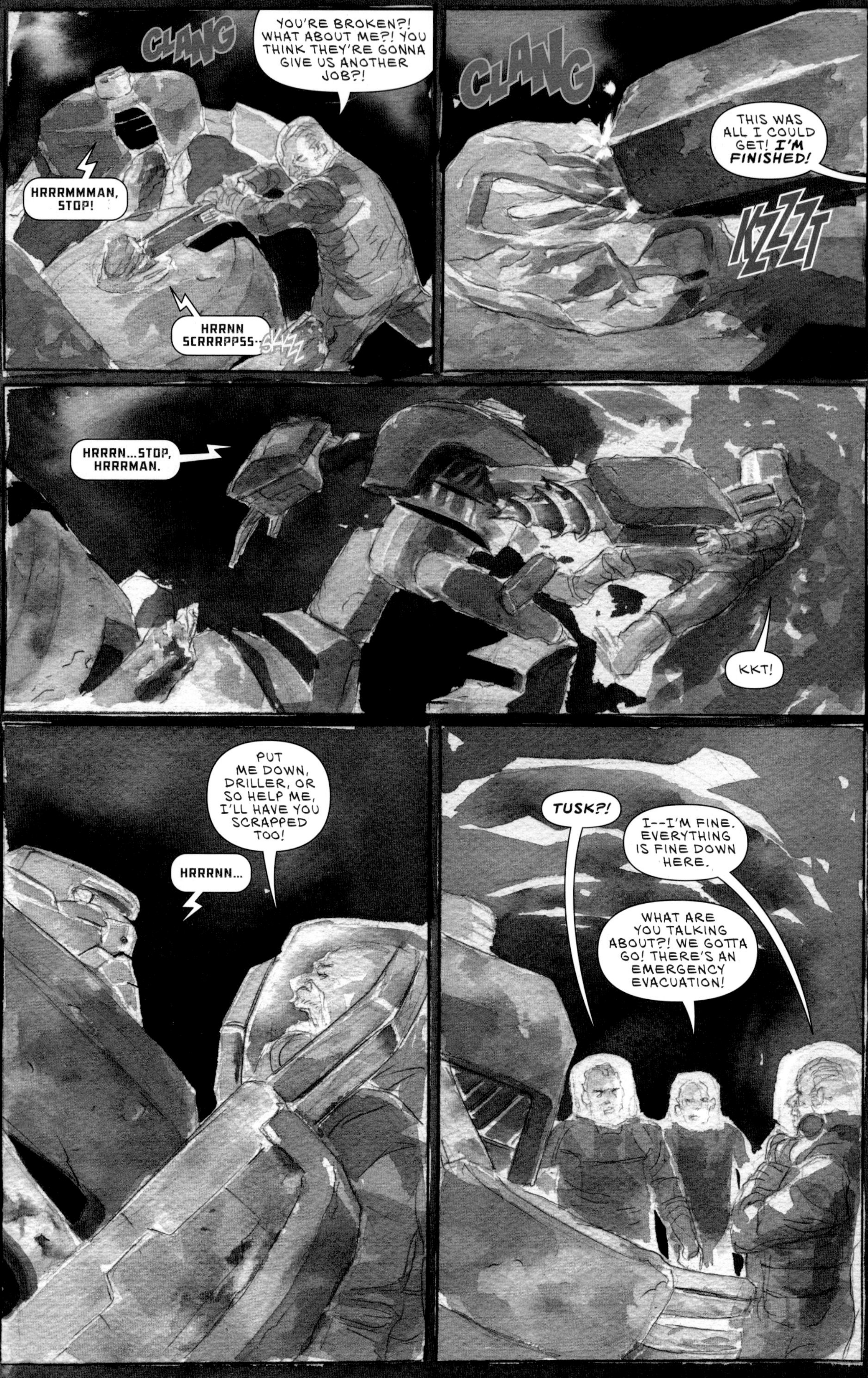
CLANG
YOU'RE BROKEN?! WHAT ABOUT ME?! YOU THINK THEY'RE GONNA GIVE US ANOTHER JOB?!
HRRRMMMAN, STOP!
HRRNN SCRRRPPSS--
CLANG
THIS WAS ALL I COULD GET! I'M FINISHED!
KZZZT
HRRRN...STOP, HRRRMAN.
KKT!
PUT ME DOWN, DRILLER, OR SO HELP ME, I'LL HAVE YOU SCRAPPED TOO!
HRRRNN...
TUSK?!
I--I'M FINE. EVERYTHING IS FINE DOWN HERE.
WHAT ARE YOU TALKING ABOUT?! WE GOTTA GO! THERE'S AN EMERGENCY EVACUATION!

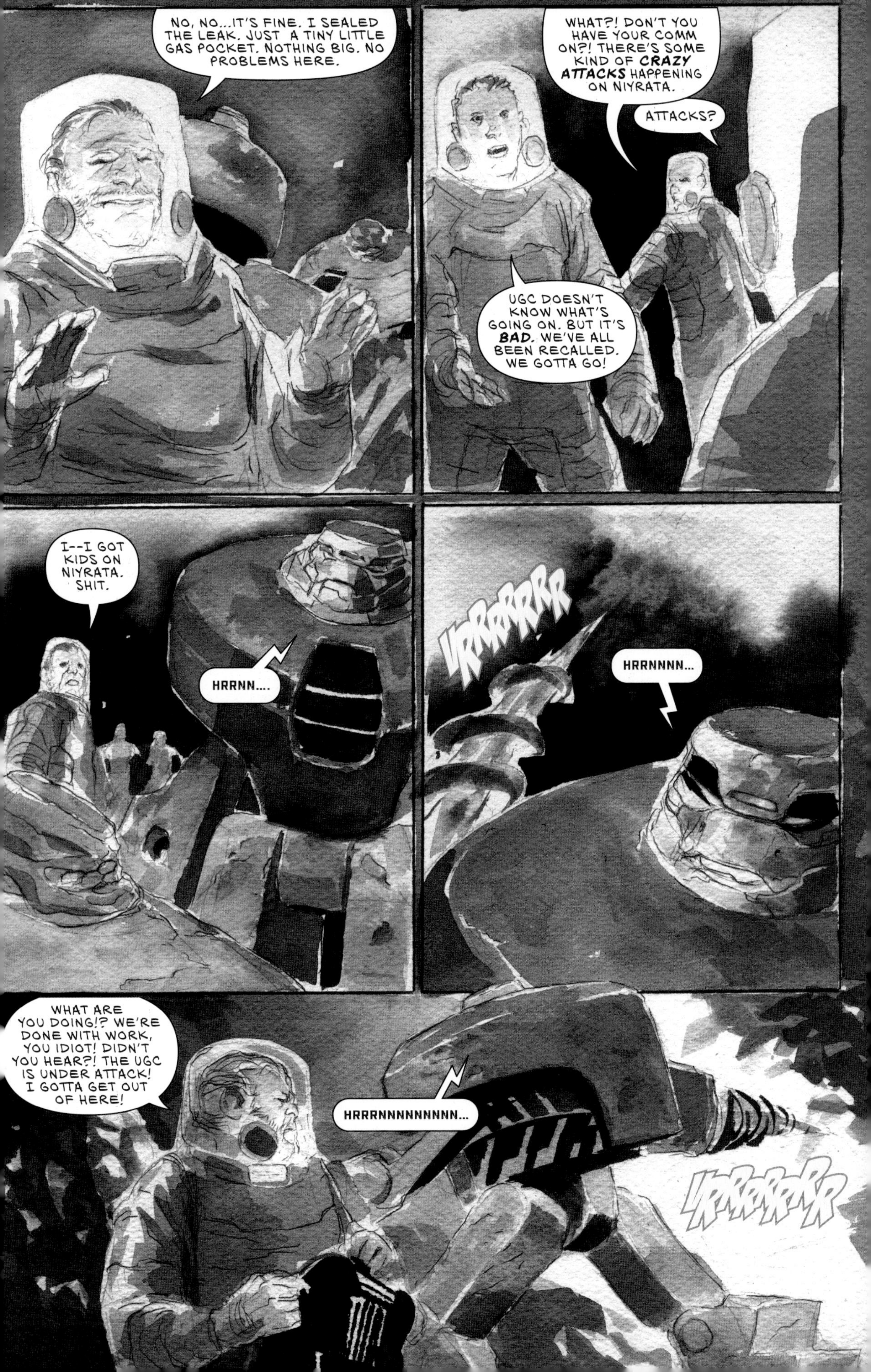
NO, NO...IT'S FINE. I SEALED THE LEAK. JUST A TINY LITTLE GAS POCKET. NOTHING BIG. NO PROBLEMS HERE.
WHAT?! DON'T YOU HAVE YOUR COMM ON?! THERE'S SOME KIND OF **CRAZY ATTACKS** HAPPENING ON NIYRATA.
ATTACKS?
UGC DOESN'T KNOW WHAT'S GOING ON. BUT IT'S **BAD.** WE'VE ALL BEEN RECALLED. WE GOTTA GO!
I--I GOT KIDS ON NIYRATA. SHIT.
HRRNN....
URRRRRRR
HRRNNNN...
WHAT ARE YOU DOING!? WE'RE DONE WITH WORK, YOU IDIOT! DIDN'T YOU HEAR?! THE UGC IS UNDER ATTACK! I GOTTA GET OUT OF HERE!
HRRRNNNNNNNNN...
URRRRRRR

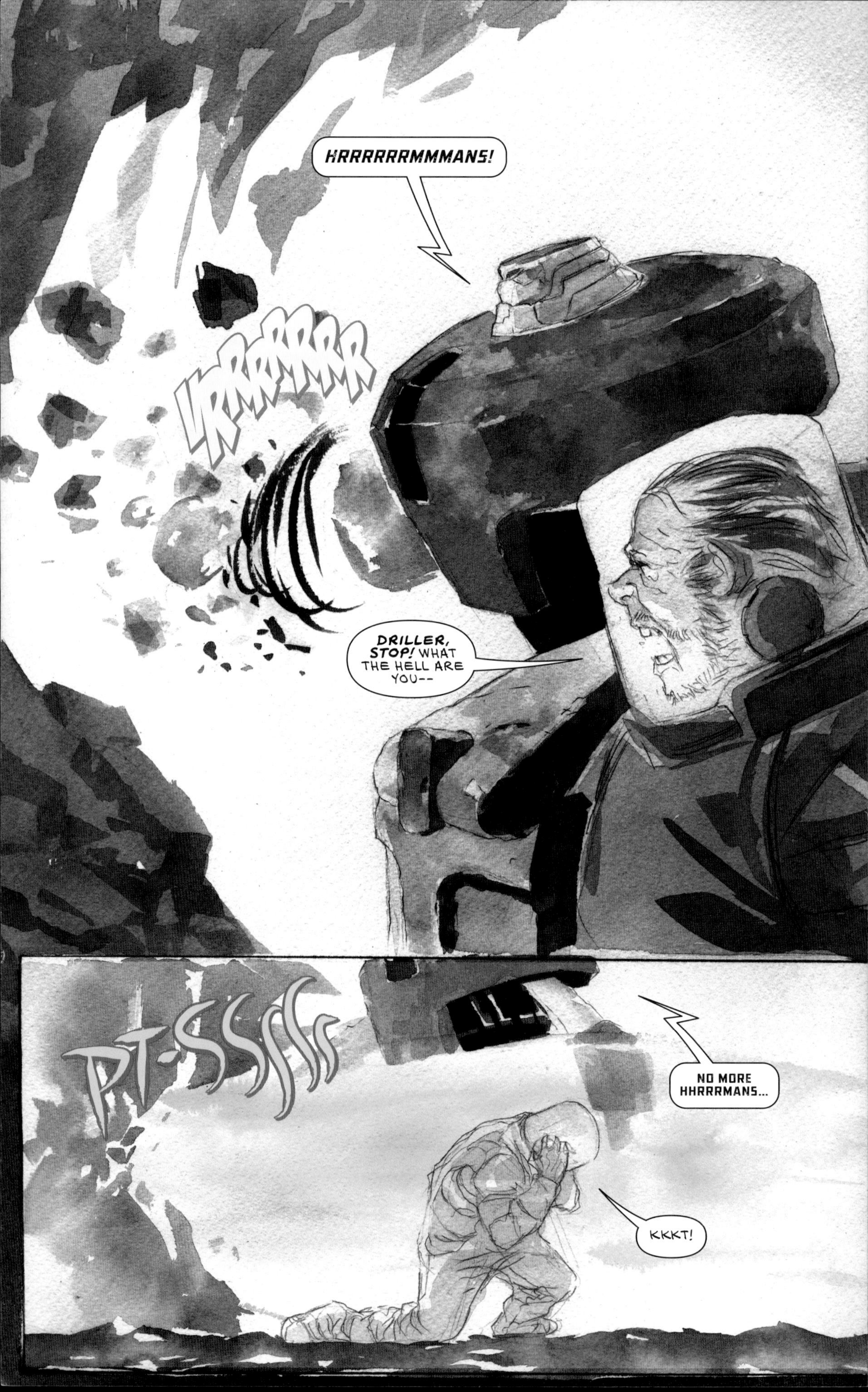
HRRRRRRMMMANS!
URRRRRRR
DRILLER, STOP! WHAT THE HELL ARE YOU--
PT-SSSSS
NO MORE HHRRRMANS...
KKKT!

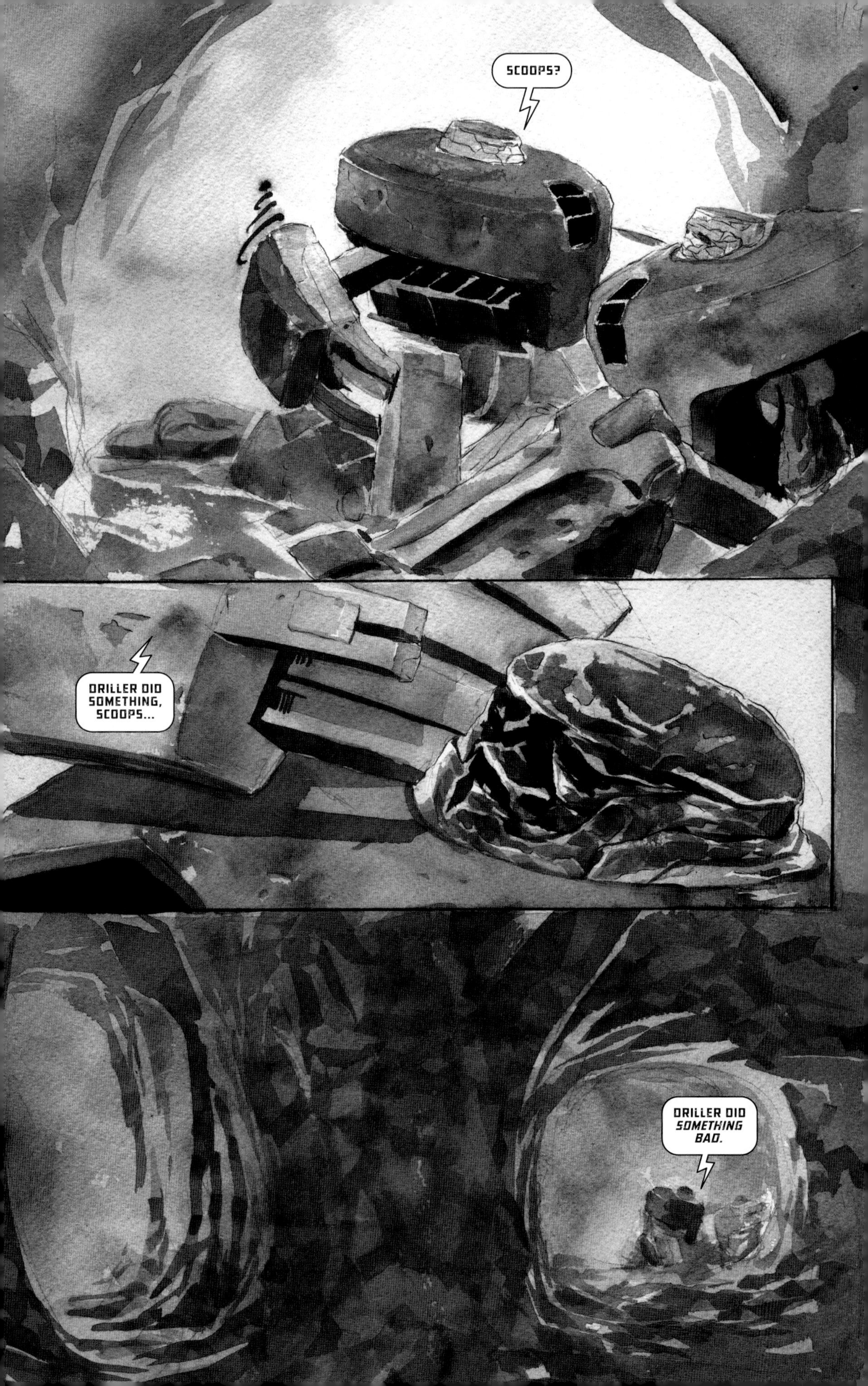
SCOOPS?
DRILLER DID SOMETHING, SCOOPS...
DRILLER DID SOMETHING BAD.

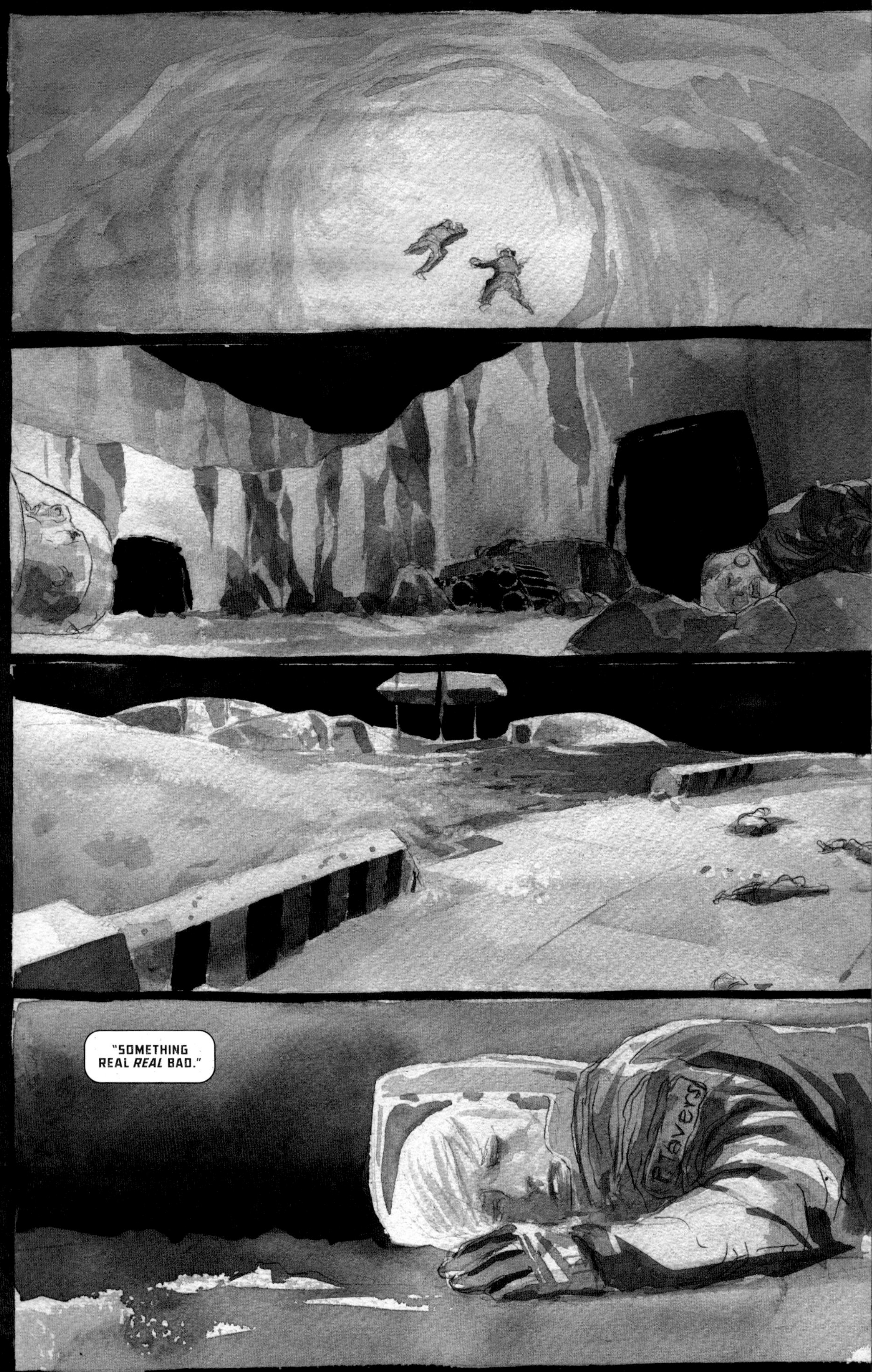
"SOMETHING REAL *REAL* BAD."

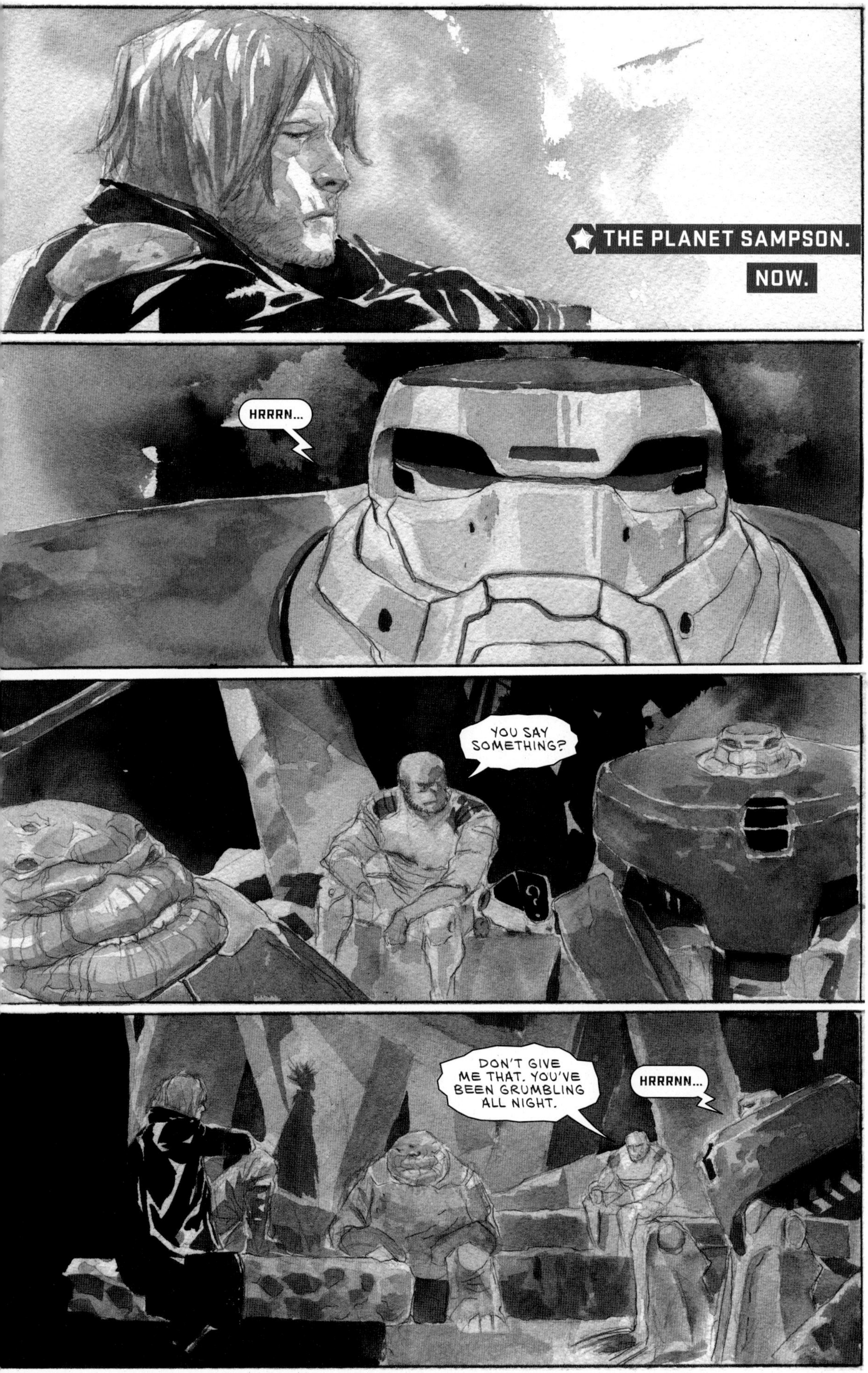
THE PLANET SAMPSON.
NOW.
HRRRN...
YOU SAY SOMETHING?
?
DON'T GIVE ME THAT. YOU'VE BEEN GRUMBLING ALL NIGHT.
HRRRNN...

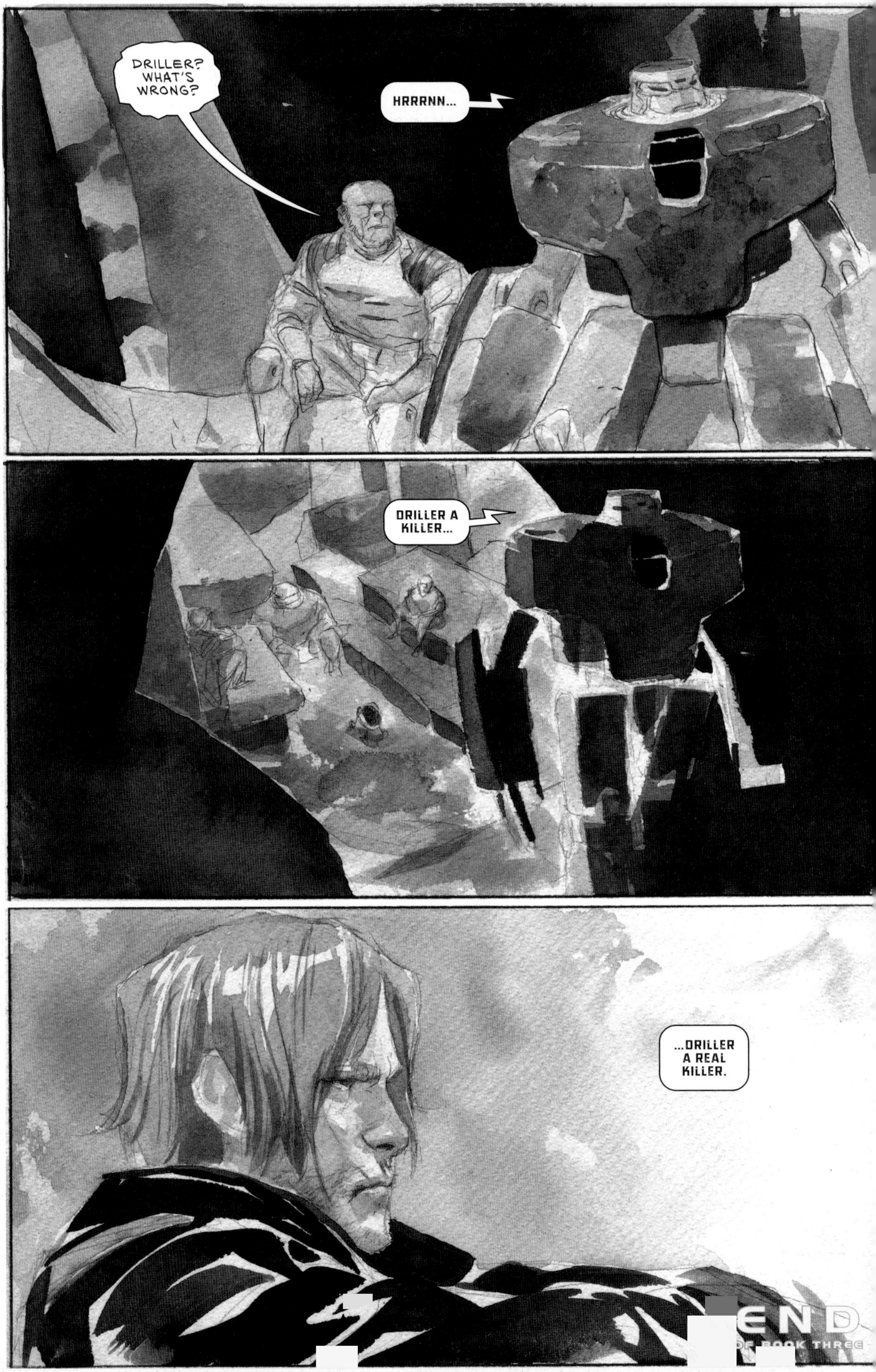
DRILLER? WHAT'S WRONG?
HRRRNN...
DRILLER A KILLER...
...DRILLER A REAL KILLER.
END
OF BOOK THREE

ATLAS OF THE CORE PLANETS OF THE UNITED GALACTIC COUNCIL

NIYRATA (THE HUB WORLD): Former technological and cultural hub of the UGC and former home of the nine Embassy Cities. One city state for each of the core planets and races representing UGC. Now a devastated world, what's left of the UGC still resides there, clinging to power.

PHAGES (THE GHOST WORLD/HAUNTED PLANET): Home to a gaseous race called THE PHAGES. Their spectral, ghost-like appearance scared early explorers into thinking the planet was haunted. Basically a world full of ghosts with no solid matter. Cities and aliens all made of gases. The only non-gaseous species are a race of hostile 20-foot tall giants.

MATA: An aquatic world. Was once home to a great empire and a baroque, almost renaissance-type world, but long ago was flooded and turned into a water-world. The descendants of this monarchy now survive on a floating, mobile kingdom. The ruins of the old cities still lay below the water.

SAMPSON: Home to the original colonists from Old Earth. Sampson is a massive planet and the military center of the Megacosm and home of the largest human cities.

KNOSSOS:
The smallest Core planet in the Megacosm.

SILENOS: The unique atmosphere on Silenos makes all sound and vibration impossible, creating a totally silent world where the native race communicates by projecting telepathic hieroglyphs into the air.

AMUN: The greatest ally of the GNISHIANS.
An insect-like race that lives in underground hives.

GNISH: The largest planet and the home of the largest military force. Leaders in the anti-robot, anti-technology movement in the wake of The Harvesters. A race ruled by luddite zealots who preach independence and sovereignty for all worlds all the while working for more and more control of Megacosm space. Main funder of the Scrappers. Home to the MELTING PITS, massive gladiatorial arenas where robots are made to fight to the death.

OSTRAKON: A desert wasteland devoid of all life. Contains the ruins of an ancient civilization that has long since gone extinct.

• THE DESCENDER TEAM •

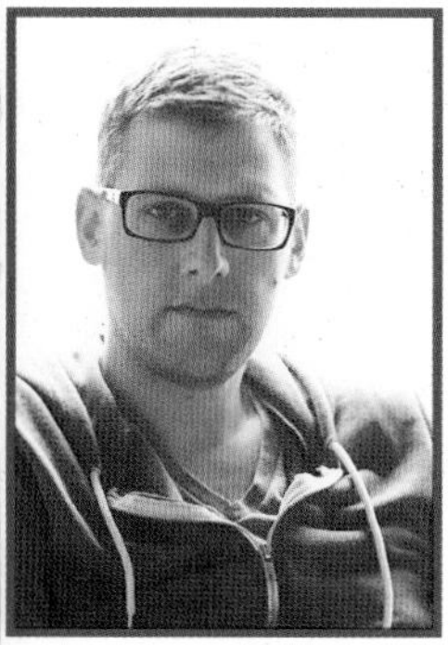

JEFF LEMIRE : *New York Times* bestselling author Jeff Lemire has built a unique career as both the writer and artist of acclaimed literary graphic novels like *Essex County*, *The Underwater Welder*, *Sweet Tooth*, and *Trillium* and also as one of the most popular writers of mainstream comics with acclaimed runs on such titles as *Extraordinary X-Men*, *Green Arrow*, *Animal Man*, and *Hawkeye* for Marvel and DC Comics.

His next original graphic novel, *ROUGHNECK*, will be published by Simon and Schuster in October 2016.

In 2008 and in 2013 Jeff won the Shuster Award for Best Canadian Cartoonist. He has also received the Doug Wright Award for Best Emerging Talent and the American Library Association's prestigious Alex Award, recognizing books for adults with specific teen appeal. He has also been nominated for eight Eisner Awards, seven Harvey Awards, and eight Shuster Awards.

In 2010 *Essex County* became the first graphic novel to be included in the prestigious Canada Reads contest, making it to the final five and winning the people's choice vote as best Canadian novel of the decade. *Essex County* is currently in development at CBC as a live-action television series with Lemire attached as executive producer.

He lives in Toronto with his wife and son.

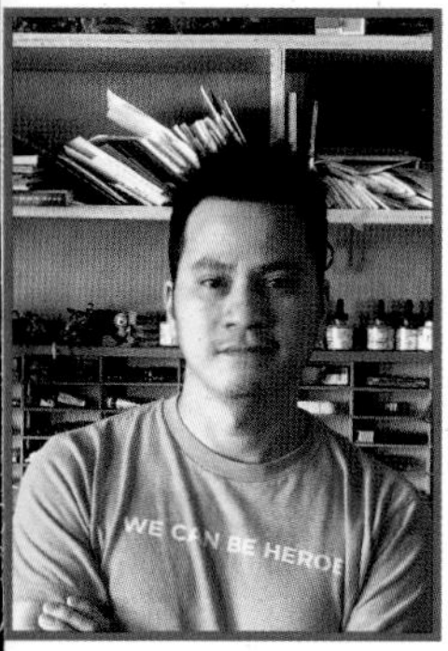
WE CAN BE HERO

DUSTIN NGUYEN : Dustin is a *New York Times* bestselling American comic artist whose body of work includes *Wildcats v3.0*, *The Authority Revolution*, *Batman*, *Superman/Batman*, *Detective Comics*, *Batgirl*, and *Batman: Streets of Gotham*. He is also credited as co-writing and illustrating *Justice League Beyond*, illustrating Vertigo's *American Vampire: Lord of Nightmares* with writer Scott Snyder, and co-creating DC's all-ages series *BATMAN: Lil Gotham*, written by himself and Derek Fridolfs. Aside from providing cover illustrations for the majority of his own books, his cover art can also be found on titles ranging from *Batman Beyond*, *Batgirl*, *Justice League: Generation Lost*, *Supernatural*, and *Friday the 13th*, to numerous other DC, Marvel, Darkhorse, Boom, IDW, and Image Comics' covers.

Currently, he illustrates *Descender*, a monthly comic published through Image Comics in which he is also co-creator alongside artist/writer Jeff Lemire.

Outside of comics, Dustin also moonlights as a conceptual artist for toys and consumer products, games, and animation.

He enjoys sleeping, driving, and sketching things he cares about.

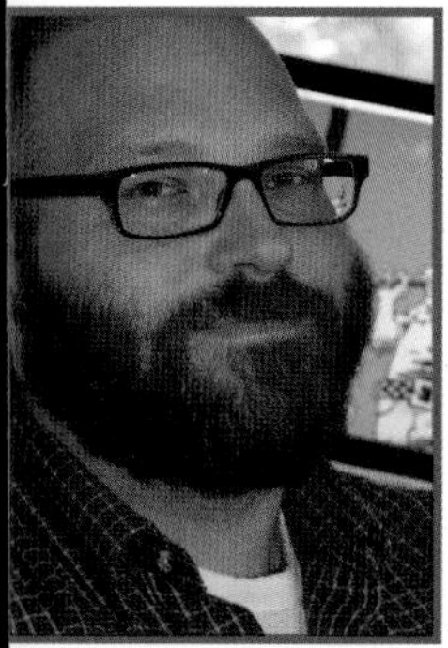

STEVE WANDS : Steve is a comic book letterer. Working on top titles at Image Comics, DC, Vertigo, BOOM! Studios, Archaia, Random House, and Kodansha Comics (to name a few). He also designs, inks, and illustrates for those, and other, companies. When not working like a maniac he spends time with his wife and sons in the greatest state known to man...New Jersey. Oh, and he drinks a lot of coffee.

DESCENDER